The Confederate General Rides North

A NOVEL

Amanda C. Gable

Scribner

New York London Toronto Sydney

SCRIBNER
A Division of Simon & Schuster, Inc.
1230 Avenue of the Americas
New York, NY 10020

This book is a work of fiction. Names, characters, places, and incidents either are products of the author's imagination or are used fictitiously. Any resemblance to actual events or locales or persons, living or dead, is entirely coincidental.

First Scribner hardcover edition August 2009

SCRIBNER and design are registered trademarks of The Gale Group, Inc., used under license by Simon & Schuster, Inc., the publisher of this work.

For information about special discounts for bulk purchases, please contact Simon & Schuster Special Sales at 1-866-506-1949 or business@simonandschuster.com.

The Simon & Schuster Speakers Bureau can bring authors to your live event. For more information or to book an event, contact the Simon & Schuster Speakers Bureau at 1-866-248-3049 or visit us at www.simonspeakers.com.

Text set in Goudy Old Style

Manufactured in the United States of America

1 3 5 7 9 10 8 6 4 2

Library of Congress Control Number: 2009012257

ISBN 978-1-4165-9839-8
ISBN 978-1-4165-9842-8 (eBook)

For Julie,

for my parents, Joan and Joseph Gable,

and for Esta

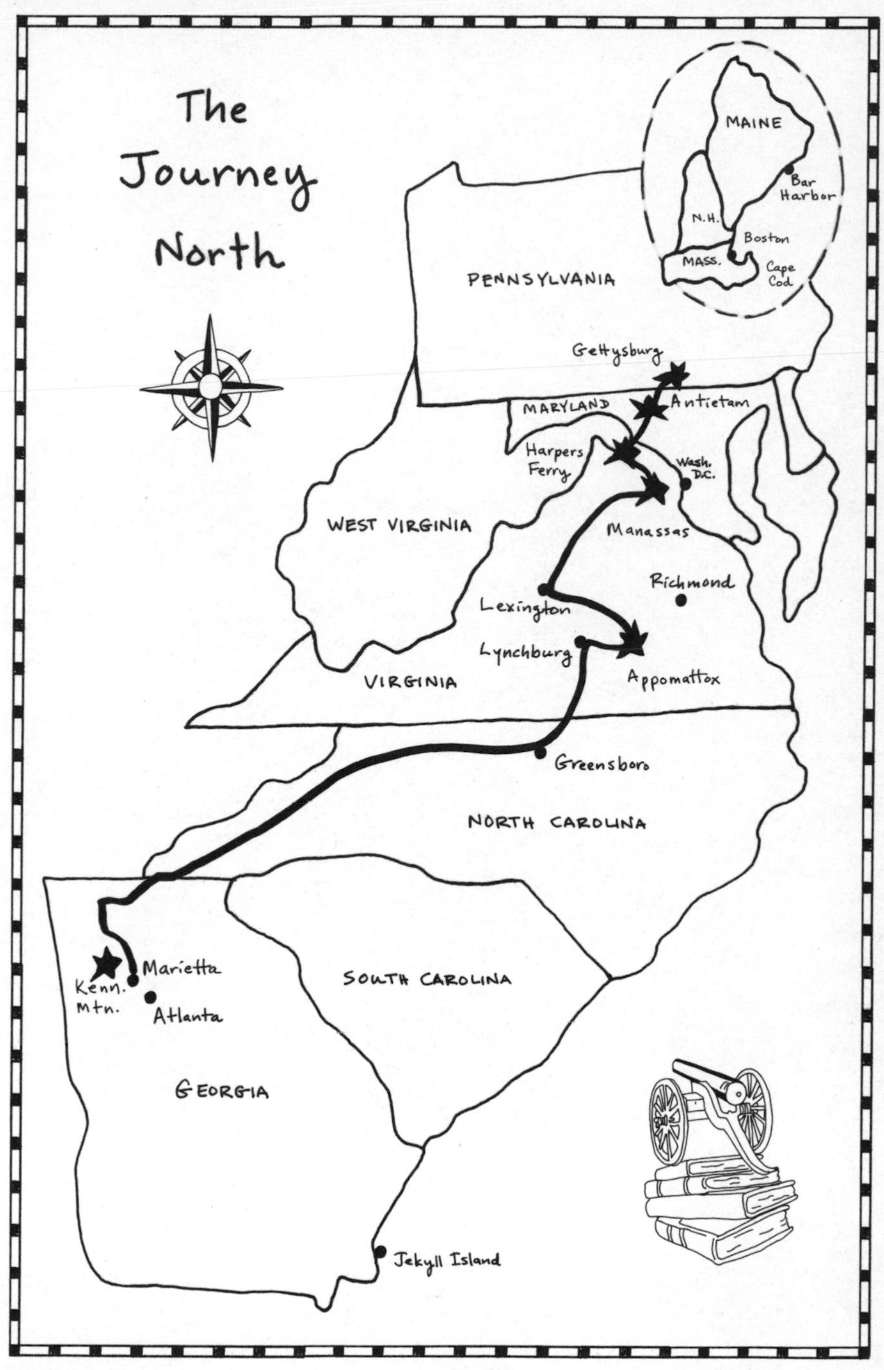

The Journey North
MAINE
Bar Harbor
N.H.
Boston
MASS.
Cape Cod
PENNSYLVANIA
Gettysburg
MARYLAND
Antietam
Harpers Ferry
Wash. D.C.
WEST VIRGINIA
Manassas
Richmond
Lexington
Lynchburg
Appomattox
VIRGINIA
Greensboro
NORTH CAROLINA
SOUTH CAROLINA
Marietta
Kenn. Mtn.
Atlanta
GEORGIA
Jekyll Island

The Confederate General Rides North

Chapter One

Get up, baby," Mother says. "We're going on an adventure." She has my suitcase out and is already pulling clothes from my dresser drawers before I've even rolled over and put my feet on the floor. It's six a.m., still dark outside. Only a few minutes earlier I'd woken up to the noise of Daddy's truck engine turning over and over until it finally started and he revved it hard once. Now that he runs his own construction company, I never see him in the daytime unless it's Sunday. "Well, come on," Mother says. "Get dressed and help me pack your things." I wonder where we're going this time. Wherever it is, I wish we could leave later.

Yesterday Mother was touchy. Usually she likes me to be in the basement with her while she's painting, but after only a few minutes she made me pack up my watercolors because she said the way my paintbrush tapped against the jelly glass got on her nerves. Then she and Daddy had a fight at dinner, not as bad as the worst ones, but she was quiet afterward. Now her cheerfulness so early in the morning surprises me a little, except that Mother's moods can change fast. I have to watch for that. Her mood can make a difference in what I say or whether it's best to say nothing at all. The good thing is that Mother never stays mad at me for long. Like Daddy says, she shifts gears a lot. Whenever Mother gets a notion, she'll change whatever she's doing, right then and there. She'll wake me up in the middle of the night to go to Dunkin' Donuts, where we sit on the pink stools next to truck drivers and order our favorite donut, toasted coconut. She tells me she thinks best then. I like watching her sketch on the folded pieces of typing paper she brings along in her purse. In those moments it's just the two of us, like grown-ups together, and she tells me her ideas for making money. It's hard to make a living only on your art, she explains. You have to do something else to bring in steady money. And you need to make your own money, be independent, have your own bank account, she says. I don't think Daddy knows that we go; we're careful not to make noise when we leave.

Over three years ago when I was in third grade, on an October Saturday when Daddy was still a crew boss for Old Man Price, Mother packed us an overnight bag and we drove four hours to Pisgah National Forest in North Carolina. "I had to see the mountains, Bill," she told Daddy on the phone in the lodge. "I wanted to see the beautiful leaves. I had to get out of there." We stayed a week. During the day we went hiking, rode horses, and drew landscapes on large sketchpads with thick sticks of charcoal Mother brought. At night we ate dinner in the lodge dining room where the tables had starched white tablecloths and napkins, and we chose books from the shelves on either side of the lodge's huge stone fireplace. I missed that whole week of school. Daddy and Mother had a huge fight in the kitchen when we got home. I heard Daddy yelling, "Damn it, Margaret, I don't care. I forbid it! You can't go off like that, spending money I don't have." He got so mad he threw a can of frozen orange juice that smashed out the kitchen window; but the next day he whistled while he put in a new windowpane, and he asked me did I have a good time, off with my wild artist mother.

As I pull on my shorts and find my favorite blue T-shirt in the pile of clothes on the floor, Mother takes my book bag out of the closet. "We're going all the way to Maine," she says. "Now that you're out of school for the summer, we can take off. Isn't this great? I've got it all planned out. We're going to buy antiques and open a store like I told you about." Mother has a lot of business ideas. Of all her plans, the antique store is my favorite—it sounds more fun than opening an art gallery or a picture-framing shop. I love old things: the wavy grain of the wood in the pine boards of our dining room table, the marble-top dresser at Gramma's with the brass drawer pulls you can spin, or the richly colored oriental rug in my aunt's living room where I lie on my stomach to count all the tiny birds in the design.

Mother grabs my dirty-clothes bag, dumps everything out of it, and begins stuffing it with sweaters and my coat.

"Hey, why do I need those? It's summer!"

She stops stuffing for a minute. "Honey, even in the summer it gets cold at night up North. Don't you remember me telling you about Boston?" I don't remember her saying Boston's cold in the summer. I remember her stories about foot-high snowdrifts in the winter and how wonderful it was to grow up in a city where you could go to a different art museum every day of the week.

Daddy hates it when she talks about Boston. "Just quit with the Boston crap," he says. "You think *anything* in the North is better than *everything* in the South."

She tightens the drawstring of my laundry bag and lays two pairs of folded pajamas in my suitcase. "Fit in as many outfits as you can. Pick out a few school dresses."

"School dresses? I hate them."

"We might need to get dressed up some," she says firmly. "I'm going to be making contacts for my new business."

I take two jumpers, both plaid, off their coat hangers and fold them on my bed. Mother adds two white shirts to the stack. I open my desk drawer and pull out my colored pencils and sketchbook.

"Katherine, you're going to see Boston and Cape Cod and all the places I went when I was growing up." Mother's tone is soft and serious, as if she's telling me a secret.

I put my art supplies in my book bag.

"I'm so glad I'm doing this. You'll see, Kat. It's going to change everything." Mother's eyes are bright this morning and she's excited.

For the last few months she hasn't had any energy, sometimes spending all day in her slippers and bathrobe, and leaving half-finished drawings all over the house. She's hardly painted at all. Daddy has started saying again that nothing suits her, that nothing is right with her. Maybe if she starts an antique business, it will change everything and she can be happier. After all, Daddy said he'd never been happier than when he told Mr. Price he was quitting to start his own company.

"How long are we going to be gone?" I ask.

"As long as it takes." She clicks the locks on my suitcase and looks at me. Her face breaks into a grin. "Yeah, as long as it takes," she says. "To get a new start." I wish she would tell me exactly how long we'll be gone, but when we take a vacation Daddy always figures out when we'll leave and when we'll arrive. Mother's not much for that kind of detail. She tosses me my tennis shoes. "Come on, we need to eat some breakfast."

In the kitchen, Mother opens up the Allstate road atlas in front of me on the table. "Up the East Coast, sugar, heading to Maine. Why don't you look and see what you think is an eight- or ten-hour drive for today. We have to go pick up the trailer in Cartersville first." She pauses. "Remember, we want to find good bargains on antiques, so make sure we go through some small towns."

It's easy to read a road map. Daddy taught me. Just add the little red numbers together to find the distance and then figure maybe fifty miles per hour and come up with the time. I begin with the dot for our town, Marietta, Georgia, and write down the numbers on a pad Mother keeps for phone messages. I pick a highway heading northeast from Cartersville and follow it to places that might be around eight hours away, which is all Daddy says you ought to drive in a day. After I calculate on the pad, it turns out Greensboro, North Carolina, is the right distance. Mother keeps walking through the kitchen, taking boxes and bags to the carport. When she stops to drink the rest of her coffee, I show her Greensboro on the map.

"That's exactly where I thought we should stop," Mother says. "Exactly." She picks up the ballpoint click pen and circles Greensboro. I don't like her marking on the map because it ruins the way the page looks, everything printed neatly, and there in the middle, her off-kilter dark blue ink circle. She stuffs the atlas in her tote bag and takes it to the car before I have a chance to look at the places I might want to visit. We're bound to pass some Civil War battlefields on the way to Maine, but I can't just come out and ask about them, because Mother doesn't like Civil War history. Whenever I go to the Kennesaw Mountain battlefield, only a few miles from where we live, I go with Aunt Laura. She teaches history at the high school, and Daddy says his sister got all the brains in the family.

The summer before third grade when Aunt Laura asked to take me to Kennesaw Mountain for the Civil War Centennial Celebration, Mother argued with her. I overheard her say that a celebration of war was nonsense—that it was gruesome to pretend men were dying all over again, especially when we're in the middle of a real war. It's about history, Aunt Laura replied; it's important to remember how and why things happened. Mother said she still didn't want me to go, that the segregationists used these spectacles to whip up people's emotions. Finally Aunt Laura said it was better that I learn history from her than from someone who was prejudiced, *if you know what I mean*, and Mother gave in.

On Kennesaw's rolling green field, inside a split-rail fence that bordered the road, men dressed in dark blue Union uniforms marched with their rifles on their shoulders toward butternut-clad Confederates who were lying in shallow depressions or crouched behind trees at the base of the mountain. On the first ridge, two small cannons were visible. Aunt Laura and I stood outside the visitor center looking down on the field, and the big crowd around us yelled and whooped. "This isn't exactly how the battlefield looked," Aunt Laura told me, "but the Park Service didn't want to ruin the field by digging trenches." It didn't matter to me. To me it was all spectacular—the noise of the people, the uniformed soldiers with their rifles, and not knowing what was going to happen next.

The lines of Union soldiers stopped and fired their rifles. Small white puffs of smoke filled the air. A round of shots came from the Confederates, marked by more puffs. Some Union men dropped to their knees to reload, but others clutched their chests and fell flat on the ground as if they were dead. Aunt Laura had told me that everyone would be using blanks—powder, but no minié balls, only paper wadding. The Union troops started running toward the Confederates and the cannons fired, making a huge noise and creating so much smoke we could hardly see what was happening. "How do they know what to do?" I asked Aunt Laura.

"They obey their officers, who follow battle plans that the generals have made. The generals are in charge of everything," she told me. Lots of Union soldiers were lying on the field and the Confederates came from behind the trees to chase the few blue coats that were still upright. "Hooray," I yelled with the crowd.

When the dead men stood up and all the soldiers started shaking hands with one another, we went to the museum. Aunt Laura bent down and spoke quietly in my ear. "It's okay to cheer—after all, our relatives fought as Confederates—but you need to know that it was a good thing that the North won the war, otherwise slavery would have lasted a lot longer." I nodded. "That's my girl," she said and patted me on the back.

In the museum, I stood staring for a long time at a wooden box with medical instruments resting in blue velvet compartments. The box was so beautiful, the velvet lush and unstained, the knife blades glinting, and the steel teeth on the saw still shiny. It was almost impossible to imagine that small saw cutting off arms and legs a hundred years before. It frightened me and I peered at it for signs of blood.

We looked at the uniform exhibit and I tried to like the Union private's dark blue sack coat because Aunt Laura said the Union soldiers did such a good thing for the country, but I couldn't. It was plain, with moth holes and threadbare edges on the sleeves. Next to it was a magnificent Confederate general's full uniform: a gray wool coat with brass buttons and braid, a sword in a decorated scabbard, and the general's hat, its gold tassels with acorns at the ends hanging over the brim. All were in perfect condition. Aunt Laura said the everyday uniforms like the Union private's were much harder to come by and more valuable, but I didn't care. I would want a general's uniform, especially the hat. "If I had been a Confederate general," I told Aunt Laura, "I could have saved Atlanta." She chuckled. "That's fine," she told me. "But remember what I said, the way the war came out was for the best." In the gift shop she bought me a biography of Robert E. Lee. "This is the general you'd want to be," she said. "North or South."

I like to imagine the lives of generals, conferring with one another inside their tents, their horses tied up nearby; writing out orders to be delivered to their trusted lieutenants, and then leading their troops into battle. They were in control, responsible, resourceful, and strong. Even when things went badly, they could figure out what to do. I think a lot about being a Confederate general, someone in a beautiful gray hat on a tall horse who would have commanded my great-great-grandfather, someone who knows how to defend his homeland and family.

Maybe if Mother keeps letting me plan the route, I can make sure we just happen to go through some of the battlefield towns—Manassas, Harpers Ferry, Sharpsburg, Gettysburg—and I can visit the museums and take the battlefield tours.

When we start packing the car, I ask about stopping by Gramma and Poppa's house across the field to say good-bye, but Mother shakes her head. "No, it'll take too long. We need to get on the road."

I write a note to Daddy and leave it for him with the one Mother seals up in an envelope and props between the sugar bowl and the salt and pepper shakers on the kitchen counter. On my note, I draw a border of flowers and ivy and write:

When we get back I'm going to help Mother run the antique store. We'll make lots of money. Scout will keep you company while we are gone. I think you're the greatest.

Love, Kat. S.W.A.K.

"We could leave a note in their mailbox," I suggest.

Mother scowls at me. "They'll come out as soon as we stop. They're always watching out their windows to see what I'm up to. They're probably looking at us right now wondering why we're putting so much stuff in the car. Soon as you get to their mailbox they'll run down the driveway calling, 'Yoo-hoo, where're y'all off to?'" Mother mimics Gramma's voice. "And then the next thing you know we'll be stuck here, waylaid, looking out for everybody else's interests." Mother is red in the face. "Those two fill your head with guns and dogs and hunting and that, that Confederate ancestor worship of theirs. I'm glad I'm getting you away from them. I should have done it years ago."

"They don't sit around looking out the window," I tell her. "They've got better things to do." Mother always thinks Gramma and Poppa are checking up on her, and she and Daddy argue about them a lot. She says she wants me to spend less time with them, but I still see them almost every day.

"Doesn't matter what you think. I know what *is* and you're not putting a note in their mailbox and that's final. This is *our* trip." She slams the trunk.

I don't want to leave without saying good-bye to Gramma and Poppa, and I think about not seeing them while Mother goes through the things in the glove compartment. She spreads out combs, lipsticks, and papers on the dashboard. I decide they won't be worried, because Daddy will tell them that we're off antiquing and I can write them postcards like I do when I'm gone for two weeks at summer camp. I can write Aunt Laura too, and if we stop in the battlefield towns I'll send her postcards of all the Confederate generals.

Mother opens the back door of the car. "Did you get your drawing supplies and books that you want?" I nod. "Go check your room and make sure." She follows me into the house. In my room, she opens all my desk drawers. "You'll want an extra pad of paper," she says, "and more pencils." I add my *Golden Book of the Civil War*. Mother sits on my bed and pats the spot next to her. "Come sit here." She puts her arm around me and hugs me hard. "You have to trust me on this," she says. "I love you. I want the best for you. This trip is a chance in a lifetime for both of us." I don't know exactly what she is talking about and that worries me a little. But I do know that she means this trip is important for both of us, that I'm going to help her do something she's always wanted to do.

"I know you'll miss everyone while we're gone, but it's like a vacation—you won't be lonesome, because we'll be having so much fun together." She pushes my bangs back a little with her fingertips, smiling. "Okay?"

"Okay," I tell her, smiling back. More than anyone, I'm the one Mother wants with her. I sit on the bed with her and she pulls me into her body again. She smells like coffee with a hint of lavender in her shirt from the sachet she keeps in her drawer. I stare at the open door of my bedroom and think about Mother and me on the trip together.

The Confederate general buckles her belt and adjusts her sword. Her orderly checks to make sure all her gear is stowed in the trunk. In a short time her army will be on the march once again. It feels good to be poring over maps and having strategy meetings with her staff—they are about to embark on an important Northern campaign. It's true that they are outnumbered, but it is also true that if they keep their wits about them, they can be victorious. The spirit and heart of the troops is what is most crucial, not how many there are. As she swings onto her steed, she says to herself, "There can be no more valiant troops in the world than those before me now."

• • •

We're in our shiny white Impala with its fire engine red interior, ready to go, when Mother pauses and twists the rearview mirror toward her. I watch as she takes her lipstick from her big leather purse and slowly touches up the frosted pink that looks so good against her tan. She examines her long blond hair, held back in a black velvet ribbon, and pulls a few strands out above her ears, making it look softer around her face. She is beautiful. Sometimes when we are in public and people look at her a little too long, I see how much she enjoys it. I feel her drawing attention to herself and I wish she wouldn't. I don't want her to care what strangers think. She often makes me sit with her in front of her vanity at night, going over the finer points of hairstyles and makeup and what colors of lipstick are in fashion, all things I don't care about. Most of the other kids' mothers are older and wear their hair short in what Mother calls beauty-parlor dos, but Mother has straight blond hair down to her shoulders. When she's driving she pulls it back into a loose ponytail, and when she's going out to a party or to Christmas dinner at my grandparents' she gives it some curl with big pink rollers and wears it down.

Everyone remarks on how much I look like her. I have her dark brown eyes, long slender nose, and my hair is blond too, but with a slight curl I get from Daddy and cut short with bangs. Mother's been after me lately to grow my hair long, but so far I've resisted. She lets Aunt Laura cut it.

"You want to look your best, Kat," she always tells me. "Greet the day right. If your face is on, then you're more confident. Spend a little extra time putting on your face. You'll be glad later." But Mother doesn't always put her face on; sometimes she stays in bed all day long, harnessing her creative energy, she says. This morning, though, she's in one of her good moods because we're heading out for a great adventure. Daddy will be surprised; I can feel it, Mother is going to follow through with her plans this time.

As we sit in the driveway while Mother checks her makeup, my dog, Scout, watches us from her pen, her nose right up against the chicken wire. She knows we are going away for a long time, not on a trip to the store. When Mother first took the suitcases to the carport, Scout barked a weird bark with a whine at the end of it and I went into her pen to give her a long hug and to gently scratch her muzzle. "We'll be back before you know it," I told her.

Around us the day is heating up fast. The sun's rays angle through the windshield onto my bare legs. I check my pocket for my pocketknife and the money from my cigar box. Mother said we don't have time to go to the real bank where I have my birthday and Christmas money stashed, earning interest.

"I'll get you what you need," she said as she stacked our cereal bowls in the sink without even rinsing.

I'm excited about going to places I've only read about, maybe even walking on battlefields where my great-great-grandfather fought. Mother readjusts the mirror and twists around to back out of our driveway. I'm already itching to look at the map again. Once we are on the highway I'll get it out of Mother's tote bag and make notes on the battlefields we can intersect. Around us there is a buzz in the air, like a million clicks of insect wings or the vibration of a long thin wire that reaches for miles and miles. It is a sound that goes with the cloudless pale blue, almost white, sky of summer and the kind of day that stands still without a hint of breeze.

Chapter Two

While Mother drives north up the four-lane highway from Marietta, I look over the atlas. All the way up the Eastern Seaboard, I can name the major battles of the Civil War by their Southern and Northern names and recite the biographies of the generals who led the troops. I can tell you who sucked lemons, who had heart trouble, who was reluctant to send his troops into fire, and who used men like so much cannon fodder. I've grown up with stories and facts about the war all around me—our church being used as a hospital after the battle of Kennesaw Mountain, my great-great-grandfather wounded at Gettysburg, my great-great-grandmother carrying the mail on horseback through enemy lines when she was only fourteen—and Aunt Laura's bookshelves full of Civil War history, filmstrips at the Kennesaw Mountain visitor center showing Sherman's Atlanta campaign and the fall of the city, and our field trip every year with my school class to the Confederate Cemetery on Confederate Memorial Day. In the years since Aunt Laura took me to the Centennial Celebration, I've read every book on the Civil War in the kids' section of the library. I love that I can connect the Civil War history I read in books to my family and our town. The history is a part of us, a part of me.

I turn to the two-page spread in the atlas that shows Delaware, Maryland, Virginia, and West Virginia. The windows of the Impala are rolled down, the wind blowing our hair. Mother has on what she calls her ballet shoes, the ones she says help her feel the accelerator better. She loves to drive, and sometimes she drives way too fast, Daddy says. But I like being in the car with her. The speed is exciting, and she's almost always happy while she's driving.

I rest my finger on Richmond, Virginia, the capital of the Confederacy. Below it is Petersburg, where at the end of the war Lee couldn't hold the line and was forced to retreat to Appomattox to try to find supplies. Sliding my finger due north, I hit the cluster of red-ink names of battlefields—Fredericksburg, Spotsylvania, the Wilderness, and Chancellorsville, where the Confederates won but Stonewall Jackson was accidentally killed by his own men. Moving north, my finger finds Manassas, the first real battle of the war, Harpers Ferry, then Sharpsburg, which the Yankees called Antietam, until finally I run into the thin horizontal sliver of pink that is the bottom of Pennsylvania. There, just over the border, lies Gettysburg.

Mother is singing along with Gladys Knight and the Pips to "I Heard It Through the Grapevine." She looks over at me as she finishes the chorus and smiles. She and Daddy have lots of records. Sometimes I lie on the carpet in the living room in front of the fireplace and listen to music: Bob Dylan, Sam Cooke, Elvis Presley, Joan Baez, Aretha Franklin, Caruso, B. B. King, and Gladys Knight. Daddy built the stereo himself from components, and when you turn it on you can see the orange lights flicker alive in the clear glass tubes. With music I can feel any way I want—I just have to pick the right record.

I fold the atlas back on itself so that I can rest it on the red vinyl seat next to me with the eastern part of Virginia facing up.

" 'Cause you mean that much to me," Mother sings and turns up the radio a little more.

Mother keeps singing, but instead of joining in I look out the window at the pine tree woods that line my side of the highway. Shortly, the woods end and we pass a farm where several horses stand next to a white fence. The palomino in the group stands with his back hoof slightly raised just like Big Boy, Daddy's horse, when he's sleeping, and only then do I realize that I didn't say good-bye to Rebel before we left.

The summer I was seven, my father bought Rebel for me. I sometimes rode in his lap on Big Boy, a huge solid-white quarter horse, but he had begun pushing for me to have a pony. Mother thought buying the pony should wait another year, but Daddy's friends at Willow Farm offered him one for cheap. I remember standing outside the Willow Farm riding ring, looking at two ponies. One was light gray with liver-colored spots all over. "She's real sweet," my father's friend Mr. Frazier said. "Her name's Nelly." The other pony was white and he tugged a little at his lead rope. I walked toward him. He pushed his muzzle forward and I rubbed his nose. "I want this one," I said. "Well, now," Mr. Frazier said to my father. "That's Rebel." Rebel rubbed up against me in earnest. "He looks like Big Boy," I said.

Before long I started imagining myself a Confederate general leading charges on Rebel. I was reading the Robert E. Lee biography that Aunt Laura had given me at the Centennial, which gave me plenty of ideas, and because we were way out in the country with no other kids close by, I had a lot of time to myself to put together battle plans. Some days my best friend, Milly, came over, but after she got in trouble for ripping her new cowgirl outfit on barbed wire, she wanted to stay out of the woods and pasture, so I was alone for my campaigns. I sketched the terrain of battlefields in my notebooks and drew tiny rectangular boxes to mark the position of troops. With my colored pencils I shaded the hills and valleys and made the boxes a light gray or blue depending on whether they were friend or foe. Each morning I grabbed my toy shotgun and six-shooters in a holster to fight the Civil War from Rebel's back.

I still ride Rebel almost every afternoon after school. I hurry to change out of the shirt with a Peter Pan collar, jumper, ankle socks, and oxfords that I hate and put on my jeans, T-shirt, and boots. When I grab on to the saddle horn and swing up on Rebel's back, I'm a general, respected and ready for action, riding my dependable white steed who never wavers under the noise of whistling shells or rifle shots. Sometimes I am Lee on his spirited horse, Traveller; sometimes I suck lemons and am Stonewall Jackson; but other times I am myself—General McConnell. I point Rebel's nose toward the barn and give a few swift kicks. "Save Atlanta, Atlanta's burning!" I yell. With the bright sun warming my bare arms and the wind in my face, we charge through the pasture—breathless, sweaty, smelling grass and leather.

The Confederate general gallops across a field of young corn astride her sleek white quarter horse. The roar of exploding cannon balls reverberates in her ears. Her army is being fiercely shelled and can hold up to the bombardment no longer. Not far in front of her she sees an opening in the pinewoods that her army can cut through.

Even though I imagined myself as a general, I wore a small Confederate private's cap. The gray felt was no longer stiff and I had to hold it on when I ran, which made it impossible to pull both pistols at the same time. It was a poor substitute for a Confederate general's hat. I yearned for one with gold braided cord, the tasseled ends resting on the brim. I had seen one only in the museum at Kennesaw Mountain, but I thoroughly searched every store I entered. You never knew.

The next October, after I started fourth grade—when the leaves had turned to molten yellow, orange, and red—Mother, Daddy, Gramma, Poppa, and I went to the North Carolina mountains for a weekend to see Gramma's sister, Aunt Lida. We drove north on the same highway that Mother and I are on now.

On the way, Poppa stopped at a roadside store and gas station, the kind that sold Indian headdresses and stuffed black bears with red collars and gold-link leashes. This one had a real black bear in a cage near the road to attract customers.

Mother was upset about the bear.

"It *is* barbaric," Gramma said as she got out of the backseat. "But up here a lot of the places do it."

Mother followed me into the store. "That bear doesn't have any water!" she angrily told the man behind the counter. "At least give it some water if you're going to keep it in a miserable cage."

"As soon as I ring up these customers, lady," he said.

"How would you like to be left out in the hot sun without any water? You need to get a dish of water for that bear." Mother was talking loudly and people were staring at her.

While Mother complained, I combed the aisles, moving away from her, passing outhouse ashtrays, rubber snakes, and Daniel Boone caps. Then I saw the Confederate generals' hats. Around the corner from the raccoon-tail hats were rows of Confederate privates' caps and just a few, maybe five, generals' hats, proud gray felt Stetsons with little crossed gold rifles. The hats didn't have any tassels or braided cord, but it didn't matter. They had an elastic chinstrap, the kind that held on Halloween masks, perfect to run or ride in. I stood there not touching any of the hats for a few seconds, almost not believing I'd found them.

The clerk slammed the cash register drawer shut and walked to the back of the store. "Hey, we're in a hurry," somebody in line said, and glared at Mother.

Gramma came back from the bathroom and went to the car as Daddy came back into the store. "Are we ready to go?" he asked Mother.

"I'm waiting for the man to get a dish of water."

"Well, I never," complained a woman in line. She plunked down on the counter a salt and pepper set woodburned with "Smoky Mountains" and an Indian tomahawk painted with bright red, yellow, and blue stripes. "Seems that bear is more important than we are." She looked at the other customers and nodded for emphasis.

Poppa had been at the front of the store the whole time, standing apart from Mother and not saying anything. Now he silently packed tobacco into his pipe. As he lit it, I walked up with the general's hat—the hat I had to have, the hat that cost five dollars, two dollars more than I had in my pocket.

Mother and Daddy went outside. I could see them through the screen door standing by the bear's cage. I heard Mother's loud voice. "Does the Humane Society know you're keeping this bear like this?"

"Lady, I don't own this bear," the clerk replied and bent down by the cage.

"May I borrow two dollars?" I asked Poppa.

Smoke rose from Poppa's pipe, and he shook out the match. "Depends on if you can pay it back, little Hawkshaw." He calls a lot of people Hawkshaw.

"I could work in the garden." Sometimes he paid me to help weed or put out fertilizer.

"You'll have to work one full day," Poppa said.

"Yes, sir." I saw him reaching for his wallet.

Daddy came back into the store. "Let's go," he said in a voice that meant there would be trouble soon. I panicked. The clerk was nowhere in sight. Poppa had his wallet in his hand but not opened, and he paused, looking at my father. "Short stuff wants to get this hat. We'll be right out."

My father said in a quiet, controlled voice, "That guy's not gonna come back until we leave. We'll get the hat somewhere else."

"But this is the only place I've ever seen one!" I stood still and clutched the brim of the hat. Daddy shifted his weight.

"Are you coming?" Mother called through the screen door. My eyes caught hers. She opened the door. "Katherine, you're not buying *anything* here."

Poppa looked at her out of the corner of his eye, took two ones from his wallet and a quarter from his pocket. "Where's your money?" he asked and motioned me over to the counter. A boy and his girlfriend were still waiting to buy one of the stuffed bears. They had on matching T-shirts printed with a scene of mountains resting on the word *Gatlinburg*.

Poppa said, "Put it up here, sport." He placed the quarter on top of the bills. "That shot got it. Let's go."

I had my hat. In the car I wore it down over my eyes. Mother said in a low voice to Poppa, "I can't believe you let her buy something there—and a Confederate hat! It isn't right."

Gramma sympathetically patted me on the leg. "I think it's a fine hat."

I moved rocks out of the garden to pay for that hat. All day long I tramped around in my cowboy boots, lugging the rocks to small piles at the ends of the rows. That night my white socks were clay-red. Poppa wrote out on a piece of paper, "Paid In Full," and signed it. I folded it carefully and put it in the leather change purse that I'd made a long time ago when I went to day camp. Poppa also gave me his old knife, sharpened so much the blade was thin and developing a gentle U shape. I was fully equipped now as a general, but I wore my hat only on special occasions—important charges, parades, inspections of the troops, and scouting.

Occasionally the general chose to do her own scouting when it was a sensitive mission. From the observation tree she would carefully climb into the gondola of the hot-air balloon that would carry her over enemy territory. With luck she could maneuver into a strong air current and stay high enough to be out of range of enemy sharpshooters. "Suicide balloon," some of the scouts called it. It was the only way she could get fast, accurate information on troop movements and artillery strength, so the general continued going up. She liked the way the woven basket of the gondola creaked and swayed. She liked holding on to the thick ropes stretched upward by the constant tug of the inflated balloon. The gentle movement of her perch soothed her, and she wanted to stay up there forever.

In the spring of that year Daddy suggested building me a tree house. He'd come out to the pasture after work one evening when I was sitting in the fork of my favorite tree. "How'd you like a tree house? We could pick out a bigger tree and do up a fancy one with walls and a roof and everything. What d'you think, Kat?"

"Sure," I told him and scrambled down to go inside with him. It was a great idea.

Mother disapproved. "Keep her acting like a monkey."

But Daddy looked excited, and I knew he liked to build things out of two-by-fours. "You could even put an old table and chair up there," he said.

The next evening we went tree hunting in the woods behind our house. By the creek Daddy stopped at an oak tree that rose thick and straight for eight feet then spread into three main branches. Even my inexperienced eye could see how a tree house would nestle there. As my father pointed to different spots on the tree where the ladder could be nailed and supports could span, I saw the possibilities too. Generals need a place for important private meetings, and the table Daddy had talked about would be perfect for spreading out maps and for the signing of surrenders.

Good Friday was building day. Daddy was off from work and I was home from school. Daddy climbed up the tree first and sawed off limbs. The weather was awfully hot, and when he climbed down he pulled out his handkerchief and wiped his whole face and neck. He handed me a small hatchet and showed me how to hold a downed limb carefully and chop it into lengths. "Cut on the diagonal, like this," and he took four strokes with his big ax to chop a limb in half. "You see how the cut looks like a vee?" I did. The small white chips of sappy wood flew up as I whammed my hatchet into a limb. We piled some logs under the tree and nailed others to the trunk to make a ladder. Daddy arranged the two-by-fours in the branches that would hold the plywood flooring. I helped by handing him nails, lengths of rope, a pencil. "Even with this kind of job, Kat, you've got to measure carefully." He had a carpenter's rule that I loved to fold up and back out again. When the plywood flooring was nailed securely down, we took a break for lunch.

Mother was making a carrot cake for Easter Sunday dinner and the kitchen was hot. She had the box fan in the doorway on high, and her hair was pulled back with yarn into a ponytail. The cream cheese frosting oozed down the sides of the cake to join in puddles all around the plate. "I can't get the frosting to do right, damn it," she complained. "Why is it so hot in this house?"

"Shouldn't be this hot this time of year." Daddy got out the mayonnaise, bread, tuna, and pickle relish.

"There're no trees close to the house, that's why," Mother said. "And you're building a useless tree house when there are things to be done around here." While Daddy made tuna salad sandwiches, Mother opened the refrigerator, put the cake on the top shelf, and refrosted it from the puddles on the plate as it sat in the cold.

We worked more slowly in the afternoon. The heat of the sun had forced its way through the leaves and a humid glaze settled on our skin. I held studs while Daddy toenailed them. We talked about where the windows should be. "We'll fix them across from one another so you can catch a breeze through your house." Daddy laughed, droplets of sweat rolling down his temples. "No fans up here, Kat." I spied a branch and climbed up onto it to rest for a little while. With my back against the trunk I was balanced well. I listened to the rhythmic *pound, pound, pound* of Daddy's hammering and the occasional *ping* of a dropped nail. He looked at me and smiled, wiped his forehead, and went back to his work. I closed my eyes and put my hands into my pockets.

I heard a loud noise like the crack of the whip Poppa kept in the wagon in his barn. My eyes opened wide. Things were rushing past me. On my cheeks and arms and legs I felt the slaps of a switch. Then something underneath me moved like waves, but bit through my shirt roughly. I looked, and Daddy was flying toward me—a cartoon character screeching and flinging his arms and legs in every direction. He was so funny-looking I wanted to laugh, but I couldn't get a breath. He touched me, drew me toward him into his arms, and pain tore through my middle. I opened my mouth but nothing came out. I felt his sweat on my face.

He ran with me in his arms, and each time he put a foot down it hurt my stomach. Mother threw open the side door. "The baby fell out of the tree," Daddy said, his voice so high it cracked. Mother was touching my hair and crying, "Where are the keys? My baby, her arm's broken." I caught my breath and started crying.

In the car Daddy held me. "What happened?" Mother screamed.

"Limb must have been rotten," Daddy said softly, as if talking to himself.

"What limb? Why was she on a limb? Why weren't you watching her?"

"I was. It had green on the end of it. It looked okay. Fooled both of us, huh, Sport?" He smiled at me. "We'll be there soon and get you fixed up."

I tried to smile back, but I couldn't.

"My baby," Mother wailed.

At the hospital they put me on a cold table. "Do something about her arm," Mother yelled. She was crying loudly.

Dr. Blair put his hand gently on my stomach. "Does it hurt here, Katherine?" he asked.

"Look at her arm, broken to pieces." Mother sobbed louder.

"I have to determine the internal injuries; the arm will wait. You're upsetting her." Dr. Blair asked Daddy to take Mother out of the room.

"Where does it hurt?" Dr. Blair asked me quietly after they left.

I pointed to the part of my stomach that burned with pain.

When Mother and Daddy were together in my hospital room they whispered to each other. I dozed a lot. Dr. Blair had removed my spleen, which ruptured when I landed on the pile of logs we had stacked under the tree. I pretended I was in a field hospital, having taken a Union minié ball in my gut.

"This is what your idiotic notions lead to," snapped Mother. "She runs wild and you don't even notice."

"She plays like other kids."

"No, not like other kids. By herself, in the woods, where God knows what might happen. Look what happened with you right there. My baby. She should join the Girl Scouts. Something supervised."

"Sssh, you'll wake her."

While my body learned to live without its spleen, I had to be flat on my back. I imagined that Daddy had finished the tree house and set up the table and chair inside.

The troops were heartened their general was still alive. She coordinated what she hoped to be the last battle of the war from her cot in the makeshift hospital. She wouldn't be able to ride her charger for a long time, her surgeon had said. That was bad for morale, she thought, especially at such a critical time. All she could do was study her maps and wait.

When I was back home recuperating in my room, every evening Daddy came in and talked about my homework and whether I wanted to join the Girl Scout troop. He overflowed the small pink chintz-covered armchair by my bed, his legs stretched way out in front of him. He read to me from the newspaper—"Dear Abby," the horoscopes, and the editorial page. "I know it's terrible to be cooped up. You'll be well before you know it, though," he said. "Then you'll be back at school getting your friends to sign your cast."

Milly came to visit me. She signed my cast with a hot pink marker she had with her in her purse. She took one of my markers, a yellow one, and began drawing a smiling sun at the end of her name. Milly had just become a Girl Scout, and I asked her what it was like. She was bent over my arm, concentrating. "I like the uniform," she said, "especially the sash." The sun was bleeding into the pink of her name.

At dinner Milly asked my mother if she'd been a Girl Scout. "My mama was a Girl Scout too." Milly picked the breast from the platter of chicken.

Daddy reached for the butter. "I don't know when we've had fried chicken."

"Your mother is one of the leaders for the troop, isn't she?" Mother passed Milly the green beans.

"Yes, ma'am. She invites speakers to come in and talk about arts and crafts, and we sell cookies."

"How long do the meetings last?" I asked.

Before Milly could answer, Mother said, "Girl Scouts is the perfect place for all your energy. And you'll be well in time to join Milly's troop this year." Mother raised an eyebrow at Daddy, who looked down at his plate of food and cleared his throat.

"Depends on what Kat thinks, I guess." He looked at me. "What do you think?"

Mother was staring at me.

I didn't say anything. I hated the green dress the Girl Scouts wore with the sash across the chest and I couldn't imagine having to wear it after school to meetings.

Daddy put down his fork. "If you don't like it, you don't—"

Mother interrupted. "Oh, she'll like it. They'll do such fun things."

Daddy stayed with me while Mother took Milly home. We sat in the den with the evening news on. "I believe the Girl Scouts do some camping out," he said.

"Yeah? Do you think they'd make us wear our uniforms while we're camping?"

Daddy laughed. "No, Kat. They wouldn't make you wear the uniform then."

The general put on her hat and climbed up the ladder to staff headquarters. It was an important day. A surrender was to be signed. There was peace. After the signing, the tired general climbed down, careful not to hit her right arm, which was still in a cast. The troops cheered.

Three weeks after the accident, Dr. Blair put a half-cast on my arm and looked at the scar on my stomach. He'd finished taking the last of the stitches out. "She's perfectly fine," he said to Mother. "That red will fade a little with time." He motioned for me to sit up. "Now you can go back to school and play outside some." He paused. "Within limits." He held out his fingers to count. "No riding the pony yet.

No climbing trees or anything else that would risk a fall. No roughhousing at school. Do you understand what I mean?"

I nodded.

On the ride home from the doctor's I felt the way I did before a test at school—nervous, worried that I might not be able to answer some of the questions. I wanted to go down to the tree house to see if Daddy had finished it. He seemed so upset by my accident that I hadn't wanted to ask him about it, but I needed it to be finished—I needed that table to spread out my books and maps. I wanted to have my staff headquarters in the woods, away from the house, so I could think in peace. I left the carport and headed to the woods, first walking and then, out of sight, running.

In the tree, the platform rested securely on its supports, but the framing listed without walls to balance it. The wood hung there, not even forming a complete shell. The jagged stump of the limb I had sat on jutted out above the scattered pile of logs on the ground. The limb itself lay in the moss and dirt, all of its leaves brown. It had fooled both of us, Daddy said. I was panting. I was angry with Daddy. He didn't understand how much I needed this place of my own. A shelter I could come to when I needed to figure things out alone.

I practiced a Rebel yell. It was loud and clear and satisfying, even though I could feel my incision pulling as I yelled. When I emerged from the woods and onto the lawn, I saw Mother hurrying toward me. "Don't scare me like that!" she said angrily. She stood for a minute holding my good arm, fixing me with her stare. "Don't scare me like that," she repeated and loosened her grip. She drew her hand back to her side and put it on her hip. I looked at the white marks that her fingers had left on my arm. We were locked together for that moment, her eyes on me, my eyes on her marks on me. I stared at my arm until the pink came back to my flesh.

"Well," Mother said, "come on," and she turned and walked toward the house. I followed because that is what she wanted from me, but I let a few yards separate us before I swung my cast into motion and began scuffing along through the tough crabgrass.

Chapter Three

I don't think I will miss Daddy much while Mother and I are on our adventure. Lately he hasn't included me in any carpentry projects around the house and he's been getting mad at the least little thing. He doesn't even sing to the radio anymore. Almost every night he and Mother have a fight at dinner.

Before dinner last night Daddy drank part of a six-pack in the den while he watched the news. He had taken off his work boots on the back porch and was padding around in his white socks dirty to the ankles with red clay. There were deep sweat lines under the arms of his dress shirt. Even though he was the boss, he often had to work along with his crew because he couldn't afford to hire many men.

At supper he poured another beer in a chilled glass from the freezer and told us about his subdivision. It's going to have fifteen houses in it, all of them brick, because brick is the latest thing people want. He's going to call it Chateau Ridge.

Mother was putting paper towels on top of the hamburgers to soak up some of the grease when he told us the name. "Who are you trying to fool with a name like that? They're just ranch houses." She took off the greasy paper towels and put the platter of hamburgers next to Daddy's elbow.

I saw Daddy's face redden and his left eyebrow twitch a little. He speared a hamburger. Mother walked around the table with a pot, spooning out baby green peas onto our plates.

"Is this it? Dried-up hamburgers and pissy peas?"

Mother stopped spooning for a moment, then she plopped more peas on my plate. I started to complain but then thought better of it. When they're working up to a fight, it's best to be invisible. Mother went back into the kitchen and Daddy yelled, "Bring the ketchup."

I wanted the platter of hamburgers but I didn't want to ask him to pass it, so I moved the peas to one side of my plate and looked at the pair of pastel drawings of flowers on the wall that my grandmother Carter did when she was a teenager. I was named for her and I can tell from her photographs that I look like her—short, stocky, though my blond hair is wavy, not straight. Mother says we have Grandmother Carter's drawing gene and that if her mother hadn't died so young she'd be a famous artist today. One flower is a camellia and the other is an orchid. Both are soft-looking, very pale, and the edges seem blurred. Mother says you do that with a piece of Kleenex after you make your drawing. I heard a noise in the kitchen like something breaking in the sink and I hoped it wasn't the platter of french fries Mother had been fixing. I watched Daddy's reaction to the sound of the crash, but he didn't act like he had heard anything, which was good. Sometimes when they fight at dinner she gets really mad and throws plates of food in the sink. One night when she did that, Daddy overturned the table and made everything crash to the floor. When that fight was over, I ate cereal in my room.

Daddy was tapping his fork hard on his plate with every bite he took when Mother walked in with a platter of french fries. She buys the crinkly kind frozen in square boxes and when she fries them she puts a screen on top of the big black skillet so the grease won't spatter as the frozen fries spit and crackle. I love the ones that get a little too brown. They crunch when you bite into them and then are hot and soft inside like mashed potatoes.

"I guess it'd be too much to ask to have all the dinner on the table at the same time," Daddy said and then downed the rest of his beer. I wondered what Mother had broken in the sink.

Mother put the fries down next to me and went back to the

kitchen. I kept my head down so I wouldn't have to see his twitching eyebrow, wondering what kind of fight it would be.

If it isn't a bad fight, they might just stomp off to different rooms at the end of dinner. Sometimes I like it when they leave before we've eaten much. By myself at the table, I can relax and eat my food slowly.

Mother came back in and set the ketchup bottle right in front of Daddy.

"Work hard all day to make money and come home to hear crap. Chateau Ridge will make people think they're moving up in the world, getting somewhere. It's smart business. Not that you would know anything about that." He bit into his hamburger. I went ahead and ate my fries without ketchup.

Mother ate her hamburger with a fork. She didn't have a bun and she didn't take any french fries. While she ate, her left index finger sketched tiny patterns on the wood of the table next to her plate. She had been in the basement painting most of the day.

"Quit that fiddling with your fingers," Daddy blurted out. "I hate that infernal fiddling all the time."

Mother looked at him blankly like she was way off in another world. Her left finger kept up its sketching. Without inflection she said, "Oh just hush."

Daddy jumped up out of his chair so fast it fell backward with a crash. Mother looked at the chair. "I come home dog-tired, wanting a little dinner and rest, and what do I get—a crazy." He leaned over toward Mother. "You ought to be happy as hell that I'm working my ass off for you."

I watched him walk out of the room toward the den and a few seconds later I heard the television blaring. Mother looked at his chair for a long time until I picked it up and put it under the table. I could tell she was in one of those moods where she would sit and stare for a while. Just in case Daddy came back in to start the fight again, I took my plate to my room and shut the door. While I ate at my desk, I stared at the cover of my biography of General Lee. Thinking about him and all the soldiers he commanded helped me forget about the fight at dinner and I let the details from the biography calm me. I imagine my favorite stories, even putting myself in them, retelling them so they're all my own. I like the one about Lincoln offering Lee command of the Union army at the beginning of the war.

It was an honor, the Confederate general thought, but not one that she could accept. Virginia has not yet seceded, but other Southern states have and she cannot fight her fellow Southerners. She writes to her sister, "I hope I may never be called on to draw my sword," but the day after Virginia secedes, she says no to Lincoln and resigns from the U.S. Army. She will fight for Jefferson Davis.

After we drive north on Highway 41 for less than an hour, Mother turns off, heading for the town of Cartersville. We pass signs for the Etowah Indian Mounds. I've been to the mounds before on school trips and looked down into the dug-out earth at the Indian mummy in a glass case like a coffin. The mounds were disappointing. For one thing, they were a lot smaller than I thought they should be, and the artifacts on display looked completely worn out—like things the Indians had used up and thrown away. In books everything to do with Indians is brightly colored—bright beaded clothing, bright rainbow-colored feathers, bright designs on blankets. But at the museum the dusty display cases with brown pottery and brown rawhide clothes were dull. Maybe the Etowah Indians didn't have time to make nice clothes. Maybe life was too rough for them to be artistic. Maybe they were sad Indians who didn't want cheerful colors.

"Here we are, Kat." Mother pulls into a gas station. "That's what we want to put our antiques in." She points to a row of small rental trailers off to the side on the grass. Each of their hitches rests on a single concrete block. "You wait in the car." She digs in her purse and pulls out her oversize wallet that holds her checkbook and pen and change and gas charge cards. She has hidden the wad of money in the trunk, in a box of Kotex. "No thief'll go under there," she'd said, laughing.

All our suitcases, duffel bags, and a cardboard box with a loaf of bread, can opener, salt and pepper, paper plates, a roll of paper towels, and some utensils are in the trunk. The small metal cooler is on the floor behind the passenger seat. In the backseat are a pillow and a sheet in case I want to take a nap while she drives, and my book bag too. In it I have my notebook, two Civil War history books, *The Guinness Book of World Records*, and a book about mapmaking. Having them near reassures me.

I watch Mother talk to the man inside the gas station. She has on her pink sleeveless cotton shirt and black pedal pushers and as she talks she keeps her weight mostly on her right foot and gestures with her wallet. He likes the way she looks, I can tell. It is the same way Kurt at the gas station near our house acts. The man leans toward her a little, swaying slightly when she gestures, as if he were completely in tune with the rhythms of her body. Kurt always tells me he'll marry me when I get older, but I know he's just trying to make Mother laugh. Kurt likes to talk to Mother while he fills the gas tank, bringing his face so close I can see how his blond eyebrows grow together.

"Hey," the gas station man says to me as he walks around to look at our back bumper. He isn't as young as Kurt. He motions to Mother. "Pull her in and I'll put 'er on the lift."

I want to stay in the car to see what things look like from up on the lift. "It isn't safe, Katherine," Mother says, and I catch her tone. She is irritated and I don't argue.

The man attaches a hitch to the bumper of our car. "I was thinkin' you already had a hitch when I said it wouldn't take but a minute, you know." He has started sweating and Mother stands with her arms crossed.

"Well, I hope you'll give me a break on the price."

"Sure," he says. "Sure." When he finally finishes hooking up the trailer and making sure its brake lights and turn signals work, we've been there almost forty-five minutes. I stand inside with Mother and watch him write up the ticket. Behind him is a Coke machine with bottles in round slots; you can open the clear door once you put your money in. That kind of Coke machine isn't as satisfying because you don't get the sound of the bottle dropping down. It reminds me of the display cases at the Indian Mounds.

"Okay," he says, tearing off a paper for my mother, "you've got the baby for a month. Here's a list of places where you can turn it in."

Mother says thanks as she heads out the heavy glass door. "Stupid redneck," she says when we get to the car. "Couldn't get the damn hitch on for staring at my boobs." We take off from the gas station and the empty trailer bumps like mad behind the Impala. "Four-eleven north," she sings out. "We're off to Asheville. Isn't that the next big town?"

I get out the map. "Well, yeah," I say, "but first, we have to make our way over and up to Highway Nineteen."

"That's great," she says, "you're right on top of things." At the traffic light she turns and looks at me. "We'll do well in antiques, Kat. I've got a knack for knowing what to buy and buying it cheap. You saw how I handled that guy back there. We got this trailer for ten dollars less than it's supposed to be. I planned it that way." She starts up and I look back at the trailer following behind us. "Yep," she says, "we'll stay off the main roads, take in the small towns. Not too out of the way, but dinky enough to get good prices." We are veering toward the side of the highway, which is overgrown with orange daylilies, and she jerks the wheel to get us back on course. "Maybe we'll go to the general store and find out where the local auctions are. We're going to open up that shop. Sell the stuff for loads of money."

I hold my hand out my window and feel the wind trying to beat it back. Mother's plan is a great one. I love antique stores, the way they smell a little dusty, but also like furniture polish. I can imagine our place with a bell on the door, a cat sleeping in the bay window, and an old-fashioned black cash register that shows the amount of the sale in big bold numbers. While I wait for customers to come in, I will read in one of the overstuffed leather chairs we have for sale. We'll collect books, china, furniture, and oriental rugs. But right now, while we are on this wonderful trip, every night I'll read road maps and pick the route for the next day. I will figure the mileage and time carefully. I will get detailed maps of the areas and not just depend on the Allstate road atlas. It will be like a military campaign with objectives and strategies. We will advance in the Impala, our trailer loaded with needed supplies. We will rely on information we get from the locals, our own noses for choosing good antique stores, and, like any good officers, we will be pleased to have a lot of luck and God's help. Like Stonewall Jackson. The biography I read said Thomas Jonathan Jackson was a religious man who didn't like to fight battles on Sunday. Sunday was the Lord's Day. The biography used the word *fervent*. I will ask Mother what *fervent* means exactly. At the first battle of Manassas, Jackson and his troops were like a stone wall against the damn Yankees. I realize as we speed down the highway that after not too many days I'll start seeing a lot of Yankees.

Chapter Four

Mother passes up a few promising-looking antique shops; the sign's too fancy, she says—or, looks like they have crafts, or, we've got to make some time right now. North of Ellijay, over the North Carolina line, though, she stops at a small sign that says BOIL PEANUTS AND ANTIQUE. A big house and barn are set back from the road behind the ramshackle peanut stand where an old man sits in a beat-up lawn chair chewing tobacco, a small trace of juice in the wrinkle at the corner of his mouth. "How 'bout some peanuts?" He stands up and wipes his hands on the sides of his pants. It seems to be a habit—he keeps doing it, rubbing the denim with the palms of his hands.

"We wanted to look at your antiques," Mother says.

He sits down quickly and motions with his thumb. "They's in the barn. Ring that bell and my wife'll come out of the house."

We walk up the driveway to the barn, which leans to the right and is plastered with old license plates from all over—Georgia, North Carolina, New Mexico, Arizona, Louisiana, Minnesota. We ring the school bell that is mounted above the big doors of the barn and a tall, rail-thin woman with a cap of black hair comes out the side door of the house. Her hands are dusted with flour like she's been making biscuits.

"You'd think he could help people himself—him down there doing nothing but chewing and whittling and me a-trying to get us some lunch together, but you know the men, if they don't want to do something they act like they don't know how. He's always saying he don't know nothing about antiques, that's my area, but it ain't nothing more than laziness on his part. Pure teetotal laziness. Sellin's sellin', I say." She opens the big barn door. "So what are you ladies looking for today?"

Mother smiled. "Oh, maybe some old dishes or a desk for Katherine here or a bureau." She pauses and puts her hand on my shoulder. "We're moving, starting over, you might say—it's a long story. But the short of it is that we need some furniture and don't have too much money." I'm a little surprised at how smoothly this whopper comes out of Mother. Maybe as we've been driving she's been thinking about ways to get better deals.

The thin woman's eyes squint a little. "Did he leave you now? Men is trash. If that one out there wasn't so lazy, he'd leave. I dare say I'd be better off if he *would* leave. Then I wouldn't have to cook three meals a day. Me, I can go with cold biscuits and coffee in the morning and maybe scramble me some eggs at night. I don't have to have roast beef, potatoes, and biscuit at lunch and pound cake after supper." The whole time she's talking she is walking through the barn looking under boxes, moving picture frames, and fingering pieces of furniture. Mother and I follow her.

"Now here's a nice set of china." The woman picks up a big cardboard box covered with dust and puts it up on a metal-legged kitchen table. She rummages in it until she pulls out an octagonal dinner plate—cream with a deep burgundy-flowered design swirling in the middle. Mother cocks her head. "Mm-huh," she says, "I like that pattern. The color's a little funny, though."

"Well, them are in good shape. Nary a chip. You can unpack them and look at 'em if you want. Whole set of eight. Dinner plate, salad plate, bowl, cup and saucer."

"Well," Mother says and picks up the dinner plate, puts it back down. "Maybe I better look at furniture first."

The woman holds out her arms. "Look at whatever you uns want to look at. I'm goin' get my biscuits out. Be right back." When she's gone Mother picks up the plate again and turns it over. "Royal Doulton," she whispers to me. And then, "Don't let them know what you're thinking," and she winks. Before the old woman gets back we pick out an oak mission desk, a plain plank table that Mother says is valuable because of how wide the pine boards are, and a cherry veneer dresser that she says is in the Empire style. She also decides on the china. That is, if she can get the right price for everything. I like how sure Mother seems about the things she wants. And she will get a good deal—no one can fool Mother when she's paying attention, focused on what she's doing.

"Where do you get your things?" Mother asks when the woman comes back in. "You have so much!"

"Oh, well," the old woman begins, and she pushes a table out of the way to reveal another stack of cardboard boxes. "I watch the obituaries. And after a week or so me and Mr. McMillan take the station wagon and drive to visit the family. We know most of the families around here." She starts unwrapping something in a dusty cardboard box. "We pay cash money and we give a heck of a lot better than the Yankee dealers that drive through here ever so often looking to flimflam people by telling them their stuff is old and no good." She begins showing Mother some dishes that are white with a border of pink and yellow flowers. "Got so now people'll give us a call if they want to sell something. People fall on hard times and they sell their wedding china or something that some rich relative in Atlanta or Charlotte give them."

Mother smiles and examines the pink and yellow china. "I don't really need two sets of china, but this is nice too." The woman watches her handle some of the china and then wrap it back up. The barn smells like hay, reminding me of Poppa's barn, where I sit on the bales of hay and read a book, or sometimes I try to figure out what the rusty tools hanging on the walls have been used for. I wander off from Mother to look at a group of little iron soldiers whose paint is beginning to flake. They hold ramrod-stiff poses, their rifles pressed against their bodies, bayonets reaching for the heavens. World War I doughboys—the only thing you can do with them is line them up in parade formations. Not suitable for realistic battles. Mother is talking seriously with the old woman. They are dickering now. I walk closer; I want to hear Mother bargaining. She is offering several dollars less than each price sticker says.

"Well, you drive a hard bargain." The old woman laughs. "But I s'pect that's fair."

Mother nods and opens up her purse. She counts out one hundred and twenty dollars to the woman.

"I'll get that lazy ol' man of mine to load up for you. You got any rope?"

Mother shakes her head no.

"No matter. We've probably got enough pieces laying around."

The old man chews and spits and then picks up the furniture like it was made of balsa wood. Mother gets out some of our towels to protect the furniture from rubbing on the rope that the old man pulls taut against it. As we shut the trailer's door, it looks surprisingly full.

Mother hums a little as we drive away and when we get back on the two-lane she turns on the radio loud. "We did well, Kat. We can sell this stuff for a whole lot more than we paid. Yes sir, I'm going to have a moneymaking enterprise."

We are heading out for parts unknown. Mother is a savvy trader and I am the navigator. We're a team, yoked together. When Mother is in high spirits like this, I feel perfect. When she is like this, everything goes right around her. I'd felt it at her first art exhibition when I was in third grade. The gallery was in downtown Atlanta. Daddy had on his dark blue suit and Mother had on a burgundy velvet dress with spaghetti straps and a cape with a white satin lining that she'd made. She was beautiful. All of her paintings sold, even the ones that Mother called her boring representational landscapes. Daddy brought her glasses of wine, and she stood in front of her paintings and talked to the guests. Daddy was grinning and red-cheeked from the wine. "Isn't this something, Kat?" he kept saying to me. I got to skip school the next day because we got home so late.

Outside my window I can see the Blue Ridge, the low, purple-and-blue mountain rises that are sometimes covered with white wisps of clouds and fog. These mountains have been our destination on fall and summer trips before—mostly visiting Aunt Lida. Daddy says that seeing them again after a long time is like you've died and gone to heaven. I love the scenery here in North Carolina, the way the occasional knolls turn into rolling hills, and then into looming mountains and carved-out valleys. The way the temperature drops steadily from the hot, humid nineties to the breezy seventies. When I'm not in school, I spend most of my time in the woods around our house—turning over rocks in the creek to reveal crayfish, walking the trails through the pine and hickory trees, and crawling through tunnels in thickets of vines. I like the cool of the woods with the quiet broken only by the soft sounds of birds or small animals running through leaves.

It is turning dusk when we pull up to a gas station in Greensboro—a Sinclair Oil with the green brontosaurus—and Mother is happy because she has their charge card. The teenager pumping gas tells Mother about the Carolina Inn. "It's not expensive," he says, and we wind our way through town as the streetlights come on. We pass the bank sign flashing the time, 8:23, and the temperature, 77°F. By the time we unlock the room and throw ourselves down, each on a double bed, we are both ready to eat a horse.

"How about a steak?" asks Mother. "To celebrate." While she gets out her train case with her makeup, I go to the television and turn the dial through all the channels; it makes a big click each time I turn it. Nothing that I recognize is on.

My favorites are old movies. Whenever I'm home sick from school, Mother and I watch *Dialing for Dollars*. If they call, you have to know the count and the amount. They have the telephone book cut up with the pieces in a huge spinning barrel; the host reaches in and pulls out a slip of paper and counts from the bottom—one, two, three, four, five—whatever it is. He has never called us, but we have always been ready. In between calls, we watch Fred Astaire and Ginger Rogers, Edward G. Robinson, and monster movies with huge spiders and bees. Sometimes Mother paints while we watch television. If it is a large canvas, she sets up in the basement and we take the TV with us and put it on top of the washing machine. I sit in a lawn chair with nylon strips that make creases on the back of my thighs. It's cool in the basement but Mother still works up a sweat as she globs her brushes with acrylic and frantically drags them back and forth on her canvas. Sometimes she starts with a scene of the beach, but usually she ends up with wild lines and splatters. "Abstract," she says. "Only blue-hairs paint stuff you can recognize." A lot of her paintings give me the creeps, especially the ones where she uses a lot of black and purple and tiny spots of red here and there. Even though they are flat objects sitting on an easel or leaning against the wall, it seems the shapes are flying out at you—angry, out-of-control beasts that are nothing but blobs of color.

In Greensboro we end up at a drive-in hamburger place because all the regular restaurants are closed, and Mother is indignant. "The very idea," she says, "after all day in the car, I eat dinner in the car." She hands me my chocolate milkshake and hamburger, and as we eat we watch people walk into the restaurant—boys in white T-shirts and girls in tight jeans.

"We could go inside."

"We're not going to sit with a bunch of teenaged hoods and criminal lowlife." She sucks on her straw and I can see the lipstick marks on the end of it. The red plastic tray with silver metal clips perches in Mother's window. I think it would be nice to eat here every night. I love the food, but even better is watching the comings and goings of the teenagers. I'd like to sit inside and listen to them talking and laughing. Mother's wrong about them being lowlife.

"Tomorrow night," she says as she wads up her hamburger paper, "we'll stop early and find one of those five-star diners and have a steak and a baked potato. We'll look in the parking lot and check to make sure all the tags are local and then we'll know it's a good place."

"All the cars here are local," I say.

"This kind of place is not what I mean, Kat. I swear, sometimes you're so dense." She cranks the Impala. I wipe up a few drops of milkshake that spilled onto the red vinyl seat. Then Mother drives out from under the brightly lit Chick, Chuck & Shake canopy into the dark street.

The troops are marching happily, making good progress north, bellies full of bacon and cornbread. Even the weather is cooperating with this campaign. The Confederate general sits back in her saddle, smiling. Maybe the war will end soon, as everyone in the South thinks. Still, she will be on the alert, utilizing her scouts effectively.

Chapter Five

When we check out of the Carolina Inn in Greensboro, the clerk calls Mother Mrs. Dunfey instead of Mrs. McConnell, which makes me nervous. As we go to the car with our suitcases, I consider why she used a different name. If you use your real name, detectives can track you, like on Perry Mason. Mother must think Daddy will track us and make us come back before she has bought enough antiques to open the store. Her paintings haven't sold for the last couple of years and Daddy keeps telling her she needs to think about going back to work as a full-time secretary. Mother says she doesn't want to be a secretary again, that she wants to do something that will leave her enough time to paint, like running an antique shop, she says, or typing people's college papers. But it's the antique shop idea she has talked about the most. Daddy always laughs about it. "You think people around here will buy a bunch of old furniture? Naw," he says, "they want the shiny new stuff."

Mother must have known that if she explained all her plans, Daddy would talk her out of it—he might even have said no, as he always does about her wanting to go to Cape Cod. She had to run away to show him how serious she is.

If at all possible, you must plan so that the enemy will not be able to anticipate your next move. This is the way the Confederate general planned the second battle of Manassas and lured General Pope into a trap. She figured Pope would never guess that she had split her army in half to flank his troops. And she knew that McClellan was too cautious to be any threat. Of course, to be so successful, you need good commanders under you like Stonewall Jackson.

In the Impala, Mother ties a gauzy scarf around her head. "Well, Kat, off to Virginia. What's my first road?"

"Highway Twenty-nine north to Danville," I say, rechecking my map.

"Okeydokey," she says cheerfully. "Say, let's stop for breakfast after we've been on the road a bit. You're not too hungry now, are you?"

"I can wait," I say and watch in my side mirror as Mother backs the trailer out of the parking place and pulls neatly onto the main street.

The scenery today is dull compared to the Blue Ridge yesterday. I stare at the land, flattened out with scrubby-looking woods every so often. The towns we go through are small with only a post office, a feed store, and maybe a restaurant. My legs are sticking to the vinyl seat from the heat.

As soon as we get back home and become successful businesswomen, everyone will be happy. Gramma sometimes worries that Mother can't follow through, like the way she didn't paint for a long time after her first show even though the gallery wanted more of her work. Lost opportunity, Gramma said. This time is different, though—Mother planned this trip, rented the trailer, knows what she wants to buy. She's not up in the air like she was after that show, wanting to do something completely fresh with her art, but not knowing what it would be. Before long, I think, maybe two weeks, we'll be back home, with Mother showing everyone how she can follow through after all. We're going to buy wonderful antiques, go home, rent a store downtown in one of those redbrick buildings with a second story, and start making lots of money. Plus, she's got me to help her. I'm a good companion for her; I keep her steady. Everyone's in for a major surprise now that I'm teamed up with Mother.

• • •

Her favorite colonel has come to the farmhouse she's been using as a temporary headquarters. As they look over the maps laid out on the round oak table and discuss the options of their newly launched campaign, the Confederate general realizes that she has been lonely without him. She hasn't seen him often in these last months, and even when they were together the colonel has been distracted and lowly. The give and take of their ideas always makes her think better. She is bolder, better equipped to come up with strategies that will overwhelm the enemy.

I fibbed to Mother about it being fine to wait for breakfast; my stomach is growling and I'm thirsty. I try to distract myself by thinking some more about her plan. It's like she says sometimes; you have to go out on a limb if you want to accomplish anything. That's the way General Lee thought too. Mother is singing loud to the radio and we're flying down the highway. I rest my head in the space between the door and the seat and let my mind wander. We pass a construction site, already baking in the sun, and I think of the time when I ran away.

That morning Daddy had driven and Mother had nagged him about the gears. "You're gonna strip 'em," she said as we drove down Slaton Road. The night before, they told me that I was going to a preschool run by a woman named Miss Nan. "You'll love it," Mother said. I had been staying at Gramma's just up the hill from our house while Mother worked as a secretary for a law office. She hated it but we needed the money and I loved staying with Gramma. I didn't want to go to Miss Nan's preschool.

Mother talked to Daddy as we drove. "I want her to play with other kids. She's only around adults all day long."

"We're wasting money," he grumbled. "My mother loves to keep her."

"She spoils her," Mother whispered loudly.

"Oh, that's it—that's the truth," Daddy said. "Nothing my family does suits you." Mother folded her arms and didn't say anything else.

"Well, like everything, Margaret, we're doing it your way." Daddy ground the gears. We made one turn and went straight for a long time before we had to stop at a traffic light. Next to us was a huge construction site. Daddy pointed. "See there, Kat, they're building a Thrift City."

"We could have bid for some of this work," he said, "but old Mr. Price said, 'No, we only do residential, Bill.' I told him it wouldn't hurt to expand a little." Daddy imitated Mr. Price's scratchy voice. " 'Poppycock! We have enough work.' "

The preschool was in a little house on a side street across from the construction. I stood by Daddy as he held open the front door for Mother. The sun was shining in streaks across his brown work boots. One of Mother's black spike heels had a tiny bit of mud on it; otherwise she looked perfect in her black skirt and the soft black leather jacket that I loved to touch. I wanted to grab hold of her jacket, make her bend down, and whisper in her ear that I could go to work with her. That I would be quiet and good.

We walked down a hallway through the center of the house to a back screen door and there they were, the kids I was supposed to play with, hanging from monkey bars, sitting in a sandbox, chasing one another. I fingered the cap gun in my pocket that Mother didn't know I'd brought. I didn't want to be left here. Mother smiled at me. "See all the kids having fun?" Two girls in dresses playing tag stopped to look at me, and Mother leaned down and told me to take my hands out of my pockets.

The week before, as Gramma lowered herself into her favorite chair to begin a crossword puzzle, she had told me it was time for me to go to preschool. I was five now, and when you are five you need to start playing with other children. "You won't be staying with me so much anymore," she said. I was sitting on the floor next to her chair, playing with the soldiers I had arranged on the rug. Cannons sat on the sill of the picture window that looked out onto Gramma's front lawn, and the afternoon sun spilled past the sill, searing some of the soldiers with light and leaving others in shadow. I gently knocked over a column of ramrod soldiers one by one with my index finger. "I don't want to go," I said, concentrating on the fallen men.

"I know." Gramma leaned slowly forward in her chair. She righted a soldier close to her foot. "But I think it's a good idea. And I believe you'll like it."

I didn't respond, just lined up my soldiers behind Gramma's, and she sat back, licked her pencil lead, and began the crossword puzzle.

Miss Nan saw us from the backyard and came in to lead us to her office. She was huge. As tall as my father and with a voice almost as deep. She laughed a lot and slapped me on the back. "You'll have fun here." Mother and Daddy sat in front of Miss Nan's desk and she offered me a smaller chair next to hers. "Today we're doing the twist."

"Won't *that* be fun," Mother chirped, and Daddy pointed to his watch. Suddenly both Mother and Daddy stood up and kissed me. "Bye-bye," they said. Miss Nan took my hand and they were gone.

We went to the front room of the house, where all the children were now massed in clumps and a red-haired woman was leaning over a table, placing a small record on a blue plastic record player. Chubby Checker's "Let's Twist" came blaring out. All the kids began twisting wildly, hitting one another with their elbows and spinning madly across the room. I moved to the window and looked out toward the construction site. I wanted to catch a glimpse of the bulldozers roaring around eating dirt, but I couldn't see over the rise of the side street. I imagined the cranes swiveling around with their bundles of girders rising higher and higher. Miss Nan came over to me. "Do you know how to twist?" It was hard to hear her because the kids were making so much noise, screaming as they danced.

"No," I shouted.

"I'll show you." She began a slow and careful twist. I saw how she moved her hips in one direction and her arms in the other. I copied her then speeded up the rhythm. "That's a girl. Do the twist!"

I twisted more to the center of the room and enjoyed myself for a few minutes. The dancing felt good, but kids kept ramming into me.

I thought they were doing it on purpose. By the time I'd worked my way back to the edge of the room, the red-haired woman came back and snapped the record player off. Some kids immediately raced down the hall and slammed out the back screen door. I followed them.

The backyard wasn't very large and there was a chain-link fence all the way around it, overgrown with honeysuckle vine. I walked around looking at the fence and stopping occasionally to taste honeysuckle blooms. When I'd gone around the entire yard, I went over to one of the sandboxes and sat on a corner seat. With a stick I'd picked up on my tour of the fence I began to draw maps in the sand. All I could think about was leaving. I wanted to be back with Gramma.

I was thinking of the way we had driven to Miss Nan's—we were on Slaton Road most of the way, that was Gramma's street. Then we crossed the four-lane highway, passed the construction site, and turned right on Miss Nan's road. Slaton Road led back to Gramma's house. It wasn't far, I thought. I would cross the small street first. Just look both ways. It would be easy. Then I would cut across the construction site and get to Slaton Road at the traffic light where it crossed the four-lane.

I drew, wiped the sand clean with my hands, and then drew some more. I drew and drew until I had the roads right.

"Sad that your parents left you here?" a voice behind me boomed.

I jumped a little, dropping my stick. Miss Nan knelt down beside me so she was at my eye level. "I didn't mean to startle you," she said in a softer voice. She put her hand on my shoulder. "Are you a little sad?" she asked. "Is that why you're not playing with the other kids?"

"No," I told her. I didn't want to play with the kids because they all seemed loud and strange. I liked being alone with Gramma much better.

"Your mother will be back to get you early this evening," she said.

"I know," I told her.

Miss Nan hung around for a few more minutes. I picked up my stick and started sketching little figures in the sand. I was trying to draw a bulldozer but it kept looking like a dog. Miss Nan watched me and smiled. "Do you like to draw? When you come inside you can get some paper and crayons and draw all afternoon if you'd like." She turned away to go back inside the house.

I worked a little more on my map. It looked right. There was the diagonal shortcut through the construction site, which would lead me to the four-lane highway. At the traffic light I would cross on red and walk on Slaton Road toward Gramma's.

The screen door was shut and I didn't see Miss Nan. Kids were playing tag and screaming.

I climbed the fence quickly and snuck around to the front of the house. It was easy, like climbing the fence around our pasture. Before I crossed the side street, I looked both ways, then I ran down the embankment that led into the construction site. The slick, moist clay smelled like the compost pile at Poppa's when he turned it over with a pitchfork. At the bottom of the bank I found myself on a large square of land with a few bulldozers roaring close by. They were much bigger and louder than they had seemed from the car, and I checked for my cap gun in the pocket of my shorts. At first I wasn't sure where the four-lane or Slaton Road was. The cranes were far away, next to the skeleton of the building, and they looked smaller than the bulldozers. I looked ahead of me, and finally when one bulldozer chugged out of my view I could see a tiny traffic light swinging. The construction site didn't seem like a shortcut anymore, but I started walking toward the speck of the traffic light.

"Hey, kid!" To my left a man in a yellow hard hat was walking quickly toward me and pointing. I began to run in the direction of the traffic light. He can't catch me, I thought, I'm too fast. I heard another person yell, "Kaaaatherrrrine." I looked over my shoulder and saw Miss Nan at the top of the bank. "Turn on the speed," I said out loud to myself and began running as fast as I could. Several men ran toward me. I tried to run around them but one caught me by the waist. Miss Nan ran up panting and grabbed my hand. She was red in the face. "What d'you think you're doing?"

When the guy grabbed me around the waist, I had lost my breath.

"Crazy kid," the man said. "Could've gotten killed out here."

Miss Nan put her hands on my shoulders and stared into my eyes. "She's safe now." She gripped my hand so tight I yelled, "Ow!"

"Just wait until I get you back to the house. You'll think *ow* then." We started walking.

One of the men followed us. "How old is she anyway?"

"Five," Miss Nan told him over her shoulder.

"Jeez. Spunky little thing."

At the house Miss Nan took me to her office and got out a wooden bolo paddle without the elastic string and ball and gave me hard licks on my bottom. I cried because it hurt but also because I was so mad. I wanted to leave and she wasn't going to let me. Instead, I had to stand in the corner while she did paperwork. I was still sniffling and tried to stop but couldn't. "You think about what you did," she said. "It was dangerous, and you don't want to run away from Miss Nan's. Now you stay right there." She left her office and shut the door.

I could hear faint noises of kids playing and occasionally Miss Nan's deep voice, but the office was mostly quiet and peaceful. The walls were very pale blue and I was standing so close I could see the tiny bristle marks the brush had made on the surface. I began to think about the landmarks on the way home and then to Gramma's. In my mind I tried to picture everything we would pass on Slaton Road; on the way home I would check to see if I was right. There was the big, tall building shaped like a chicken with eyes that rolled and a beak that opened and shut—the Big Chicken—where we went to get fried chicken and biscuits. Then there was Sears, where Daddy bought the lawn mower and I sometimes got clothes. Then the gas station, where Kurt says he'll marry me when I grow up. Then the big cemetery for soldiers, where Daddy says he might be buried someday. And Bob and Joe's used-car lot with the red triangle flags flapping in the wind and the little trailer behind the rows of cars where Bob and Joe have their desks and the candy machine with M&M's for ten cents. As I drew the invisible map on the wall, I knew there were long spaces in between things and I couldn't remember what went in the spaces. I didn't want to miss anything. I was so intent on the landmarks that I forgot to listen for footsteps until the door opened and Miss Nan and Mother hurried in. Mother's voice was high-pitched like it was when she was angry with me and all of her lipstick was gone and one eyebrow was raised. "Sit down," Miss Nan told me. I sat and my mother sat next to me.

Mother shook her finger at me. "I'm going to wear you out when we get home and then your father will have at you."

"Well, she's had a paddling and stood in the corner for half an hour," Miss Nan said.

Mother leaned closer to me, and I smelled her perfume and the cigarette smoke from her boss that she hated. "Your father is going to be mad."

"I've never had a child climb the fence before," Miss Nan said. "She's a strong little girl. Obviously she needs an eagle eye on her."

"She climbs everything." Mother turned to face Miss Nan. "She climbed up to reach the top shelf of the cabinet in her grandmother's kitchen and ate aspirin—she had to have her stomach pumped. She goes up the ladder into the hayloft, where she's not supposed to play. She stands on her Wonder horse in the basement to climb out the window and go up to her Gramma's house when I've told her she can't go."

Miss Nan got something out of her drawer. "I'll understand if you . . ."

Mother didn't let her finish. "You'll keep her, won't you? I can't afford to quit work."

Miss Nan looked at me and then smiled like we might have a secret together. "Well, yes," she drawled out slowly, "I suspect Katherine and I can work things out."

On the drive home I had a hard time looking out the window to check the landmarks. Mother was screaming at me about trying to run away. She said I didn't love her. "Look at me when I'm talking to you," she yelled.

I had to look at her because she was so mad, and I discovered that

Mother was crying. Her makeup streaked down her face; black lines ran from her eyes to the tiny wrinkles at the corners of her mouth. I hadn't meant to make her cry, didn't want her to be unhappy. She ground the gears of the car. "This damn thing," she said. "Your father has stripped its gears I'm sure."

I looked past her, out the car window, watching for the wagon-wheel mailbox that meant we were almost home.

"You have to be good, Katherine, and not do things like run away," Mother said between sobs. "I just can't take it."

"What do you think about stopping at this next town?" Mother asks.

I open my eyes with a start. I hadn't felt asleep, but I must have dozed while I was thinking about running away. When I ran away from nursery school, I was only thinking about leaving and being by myself again with Gramma. I had no idea how far I had to walk to actually get to my grandmother's, and I hadn't thought of how it would upset Miss Nan and make my mother cry. It's a different thing for adults to run away, I'm sure. Adults are supposed to have a better idea than kids of how things are going to turn out in the end.

Chapter Six

We stop for breakfast at a diner in Pelham, which is not far from the border of Virginia. Robert E. Lee and Stonewall Jackson were from Virginia. It's the place of Jackson's Shenandoah Valley campaign; Manassas, where Jackson got his nickname; and Richmond, the capital of the Confederacy. It was also the place of Lee's surrender. I glance at the road atlas tucked beside me on the vinyl seat of the booth. Can I figure out a route to take us to these places that Mother will follow? I see how close we are to Appomattox; surely I can convince her to go there.

The Confederate general and Stonewall dismount. Her aide brings them two cracker boxes to sit on. It's early in the morning. She's hungry, but there isn't time for breakfast yet. They discuss General Hooker. He's an arrogant man, she tells Stonewall. Too confident, Stonewall says. Yes. We can outmaneuver him, she says, but it will be risky. Stonewall is my right hand, she thinks. I cannot do without him.

"Quit looking down at your seat or whatever you're doing and decide what you want for breakfast," Mother says.

I look up and a waitress is there with her pad and pencil. She smiles and nods at me. "And what'll ya have?" I haven't looked at the menu, but I know I want a fried egg and toast. "Somethin' to drink?"

"She'll have orange juice," Mother says.

"Okeydoke," the waitress says and hurries away.

"What do you keep looking at?" Mother asks.

I pick up the road atlas and put it on the table. "I was looking at where we're going."

"Well, tell me." Mother sits back and sips her coffee. Usually nothing happens until Mother gets her first cup. Getting on down the road this morning must have been important or she wouldn't have skipped it until now. The way she is settling herself in the booth, I know we will be relaxed at breakfast and not in a hurry.

"We keep going on Highway Twenty-nine and we head . . ." I look down at the map. ". . . toward Lynchburg, Virginia." I enjoy saying "Virginia." Virginia, the place that Lee considered his country. The place that made Lee turn Lincoln down when he asked him to be the commander of the Union armies. I want to see Appomattox, where my great-great-grandfather had to lay down his arms, where Lee met with Grant to sign the surrender, Lee in his dress uniform and sword and Grant still in his muddy battle clothes, apologizing that in his haste he hadn't been able to change. "We'll be near Appomattox. Could we go?"

Mother sips her coffee. Lots of people are coming in and out of the diner and the bell on the door keeps jingling.

"We'll be on little roads. Maybe we could find some good junk shops," I say, hoping to sway her.

Mother cocks her right eyebrow and grins. "How far?"

I count up the mileage quickly. I wish I had brought my ruler in, to make it easier to estimate. "About twenty-five miles, maybe thirty at the most."

"Sounds good." Mother chuckles. "Yeah, that's a good idea. Let's go see where the Gresham and McConnell families had to eat crow." She laughs a little louder. "Poor ol' Great-Great-Granddaddy Monroe Gresham and his buddy Jed Pendleton, who had to walk home to Georgia from Appomattox."

The waitress comes to our table juggling both our plates. Mother says, still grinning, "If I've heard that Appomattox story once I've heard it a thousand times. After four years of combat, no food worth eating, dead and maimed friends, and Monroe's wounded leg, somehow walking home was the big story."

Mother may hate it, but I love the story about Great-Great-Grandfather Gresham. Sometimes I use a long stick as a crutch when I play in the woods behind our house. I limp around with my crutch for a little while, fall crumpled to the ground, and then crawl to the nearest tree, pulling myself up.

Once, after I'd begged for months, Daddy took me camping overnight in the woods behind our house. We took sandwiches for dinner—he said it was too dry to have a campfire—but we had fun staying up late listening to the owls and looking at the few stars from our sleeping bags spread out on a tarp in a small clearing. Daddy seemed relaxed and happy, and he told me the long version of the story about Monroe Gresham walking home from Appomattox with his buddy Jed.

Daddy said they had shoes, unlike some of the Confederate soldiers, but they were hardly more than pieces of leather tied together with string. And their clothes were in shreds, rags really. Nothing like the dress uniforms in the Kennesaw Mountain museum. That's the stuff people saved, Daddy said. They never wore those uniforms except for getting their pictures made. Daddy told me that when Lee surrendered the Army of Northern Virginia, he arranged for Grant to give the Confederate troops rations because they hadn't eaten anything other than parched corn for days. They had been trying to get to a supply train at Appomattox Station but the Yankees got there first. "Can you imagine it, Kat?" he said. "Nothing but a handful of parched corn every day for a week when you're marching ten, fifteen miles a day. I honestly don't know how they lived." Daddy sighed. "Anyway, Monroe and Jed started home with Yankee coffee, bacon, and hardtack and each had a parole pass saying that they should be allowed to go home. But their guns had been taken up, so they didn't have a way to kill game, and they had at least five hundred miles to walk to get to Marietta. It rained almost every day—the roads were deep in mud and afterward Monroe told his mother that he thought his clothes would grow moss on them before he got home. His leg kept aching—he had been wounded at Gettysburg, but recovered enough to stay with his regiment until the end—and that slowed them up some. On the third day their supplies gave out but they found a household that had food to give them. A young woman, only a few years older than they were, fried them a chicken, made biscuits and gravy, and let them sleep in the barn. Her two brothers and father had been killed in the war. She was running the farm with her two younger sisters and taking care of her invalid mother who was tetched in the head. When Monroe and Jed first walked into the house toward the kitchen, they passed the old lady's room and nodded to her. She mistook them for her sons and commenced to hollering and crying. It took an hour for the younger girls to get her quieted down. 'It gets worse and worse,' the young woman, Marie, told them. 'She's been out of her head ever since we got word that Bennie, the youngest, was killed at Spotsylvania, and lately she's been wandering out of the house and into the woods at night. We don't like to, but we're locking her in to keep her from going to look for him.' Apparently, Jed took a liking to Marie and wanted to stay and help her through planting season, but Monroe was itching to get home. Still, they stayed a few days. Jed fixed the barn roof and Marie made loaves of bread for them to take with them. When they left, Jed took a cutting of the camellia bush in Marie's front yard. Jed was a nut about plants. Camellias from that cutting are still on the Pendleton place."

I watched the lightning bugs that rose at the edge of the woods near us. It took Monroe and Jed two months to get home. By the time they made it, it was the middle of June and the war was completely over. They hadn't found out until May that Lincoln had been assassinated. The first thing they did when they got to Monroe's place was scrub with lye soap in tubs outside while Monroe's mother burned their clothes. They put on some things Monroe had left behind which were baggy on both of them. Jed stayed for a few days, deciding what to do since his mother, his only family, had died in the first year of the war. He ended up working at the Marietta sawmill and years later started a nursery business.

Every time Daddy told the story, details changed. That's what I liked most, that each time it was new. Sometimes he described Marie crying by the gate when they left and sometimes he said Jed sent her money after he'd worked a few months at the sawmill. Sometimes he said the camellia bush cutting was what gave Jed the idea to start a nursery business. Sometimes he talked about the miles they walked each day—up to thirty miles they would do in a day, he'd say. They would get up at four thirty to start walking, stopping at nine or so to eat breakfast. That everywhere they stopped, people would give them whatever they could. At the ferries where they crossed rivers, they saw hundreds of other soldiers walking home.

Mother pours syrup over her stack of pancakes. "Yes sir, you need to see Appomattox, honey. You need to see where the South had to admit they were licked. It'll do you good." She cuts a bite of pancake with the side of her fork in two easy movements. It doesn't matter to me what she says; all that matters is that we're going.

"Don't cut your egg up all at once and mix it together like that." Mother scowls at me. "It doesn't look nice." Poppa and Gramma never bother me about the way I eat my eggs. I think about when I will see them again. Our trip to Maine and back may take longer than two weeks. It may be a month before I see them. That's twice as long as camp, where you're doing things every minute so you don't have much time to miss anybody.

For the last three summers I've gone to Camp Summit in the north Georgia mountains near Rabun Gap. A lot of the same girls go every year, and my friend Fran and I always get to be in the same cabin. I wish Milly would come too, but her mother says she would be too homesick. I can't understand that. Every time I go I'm always sorry when it ends. We have a schedule and practically every hour during the day we switch to a new activity—swimming, canoeing, archery, games, riflery, arts and crafts, and horseback riding. Every night there's a different event like movies in the gym or an all-camp scavenger hunt or counselor skits. At meals we sing. If you get a good counselor she'll let you stay up late and ask her questions about college, what the dorms are like, and what she's studying. I write a letter every night, to Gramma and Poppa, Mother and Daddy, or Aunt Laura, and most days I get at least two letters at mail call.

Being on this trip with Mother isn't busy like camp. There's more time to think while we're in the car, and to wonder about things. I'm starting to wonder how much Mother has really planned and how much is just happening to us, and why Daddy isn't supposed to know where we are exactly.

I eat more of my egg and watch her. She is gazing out the plate-glass window with her coffee mug in her hands.

"Mother," I say. She turns away from the window.

"What?" She puts her mug down and picks up her fork.

"Are we running away?"

Her laugh sounds forced. The waitress comes by our booth and fills up Mother's mug. "Didn't you like your orange juice?" the waitress asks me.

"It's fine," Mother says, "she'll drink it in a minute."

Mother turns back to me. "I *told* you what we're doing. We're going to buy a bunch of antiques and open an antique shop." She puts more sugar in her coffee. "We're not running away. We're breaking free," she says and her eyes are serious as she leans toward me. "I've got most of the money from my exhibition and I'm going to buy us a whole new life." She leans back against her seat and she raps her index finger against the table a couple of times for emphasis. "I mean it—a whole new life. I'm not going to be stuck with your father's family telling me what to do, where to go, who to see, how to act. And trying to steal you away from me. You're *my* daughter. *I'm* going to take care of you."

Her voice rises and it sounds sharp. The man in the booth behind Mother turns around to look at us.

She stares at my plate. "Quit cutting your toast that way. That kind of stuff is for little kids." She pushes her plate over to the side. She's eaten only half of her pancakes. "Hurry up and finish," she says.

I start eating and even drink some of my juice. I've said the wrong thing and upset her. When she's upset she will say anything, wild things that she can't possibly mean. It's best to be quiet now.

The general must keep her strength up. She has many important decisions to make in a day and she must remain aware of not only the enemy, but also what's going on within her own staff and among her troops. She needs to understand the generals serving under her and monitor the morale of the men. She needs to remain vigilant so that she always knows which way the wind is blowing.

"I'm going to have a separate studio with lots of windows where I can paint. No more basement for me, no sirree. My shop will be at the edge of town in a stone house. I love stone houses. That'll be the name, Stone House Antiques. I'll paint a sign and come up with a logo for our business cards. You'll be a partner, Kat. We'll have flower gardens out front and wrought-iron furniture for people to sit on. I want a weathervane too. Some kind of unusual weathervane. We'll hunt for one." She looks at me, beaming.

As she talks she gestures with her hands. On her left ring finger, above her wedding band, she wears a garnet ring with gold prongs holding the stone in the setting. An artist friend made it for her. The gold's valuable, she says, but the garnet is junk. On her right ring finger she wears an amethyst that was her mother's. It's a large stone cut in a rectangle and the setting is simple, almost invisible. Her mother's ring, she told me once, is very valuable. I drink more of my orange juice. I'm getting hot sitting by the window.

Mother stops talking when the waitress leaves the check. For a minute I listen to the noises around me: the bell of the cash register, the sound of forks and knives tapping plates and glasses being set down on the Formica tabletops, the murmur of people talking and laughing, feet scraping the floor, and the door opening and shutting with its jingle.

She opens her purse. "You'll see, Kat." She pulls bills out of her wallet. "I'm going to be a real success."

Mother needs to be away with me on this trip to get the stock for her business. She knows what she's doing. In a few days she'll probably call Daddy to tell him where we are and when we'll be home. He won't be so mad then and will be able to listen to her plan. I'm her partner in this, and everything is going to work out.

Chapter Seven

Just north of Chatham, Virginia, Aretha belts it out above the hum of the wheels and the whoosh of the cars passing in the opposite direction. I tap my foot and try to sing along like Mother, but she hits all the notes and knows the words better. "Let your mind go," Mother sings. I catch up on the chorus and sing it loud. Mother can scream just like Aretha. "Ooowaah," she hollers.

"You better think," I jump in right on cue with Aretha and Mother.

When the song is done, Mother clicks the radio off. Even with the road noise, the inside of the car is a sudden empty space. We ride in silence for a few miles. We're not far from Lynchburg, which is the last big town before we turn off to go to Appomattox.

"Your hair," Mother says, looking over at me with a wistful expression. "Your hair blowing looks just like my mother's—wispy, fine hair." I hope she doesn't start thinking too much about her mother—that always makes her sad. I open up my *Golden Book of the Civil War.*

"Mother loved Cape Cod," she begins.

I try to concentrate on my book—the chapter is about the Confederacy's and Union's ironclads, the *Merrimac* and the *Monitor.*

The general watches from shore as the Merrimac *and* Monitor *clash. The day before, the* Merrimac *had sunk the* Congress *and left another ship in flames. The* Merrimac *is the Confederate hope to break the blockade. Now the two iron ships pound each other with shot at close range. She can't see well through the clouds of smoke, but neither ship seems to be able to maneuver very well. And now what's happening? The* Monitor *escapes into shallow water where the* Merrimac *can't follow. Finally, the* Merrimac *retreats, unable to end the blockade.*

"Almost every summer Mother went to the Cape. The summer before my father left us, I was younger than you are now; only nine. For two months we stayed in a cottage that belonged to my father's parents. It had gray shingles. They weren't painted, the wood had weathered that color. I loved those shingles." Mother pauses. I keep my book open but I am only staring at the illustration.

"She painted watercolors that summer. She painted the shore with the grassy dunes over and over. On weekends Dad would come out and stay. He took me to the Sandwich glass museum and one Saturday night a lot of Mother's artist friends came over for a spaghetti dinner. Everyone drank a lot of wine and Dad grabbed two paintbrushes and beat a rhythm on the wood plank table in the dining room when Mother put 'Sing, Sing, Sing' by the Benny Goodman Orchestra on the record player. It was the only time I ever saw him drum. Mother said he had been wonderful in college and could have gone professional if it hadn't been for his family wanting him to run their bank. He always wore a three-piece gray suit, but that one summer weekend I remember him in khaki pants and a dark blue T-shirt twirling those paintbrushes in his fingers.

"I was only thirteen when she died," Mother says softly. "Only two years older than you." She has often told me the story of how my grandmother Carter died unexpectedly of a stroke. How my mother found her on the floor of the parlor when she came home from school. I hope she won't tell it again now. The fact that she died doesn't bother me; after all, I was born long after that. But hearing Mother tell the whole story with all the details of what kind of rug it was and what she'd been doing at school before she came home, how she had no warning, makes me nervous somehow.

• • •

We need a diversionary tactic, the general thinks; something to confuse the Yankees, put them off track. She calls her cavalry general—it's time for a brief raid at the edge of the enemy lines, she says, have the men saddle up. Remember, nothing very sustained, just give us enough time to move our cannons into position before they notice what we're doing.

I pull out the atlas and open to the map of the whole United States. Mother wipes her eyes with her finger; she is crying a little. "We're not many days from the Cape," I remind her. "When we get there you can show me your favorite places. We'll go all the way to the end and walk straight out into the ocean. And you can find the weathervane for the shop, I bet."

Mother laughs out loud, her cheeks still wet. "You're a little genius, Kat. You know just the right thing to say. Where do you get that?" She pokes me gently where she says I might get love handles if I keep eating french fries like a field hand. "Yup, on Cape Cod we'll find great antiques. Sandwich glass, ship models, and old corks from fishing nets. And we'll eat fried clams like you've never seen before."

I turn the pages of the atlas to Massachusetts. Mother grew up somewhere in Boston. I look at the cities and towns on the map near the Cape and around Boston: New Bedford, Plymouth, Brockton, Rockland, Weymouth, Lynn, Salem, and Gloucester. My grandmother exhibited her watercolors at the library in Boston; I wonder where it is in the city.

"Your grandmother liked to get up very early and walk on the beach while the sun rose," Mother says softly, more to herself than to me. "Sometimes she woke me up and I went with her, but more often I woke up and realized she'd already left. I could tell that the house was empty. It was like Mother filled up wherever she was with invisible energy or electricity. You could sense it. Daddy said it too, but he said that she was just too much. That she went too far with everything."

I don't like the way Mother's tone of voice sounds. Now it has an edge, like she is drifting into anger. Sometimes she says it was her father's fault that her mother had a stroke. His leaving her did it, she says.

The cavalry does a wonderful job and gets back with only one soldier wounded, and the cannons are almost in place on the short knoll. The general considers her options. Yes, it's time to move out a corps of her infantry to be ready to surprise the Yankee left flank right after her artillery lets loose.

Mother clicks the radio back on. "All You Need Is Love" by the Beatles is playing.

As quickly as she had shifted to anger, Mother seems to catch herself. "Hey, Kat," she says in a fake cheery voice. "Let's keep our minds on what we're trying to do right now. Look at that map. How far are we from the scene of the South's awful, terrible defeat?"

If Mother didn't get so upset when she talked about her parents, I would ask her about them. I think about what they must have been like, especially my grandmother, because Mother tells me I look just like her and because all three of us can draw so well. Sometimes my drawing embarrasses me. The other kids stare at my art projects and ask me how I do it. Teachers gush over the simplest things. Mother says not to worry, that we are born being able to see all the lines out there in the world. "Lots of people can't see the lines to save their life," she says, "even when you show them right where they are."

In my notebook I am drawing portraits of all the major Confederate generals. I started with Stonewall Jackson and Robert E. Lee and now I'm drawing Jeb Stuart. When mother saw my first sketches last night she insisted I add Abraham Lincoln. In the back of my notebook, she made a quick full-body sketch of Lincoln with a top hat. "Look at the pictures in your book," she told me, "and then put the book away and see if you can sketch the face quickly. That way, you'll train yourself to look more carefully and to remember what you see."

Most of my sketches are copies of photographs in my American Heritage Junior Library book about the battle of Gettysburg and my

Golden Book of the Civil War. Aunt Laura gave me the American Heritage book—it's exactly like the one she has. Aunt Laura has a lot of Civil War books. She teaches American history at the high school and was a history major in college. We live out in the country, but Aunt Laura lives in an apartment house for teachers off Marietta's downtown square. Some weeks I spend more nights at her apartment than I do in my own bed, and from her room I can hear traffic noises and, three times a night, after I go to bed, the train going by. At home the nights are quiet. We live on twenty acres that belong to Poppa and the only night sounds are crickets and maybe once in a while a siren on the main road a couple of miles from our house. Aunt Laura's apartment is sophisticated and she lives all by herself. I want to be like her when I grow up.

Aunt Laura is eight years older than Mother and her hair is short and curly, brown with a few strands of gray. Her mouth and eyes are almost always smiling, even if she's staring off into space. When I've been the most confused, Aunt Laura has been the one who understands me. Of everyone in my family she seems to be the calmest, especially around Mother. And I never have to worry about paying attention to Aunt Laura's moods. It seems like she pays attention to mine.

When I'm with Aunt Laura, we do grown-up things. She took me to see *Gone With the Wind* at the Loew's Grand in Atlanta, the movie theater where it has played continuously since its premiere in 1939, and we sat in the balcony. Afterward she took me to Rich's department store restaurant, the Magnolia Room, for a late lunch. When I spend the night with Aunt Laura I look at her books. She has several books with nothing but photographs from the war. My favorites are Mathew Brady's and Alexander Gardner's Civil War photographs. I read about the wagons full of photography equipment they used to follow the fighting and take pictures right after the battles were over. I can't get enough of these photographs. I stare at the dead soldiers in the crevices of rocks, rifles lying useless against their drooping bodies. I dip into Allen Tate's biography of Stonewall Jackson, and Shelby

Foote's first volume of Civil War history. Aunt Laura is proud of how well I read aloud. "Hey, Louise," she calls, knocking on the door across the hall, "I want you to listen to this." Louise invites us in to sit on her sofa and I read from one of the books. "The kid's never seen this before; isn't she great? Some of my high schoolers can't read this well." Louise gives us Neapolitan ice cream or a Coke float. When I grow up I want to live in a boardinghouse with other women who have Cokes in their refrigerators and bookshelves everywhere. Louise even has bookshelves in her bathroom.

Aunt Laura visited a lot of the Civil War battle sites while she was in college, and her bookshelves are full of the guidebooks that she bought. I never get tired of reading them. The cover of the one from Gettysburg has the Union and Confederate flags crossed. Others have black-and-white sketches of a general or a battle scene on the cover. They tell stories about the generals, have diagrams of the armies' movements and lots of photographs—some of monuments, others of cannons with soldiers in jaunty caps leaning against them, and always photographs of bodies lying on the ground. So many times I've dreamed that when I grow up I'll tour all the battlefields Aunt Laura's been to. Now I may have a chance to see at least a few before I'm even old enough to drive.

The beautiful, gently winding road heading to Appomattox seems to soothe Mother. She hasn't told me any more of the story of her mother's death, which is a big relief. Mother is handling things fine. Daddy says if she would just concentrate on what is right in front of her she would be okay. "Reliving the past," he says, "doesn't do anyone any good." Outside the car window, we aren't passing any more gas stations, restaurants, or businesses. We have entered a world that looks a lot like pictures of the countryside right after the surrender. Rolling fields, wooden fences lining the road, houses far apart, horses grazing here and there.

"Hey." Mother points to the side of the road. "Did you see that sign, 'Antiques Bought and Sold'?"

She turns around where the shoulder of the road widens, and grins as she drives down a gravel driveway that leads to a run-down rambling farmhouse set far off the road. Old shade trees in the front yard partially hide the wraparound front porch. At one time, the house must have been impressive, but a large ramshackle shed has been built on one side and the house hasn't been painted for years.

"This will be a great place for bargains," Mother says. Her face is so hopeful and excited that it is hard to believe she was sad earlier. As we walk up the steps I smell cat pee and when we open the front door, the smell rushes out at us. "Hmmh," Mother mutters and forges ahead.

The place is dim and full of furniture—tall corner cabinets, marble-topped bureaus, ornate mirrors edged with gilt, and old children's toys lined up in rows on sideboards and long dining room tables. An orange tabby cat jumps from a bookshelf and lands in the middle of a maroon brocade sofa. His tail stands straight up and quivers as I walk by. I pass a metal windup rocket ship with wheels, dolls in boxes still wrapped up in their brittle cellophane, and a clump of junior football pads with a helmet next to them. Dust covers everything. Two tiny gray kittens chase each other under the legs of one of the dining room tables. In the corner of the second big room, a huge man and woman sit in metal fold-up chairs watching a black-and-white portable TV on a rickety card table. They keep their eyes glued to it until we get right up next to them. They are watching a stock car race.

"Lap 'em, lap 'em, you sorry sonabitch," the man shouts and slaps his wide thigh.

"Hush, Larry. We got customers."

The man reaches into his shirtfront and I see the wire leading from his shirt to his right ear. My great-aunt Mabel has a hearing aid like this and she is always reaching into her bosom to adjust it.

"Sorry," the man says. "Had my aid off. Didn't know anybody had come in."

"What can we help you with?" the woman asks with one eye still on the television.

"We're just looking." Mother walks over to a dining table covered with glass dishes. The sun peeks through the top of a window that isn't blocked by stacks of boxes or mammoth furniture and illuminates a cranberry red cup and saucer here, a cobalt blue dresser set there. I watch Mother as she begins to casually finger the glassware. She moves slowly down the length of the table. Both the man and the woman are again staring at their TV. Mother stops, picks up a plate, holds it up to what light there is, runs her finger carefully around its edge, and then puts it back down on the dusty table.

I go over to a table of toys and examine the brightly colored metal racers and the huge Chatty Cathy dolls standing mute, waiting for someone to set them free. Then I see the rows of shoe boxes full of baseball cards.

Baseball cards are okay. I have a small collection stored in a Russell Stover candy box on one of the shelves in my closet. My closet has wooden louvered doors and if I squat up and down in front of them really fast, I can see the contents through the slats. But I can't go up and down for very long and sometimes I wonder if I'm really seeing or only remembering the inside of my closet. I like the idea of being able to see through things. I ordered X-ray glasses from Bazooka bubble gum after collecting a hundred wrappers and sending a dollar. The glasses were a huge disappointment; all they did was add a fuzzy halo around things.

I flip through the contents of a box divided by cardboard pieces with the name of the team at the top of each in red handwritten letters. The lettering is a mix of cursive and print, with capital and lowercase letters used randomly—cinciNNaTi reDs. There are only a few Atlanta Braves cards and they are ones I already have: Hank Aaron, Joe Torre, and Felix Millan. Under the St. Louis Cardinals I look for Bob Gibson. His card isn't there. Two Lou Brocks, but I already have him. Every summer Poppa takes me to two or three baseball games at Atlanta Fulton County Stadium. Once my parents went with us to an Old Timers' game where Satchel Paige pitched. After the game I went down and leaned over the fence to get him to sign my program.

"He's famous, Kat," my father said. "He would have been more famous if they'd let him in the major leagues before he got old. He was something when he was younger. I used to go to Negro League games in Alabama to watch him."

"Save that program," Mother said. "It'll be worth a lot of money someday."

I have put the program somewhere safe, but now as I flip through the baseball cards I can't remember where it is. Maybe in my closet underneath my Russell Stover box. My face begins to heat up. If I can't remember, Mother might ask me but I won't be able to tell her and she will be angry. Maybe it's in my desk. In the bottom drawer I keep my photographs and scrapbooks from summer camp. In the second drawer I put all my school notebooks and I have a cigar box with pencils and pens. Next to the desk is a small bookshelf with my *Golden Book Encyclopedia of Science* and the *Golden Book Atlas of the World* set. Then I remember where the baseball program is. I put it next to the last volume, the atlas of Asia. I am relieved. My face cools off. I glance quickly at Mother. She is still inspecting glass dishes and the woman stands up and walks over to her.

"Finding everything?"

"Yes, you have so many nice things," Mother says.

The woman nods and walks to the front door, calling for her dog.

In the next few rows of shoe boxes are football cards, which don't interest me, but at the end of a sideboard, the boxes contain Civil War trading cards. I look at each one carefully. I have never seen this kind of card before, and for the first time I think that maybe there are other kids as interested in Civil War history as I am. Each card is set up like the front page of a newspaper called the *Civil War News*, with a date and a major headline with two columns of story underneath it. On the other side of the card is a scene in color to illustrate the article. One card shows General Lee on a horse, visiting his wounded soldiers. The article tells a little of Lee's biography and that he lifted the men's spirits so much that day when he visited them at the temporary medical station next to the battlefield. I turn this card over several times, examining it. The date is April 1, 1863, the location, Southern headquarters. I don't know what battle that could have been. I examine the picture on the front of the card again. The artist has made Lee's horse brown with a white star in the middle of his forehead, though I know that Lee's horse, Traveller, was light gray. Everyone knows that. I wonder how the artist could have made that kind of mistake. I consider that the card might be a joke—it's dated April Fools' Day.

I pick another card, "Badly Battered Union Retreats." It is dated May 10, 1863, from Chancellorsville, Virginia. The picture shows a charging Confederate officer getting ready to slash a Union foot soldier with his raised sword. The officer has on cavalry gloves with wide bands that protect his wrists and forearms. His red sash is streaming behind him. The colors on all the cards are intense, lots of deep purple, bright reds. The battle scenes are gory: a Confederate soldier run completely through by a Union bayonet, bright red blood dripping off the silver blade and soaking his shirt.

I keep flipping. Soon I come across a card unlike the others, "15-Year-Old Boy Hanged as Spy," dated June 29, 1862. The picture shows a defiant teenager, a noose around his neck, with his mother and little brother kneeling in front of him, grasping his knees. He is being hanged for giving information to the Confederates. Location: Eden, Pennsylvania. Deep in Yankee territory.

Mother has left the table of glassware and is talking to the woman. The television is still blaring the racket of stock cars making their endless laps. The man gestures to another part of the store and Mother nods. I have at least a few more minutes with the trading cards. On the front of the shoe box is written: "Most 50 cents." The General Lee card is in a plastic sleeve and has a sticker marked $1.00. Each card is numbered, so I know the set goes up to at least #86. I have eighteen dollars, but it has to last the whole trip. I pick out cards showing the battles of Gettysburg and Chancellorsville, the odd one of General Lee on the brown horse, and the boy spy being hanged. I also choose the balloonists, the fall of Atlanta to Union soldiers, and

General Sherman. Another in my pile shows General Stuart dying of his wound, still another is titled "North Blasts Rebel Army at Petersburg." As I stand with my choices laid on the table, I shuffle through the ones I will be leaving behind. If I had more money, I would buy them all and then try to collect the rest of the eighty-six.

Mother comes over to me carrying a mantel clock that has a reclining figure of a woman on top of its wooden case. "Isn't this great? It has the most unusual ornamentation I've ever seen and it's in good working order. See, it's got its key." She holds up a small brass winged key that doesn't look like a real key, but has a round hollow end that fits into a slot on the back of the clock to wind it.

"What'd you find?" Mother asks as she looks at the Civil War cards I have spread out on the table. She picks up the cards and then puts the clock down on the table so she can look through one of the boxes. "These are interesting, Kat." She examines a few of the cards. "Someone painted these scenes, probably on canvas, and then they reproduced them for the cards. They're obviously done fast, but the compositions are complex." Mother smiles at me. "Do you want these?" In one hand she picks up the cards I had laid out and in the other hand she grasps her clock.

"Yes, please," I say, hoping she means to buy them for me. I wish desperately I had chosen more.

"Come on, I want to show you what else we're going to get." I follow her to the large dining table where she had been studying the glass dishes.

"This is cranberry and cobalt glass," Mother whispers to me, bending down. "The woman's got it marked so cheap, she must not know what she has. Not many pieces have chips and in the cranberry there's a complete set." She reaches to the middle of the table to pick up a large dark red glass bowl. "Look at this," she says. "Isn't this wonderful?" I nod and notice that the fat woman is making the little dog stand on his back legs to beg for a tiny dog biscuit. He only has one front leg, and he waves it madly.

As Mother pays the woman, the man shuffles over with an empty box and stack of newspapers to wrap up the glass. "We're traveling a long way," Mother is saying. "We need it packed very tightly." The man grunts. Some of the pieces of newspaper have faint yellow stains on them.

"My daughter is interested in Civil War history. We're going to Appomattox."

"Well, you're practically right there," the woman says and watches her little dog root around in his bed. "Get settled, Joey," she says and then looks up at Mother again. "The McLean House and all the other buildings—where they signed the surrender and all—are down the road a short piece."

Three-legged Joey follows his master out to the parking lot as the man presses the box of glass against his Santa Claus stomach and turns red in the face. After much discussion, he and my mother wedge it safely in the trailer. He lumbers, swaying from side to side, back into his antique shop. Joey hops behind him.

Chapter Eight

"I thought that guy was going to have a heart attack," Mother says as she starts the car.

The air is so fresh outside. I roll my window down despite the dust from the driveway. No more smell of cat pee. I get out my Civil War trading cards and shuffle through them slowly, stopping on the hanged boy spy. I wonder how long it took for him to die. Do you die right when you drop and the rope breaks your neck or does it take longer? I held my throat, took a deep breath, and let it out. Maybe you just suffocate.

"What are you sighing about?" Mother asks. She looks over at me like she's a little mad.

"Nothing," I say quickly. "The antique place stunk so bad that I was taking big breaths of air."

"Boy, did it ever." Mother laughs. "That's what you get when you don't neuter your male cats. Marking their territory all over creation."

We follow the signs to Appomattox Court House National Historical Park, but before we get there Mother spots a pull-in next to a grove of trees and a small cemetery. "Here's a good picnic spot," she says. The cemetery has an ornate iron fence all the way around it and outside the fence under the biggest tree is a granite boulder with a brass plaque that says this is a Confederate cemetery. Beyond the grove of trees is a split-rail fence and someone's field of half-grown corn. Mother gets the cooler out of the backseat and opens a jar of green olives, which she eats one by one while she gets out the lunch meat and bread for sandwiches.

The wrought-iron cemetery gate is chained shut. I trace its elaborate design of a weeping willow tree and crossed swords and look at the lines of graves. Rosebushes are blooming between some of the headstones.

The plaque on the boulder says that it's from the United Daughters of the Confederacy. APPOMATTOX. HERE ON SUNDAY APRIL 9, 1865 AFTER FOUR YEARS OF HEROIC STRUGGLE IN DEFENSE OF PRINCIPLES BELIEVED FUNDAMENTAL TO THE EXISTENCE OF OUR GOVERNMENT LEE SURRENDERED 9000 MEN THE REMNANT OF AN ARMY STILL UNCONQUERED IN SPIRIT. At the bottom in smaller letters it says: ERECTED JUNE 1, 1926 BY APPOMATTOX CHAPTER UNITED DAUGHTERS OF THE CONFEDERACY. Aunt Laura said I'll be a UDC when I get old enough. It was started after the Civil War to support Confederate veterans. Over Aunt Laura's mantel are two framed UDC certificates—one hers and one Mildred Gresham McConnell's, Monroe Gresham's daughter. She has already shown me the family history I'll have to send in to prove I'm a descendant of a Confederate soldier. Great-Great-Grandfather Gresham fought in First Manassas, Second Manassas, Fredericksburg, Chancellorsville, Gettysburg, Petersburg, and Appomattox Station.

When he was recuperating from his leg wound after Gettysburg, he sent my great-great-grandmother a picture of himself lying on a cot outside a white medical tent. Aunt Laura had the photograph framed. You can see the other men lying on cots, some of them propped up a little on their arms so they can look at the photographer, others lying flat on their backs like maybe they can't move at all. A man in a white shirt and a dark vest with his sleeves rolled up is standing between two of the cots. He must be the doctor. Aunt Laura told me that after my great-great-grandfather Gresham got home from the war, they took him to Atlanta for several operations, but his leg was never right. He farmed a little, the best he could—one leg was shorter than the other and if he wasn't behind the plow he had to use a cane.

People said he was mean, Aunt Laura told me, but it was probably because his leg was always hurting. When he died at fifty-five, the doctor said it was because of an infection that developed in the old wound. My great-great-grandmother lived forty-six more years and died when she was ninety-five on a Sunday morning while she was getting ready for church. Aunt Laura says she wants me to know all the family stories, especially because my father doesn't care about remembering them, but I tell her that she's wrong about Daddy. That he has told me all about Monroe Gresham walking home from Appomattox, and stories about them as kids, like the one when he and Aunt Laura were supposed to carry a bowl of potato salad through the pasture to their grandmother's house. They got into a fight about who was going to open the gate, and set the potato salad on the ground. While they shoved each other around, one of the cows came over and ate it. Aunt Laura laughed when I told her this story and said that she stands corrected about my father.

But Aunt Laura is right that I care more about remembering the family stories than Daddy does. I collect them. Whenever she tells me one, I write down the outline of it or sketch it out as a cartoon. Sometimes when I'm staying overnight at her apartment, she'll tell me two or three at a time. She says I'll be the repository of the family history; I'll pass it on to my children.

"You want a Coke?" Mother asks. At home Mother never buys them, but she got six Cokes and six Tabs to put in our cooler. "Cheaper from the store than from the Coke machine," she tells me.

Mother asks me about the plaque while we eat lunch.

"It's about the surrender," I say. "The Appomattox UDC chapter put it up. It says Lee's army was unconquered in spirit."

"Typical," Mother says. "Making war seem wonderful."

I get my pocketknife out to peel my apple. Poppa can peel an apple in one long strip. Though I often try, at some point I always cut too shallow and break my spiral.

"Kat, you understand that all this Southern honor stuff is crazy, don't you?"

I'm not really sure what she means and debate whether I want to ask her.

"Are you listening to me?"

"Yes, ma'am," I answer quickly. "But which honor stuff is crazy?"

"Okay. You know the Civil War was about slavery."

"Right," I reply.

"Well, some people in the South try to bury that fact by saying it was over states' rights. But what states' rights were they concerned about? The right to own people!"

"But what about honor?" I ask.

Mother walks over to the plaque. "Principles. The principle they fought for was slavery."

I didn't want to ask her a third time, but I still didn't understand why being honorable was crazy. Wasn't Robert E. Lee right to fight for the South, to not fight against men from his home state of Virginia? I consider this as I peel my apple. My hand is steady and the spiral is hanging down beautifully. After Poppa peels his apple, he cuts sections, spears them, and lifts them to his mouth to eat from the tip of his knife. He says I shouldn't do this because I might cut my lip. I miss Poppa.

"It's the same kind of backward thinking that killed Martin Luther King, Jr.," Mother says. "The South doesn't want to let go of segregation—they can't have slaves, so they've set up the next thing to it." When Martin Luther King, Jr., was assassinated, Mother was shocked. "There will be riots for years," she said. "I hope they burn the South down." She kept me home from school to watch King's funeral and procession through the streets of Atlanta and I stared at the images on the television, knowing that I was viewing history. Mother cried, but she also said angry things about idiot Southern white people. I was angry too—but I didn't like it when she said those things about

Southerners. I'm a Southerner, and so are Daddy and our whole family.

I had talked to Aunt Laura about civil rights before Martin Luther King, Jr., was assassinated. Separate but equal wasn't right, she said; the Supreme Court overthrew it years ago but our schools in the South had only recently integrated. She had done a week in her class on the history of civil rights, and taught her students all about the Civil Rights Act of 1964 and the Voting Rights Act of 1965. "Next to constitutional amendments, these are the most important pieces of legislation in the last hundred years," she told me. "And King and Lyndon Johnson were responsible for making them happen."

Only two months after King's death, right before our trip, Bobby Kennedy was assassinated too, and even though it was after midnight when the news reports came on television, Mother woke me up and called Aunt Laura. As we watched the footage of Kennedy lying on the floor with the crowd of people all around him, Mother sobbed and told me she didn't know what the world was coming to. On Saturday morning Mother, Aunt Laura, and I watched Bobby Kennedy's funeral on television. I was as transfixed by it as I had been by King's. It was as if I had known both of these men and in that moment it seemed that anyone who was trying to do good things for the country might be killed.

When Bobby Kennedy had entered the nomination race, Mother decided he would be better than Gene McCarthy. Daddy told her she was a damn fool for supporting a Kennedy. "You just want to vote for him because he's a Yankee," Daddy had said. "A Yankee from Massachusetts. His family got their money from bootlegging. They're no better than mountain moonshiners. Crooks that sent their kids to Harvard." When he ranted about the Kennedys, it felt like he was yelling directly at Mother about something she had done.

Mother never tried to argue with Daddy when he berated the Kennedys. She told me he was irrational when it came to them, that he didn't disagree with their politics—he just had it in his mind that they cheated to get where they are. I wasn't sure she was right about why he disliked them, but I did know that one of the worst things he could say about a man was that he had cheated. Daddy was also against George Wallace, and called him a hatemonger. He and Mother agreed about that. I heard him talking with Poppa, saying that it slayed him that other people in the country would think everyone in the South was like Wallace.

I lose my concentration and with only one inch to go I cut too shallow on my apple peel. Still, the spiral turned out fairly long. I dangle it in the light.

"You and your pocketknife," Mother says. "For heaven's sake, eat your apple." She crumples her paper plate and walks over to the trash barrel.

I think about honor some more. No one in my family considered George Wallace to be honorable because he wanted to keep Black people down and not give them their rights. But Aunt Laura said Robert E. Lee was an honorable man, and at the same time said it was right that the North won the war and ended slavery. Could the Confederates have been wrong and still honorable?

"Come on, kid. Let's hit the road." Mother's voice interrupted my thoughts.

After the short drive to Appomattox, we park and walk up to the McLean House, where Lee surrendered to Grant, a stately three-story brick home with a large porch on the front. The McLeans must have been well off. Mother carries her sketchpad and a zip-pouch of several black drawing pencils. In addition to the McLean House there is a cluster of buildings, most of them brick, with paths leading to each through mown grass.

"You go on," she tells me. "See all the exhibits. I'm going to sit under that tree and sketch." She points across the dirt road that runs in front of the house.

I buy a ticket at the visitor center, which is a replica of the Appomattox County Court House, and hurry back to the front of the McLean House to join a group guided by a National Park ranger in a Smokey Bear hat. Mother waves at me from under her tree.

"Here on this road the Confederate soldiers turned over their weapons and their flags," the guide says. A man next to me in plaid Bermuda shorts and black socks takes a picture of the guide. A little girl in a yellow dress with white polka dots tugs on her mother's arm, saying, "When are we going?" The sun has come out from behind the clouds and the top of my head is getting hot. Beyond the sturdy brick buildings are rolling fields. It smells like hay bales and mown grass.

"General Joshua Chamberlain of Maine was in charge of receiving weapons from the Confederates, and his brigade was lined up on this side." The guide points. "When the first group approached, commanded by General Gordon of Georgia, General Chamberlain ordered his troops to salute the Confederates. General Gordon, who was on horseback, returned the salute by dropping his own sword point to his boot and then ordered his own brigades to perform the marching salute as they approached to give the Union soldiers their arms. All day long the Confederates marched by and stacked their weapons. The men cried when they had to give up their regimental flags." The guide pauses. "Here, more than one hundred years ago, with respect and honor, the Union began to come back together as one nation." The Union general thought the Confederates were honorable, so much so he made his men salute them. I take this story as an answer; the men who fought one another knew honor and there was honor on both sides.

In front of me, a man in a ponytail and a brown suede fringed vest turns to his friend and says, "Boy, is this a lot of hokey crap. Let's split."

"Does anyone have any questions?" The guide looks over the group. "Well then, I thank you for joining the tour." The guide takes off his hat and wipes his brow. I ask if I can see where the surrender was signed. "You missed the first part," he says to me. "I start up again in an hour."

"Oh, I don't think Mother will want to stay that long." I point to Mother sitting under the tree with her sketchbook. I really don't want to miss seeing the surrender room.

"Well, now," he says, looking at Mother. "You could go through the house yourself and read the display cards. Or maybe we should go ask your mother to let you stay longer." The guide begins walking toward Mother before I can respond. She won't like him talking to her about the next tour; she'll think it's my idea, that I have cajoled him, and she might be angry.

I catch up with the guide. "Don't say anything to her about the tour," I urge him.

He stops and smiles at me. "Don't worry. She won't get mad. I'll ask her nicely. What's your name?"

"Kat."

"Kat what?"

"Kat McConnell."

"Good Scottish name, me lassie."

Mother is leaning back against the tree trunk with her sketchpad propped on her knees. She looks up as we approach.

"Is there a problem?" she asks.

"No, ma'am." The guide takes off his hat. "Thought I'd offer my services. Your daughter missed the first part of my talk and it'll be an hour before I start another group tour. She seems to think you will be leaving before then."

Mother nods.

"I'd be glad to give the two of you an informal tour now if you'd like." Mother's expression hasn't changed, and he pauses. "Just enough to cover the part your daughter missed."

The corners of Mother's mouth lift slightly in a smile. I doubt the guide can even tell. "I'm sure Kat would love it if you would give her the first part of your talk. We will have to leave shortly." Mother resumes drawing. She always sketches quickly and I rarely see her make a line that doesn't look right. I am so much slower and she often tells me that I need to hold my pencil lightly so that I can sketch faster. "You don't look at something and then transfer it to the paper," she says. "You feel it. It's one big flow."

"It's better to have more than one in an audience," the guide says cheerfully. "My name is George Collier. I'm a Ph.D. student in history at the University of Virginia—was born and raised right here in the burg of Appomattox."

Mother keeps sketching without looking up. George seems to be waiting until she reaches a stopping place. I know she won't.

"And your name is?"

"Dunfey, Carrie Dunfey." She taps her pencil on her sketchpad.

"I thought your daughter said McConnell." The guide glances at me, confused.

"She pretends a lot," Mother says without skipping a beat.

I had forgotten that Mother had used Dunfey to sign the motel register. The guide, in his green uniform, shiny silver badge, and polished black boots, will think I am a liar now, when she is the one hiding the truth.

"No harm done," he says to me. "Well, y'all ready for the tour?"

"Actually," Mother says, "my daughter is the Civil War buff. I'll stay here and finish my sketches."

The guide seems surprised and pauses as Mother begins to rapidly fill another page of her pad.

"You'll miss the best guide Appomattox has to offer," George tries.

Mother ignores him and looks at her watch. "Kat, we need to leave in twenty minutes or so. You'd best hurry to see everything you want to see."

George puts his hat back on as he strides heavily toward the back of the McLean House. I have trouble keeping up with him. When we get to the back door, he hurries in.

"Hey, Hal," he greets another guide in a green uniform who is leaning against a door frame. "The surrender room's up there, kid." He points without looking at me. "Here, take this description." He gives me a flyer from the table. "I'll be there in a minute." His voice is gruff now and I know that the only reason he offered us the tour was because he wanted to meet Mother.

I walk up the stairs to the room, where the door is blocked with a velvet rope. A painting on the wall shows where each of the generals and their staff stood and a display card says the pieces of furniture are replicas of what was in the room at the time. I hear footsteps on the stairs, and George enters. He has loosened his tie and is drinking a Coke.

"Lemme tell you a story not in the flyer," he says. "After everything was signed and Lee and Grant had left, the Union officers took dibs on the furniture in the room. Some of them gave Mr. McLean money for what they took, but others just stole things. They hauled it off on horseback, gave the stuff to their wives or mothers or sweethearts." George takes a few swigs from his Coke. "They don't want to tell you that part of history, that the soldiers were stealing candlesticks and anything else that wasn't nailed down." He turns to go. "I gotta take a break before my next tour. Look around all you want."

I go downstairs to the first floor to see the warming kitchen and the dining room. In the hallway, a woman is looking at a wreath that is framed and hanging on the wall. "It's hair, Roger. Come look," she says to her husband.

I wait until they leave, then I lean close to the wreath in the frame and see that it really is made out of intricately braided hair. Human hair, the display card says. The screen door slams and I see Mother backlit by bright sun.

"Well, Squirt. You about ready?"

"Look at this."

Mother glances at the wreath and George appears. "Isn't that interesting? Women in the nineteenth century often made elaborate keepsakes out of human hair and dried flowers. This is larger than most. Usually they're the size of a small brooch."

"It's gross," I say.

"Mmm," says Mother. "I suppose they're valuable." I can tell she's not interested.

"Well, yes. Intricate ones with good artistry."

"Hey, George. Group forming," a voice from the porch calls out.

"If you're staying in town," George says eagerly to my mother, "I'd be glad to escort you to our local steak house. I'm living with my sister and her two kids. One is Kat's age and my sister wouldn't mind an extra kid at dinner while we go out." It all comes out so quickly that each sentence sounds like one word. He ignored me before and now he thinks he'll get Mother to leave me with strangers. Can't he see her wedding ring?

"George?" someone says again.

Mother raises her eyebrow. "Seems you're wanted outside."

"How about tonight?" George asks.

"I don't think so," Mother snaps and walks by him. "Come on, Kat," she says. "Let's go."

"Twenty-four," I tell Mother once we get into the Impala. "And then after that, we take Sixty west to Lexington." We are on our way to the Virginia Military Institute, where Stonewall Jackson taught before the war.

Mother has taken an icy Tab and a Coke out of the cooler. I drink mine so fast it makes my forehead feel like it is going to crack in half. Mother drives with one hand, taking us away from Appomattox and toward our next adventure. "What about George, the guide?" she says. "How old do you think he was? Twenty-three, twenty-four?"

"He said he was a Ph.D. student."

"Maybe twenty-four or -five, then. Goodness." Mother smiles.

Mother is thirty-one, but she tells me not to tell anybody. When she goes into liquor stores she still gets carded, she says, as long as I'm not with her. At Easter the sales clerk at Rich's department store told me that I looked just like my big sister. Mother went home and told Daddy. I've heard her say she hates men always staring at her, trying to talk to her, but I can tell, despite the way she acted, that she liked it when George asked her to dinner. I knew she wouldn't accept the dinner, but if she had agreed to the personal tour I would have gotten more stories about the surrender. Since she takes advantage of how men look at her sometimes, I wish this time she'd done it for my sake.

I stare out the window as we pass fields and then the cemetery where we had our picnic.

The Confederate general doesn't consider surrender. Her mind is on the clash of armies, the galloping cavalry, the quick march in the dead of night to prepare for a surprise dawn attack. In the heat of battle, the soldiers are fighting for their brigade, for a hill, for a field of wheat, for a town. It's hard to see farther than that in the white-hot moment of a fight. But from time to time back in her tent she thinks about why they fight. Sometimes she's troubled by the thought that maybe they shouldn't win. That she's fighting for the wrong reasons. She makes herself turn away from these thoughts because she needs to fulfill her responsibilities as a commander.

Chapter Nine

The highway to Lexington snakes up and then back down a steep mountain and Mother keeps asking me to look back at the trailer. She takes the curves smoothly so it won't fishtail, but there are two big trucks behind us and I can feel them pushing us to go too fast.

"This is awful," Mother says. "How much longer?"

I try to read the map but the tiny red numbers blur against the wiggling blue line of the road. I'm feeling a little queasy, even though I usually don't get carsick.

"I can't tell," I say. "Reading the map is making me sick."

"Put it away, then. There'll be a sign soon. Keep watching the trailer. It wants to pull us over the side."

I turn around, knees on the seat. The trailer's wheels drift close to the edge of the road when we go around a curve.

"As soon as we get to Lexington, we're going to check into a nice motel and take a bath and go out for a big dinner." Mother grips the steering wheel hard and watches the road carefully. "This drive is giving me one major headache."

I have been worried about Mother getting a headache. Sometimes they are so bad she can't get out of bed all day. But when we leave the mountain and enter Lexington, she seems calm and even relaxed. It's still light, but the evening has begun and the air is cooling off, which is a good thing. I'm sweaty even though the windows are rolled down.

We pass signs to the Virginia Military Institute and I point them out to Mother.

We end up at the Shenandoah Court Motor Lodge, which has ten rooms strung out on either side of a small two-story building with white columns and a neon sign blinking OFFICE and VACANCY. A few cars are parked in front of the room doors. Off to the side is a pool with a tall slide, but I don't see anybody swimming.

Our room is big but smells musty. Mother cranks the air conditioner to high and the whole thing vibrates to life so loudly I think it may blow up. I sit at the small wooden table next to the window, cracking the curtain to look out. The air conditioner blows cool air on my legs. As Mother goes to run her bath, she turns on the television. The evening news is on; I'm not really listening to what Huntley and Brinkley are saying but their voices make me feel good, as if I am in my grandparents' living room, spread out on the brown-and-gold braided rug in front of the fireplace, watching their big TV in its wooden cabinet.

I spread out my books, sketchpad, pencils, pens, and trading cards. I want to draw a Civil War scene like the ones on the cards. My sketches of generals are all done with a black drawing pencil, but if I create a full scene, I can use my colored pencils. I have a set of watercolors with me, but I don't think I can get the right amount of detail with them.

The story that George the guide told would be challenging to draw. General Chamberlain from Maine and General Gordon from Georgia—the salute from the Union soldiers returned by the Confederates, and the stacks of Confederate rifles and cartridge belts. Gordon's horse could rear slightly while Gordon touched his sword tip to his boot. Chamberlain would be at attention, he and his horse stock-still. I will have to find out what they looked like, and if there is any mention about the size and color of their horses.

General Gordon is listed in the index of my Golden Book, but it doesn't include the story of the salute between the enemy brigades at Appomattox. If I were at home, I could call Aunt Laura and ask her about it. She would have a book that went on for pages and pages about Gordon and Chamberlain, including pictures of them both. She would be able to tell me if the story was a legend or fact.

Mother comes out of the bathroom with her hair wrapped up in a towel like a turban and another towel wrapped around her body—the end neatly tucked above her right bosom.

"Baby," she says. "The hot water kind of petered out toward the end of my bath. You wait for a few minutes before you start yours." She leans over the table and turns down the air-conditioning a notch. "I think everyone who's rented this room for the last ten years has been a chain-smoker. Seems like the AC would clear it up."

I contemplate my Chancellorsville trading card. Stonewall Jackson died there, shot by Confederates from North Carolina who thought he was part of the Union cavalry. I will try to get Mother to take me to the museum at the Virginia Military Institute. Aunt Laura told me about it and I read in one of her guidebooks that Stonewall Jackson's horse was stuffed and on display. "Jackson's coat is there too," Aunt Laura told me, "with the bullet hole through the left sleeve."

Mother props all the pillows behind her on the bed and brushes her hair while she watches the news. "Everything's going to hell in a handbasket, Kat. We'll never get out of Vietnam because of Johnson's precious sense of honor. In the meantime the students will have torn up all the college campuses." She rubs her hair vigorously with her towel and starts brushing again. "They don't know how good they've got it." She points to the screen. "I bet every one of them prancing around with those signs gets a big fat allowance from Mommy and Daddy."

Daddy's cousin Danny is a helicopter pilot in Vietnam with three months left on his hitch. The fighting has heated up, Daddy says. One afternoon when we were at Gramma and Poppa's, Poppa read Danny's latest letter. He told about evacuating the wounded. On the news I sometimes see soldiers carrying stretchers to helicopters that make the tall grass around them blow wildly and I wonder if Danny is the pilot. Everyone in the family thinks Danny is brave to serve instead of running away to Canada to avoid the draft, but everyone also thinks we have no business fighting in Vietnam. I asked Daddy why we are fighting, and he said to keep the Communists out of Southeast Asia, which he says is useless. The French failed and we'll fail too, he says. Aunt Laura loves Lyndon Johnson, but says he's ruined his legacy with Vietnam. I can't figure out why we would go fight in another country that hasn't attacked us. Sometimes in his letters, Danny says hello to me and that I can ride with him on his motorcycle when he gets home. My whole class at school wrote him once, and I write him every few weeks.

I get out my notepaper and write to Aunt Laura, telling her all about visiting Appomattox. It would be wonderful to go with her to the battlefields. She probably knows more about the Civil War than even the park rangers. Of course, it wouldn't work on this trip; having Aunt Laura along would change everything. Not that she and Mother don't get along, they do—Mother told me once that of anyone in the world, even Daddy, she trusted Aunt Laura the most because she knows herself and is a straight shooter with everyone. You know exactly where you stand with Laura at all times, she said. But this trip has to be just Mother and me. It's something we have to experience together.

Sometimes the Confederate general has to do without her valued captain while he goes to check on progress in another theater of operation. Things don't work as smoothly in her headquarters without her full staff—but she especially misses the captain, who has an almost encyclopedic knowledge of everything. She thinks of this before she sends him off on a mission, but her own comfort is nothing compared to the success of the entire campaign. She must send her best men to deliver her orders and make sure they are carried out properly.

"You can take your bath now. And be quick, I'm getting really hungry."

I fold the letter and stick it in my book. Maybe tomorrow when we go out we can stop by the post office to buy an envelope and stamp. The floor in the bathroom is puddled with water but I ignore it, hang my clothes on the door hook, and run my water. It's lukewarm, which is fine with me. When I get out, Mother is dressed in white slacks, a navy blue silky shirt, and her leather sandals. She has the room key in her hand.

We go down the street to a nice restaurant in the Jackson Inn for dinner, and when Mother mentions to the waitress that she is an antique dealer, the waitress points out an older woman in a pink linen suit, her white hair pulled up in a bun. "Miss Jameson over there ran an antique business just down from us for years. She doesn't have any children, never married, plenty of money. People wonder who she'll leave it to. She eats here every day; maybe she'll leave me a little something." The waitress laughs softly. "I'll tell Miss J. you're a dealer. She loves company when she eats her pie."

"What luck," Mother says as the waitress walks away.

When we first join Miss Jameson, she and Mother talk about furniture and the flow blue china displayed in the entry hall of the restaurant. "Antiques don't interest me as much now that I *am* an antique." Miss Jameson laughs. "Now I'm interested in human nature. For instance, why are you traipsing around so far from home looking for old, decrepit things?"

"I'm going even farther—all the way to Maine," Mother answers.

"Surely you don't have to go all that way for antiques?"

Instead of answering, Mother takes a bite of apple pie. She's getting angry. I recognize now that as they've talked Miss Jameson has pulled more information out of Mother than she wanted to give. Rarely is Mother at a loss.

"We're going to Civil War battlefields," I blurt to fill the silence.

Miss Jameson smiles at me. "A bit of a vacation, then. Where is your shop?"

"Oh, I haven't opened it yet," Mother says casually.

"Ever worked in an antique shop?"

"Nooo." Mother raises her left eyebrow a little, wary.

"Collected on your own?"

Mother's second no is quick, sharp.

"Then you don't really know anything about the business." Miss Jameson sets her cup down with a definitive click on her saucer.

Mother plays with the handle of her spoon while her left index finger outlines imaginary designs on the white tablecloth. I don't like the quiet between them. "I'm new to the antique business," Mother says with care. "But I'm not new to being around antiques. My mother had fine things and taught me a great deal."

Miss Jameson's expression softens.

"And being an artist," Mother adds, "gives me a better eye, a better appreciation for quality and fine things."

"Mother had an exhibit in Atlanta and one of her paintings had a beach ball sticking out of it," I say, trying to break the tension and show Miss Jameson that Mother is right. The painting with the beach ball and the red, orange, and pink swirls had been my favorite. I hoped that no one would buy it so we could keep it at home, but it was the first to sell.

"Sounds delightful," says Miss Jameson. "I don't think good art has to be stuffy." She clears her throat. "I didn't mean offense earlier. But I'd like to introduce you in the morning to a few of my dealer friends, so I wanted to know a little about your experience."

"No offense taken. I would appreciate the introduction," Mother says softly, looking at Miss Jameson with sharp eyes. It's the look she has when she goes to an art exhibit or when she is in the last stages of finishing one of her own paintings. She's sizing Miss Jameson up, figuring the best approach.

"I've gone to a lot of shops," Mother says. "Most people don't take enough care in arranging their stock. You want to entice people when they first come through the door, lead them to the different places you want them to linger. I can sell a dining room table for more if I have a gorgeous centerpiece on it."

"The problem with the antiques is that it takes a good while to make a living." Miss Jameson pauses and purses her lips a little. "Of course, you will have your paintings too. Perhaps that will make the business move along faster."

Even though she is very different—older, much smaller, and more refined—Miss Jameson makes me think of Gramma. Gramma has broad shoulders and large, loose bosoms that hang down to the belt of her shirtwaisted dresses. On Sundays she wears pearls but otherwise her only jewelry is her gold wedding band and her Timex watch with a black leather strap. She's a nurse and everything about her is practical and reassuring—the touch of her hand to my forehead, the way she shakes down the thermometer before she puts it in my mouth, the way she pours the cough syrup into the spoon. But I can see Miss Jameson, like Gramma, sitting in an armchair by the window watching the birds and working a crossword puzzle.

"It was a good thing I never needed to make a living selling antiques. It was years before I ever showed a profit. But of course, selling things didn't interest me as much as fixing them up. I liked the dirty, grimy, labor part of it. I loved scrubbing with a wire brush dipped in paint stripper. I guess it was a bit like gambling; I'd bet on something that looked like junk, everyone else thought was junk, but that, with its layers of green paint removed and its wood revealed—cherry or mahogany or oak—might be beautiful."

"Well, my priority is selling. I have the two of us to support and I haven't got years to show a profit." Mother looks defiant. When she has this expression I know she will get her way. She's told me not to accept what others say if I don't think it's correct.

"I suppose it can be done." Miss Jameson puts her neatly folded napkin on the table. I copy her because Mother always says when you're in doubt about table manners, follow the lead of your hostess.

"How would you two like to come to my house? It's just down the street. I'll show you some things I would never sell."

Mother sips the last of her coffee.

"Civil War items," Miss Jameson adds. My ears perk up.

"Please, could we?" I ask Mother.

Chapter Ten

Miss Jameson's massive front door is painted shiny black and has a huge brass ring knocker. As we enter, she takes my hand with her soft fingers. "Dear, what do you look at when you and your mother are in antique shops?"

"I like antique toys," I say. "The kind that wind up."

"Yes," Miss Jameson replies as we walk through the marble-floored entrance hall and into a wood-paneled room lined with books.

"And Civil War trading cards. That's what I bought at the last store."

"You like Civil War history, don't you?" Miss Jameson drops my hand and walks over to a desk to turn on a lamp.

"She's a nut about the Civil War," Mother says. "We spent all afternoon at Appomattox."

Miss Jameson is still looking at me, and I try to think of the right words, the ones that will tell her that I more than *like* it.

I remember what I've heard Aunt Laura say, that the Civil War is her passion. That's what she wrote in the biography that appeared in italics under her article about Kennesaw Mountain in *Civil War Times: Laura McConnell, high school history teacher, whose passion is the Civil War, particularly the Atlanta Campaign.*

"The Civil War is my passion," I say to Miss Jameson.

"Gracious," Miss Jameson says, and I know I've made the right answer. She gestures to the wingback chairs and sofa, arranged in front of the fireplace. "Please.

"Since I think you'll appreciate them, young lady, I want to show you some of the pieces that I normally don't get out. Make yourself at home," she says as she leaves the room.

While we wait, Mother examines the room. She picks up the coffeepot of the silver service. "Gorham, of course." Then she looks at the book cabinets. "She's got every reference book on antiques you could possibly own. And listen, Kat," Mother whispers, "she's too nosy. Let's not tell her any more about us than we have to."

When Miss Jameson returns she has a coat draped over one arm and in the other she cradles a large ledger book and a sword encased in a scabbard.

"Wow!" The sword looks like it should be in a museum, and I get up to see it more closely.

"I thought you'd like this." She smiles and hands me the scabbard. "You can pull it out, but don't touch the blade." Mother comes over to my side.

I carefully grip the leather-covered hilt and pull out the sword. The silver blade gleams in the lamplight.

"It's engraved with the name of my grandfather."

The ornate *J* is bigger than any of the other letters, and I lean in to try and decipher the rest of his name.

"Be careful," Mother says.

"Malcolm," Miss Jameson tells me. "It's hard to read, isn't it? Malcolm T. Jameson. He was killed in the Seven Days battle. Fought with A. P. Hill. In that battle, Jackson was supposed to cross White Oak Creek to reinforce Hill and Longstreet. He was napping and never ordered them to go across the creek, even though they could have waded without any problem. Malcolm's brother Horace wrote to their mother and said that Stonewall Jackson had killed his brother as much as if he had shot him with a pistol. My great-grandmother would probably be upset if she knew I ate at the Jackson Inn almost every day of my life.

"Here's his coat." She holds up a coat of gray wool with dull gold braid on the sleeves, and I'm surprised to see that it looks too small for Mother and only slightly big for me.

"I keep it packed away from moths and other critters. Someday all of these things will go into a museum." She folds the coat back over her arm before I can look at the buttons more closely. "Can you put the sword back in the scabbard yourself?"

Mother steps in. "It's too long for your arms." She takes the sword from me and returns it to its scabbard.

Miss Jameson settles on the sofa, the ledger in her arms. "I am the last of my family and it seems a shame that no one will tell these stories after I'm dead. Oh, there might be a few words on a card in the museum display, but there's a great deal of difference in that and in hearing your grandmother or mother tell you the story of how your family came to be who they are." She patted the ledger. "Come here," she says, "I'll show you the record of the Confederate army at Appomattox."

I sit next to her, and Mother stands behind the sofa to look over our shoulders.

"McConnell, I believe you said your name was." Miss Jameson turns the pages slowly. I am glad Mother has told Miss Jameson our real name.

"Yes, but my great-great-grandfather Gresham was the one at Appomattox," I say, reading the lists of names on the pages.

"I want to look it up for you and show you the name of your relative written in the ink of April, 1865, by one of my relatives," Miss Jameson says. She turns the ledger pages carefully. Her finger moves slowly down the list. "He's not here," she says solemnly.

"Well, whaddya know," Mother chirps. "Maybe ol' Monroe wasn't really at the big surrender. Maybe he wasn't really in the war at all."

"He was," I say, angry that Mother is trying to spoil things. "Aunt Laura said he got a pension."

"These records could be fallible, I suppose." Miss Jameson closes the book. "And of course, many Confederates"—she looks at me—

"didn't want to turn in their weapons, so they didn't go through the process of getting the parole pass." She taps on the ledger. "You see, this ledger is a record of all the Confederates who received a parole pass at Appomattox."

"What about his friend Jed Pendleton?" I ask. I want to prove that the stories are true. "That's who he walked home to Georgia with."

"It's getting late, Kat," Mother says, sounding impatient.

"Let's see." Miss Jameson ignores her and opens up the ledger again. "Pendleton, Jedediah. Yes, here he is."

The faded cursive writing is evenly slanted to the right, just like the handwriting charts above the blackboard in my classroom. I can never get my handwriting to be that neat. The ink is blue-black and its line is thin. And right in front of me is Jed Pendleton's name. Seeing it, my family's stories feel more real than ever, and a piece of them exists right here in this book.

"I take it," Miss Jameson says a little stiffly to Mother, "that you don't share your daughter's interest in the Civil War."

"I don't think war should be glorified," Mother replies.

"I had McConnell relatives in Atlanta; maybe you knew them—Roberta and Richard McConnell—brother and sister." Miss Jameson stands and puts the ledger book on the desk across the room.

"No, I'm sorry," Mother says. "I didn't know them."

Mother stands and I do too. "So nice of you to have us over." Mother smiles, but her neck has red splotches on it, the kind she gets when she is nervous or angry. Miss Jameson looks at Mother, but if she notices anything she doesn't show it.

"I'll meet you at Perry's Antiques in the morning—you have the directions I wrote out?" Miss Jameson walks in front of Mother and leads the way to her front door.

"Yes, thank you," Mother replies.

The night air is cool as we walk back past the Jackson Inn and around the corner to our car.

"I know about those McConnells," I say quietly.

"What?" Mother rolls down her window and cranks the engine.

"Roberta and Richard McConnell. They were some kind of cousins of ours who were twins and lived together in a big old house with lots of Dalmatians. I heard Aunt Laura talk about them. She said they died five hours apart."

"Your father's never mentioned them to me. Great, more batty cousins on the family tree." I'm not sure I believe her, but I don't say anything else. She is driving fast and it is very dark. Why can't she just be happy about Miss Jameson introducing her to the dealers in town? Why does she care that Miss Jameson brought out her special things just for me?

It bothers me too that Monroe Gresham isn't on the Appomattox roll. Maybe he didn't give up his gun, like Daddy said he did. Or maybe he was one of the deserters that I read about; maybe he lagged behind his company or went off looking for food and never caught back up. The Confederates were starving by the time they got to Appomattox, and Monroe Gresham had a bad leg. Maybe he couldn't keep up.

When we get back to the motel I dig out my paper and pen from my book bag and write a letter to my grandparents. I find my seal with the letter *K* and my sealing wax. "Do you have any envelopes and matches?" I ask Mother.

Mother is brushing her hair and watching *Green Acres* on television.

"What on earth for?"

"I want to seal my letters with my initial." I hold up my crimson sealing wax.

Mother jumps up from the bed and throws down her brush. "Give me those." She grabs the papers on the table. "Who are you writing?" she demands.

"Poppa and Gramma."

Mother's voice is low and she bites her words. "Why are you writing them?"

I don't want to answer because when she is this way, every answer is wrong.

"Answer me." Mother's eyes flash and she grabs my wrist.

"*Ow*. I just wanted to tell them about our trip and ask them about Monroe Gresham." As soon as I say it, I realize that I shouldn't have said anything about Monroe.

She drops my arm. "You would, wouldn't you. All worried about the family history. Get it through your head. It's not real. Listen, Missy, that family hasn't got any history except what they make up." Mother starts reading my letter. " 'I miss you. I wish you were here,' " she reads in a high, fake voice. "How many days have we been gone?" She glares at me. "Two days and already you miss them. You wish they were here?"

She crumples up the letter and throws it across the room. "What am I? Nothing?" she yells. Suddenly she sits down on the bed and starts crying. "Can't you just be with me?" She holds her head in her hands.

I try not to cry. "I wasn't going to mail them. I know you don't want anyone to know where we are." I try to reassure her. When she is like this I am afraid of her, and the only thing that helps is to stay quiet. Once when she was this angry she pulled my louvered closet doors off their hinges, threw them on the floor, and stomped on them. I climbed onto my bed as she stomped and screamed. She was angry because Daddy hadn't oiled the squeaky hinges. She was also angry because I had begged for lights on our Christmas tree like the ones Poppa and Gramma had. "You want to do everything their way, don't you?" she had yelled. "Nothing I do is good enough." She sat down on my bedroom floor and cried for an hour until Daddy got home from work. I sat on the bed, curled into my pillows, and watched her, but after she started crying she didn't look at me again.

Now Mother stops crying and stands up, looking around. "Have you written any other letters?"

I get the letter to Aunt Laura out of my book bag. She crumples it up and throws it at the television. "Is that it?" she asks, moving toward me.

"Yes." She is almost on top of me. I look up at her and freeze. She's so angry, her features seem utterly altered, and she stares past me, eyes wide. She's no longer my mother.

"Don't you understand? I've got to have a chance. I've got to have some air to breathe. I swear, that family is suffocating me." She takes me by the shoulders, shaking me. Her fingers dig into my skin. The chair bangs against the table.

"If I let them, they'll do the same thing to you." She lets go of my shoulders.

Someone knocks on our door. Mother grabs her bathrobe out of her suitcase. "Just a minute," she calls out sweetly. The instant change in her tone is as frightening as her anger.

She opens the door, and it's the motel clerk. "Your neighbors called the desk. Said they heard a woman yelling. Thought there might be some problem." He sticks his head into the room. "Is everything all right?"

"Yes," Mother replies calmly, "everything is fine. My daughter had a tantrum, but it's over now." The clerk looks at me and I look away.

"You see," Mother says to me, shaking her head. "I told you the owner would kick you out if you didn't behave."

"Oh, I'm not the owner," the clerk sputters. "And we wouldn't kick her . . ."

"That's fine," Mother cuts him off and begins closing the door. "There won't be any more problems." After the door clicks shut she turns toward me and I ready myself for what she will do next, but she just moves past me and says it's time to get some sleep. She washes her face and then looks at herself in the mirror as if she is memorizing her appearance. Her features are familiar to me again, and she is beautiful. Even the slight darkness under her eyes doesn't mar the effect.

She sits down on the bed. "Listen," she says in a soft voice. "You can mail letters to everybody later, when we get to Maine. Do you understand?"

"Yes, ma'am." I begin to relax. It's over. She just wants me to be loyal only to her right now, I tell myself. She needs a chance to show everyone what a success she can be, and I can help her. I will write the letters in my notebook, kind of like a diary, otherwise I might forget some of the things we do. Then I can copy them over and mail them one by one on our way home. Mother is calm now and I think everything will be okay; I'll just have to be more careful.

She loves to unfold her traveling desk. At this desk she writes important letters to Jefferson Davis and to her family. She writes battle orders and instructions for her aides. She even writes a sort of diary that no one knows about. Her tiny daybook has just enough room for two or three sentences for each entry. She's often hard-pressed to reduce all that has happened to that small space, but she does; she has a shorthand that only she understands. In this tiny book she writes what she cannot say out loud. She writes what she wants no one to read. These pages give her the strength to go on being a general.

Chapter Eleven

Before Mother meets Miss Jameson's antique dealer friends, she drops me off at the Virginia Military Institute museum housed in Jackson Memorial Hall, the chapel building, at the edge of a quadrangle with a wide grass field in the middle. The imposing hall, with its wide arched doorway and tall church windows in front, is not far from downtown and the Jackson Inn. "I'm in a hurry," Mother says. "Run in, find out if the museum's open, and come right back."

"It's open," I tell her when I return, "until four."

"All right," Mother says. "You look around the museum and if you want, you can sit outside." She points to a bench outside the chapel doors. "But don't you go anywhere else. I'll be back in two hours." I look at my watch. She'll be back at eleven. "Oh," she says and reaches for her purse. "Here's some money to pay for your museum ticket." She hands me a five-dollar bill. "And I want my change," she adds. The sign inside listing the museum hours said the admission is free, but I don't say anything. I might want to buy something in the gift shop.

In the entrance hall, before I go downstairs to the museum, I stand for a few minutes in the open archway of the chapel, staring at the flags hanging from the rafters and at the gigantic painting behind the altar. The painting seems out of place in a chapel—a vivid battle scene with soldiers running under heavy dark clouds, sheets of fire in the background.

As I walk down the marble stairs to the entrance of the museum, I stay on the outside edge of the steps where they are not so worn down. It doesn't seem possible that my blue tennis shoes could wear down stone, but years and years of shoes, some with tough hard soles, have made a gentle valley in each of the steps. Downstairs the woman at the museum entrance smiles at me. "Here's a brochure," she says. "Go down that hall, exhibits start on your left."

I pause. "The painting upstairs," I ask. "What's it of?"

"Oh, that's the battle of New Market where the VMI cadets helped carry the day. Striking, isn't it?"

I open the brochure. The woman gets off her stool and points at a paragraph. "Right there. That tells more about the painting." She smells like baby powder.

The brochure explains that a VMI alumnus painted the scene of the charge of the fifteen-year-old cadets at New Market, part of a desperate battle in May of 1864 when the Confederate numbers were dwindling. I've never seen a painting of a battle in a church before. And it shows such a chaotic scene, full of energy and violence.

The first exhibit case I come to contains a display of the different VMI uniforms. Some of the mannequins wear the double-breasted, brass-buttoned, blue-gray coats that the cadets wore at New Market. The collars are so high they look as if they would choke you as you ran. I open my notebook. I want to remember everything about what I've seen so I can talk to Aunt Laura about it when we get home. As I sketch the frock coats, I remember the coat Miss Jameson had.

I could rush ahead through the rooms to find the things Aunt Laura has told me about—Stonewall Jackson's horse, Little Sorrel, and his coat with the bullet hole in the left arm—but I'd rather come upon them as I move through the exhibits. I slowly examine graduation rings, pipes, dress uniforms, and fountain pens of famous VMI military men from World War II, and photographs of alumni who died in Vietnam or are still serving there.

In a side room that has a display of military medal winners, the dim light, darker than the rest of the museum, makes the edges of everything look fuzzy, rounded off—the medals under glass, the frames around the military citations, the photographs of men from modern wars. A small sign on the wall says that the Congressional Medal of Honor is most often awarded posthumously. The medal is a five-pointed star, each point connected to the next by a gold braid circle, all hanging from a powder blue ribbon. In place of the man, the family gets a medal. Thinking of it that way makes the beautiful, intricate design appear insignificant, stupid even.

I have been alone in the museum, but as I leave the gloom of that room a group of parents and their sons led by a cadet in a white uniform and shiny black shoes makes its way past the exhibits.

"Here's our room of medal winners," the cadet says. "VMI's finest."

I walk quickly around the corner away from the group and come upon Little Sorrel standing stiffly behind a short split-rail fence. He is even smaller than I thought he would be and he's dusty and not nearly as grand as I expected. It's hard to believe that this was Stonewall Jackson's famous mount. Little Sorrel is half the size of Big Boy.

In the room with Little Sorrel are Jackson's coat and the VMI uniform that he wore at First Manassas. Another case holds the black raincoat he was wearing at Chancellorsville, where he was mortally shot by his own troops. Jackson's coat is bigger than the one Miss Jameson had, but it still doesn't look like it would fit my father or even the cadet giving the tour. People were so small back then.

I close my eyes and think of Jackson being shot three times, then trying to rein the frightened Little Sorrel with his wounded right hand, his left arm shot twice and hanging broken by his side. Jackson's men had a hard time carrying him behind the lines, shells exploding all around them, Jackson unable to walk. At one point they dropped him on his mangled left arm. I open my eyes again and stare at the black raincoat with its wide lapels. He was in this coat as they lifted him onto the litter, as they tried to make their way as quickly as possible in the underbrush. His blood is probably still on it. Little Sorrel had already run away toward enemy lines, though he would be captured and returned later.

• • •

All of a sudden out of the quiet night, crack, crack, crack—and the horse takes off. It isn't like Little Sorrel to bolt, and the Confederate general does all in her power to rein him and stay in the saddle, but her left arm is useless and her right hand is slick with blood. She hits the ground. Painfully, she turns her head to the side and spits out wet dirt and leaves. More than anything she wants to get herself up before her aides find her, but she can't even turn over. Yankee artillery starts up with a vengeance in the distance. The ground is cold, Little Sorrel is gone, and for a moment she is terrified that she will die here, waiting for help to come. She had been on reconnaissance, and had seen no sign of the enemy. How will she lead her men? I need your help Oh Lord, she prays.

The group of parents and their high school sons thump noisily into the room. "Little Sorrel, Stonewall Jackson's horse," the cadet guide says, "gives us good luck on our exams. If you've got a tough one coming up, just come down to the museum, give ol' Sorrel a couple of pats, and pluck out one of his hairs."

The parents chuckle and one of the boys rolls his eyes and sighs. "Jackson had a reputation of being a bit of an eccentric when he taught here," the cadet guide starts up again as the group drifts in front of him. I see him look at his watch, and I check mine—twenty to eleven.

In the gift shop I pick out postcards of Little Sorrel and the painting of the battle of New Market. Some of the parents and prospective cadets are milling around, looking at books and tiny soldier replicas. Many of the books on the shelves are ones Aunt Laura has: Shelby Foote's *The Civil War, Vol. 1*; *The Civil War in Pictures*; and the Van Doren Stern biography of Robert E. Lee that she gave me. I recognize a Stonewall Jackson biography that is in the children's section of our public library.

Next to a window in the Marietta library, out of sight of the grumpy children's librarian, is the shelf of biographies. Many, like the one on

Jackson, are Landmark Books with a number on the bottom of the spine and a red, white, and blue eagle on the top. I take the copy the VMI has for sale from the shelf. On the front is a bareheaded Jackson charging on a horse that looks a whole lot bigger than Little Sorrel. Behind him are cannons and infantry soldiers. I have read it probably three times already, and I have copied some of the illustrations into my sketchbook, but I want to own it. The book is reassuring. I know the story almost by heart. I can sit on the bench with my old friend of a book and read until Mother picks me up. I will be marching the endless miles in the Shenandoah Valley with Stonewall Jackson.

Back upstairs, I check to see if Mother's there yet. She's not, and since I've got ten minutes I decide to go into the chapel to take a closer look at the painting behind the altar. I'm not sure whether I should bow my head before I sit down in one of the pews. I don't see a cross anywhere. It looks a lot like my church, St. Matthew's Episcopal, but if it isn't Episcopal, I think maybe I don't need to bow so I give a quick nod of my head instead of bending at the waist. If bowing is a mistake, I won't have been obvious, but if I am supposed to, then technically I have. The Episcopal church has a lot of rules you have to remember. When the cross passes you on its way to the front of the church, you have to bow your head. When you say Jesus' name, you bow your head. At certain times during the service you have to stand or kneel or sit, so you need to pay attention. Of course, being in the choir, I have the rules down pretty well. The choir is the model for the congregation, our director tells us. "As much as the priest, the congregation is looking to you to know what to do next." We keep on our toes and make sure when we pass in front of the altar that we bow deeply for Jesus.

The chapel smells of wood shavings and the air is cool. The pew makes a slight creak when I sit down, but otherwise the chapel is stone silent. The morning light streams through tall windows and the massive painting looms behind the altar.

In the foreground, the figures of the running soldier boys look odd to me; each left leg extends behind them in what might be more of a stretch than a run. And it looks like the painter has used the same left leg on three different boys. The troops run into solid white smoke with orange flashes and the background is black with a horizon of fire, and jagged red that must be shells exploding. At the bottom of the painting, the boot-high grasses vary from green to yellow to blue with patches of rust-red mixed in.

I decide finally that the rifles make the painting look so out of place. You don't expect to see guns in a chapel, even in a painting. And it is so huge, reaching all the way to the ceiling. Some of the boy soldiers have already fallen in the charge. Not many, but I can pick out two or three dead bodies. One running cadet has a bloody bandage around his head. A church ought to have peaceful paintings. Of course, Catholics have Christ being crucified in their churches and that certainly isn't peaceful. I saw him once when I went to the Catholic church with my friend Sherry. I didn't like looking at him, but I loved the lamb at St. Matthew's. There was a peaceful lamb carved in marble above the altar, and I used to see it in church on Sunday and every day when we went to chapel during school. I loved looking at the lamb.

Chapter Twelve

Every day at school when it was time for chapel we filed out of our brightly lit first-grade room, along the polished linoleum hall and down the stairs, which had bright metal strips on their edges. Everything was shiny until we reached the sanctuary—and then there was dark wood, burgundy pew covers, and needle-pointed pillows at the rail where we knelt to take communion. I would run my hands up and back on the velvety pew cushion, making the material go dark and then lighter, and my best friend, Milly, and I rubbed our initials in the velvet. The priest, Father White, was gray-haired, jolly, and drew cartoons for us as sermons. He had an easel like Mother's that he set up right below the three steps that led up to the altar—one step each for the father, the son, and their holy ghost.

What was best about chapel, even better than Father's drawings, was the marble carving of the Lamb of God way up high above the altar. The piece of marble was rectangular, but the scene carved on it was oval. The lamb was about the same size as my dog, lying down in the center with its legs tucked up. It looked so comfortable. The marble itself was mostly white with streaks of color here and there that Mother said were veins of minerals. I thought it might be the blood of Christ which is shed for you, but I didn't tell her that. Father White told us that the Lamb of God is what it's all about. He said the

Lamb would always protect us and be with us, and we never needed to feel alone.

At home, on her easel in the basement, Mother painted huge canvases of cathedrals with cows in front of them. She looked at a poster of a painting by Constable taped to the wall and copied it using acrylic paints; it really should be done in oil, she told me, but oils were harder to use. "Cathedrals are stupid," she said, "artistically, that is, but I need to work on my structures." When she finished learning, she told me, she would paint truly original art that would sell for lots of money and we would buy a new car.

Mother got me into St. Matthew's because I was too young to go to first grade in public school. "Your birthday's at the wrong time of year," Mother said, hanging up the phone. I knew that sigh of hers; something wasn't going her way. Any minute she was likely to get stony-faced and look at my forehead instead of my eyes. That's how it was when she concentrated; she didn't look into your eyes. I was eating an egg-and-olive sandwich and staring at the silver flecks in our kitchen counter. "Can you believe the school says you can't enroll until you're six?" I kept eating. I knew she was scheming to make things turn out her way. "I told them you could already read and they didn't seem to care. Now, what do you think of that?"

The next thing I knew I was in my pink frilly dress in the backseat of the green Rambler with both parents, heading to our church. In a room with big furniture we met a tall, bald man with big lips and a soft voice. Mother talked loud, and the louder she got, the softer the tall man spoke until Daddy asked him to repeat something. I was glad when he asked my parents to wait outside the room for a few minutes. When Mother got going like that, it was hard to think straight. "Katherine," the man said, leaning toward me, "are you excited about first grade?"

"No," I said. I didn't want him to think I was like Mother. "Quit getting so damned excited," Daddy often said to her.

He didn't act like that was the answer he was looking for, so I said real quick, "I mean yes." He scowled after I said that, so I decided to be quiet. "Let's get your parents," he said, and he stood up. "How do you think she'll adjust?" he asked my mother.

Mother held her pocketbook tight to her waist and looked at me. "Oh, she'll love school. She's not scared of anything."

"Sometimes she should be," my father said, winking at me.

"She seems a little hesitant," the man said slowly.

I got out of my chair and smoothed my dress. "I already read," I said as solemnly as I could.

In the beginning, Mrs. Rockwell's first grade at St. Matthew's was boring. There wasn't any dancing the twist like we did at Miss Nan's; we just sat in our seats and watched Mrs. Rockwell. When she turned her back and wrote carefully on the chalkboard, her head jiggled a little, and when she pointed the wooden stick to the row of letters above the board—the letters divided in half with a dotted line like the one on each page of our writing pads—I could see a crescent of sweat on her dress under her arm. We read about Dick and Jane, but the stories were silly, not nearly as good as the *Aesop's Fables* book that my grandmother gave me. In my desk I kept ballpoint pens, a book on dinosaurs from home, and a pencil case with a zipper that had three holes to go in a clip notebook.

The third week of school I refused to use my pencil and paper. I had been looking out the window watching workmen rebuild the steeple on the Presbyterian church next door. The night before, Mother and Daddy had a fight in the kitchen about her painting. "You're out of your mind," he said and slammed his fist on the counter. "You can't sell your paintings—look at them." Mother cried and yelled back at him, "You just don't believe in me."

Mrs. Rockwell called out, "Katherine." I looked up and she smiled. She had a silver cap on a bottom tooth that glittered a little bit in the right light. "Pick up your pencil like everyone else, Katherine." The paper was crummy newsprint with lines too far apart, and we had to use fat pencils without erasers. I was used to Daddy's ballpoints and legal pads. Almost every night in front of the television he sketched houses he said no one would hire him to build. Adults never wrote as big as Mrs. Rockwell told us to write. "I don't want to write with the pencil," I replied. "This pencil is stupid."

"Now, Katherine, don't worry, I'll show you how." She started walking back to my row.

"I want a ballpoint," I insisted.

"You'll begin with the pencil." She stared at me with her jaw tucked, making her chin wrinkle into two mounds. My huge red pencil rolled down my desk and hit the floor. "Class," she said, "be sure your name is at the top right-hand corner of the page and make your letters fit in between the lines on your paper. *Everyone*." I picked up my pencil from the dusty floor, following her rules. It was like learning the system at Miss Nan's; it was simple—you had to be in the main room with all the other kids "*par*ticipating." The better I did the twist, the nicer she was to me. Once I overheard her telling Mother, "Katherine is learning to play well with others." Mother had a system too: Wear frilly dresses without hollering about it and be*have*, which meant don't get dirty or wander off. Daddy's system I couldn't figure out; one minute he wanted me to speak up and the next minute he wanted me to be quiet. One time at his job site Mr. Price told me his granddaughter loved her Barbie doll and asked if I played with Barbie too. I didn't say anything until Daddy poked me gently in the back. "I buried Barbie in the—" I started and Daddy interrupted me. "She's got such an imagination." If I talked back, he issued the mysterious threat, "One of these days I'm going to put the fear of the Lord in you." But he rarely spanked me; that was Mother's job.

On a Sunday night the last week in January, right after my birthday, when I was finally the right age for first grade, the church burned down. Daddy said it was electrical. The wiring behind the altar shorted out. Too bad they couldn't have been more prudent and had the place upgraded, he said. I didn't have to go to school for a couple of days until Father White worked a deal with the Baptists across town to use their Sunday school rooms for our school. Daddy said our church looked like a bombed-out building.

The first time I walked into the Baptist church I felt strange because Jesus was everywhere. In pictures on the wall and life size in the big stained-glass window. I looked for the Lamb of God but couldn't find it. Jesus in the window unnerved me; he looked unfriendly and had long fingers pointing down at the ground. I sat in chapel and stared at Jesus' creepy fingers. I could barely pay attention to Father White. He wasn't drawing and he was saying something about strength, faith, counting our blessings, and the good neighbor Baptists. I was scared not seeing the lamb; Father White had said the Lamb of God was what it was all about, and it would be with us. I had assumed there was one in every church.

The Friday after the fire my mother took me over to our church after school. Mrs. Rockwell had already taken a lot of stuff out of our old classroom and we were using the smoky books in our cramped Baptist Sunday school room that had long tables and chairs instead of desks.

In our burned church, the corridor that had been so shiny was black and one whole wall, the wall that Daddy had explained was the upper wall of the sanctuary, was gone. I peered over the blackened linoleum cliff down into the rubble with Mother holding my hand tightly. I tried to figure out where it all had gone. I recognized what I thought were pews. "You see, the rafters fell into the church because the roof caught on fire," Mother said. I looked up and saw sky above us. I stepped back. Our church had become a huge cavern big enough to hold a hundred dinosaurs. "Awful, isn't it, baby?" Mother said and led me into my classroom. In it, many things were black, but nothing was burned.

"Get your things out of your desk, honey." Mother's voice sounded a little too cheery. She was at the bulletin board, untacking a picture I'd drawn. Barely recognizable beneath the paper's smudged coating was a *Tyrannosaurus rex*. I turned to find my desk and panicked. I didn't know which was mine. Nothing looked right. I looked back at Mother. "Well, it stinks in here, let's get going. Get your stuff." I inspected each desk carefully, looking into the cubbyholes below the desktop. Then I saw my mittens sticking out of one of the cubbies. I went to it, and instantly knew where I was. All the faces of the kids in the class came back to me. Harold Kemp sat in front of me—I hadn't kissed him since the fire—David Loudermilk sat behind me. Ann Wilson was across the aisle and behind her, Milly Mason. I pulled my mittens out and they stank like the books Mrs. Rockwell had salvaged. Then I saw my dinosaur book—a hardback, very special, that I shouldn't have taken to school in the first place. The part that had been sticking out of the desk was black, but other than that it was fine. Mother was always telling me that I didn't take care of my nice things, but she didn't notice the book at all. She seemed to be in a big hurry. "Come on," she said and grabbed my hand.

We peered into the sanctuary again on our way out and I couldn't see the lamb. As we went down the steps, which were tracked with huge footprints, I asked Mother where it had gone.

"What?" she said loudly and it echoed in the stairwell. We came out into the parking lot. It was cold, but the sun was shining brightly.

"Where's the Lamb of God?"

She stared at me for a minute. "What in the world, honey?"

"That was above the altar," I said.

She seemed relieved. "Oh, that. I don't know." As we got in the car, I thought she ought to be more worried about it.

On Monday at the Baptist church, while we were out at recess, I asked Mrs. Rockwell about the lamb. "It must have fallen in the fire, dear. It surely would have been broken." I hadn't thought it was gone completely, only lost temporarily. This was terrible news, but Mrs. Rockwell didn't seem any more concerned about the lamb than Mother had been. I watched the other girls jumping rope and the boys playing milk-carton football. Mrs. Rockwell had been trying to keep me out of the game all year. "Girls don't play football," she'd said over and over. I thought about the poor lamb all comfortable and resting and then suddenly falling into the fire.

Everyone else except Mrs. Rockwell had left when Mother came to pick me up from school that afternoon. She had paint on her hands, orange and pink flecks. "Mrs. Rockwell said the lamb fell and broke into pieces," I told her as I got in the car. Mother put her hand on my cheek and then took the barrette out of my hair, smoothed it, and put the barrette back in. "It's nothing to worry about, baby," she said smiling. "It's just a piece of marble." It scared me to think that Mother didn't know how important the lamb was. Now she was rubbing my shoulder. "Guess what happened today," she said.

I adjusted my book bag on the floor and positioned my feet on either side of it. "I started a real painting, not a copy." She put the car in gear. "No more cathedrals and cows, and this one's gonna get bucks. It's an abstract." I played with the handle of my book bag and imagined that I could will the lamb back together. I could remember all the details about it and make it whole in my head. "Yes sir," Mother said, "your father will have to eat his words on this one." I ran my thumbnail along the plastic ridges of the book bag handle and told Mother, "They're going to find the lamb and it's going to be okay." She stopped at a traffic light and looked at me. "Oh, they're bulldozing right now, I saw them on the way to get you. They probably won't recover it." She paused for a minute. "It's okay, baby, it's broken, it can't be used anymore."

I looked out the car window. We drove by Town and Country shopping center, which meant we would be home soon and I would go downstairs and look at her new painting. Mother said the painting would buy us a Triumph. "Let's celebrate and get dinner at the Shrimp Boat," she said. We turned into the parking lot of the restaurant built like a boat. "You wait here while I go in. I'll get hush puppies too." After she'd been gone a few minutes, I started feeling afraid, all hot and sweaty. I imagined the restaurant going up in flames.

I thought hard about Mother opening the door of the Shrimp Boat, sticking her head out to wave at me. I held on to the dash of the Rambler and thought about her green wool coat, her white shirt with the collar up, her black slacks, her black loafers. Even though it was winter, she never wore socks. I visualized her face and said out loud, "Come out that door." She didn't come out. I got so hot I took my coat off. I opened the car door and dangled my legs into the cold. By the time I ran up the steps and into the dim restaurant I was crying. When the door slammed behind me, Mother turned around from the counter to look. She seemed so far away. She frowned and bent down a little as I ran toward her.

Sitting in the pew in the VMI chapel I think about how silly I was in first grade. But just remembering the feeling I had outside the Shrimp Boat makes my face feel hot, and I get up to see if Mother has come.

It's eleven o'clock but she's not there so I sit on the bench outside. My face is still warm and my stomach hurts. I have no idea where Mother is in Lexington. If she doesn't come, I don't have anyone to call. When Mother is late picking me up from school, I wait fifteen minutes, then I call her. If she isn't at home, I call Poppa. He is almost always at home when school lets out. The only time he wasn't, Miss Reynolds, the teacher on bus and pick-up duty, was mad. "Your mother has kept me standing here too many times this year. We can't wait for your poppa to come home. Call someone else." I called my aunt at the high school and she talked to Miss Reynolds on the phone.

"Come on," Miss Reynolds said. "I'm going to drop you off at the high school on my way home. I didn't know your aunt was Laura McConnell. We used to run into each other all the time. Your aunt said you could wait for her in the principal's office and she'll get you as soon as she finishes her last class." Miss Reynolds's red Volkswagen had a baseball glove and aluminum softball bat in the backseat. On the floor underneath my feet were a hamburger wrapper and a wadded up french-fry bag.

"I've got softball practice tonight. Have to hurry to have time to eat and change." Miss Reynolds fiddled with the gear shift and gunned the motor at the stoplight.

She didn't seem angry, only in a hurry. I wondered what position she played. At six feet—that's how tall all the kids said she was, and she did look as tall as my father—she probably played first base. Usually I played shortstop in the summer league. You had to have fast reflexes for shortstop. It also helped if you were close to the ground, as my last year's coach, Mr. Darby, said.

"Do you play first base?" I asked.

"No." She smiled at me. "But that's a good guess. I play left field." She pulled in front of the main building of the high school. I'd been there before for concerts and once to my aunt's classroom on a Saturday.

"Here you go," Miss Reynolds said. "Do you know where the office is?"

"Yes, ma'am," I told her as I got out with my book bag. "Thanks for the ride." I waved as she roared down the street, a faint tail of gray smoke shooting out of the Volkswagen's muffler pipe.

The secretary in the office was so busy talking to a clump of very large boys, all wearing letter jackets, that she never asked me what I was doing. I sat on one of the wooden chairs lined up against the wall and did my math homework. Once I got up and sharpened my pencil.

"Here I am, Katherine," Aunt Laura said as she came into the office with her brown leather briefcase. For the first time, the secretary looked at me.

I take deep breaths and wait on my bench.

The general prays that her trusted spy will return soon from his scouting mission. In crossing enemy lines there is always the possibility of capture or, worse yet, death. He is already a day overdue. But he is her most clever and able spy, so she has to have faith that he will make it back safely. Nevertheless, she worries that she might never see him again and the thought fills her with grief. She tucks her hand into the chest of her uniform coat and breathes deeply. Waiting is never easy.

I know the sick, acidy feeling in my stomach and the heat on my cheeks will eventually go away, especially if I focus on something else. I pull out my Stonewall Jackson biography and begin to read. Suddenly an idea comes to me. If Mother doesn't come, I can go to Miss Jameson's house. She will know where Mother is or how to find her, and her house isn't far from here. I am sure I can find it. The woman in the museum might even be able to give me directions. I take a deep breath and then another.

When the Confederate general decides on a wise battle plan and a retreat route should her troops not be successful, she is more confident. She summons her mapmaker. What can you tell me of where the good roads are and how we are to move this army through the valley as fast as Lee wants us to? The maps are beautiful—swirls of lines showing elevation, ink marks showing passes through the mountains, block-letter names for the roads. She pores over the large sheets of paper in front of her. We must fight for our honor, she says. I believe with these maps we will find our way just fine. Her mapmaker smiles.

Chapter Thirteen

Mother finally shows up at noon, looking relaxed and happy as she pulls to the curb, as if she's forgotten that she said she'd be here an hour ago. I feel achy from waiting. She has fried-chicken box lunches from the Jackson Inn restaurant and we have a picnic right in front of the Memorial Hall. I am so hungry that I eat all of mine plus Mother's potato salad and I start to feel better. Mother couldn't help being late; she was doing business and she knew I was safe waiting at the museum. "Now come look!" She opens the back of the trailer. "Just look at this mahogany table and the Queen Anne chair," she says. "And because I'm a dealer, I got a huge discount. I didn't know about that before—but now wherever we stop, I'll ask for a dealer discount." She shows me a cherry shaving mirror that is meant to stand on a dresser, a porcelain pitcher and washbasin with tiny blue flowers, and an early American gilt-framed mirror.

Soon we are on the road again, headed to Manassas. "Read to me about Manassas," Mother says. "I've never even heard of it before."

Shocked, I put down the road atlas and dig in my book bag for the Civil War history book. I'll tell her about the battle, but I wonder how long it will take before she says all of it is nonsense. I read out loud that Manassas was the first real battle of the war, that residents of nearby Washington, D.C., came in wagons with picnics and parasols on that July day to view what they thought would be a rout of the Confederates. Generals Beauregard and Joe Johnston managed to amass the Confederate forces right under the nose of the unsuspecting Union general, McDowell, mostly by using the railroad. "It says here that this was the first time troops were moved into enemy territory by train," I told Mother.

"I'll be darned." Mother smiled. "Go on."

"Well," I tell her, "Stonewall Jackson's troops came up to save the day when McDowell had almost overtaken the Confederates. In the end, Jackson and Beauregard charged the whole Union force, broke their line, and the Union soldiers ran away in a panic. They choked the roads and bridges, dropping all their gear so they could run faster back to Washington." I read about the first civilian casualty of the war, eighty-five-year-old Judith Henry, who died in her house that was in the middle of the battlefield. Her son and daughter tried to evacuate her, but as they rode away in the wagon she was too frightened by the smoke and the artillery fire, and she made them take her back to the house. Her daughter hid in the fireplace and went partly deaf from the reverberations of exploding shells. Mrs. Henry was "mortally wounded" by shrapnel from Union fire.

"That stupid old woman," Mother says. "She should have gotten out while the gettin' was good."

"She was afraid."

"Where was her son?"

"I don't know." I read ahead in my book.

"It doesn't say anything about him going deaf or being shot does it?"

"It says here he was outside the house."

"Oh, outside my foot. As soon as they got Momma back home, he hightailed it to hide in the woods." Mother checks the rearview mirror while she holds the steering wheel firmly. She is a tough customer; people don't fool with her. I like the way she doesn't take any guff from anyone. "So what else do you know about this battlefield?"

"There were two battles at Manassas, the second one in 1862, also a victory for the South." I close my book. "Jackson got his nickname,

Stonewall, at the first battle of Manassas. The Yankees called it the Battle of Bull Run after the creek—Confederates named battles after towns."

"Well, I've heard of Bull Run." Mother turns to wink at me. "But that's because I'm a Yankee. Remember that, Kat. You're half Yankee." She laughs.

I consider this. Monroe Gresham might have been shooting at one of Mother's great-grandfathers. The possibility reminds me of the brother story at the Atlanta Cyclorama, the largest oil painting in the world. It depicts the battle of Atlanta and hangs in its own special building right next to the zoo. The sections of the painting form a giant ring that surrounds you, and real Georgia clay creates a diorama landscape in front of the painting. Miniature plaster of paris soldiers holding their rifles walk out of the painting onto the ground. Half of an army Conestoga wagon juts out into the dirt, its horses gone, frightened by the cannon fire. I've seen the cyclorama so many times I've lost count. At one point in the presentation, the guide focuses the spotlight on two figures in the diorama near the foot of the huge painting, one in blue, the other in gray—together on the field. The Union soldier is offering water to the fallen Confederate soldier, his brother. "Families torn apart like the nation," the speaker intones, and the spotlight fades and moves to another scene.

This is the first time I've thought about my ancestors being on opposite sides in the Civil War. "Did your great-grandfather fight for the Union?" I ask Mother.

"You know, I never heard anybody talk about it, but I wouldn't be surprised if someone in the family did. I come from an old Boston family," Mother replies.

I'll need to find out more about Mother's family, get more names from her, do the research with Aunt Laura. We may be able at least to find out who fought and in what battles. Once I know that, I can imagine the stories, a piece of me I never considered before.

Simon and Garfunkel are singing "Mrs. Robinson" again. Mother joins in. We have already memorized the Top 40 Billboard chart songs because they play over and over as we drive. Mother is never off-key. Sometimes she even sings harmony. "Hey, hey, hey . . . hey, hey, heeeey," we both sing.

I get out the atlas again. Before long I will be walking in Stonewall Jackson's footsteps, but I have plans beyond Manassas. I add up mileage and write down highway names. Like Lee, we can go from Manassas to Antietam and then continue north to Gettysburg. Aunt Laura has visited Gettysburg twice and Antietam once. I've read her battlefield guides and love to look through her photo album at pictures of her with her friends in front of monuments, visitor centers, and fences, and next to headstones. In one picture, she wears a Confederate kepi hat and her college roommate, Sarah, wears a blue Union cavalry hat with a large plume. Each has a toy sword thrust at the other as if they are fencing. They both are grinning, Sarah holding the edge of her hat so it won't fall off. Aunt Laura took a three-week trip to the battlefields one summer with Miss Brown, who also teaches history, but at a different high school. Beginning with Chickamauga, they worked their way north, ending with Gettysburg. Aunt Laura says you can't really understand the battle until you stand on the ground where it happened. She says the ground itself talks to you, and I want to hear it.

When we get to Manassas three hours later, I run ahead of Mother to the visitor center—I'm tired of being cooped up in the car and Mother takes forever to get her sketching supplies together. Without stopping at any exhibits, I go through the door that leads directly onto the battlefield, a rolling green field stretching as far as I can see, with clumps of hardwood trees here and there. A few people are in the distance, but otherwise I am alone in the open space. I walk out onto the field and see how exposed the soldiers were; only a few big trees to hide behind, and a group of slender ones not far from the Judith Henry house. I walk farther away from the building. This is where Stonewall and his brigade came up in the nick of time to save the day for the Confederates. I look around, amazed to think that they were right here.

Beyond an expanse of mown grass around the visitor center, hay grows on the battlefield. Wide paths arc through to the Judith Henry house, past a grove of trees, and in a semicircle to a huge statue of Stonewall Jackson on a horse much larger and more muscular than Little Sorrel. I want to follow the path through the field, but I need to wait for Mother. She'll be upset if she can't find me.

While I watch for Mother to come out of the visitor center, I run my hand over the bark of a hemlock tree next to me and think about the Union and Confederate soldiers who sought safety behind it. When the glass door of the center opens, it reflects the sun in a burst of light as I imagine a signal lamp would. The gently rolling land all around me was a farm, then twice a battlefield, and now is a national park. It's so restful here, it makes it hard for me to picture soldiers dying on this field. The hemlock tree beside me is as big as the one growing next to my grandparents' screened porch.

On summer nights we sit and rock on the porch, listening to the news on the radio or talking. Gramma might be snapping beans or cutting corn off the cob for vegetable soup. Poppa smokes his pipe and peels potatoes. I go with them to the cannery at the Atlanta Farmer's Market, where we cook big vats of vegetable soup, ladle the soup into steel cans we buy by the case, and put them on the conveyer belt that leads to the lid machine and then to the steamer. I love the hot, steamy cannery, the deep square stainless steel sinks where we wash the vegetables, and the bustle of activity all around. When you want to cool off you go outside through a screen door and sit on the concrete loading dock to watch the comings and goings in the rows and rows of farmers' produce stalls. Poppa grows most of what we put up, but occasionally we need more okra or more Big Boy tomatoes for the soup and we walk among the aisles to buy vegetables by the market basket full. The Farmer's Market is modern and concrete, but it smells like the earth: moist and grassy.

At the next signal of light from the glass door, Mother emerges.

She pauses, puts her hand up to shield her eyes. The big tree behind me rustles in the slight breeze; the sun beats down. Groups of tourists—the slide show must have let out—detour past Mother, who stands just beyond the door, not moving another inch until she knows the direction she needs to go. I hesitate for a minute before waving because I want to look at her trying to find me. In that moment, she is thinking of me and only me.

Mother holds herself differently than the people moving past her: her back is straighter, her figure more slender, her head held higher. She never scuffs her feet or moves clumsily; she glides, her long, thin legs cutting the air. Now I wave, big and exaggerated, and her head turns toward me. Even though I can't see her eyes, I can sense them. Large and dark brown, almost black, they always appear angry even if she is laughing and having a good time, but when she is really angry, I think I can see a red edge glowing behind the dark brown.

When my mother walks into a room, people notice her, men and women. They want to be near enough to smell her perfume. They want to hear her hilarious imitations of high-society Atlanta women. People want to be in the circle around her when she throws back her head to laugh, her mouth open, her glinting white teeth showing. I know what people sense—that Mother has energy to spare, a vitality that everyone wants a piece of. Too often I see her when her energy is gone, when she has nothing to give. But I still like to think of her as I see her now, mesmerizing, with a magic that can be mine.

Now she strides quickly across the low-cut grass between us. I start walking too, so that we meet in the middle. "I'm going to the Jackson statue," she says. "You go explore whatever you want and meet me at the statue when you're done." She has put all her supplies in my book bag. She throws an arm around my shoulder, something she rarely does, and gives me a hug from the side.

I walk all around the Henry house—it's not open—wondering where her son might have huddled to avoid the gunfire. I think about the daughter crouched in the fireplace, and what she went through after the shrapnel hit her mother. Did she crawl out and try to help her? Was she even in the same room? I walk away from the house, heading toward the cannons lined up beside the Jackson statue. On the way, I pause in the small stand of trees. It is cool, and I wonder if soldiers came here to get out of the sun or hide from gunfire and cannon shells. Or were these trees even alive then? Their trunks aren't very big around. When I reach the cannons, the sign says that they mark the spot where Jackson's brigade overwhelmed the Yankees. I want the battlefield to speak to me, so I close my eyes and touch the barrel of the cannon.

She strides up and down in front of her brigade. "Steady now, steady. Wait until they're closer upon us." Her troops lie low and watch the bluecoats coming nearer. "When I give the signal, rush them like devils screaming bloody murder." The bayonets glint. She knows her brigade can make the difference in this battle, but the timing has to be perfect. She watches the blue columns snaking nearer, raises her right arm. "Sir," she says to her lieutenant, "advance the troops!" The men in her brigade escape from their waiting like crazed banshees. In unison, the Rebel yell lets loose from their mouths and the Yankees hesitate, then hold their ground, firing, and finally turn and run back toward Washington, D.C.

I open my eyes. Mother calls from where she sits in the mown grass by the statue. "Look at what I'm doing." In the sketchbook in her lap she has drawn in bold black the outlines of Jackson's overly muscular figure sitting on the equally oversize Little Sorrel. Several tourists have gathered behind her, admiring her work.

"I'd like to buy that sketch," one man says. "That's better than any poster they have in that center."

"Well, I wasn't drawing with the intention of selling, but . . ."

As Mother settles into her drawing, glancing back and forth between her pad and the statue, I retreat to a rise right behind her. She looks confident and at ease, making fast, loose movements with her drawing pencil. I stick a hay stalk in my mouth and begin to braid the others that I have plucked on my walk around the battlefield. Mother carefully tears the sketch out of her pad.

"How about three dollars?" the man asks and pulls his billfold from his pocket.

"Sold," Mother says and smiles. The man walks away with his sketch, but four or five others linger.

"Could you do another one like that?" a woman asks. "My husband would love it. He's sick and didn't get to come on this trip. He thinks Stonewall Jackson hung the moon."

Mother says sure, and begins another sketch. I pocket my braided hay and lie on my back to look at the sky. With my hand as a visor I watch the white clouds lazing across the brightness. I often watch the clouds in my grandparents' side yard near the crab apple trees. As they drift by, I see how many different things I can find in the shapes. What begins as a toy poodle might change into a charging stallion or become Gramma's sofa. While Mother rapidly sketches for her audience, I watch a hunting dog point out an invisible quail, then transform itself into a *Tyrannosaurus rex*. The next group of clouds stretches itself out as it moves across the sky, first resembling my father's truck with a ladder sticking out the back, then growing into a fire engine. I can hear the murmur of voices as people walk by on their way back to the visitor center. I was so eager to get outside to see the battlefield that I skipped the slide show. Maybe Mother will let me see it before we leave, but for right now I'm enjoying the smell of the grass and the warmth of the sun. A cloud drifts by that looks like Poppa's pipe, then it runs into another cloud and forms my aunt's mother-of-pearl sunglasses.

I hear Mother tear off another sketch, and as I sit up I see a woman walking away with the white paper held carefully between her fingertips. The people who were hovering around Mother have all left and she waves me over.

"Look at that bunch coming out of the center. I'm going to make a few more sketches," Mother tells me, excited. "You stand behind me looking interested and I'll be drawing as they walk up." On her sketchpad she blocks out Jackson's horse—I love the way she draws horses; their legs always exactly proportional and shaded just right—then she adds the ramrod-straight figure of Jackson wearing a cape and a kepi pulled down tight over his forehead. The crowd of people approaches. "I'm going to make us some money," Mother whispers.

I take my position behind her, watching every move of the black pencil. Her technique is perfect. She makes flowing strokes, and her shading is economical, done with the lightest pressure. She says that with sketching, less is more. "Oriental watercolor," she told me, "has taught me more about sketching than any Leonardo notebook page. You need to give the essence with a sketch; you don't want to draw every line that's out there."

A little kid with a six-shooter in a holster sees it first.

"Hey, look here, Pa." The boy's father steps up to Mother and nods at her. She sells him the sketch, which she says is a better effort than the one she is working on. Two heavyset ladies, both in white sandals and cotton shirtwaist dresses, buy the next sketch and wait for her to produce another. Mother shifts to draw from a different angle.

"People like for drawings of the same thing to look different. Otherwise, they could have bought the mass-produced poster in the visitor center," Mother says when the ladies walk away.

Because no one comes up the path for a half hour or so, Mother is able to draw five more sketches, each unique—sometimes she changes the perspective, sometimes the background. To one she adds the cannons; another has trees; still another, the briefest suggestion of the Judith Henry house. At the bottom of each she prints a small title—MANASSAS BATTLEFIELD.

A ranger with his hat tipped back and his stomach pushing against his olive shirt walks over to us.

"Howdy, ma'am," he says.

"Hello," Mother replies.

"Folks have been talking about the sketches you're selling."

"Oh, good." Mother stops sketching and gazes at the ranger. "I'm hoping you'll carry them in your gift shop."

"Well . . ." The ranger touches the rim of his hat, pulling it down a little. "We really don't have a gift shop."

"Your bookstore, then."

"Yes, well." The ranger jingles the keys in his pocket. "The thing is, we can't let you sell these drawings on account of it not being approved by the Park Service."

"Oh," Mother says. "In that case, I'll just keep selling them myself out here."

"You don't understand," the man says. "I can't let you sell them out here either."

Mother glares at him. "Last I looked," she finally says, "it was a free country."

"Yup." The ranger chuckles. "That it is. But you see, if we let anybody that wanted to sell something come in here and set up shop, why, we'd have a snow-cone stand over there"—he points to the cannons—"and a hot dog stand under those trees."

"I don't want to set up a food stand. I want to sell a few sketches in your bookstore." Mother hands him one of the sketches.

The ranger studies it. "This is really good. One of the women showed us hers. But you have to be approved to have stuff in the center. We don't do the ordering—Washington does." Mother rolls her eyes. "I know," says the ranger, "it's a bureaucracy. You would need to write a letter to the National Park headquarters—we can give you the address—and send a sample of your work."

"Well, that's fine," Mother says. "That's what I'll do." She puts her pencils in her purse.

"Of course, you'll have to mass produce this if they approve it."

"I'll make numbered and signed prints—not a problem." Mother holds out her hand for the sketch the ranger is holding.

"Actually, I'd like to buy this one." He reaches in his back pocket for his wallet.

"Three dollars," she says cheerfully.

"And"—the ranger hands over his money—"the other rangers are interested in seeing the ones you have left."

He takes us with him to the visitor center, where we are ushered into an office behind the counter, and Mother sells her remaining three sketches. Mother's in such a good mood she lets me see the slide show before we leave.

Chapter Fourteen

On the way to the motel that the rangers recommended, Mother sings "Do You Know the Way to San Jose?" with Dionne Warwick. The windows are all the way down and the wind is blowing our hair back. Mother rips through the second verse. The trip is working out better than I could have imagined now that Mother has become so interested in making Civil War sketches. She's letting me add all the battlefields I want to the trip, as long as they're not too far out of our way. She plans to make a series of sketches in order to present a package to the Park Service. I know where I want to go next—Harpers Ferry and then Antietam. After that, Gettysburg. The trailer's almost full, so Mother says we'll only stop to buy antiques if we see a perfect shop.

"As soon as we get checked in and I change my clothes, we're going to find a really nice seafood place and we're going to eat whatever we want—lobster, crab, shrimp. We're loaded." Mother pats her pocketbook.

"Bring in your notebook," she tells me as we pull in to park. "I want to write down a few ideas I have for the letter to Washington. Tell me again the battlefields we're going to."

"First Harpers Ferry, then Antietam and Gettysburg."

At the motel, perched on the bed with my notebook, she writes a few lines, tears out the page, wads it up, and throws it at the trash can. Then does it again and again. Most of them miss. At the rate she is going she might use up my whole notebook before we go to dinner.

"I wonder if I should include the exhibit I did when I took that class at Kennesaw Community College." She gets up and turns on the television. "No, maybe not, since I wasn't really anything but a special-status student." I watch her write a few more lines, then cross them out. "Dear Sirs," she says. "You should carry my prints in your stores because . . ." She chews on the end of my Bic pen. "You should carry my prints of Civil War scenes in your park stores because . . ."

While she works I refold all the clothes in my suitcase and then place it on the low wooden dresser where Mother has put her change and keys in a clear glass ashtray. I run my finger over a burn mark in the wood at the edge of the dresser top. Mother tells me not to put my clothes in the drawers because I am likely to forget some when we leave. I open the top drawer and find some matchbooks.

Mother pulls her knees up to her chin. "Turn down the volume, I can't hear myself think."

I turn the sound off and stand in front of the TV, staring at a reporter in a bush hat and huge vest with pockets. He gestures behind him at the grass huts where Vietnamese men and women shuffle back and forth carrying pots and what looks like bundles of sticks. Soldiers wearing helmets and holding rifles are sitting off to the side, smoking. The villagers are tiny compared to the American soldiers, and have vacant expressions. They look poor, dirty, and tired. I feel sorry for them because Daddy says their civil war has been going on for thirteen years—two years longer than I've lived and nine years longer than our Civil War, they've endured bombings, their villages being burned, all their sons fighting and many of them dying. Daddy says that we don't know what we're doing over there; that we don't understand the people. "Like fighting an octopus with your hands tied," he says. "Korea was bad enough."

The Vietnamese on the television aren't looking at the American soldiers. I think it's because they know these big men can't help them, and the war has worn them out. The villagers just want to build their cooking fires, prepare their food, do the best they can to pretend there are no guns, even silent ones, in their village and that it is possible to have a normal life.

Daddy fought in Korea. I've seen the picture of him walking on a city street with his army buddy—the two of them tall, Daddy dark-haired, his friend blond. Both had rolled-up short sleeves with muscular upper arms exposed. A cigarette hung out of the corner of Daddy's mouth. Maybe the city was Tokyo. He told me that on his R & R he went to Japan. He taught me some Japanese: *mizu* for "water"; how to count to ten: *ichi*, *ni*, *san*, *shi*, *go*, *roku*, *shichi*, *hachi*, *kyū*, *jū*. In Japan he bought Mother a black silk kimono with an embroidered red, yellow, and green dragon on the back.

Mother starts reading out loud again. "Visitors to your park will want a quality souvenir of their visit." Mother looks up at me. I climb back on my bed with my Stonewall Jackson biography.

"Quality souvenir. What d'ya think of that?"

I nod.

"I can't say visitors and then visit, though." She tears out another piece of paper. "What's another word for visit?"

I open my book and think about it. "Stay," I say.

"That's it. A quality souvenir of their stay . . ." Mother writes quickly. My stomach growls. "I can produce appealing prints representing scenes from each of your parks." Mother chews the blue cap from the pen.

"I'm hungry," I say softly.

"Don't break my train of thought, Katherine." Mother tears out another piece of paper.

I begin reading about Stonewall Jackson and the battle at Antietam. My watch says it's eight o'clock. Before the battle, Lee waited at Sharpsburg to get word from Jackson, who was fighting at Harpers Ferry. Harpers Ferry turned out to be a rout; Jackson completely overwhelmed twelve thousand Union troops, who had to surrender. Lee depended on his right-hand man, Stonewall.

• • •

The Confederate general makes her troops pour out the barrels of whiskey, but allows them to take all they want of the food and other supplies that are in the Union's Harpers Ferry storehouses. Her tattered soldiers hang extra shoes around their necks and gorge themselves on tins of sardines. She sees more than one soldier fill his canteen with molasses. She feels bad that her troops never have enough to eat and is happy to see them stuffing their haversacks with tins of condensed milk and hunks of bacon. They will march tonight to meet Lee at Sharpsburg. She wonders why McClellan has moved so quickly to amass his forces. It's unlike him. He usually waits and waits before he takes any kind of action.

What Jackson and Lee didn't know was that McClellan had intercepted battle plans used by a Confederate officer to wrap up his cigars, which had, unfortunately, dropped out of his pocket. When McClellan unexpectedly moved his army, Lee was forced to take a stand at Sharpsburg, the town where the Antietam creek flowed. But even with the stolen plans, McClellan only managed a draw.

"Hand me that book of yours with all the pictures in it," Mother says. I do and she begins furiously sketching a scene from my *Golden Book of the Civil War*. "I have to give them plenty of samples of the work I might do." She tosses the sketchbook aside and begins writing again.

"Enclosed are representative samples of the work I plan to produce when I personally visit each battlefield." She goes over to her suitcase and pulls things out of it until she finds her pencil case. Some of her clothes fall on the floor, some she throws on the end of the bed.

"If I say that, Kat, then I can go ahead and send them this letter and sample sketches before we go to all the battlefields. Maybe I'll even get some money to cover our expenses. I could sell them the exclusive rights to my prints." She settles back on her bed. She is drawing Confederate dead beside a picket fence but I don't think that's the kind of sketch people will buy. Tourists want sketches of spy balloons, soldiers in different fancy uniforms, and monuments. Or a general on horseback leading the troops in a charge up a hill. My stomach growls again. Mother has forgotten about our seafood dinner. If we were at home I could go into the kitchen and make myself peanut butter crackers. I remember the cooler in the car. We have eaten all the bologna, but there is still bread and mayonnaise. When Mother is agitated like this, I can't interrupt her. I'll have to wait a little longer before I ask for the car keys.

On the television screen a dark blue cartoon sky with twinkling stars and Samantha riding her broomstick appears. *Bewitched.* I ease over and turn the volume up enough for me to hear if I sit at the end of the bed. Mother doesn't say anything and keeps sketching. Once I asked her why Samantha didn't want to use her magic all the time to cook, clean up the kitchen, or vacuum and Mother said it's because she's an idiot.

I would love to twitch my nose and go back in time. Like Endora, I'd love to be invisible and observe people whenever I wanted to. I would go back to watch Belle Boyd, the Confederate spy, run from the town of Front Royal across Yankee lines and over to the Confederates to tell General Jackson about the Yankee plans to burn the bridges as they retreated. I read that the bullets from the battle were so close to her that they made holes in her dress, but she didn't get wounded. Later she was imprisoned for spying and she wrote her memoirs there. She wrote that never before and never after did she run so fast in her life as she did at Front Royal.

Of course, right now I'd love to twitch my nose and turn our room into a restaurant buffet. Mother could keep working if she wanted, but I would eat dinner. Mostly though, I wish I could freeze Mother in time so I could go visit Aunt Laura, Gramma and Poppa, and Daddy without her knowing. I could cast a spell on them so they wouldn't remember my visit, but at least I could see them for a little while. I'd sit rocking on the screened porch in the evening after dinner, listening to the baseball game on the radio while my grandmother shelled peas and my grandfather shucked corn. On a Sunday morning I'd read the paper with Daddy and get him to give me sips of his coffee. I could pop in on Aunt Laura just to read quietly in her wing chair while she graded papers.

"Could I have the keys to the car?" I ask Mother.

Mother looks up from the notebook. "Listen to this: 'We could discuss a fee that would provide the National Park Service an exclusive contract for the custom-produced prints.'" She waits for me to say something. "Well, what do you think? Maybe I should state an amount in the letter."

"I don't know," I say. "How much do exclusive contracts cost?"

"Good question." She tears out the notebook page, but doesn't crumple it up. "I won't put an amount and I'll figure out what would cover my time, travel, and materials to produce the prints."

"I want to get some stuff out of the cooler."

"What?" Mother is watching Endora and Samantha argue over baby Tabitha's powers.

"I thought I'd make a sandwich."

"You'll ruin your dinner," Mother says and starts sketching again.

"But it's after eight o' clock."

"Oh," she says. "I'll give you some money and you can go to the motel restaurant to get us some hamburgers."

Mother doesn't remember the seafood dinner at all. Just like when she forgets to pick me up from school or when she was an hour late picking me up from the museum. She starts obsessing on something and loses time, forgets what she's promised. I know that, along with the time, she's forgotten me. She hands me two dollars from her train case without looking at me. "Here, go and get us two cheeseburgers and one order of fries. We've got drinks in the car."

Going down the stairs and along the sidewalk past rows of rooms is a little scary because the outside lights make weird shadows in every corner. When I turn the corner at the side of the building, I see that the restaurant windows are dark; the hours on the door say that it closes at 8:00 p.m. I check my pockets for change. I have three quarters and a dime, which will buy us crackers and candy bars from the Lance machine that I saw next to the ice machine. I make my way back.

The Confederate general sits outside Jefferson Davis's office. She has been waiting for hours, and Davis's aide keeps telling her that any minute the president will be back from his meeting on the other side of Richmond. The general has come from the battlefield, is dirty and weary, and not at all happy with how Davis has been managing the war so far. He has split the army into too many commands and isn't taking care that supplies and men are equally allocated. She's especially tired of hearing him blame the delay of an important decision on his migraine headaches. As she sits in the uncomfortable parlor chair and hears the clock chime half past, she wonders why she ever accepted her command.

It doesn't take me long to choose two packs of peanut butter crackers and two bags of potato chips, but I can't decide between a Baby Ruth and a Hershey bar. I end up getting two of each.

When I get back to the room, Mother has arranged her sketches on my bed. She stands over them, exchanging them for one another as if she is playing a solitaire game with giant cards.

"The restaurant was closed."

"Look at this." She doesn't respond, just waves me over to the bed. "What do you think? If I present a portfolio of sketches, I have to decide the order. What about this layout?"

I can't tell if her reordering makes any difference or not. Each grouping looks the same to me and all I want to do is eat. Mother pauses only a second or two after she switches sketches, then she switches two more. Soon she has moved every sketch at least once.

"What did you say?" She sits on the bed looking exhausted.

"I had to get stuff from the snack machine." I deposit the snacks on the end of her bed.

"Why in the world?"

On the television a toy soldier brought to life by Tabitha marches into the Stevenses' living room, infuriating Darrin and alarming Larry Tate, his boss. Samantha begins to make up a story to explain why he is there, but she can't come up with anything fast enough, so she freezes everyone except Darrin and the toy soldier.

"The restaurant was closed." I watch Samantha wave her arms in a big circle, which makes everyone unfreeze again. Darrin explains the new ad campaign that uses an animated toy soldier to sell silver polish.

"Well, get the drinks out of the car." Mother picks up the notebook. "I've got a few more changes to make to this letter. The keys are in my purse." I want her to stop writing the letter. I want her to pay attention to what time it is, to what I'm saying to her. But there's nothing I can do to make her listen to me tonight. I go through her purse roughly, not caring if I get things jumbled up.

As I open the motel door she says, "Damn one-horse town. Rolling up the sidewalks before dark."

Chapter Fifteen

Mother doesn't sleep at all, and she keeps the television on almost all night. At midnight when the channel she is watching plays the "Star Spangled Banner" and goes off the air, she clicks the dial until she finds another channel still broadcasting. At first, with a pillow over my head to block out the light, I doze to the background noise of television conversations. But whenever a commercial blares or someone shouts or a gun fires on-screen, I wake up. Finally, I give up and flip through my books while Mother continues her sketching.

They won't keep the shelling up much longer, the general thinks. But she knows her troops won't be able to get a good night's rest even if it stops. That's the point of this late-night barrage. Making them edgy, on guard; it's meant to fray their nerves. This Yankee commander opposite her is clever. Sleepless troops are much less effective. She resigns herself to it, but hopes tomorrow she will be able to find time for her and her troops to rest.

Mother sits on the bed cross-legged, occasionally jumping up to get a crumpled drawing out of the trash can, then carefully smoothing it out on the bedspread. She examines each one from every angle, sometimes adding a few lines to the sketch and sometimes tossing it again. She doesn't tell me to go to sleep; she acts as if I'm not there at all. And she talks, more to herself than to me. "You'll see. We'll make plenty of money on these sketches. And the antique shop. People will come for miles to see what we have. Stone House Antiques." She goes over to the dresser and brushes her hair. She drops the brush back on the dresser with a loud whack.

"It's a new life. New occupation. Everything's possible. In fact, everything's great. The exclusive contract with the National Park people is a cinch. And we're heading north where I can think better. Where it snows. Where it gets cold, like it did when I was a kid."

Mother turns to me. "My mother once told me that in Maine the snow gets so deep and the wind blows everything around so much that you can't see your way from the house to the barn. People get lost and freeze to death fifty feet from their own back door. So whenever they go out in a snowstorm they tie a rope around their waist and anchor it on the railing of the steps. That way they can find their way back to the house." She closes her eyes. I think about walking along holding that rope. Walking, pulling on that rope hand over hand, not letting go, hoping soon that my hand will grasp the rail. "They called those ropes lifelines. Lines that keep you alive. In the North that's what they do; they make sure you tie on to a lifeline so that you don't get lost."

I've never heard this story before, and it makes me glad we're not going to be in Maine in the winter. Thinking about people freezing to death right outside their house is awful; but I tell myself that the story is reassuring, it explains how to avoid getting lost in a storm, how to take care of yourself. Still, Mother's voice is agitated, and despite how sleepy I am I pay attention to see if she starts talking about her mother.

The Confederate general takes out her binoculars to keep watch on the mountain pass up ahead. If the enemy is coming, they'll have to use this pass. Though she is exhausted, she wipes her eyes and forces herself to focus. She and her army have had a long march through the bitterly cold mountains—no snow yet, but the icy winds have pierced the fabric of their uniforms. She hopes she doesn't see the enemy today. Her troops must rest. She must rest.

At three a.m., Mother runs bathwater and pours in a paper packet of bath beads that smell like lavender. Through the doorway, I see her sitting on the side of the tub, using her hand to stir up the water. Another "Star Spangled Banner" comes on the television and she comes back into the room, changes the channel with her wet fingers, and sits down on the end of the bed. Her voice is less edgy than before, but she's talking to herself again. "My mother never had much of a chance to sell her art," she says, "but things are different for me. I'm different from my mother. No reason I should end up like her. That's why I have to go off on my own. Take things into my own hands. We're not the same, we're different altogether. Not to worry." On the television, a huge flag ripples in a stiff wind. "Damn TV." Mother twists the knob hard, making the screen go black.

I lie down, close my eyes, and try to identify what Mother is doing by the sound of her movements. I make it a game. She's packing her suitcase, crumpling more papers. She has stopped talking; she is calming down. I drift off to sleep. When I wake up, the door to our room is open and sunlight streams in. Mother is putting our suitcases into the car. Her forgotten water is still in the tub with the light purple residue of the bath beads.

"Come on, sleepyhead," she calls. "We're heading out to Harpers Ferry." She holds the atlas toward me.

The Confederate general is as tired as her troops, but she must not act as if she is. They depend on her for leadership. She looks at the map and points with a gloved hand to Harpers Ferry—a confluence of rivers, railroads, and a major Northern supply depot. It is a worthy military goal, even if a bit chancy, and she thinks it's better to be on the move, tired, than holed up in a place where you can be bombarded again. Best to have fresh vistas, new sights—it keeps the morale of the men up, even if they're not sure what's next.

• • •

"Be on the lookout for a drugstore," Mother says. "I need mascara and a new lipstick, plus a notebook, writing paper, and envelopes." I rouse myself and look out the window. A thick white mist hangs on the mountains that rise on either side of the bridge leading into town.

"The Shenandoah River," Mother calls out.

As we drive through the Lower Town area of Harpers Ferry we see the Potomac, flowing with the Shenandoah through a gap in the mountains. The river looks eerie; fog rises just above the surface of the water, and I picture the photographs of John Brown I have seen in my books—staring out like a crazy man, his beard long and white. He tried to lead an armed uprising here to free the slaves, but it was a failure and he was captured and hanged. Maybe his ghost roams Harpers Ferry.

The narrow streets of the small town are lined with two- and three-story row houses, all different from one another, some stone, some clapboard. The whole town seems to teeter above the rivers that converge below it. A mountain rises up across the Potomac, a tunnel blasted through it for the train tracks that span the river on a trestle bridge anchored with stone piers.

Mother pulls up to the curb just down the street from a drugstore. "Thank goodness there's space," she says. "Nobody can parallel park a trailer."

Though she's had her coffee, I'm surprised how chipper Mother is, given how little sleep she got. I think about staying in the car so I can doze, but I don't want to miss looking through the magazines and paperbacks that drugstores always have.

While Mother shops I find the big wooden magazine rack and begin to scan the titles slowly. Daddy likes *Field and Stream*, *Life*, and *The Saturday Evening Post*. I like *Town and Country*—Aunt Laura has a subscription—and when I was younger I liked *Highlights*, with the "What's Hidden" puzzles. I used to time myself with my watch's second hand to see how fast I could find the hidden pictures. Usually it took me only twenty seconds. Then I would read "Goofus and Gallant," but I thought it was a dumb way to teach manners. I didn't know any kids who acted like Gallant.

Before he started working every Saturday, Daddy used to take me along to run errands—the things that Mother forgot at the grocery store, the prescription that needed filling, the nails and tools he might want from the hardware store. He was never in a hurry. And he didn't like for Mother to go along. "Me and Kat can handle it." I think a lot of the time he wanted to get away from Mother.

At the drugstore when Daddy and I shifted over from the magazine display to the book racks, I liked to watch him gently pull a book out of the rack and open to its first chapter to read several pages. He concentrated as he picked out novels with cowboys or horses or Wild West scenes on the front. The West is his favorite topic; spy novels are a close second. Even if I found a book I wanted after only a few minutes of looking, I did not interrupt him to ask for it because I knew that every time he found a book for himself, he would buy me one too. If he didn't, it wouldn't matter how much I begged or pleaded, I wouldn't get one either unless I had my own money.

Once I found *The Guinness Book of World Records* and *Ripley's Believe It or Not*. I wanted both. I watched Daddy meticulously scan the racks from top to bottom, occasionally picking out a thick paperback. He set aside a book with a portrait of an Indian on the cover. He continued looking. I was patient, going through all the titles again myself, picking up *Emma* and *Jane Eyre*, which were on the summer reading list for high schoolers, nestled next to *Sweet Revenge* and *Passionate Escape*. At the drugstore, even the classics had covers with buxom women. Soon I saw him pick up another book, *Biography of Jesse James*. He read the first few pages and then gathered it and his other book in his large hand. "You about ready?" he asked me as he always did, acting as if he had been waiting for me to finish.

Quickly I determined my strategy. "I'm trying to decide between these two." I showed him the books.

He took them from me. "It's all right," he said. "We'll get them both."

When we stood at that book rack together at the drugstore, the world felt steady. Not quiet, because people bustled around us in the store, calling to one another, clicking their heels on the shiny black and white linoleum squares, but it was peaceful. The everyday noises stayed in the background and we focused our attention on cover art, titles, and the story that the first few pages of a book tell. At the library I check out books on the school reading list. Every summer I read more of the list than any other kid in the county. Each fall the newspaper runs a picture of me holding the gold-seal certificate standing next to another kid, usually John Taylor, holding the second-place certificate without a seal. But at the drugstore, I didn't choose the reading-list books; I bought the *Best of Mad Magazine*, *Peanuts* cartoon books that I read in one hour, books on UFOs and the Loch Ness monster, and one called *Salted Peanuts* that contained 1,800 trivia facts. Daddy bought me these frivolous books, the books that weren't educational.

As I examine the paperback books at the Harpers Ferry drugstore, I notice how many are about the Civil War. One titled *Combat: The Civil War—The Curtain Rises* draws my attention. I pull it out carefully as Daddy would and turn to the beginning. It is a collection of eyewitness accounts written by real Civil War soldiers. The book is organized according to battles, each battle having a story from a Union soldier and a Confederate soldier. This book will tell me what it is really like to be in combat, to hear shot and shell all around you, and to see bloody arms mangled by minié balls. I keep the book in my hand, get out a five-dollar bill, and go to find Mother. She's already at the cash register and the clerk is ringing things up. I put my book and money on the counter.

"Oh, interesting cover art," she says, adding the book to her pile. She hands me back my five dollars. I'm thrilled at my luck.

When we return to the car Mother stashes her purchases in the backseat, handing me my new paperback. "Let's go see where old John Brown created such a ruckus. I'll make a few sketches, maybe of the two rivers coming together with the mountains on either side covered in mist. Of course, it's hard to put mist in a simple sketch, but I can probably pull it off. What else should we look for, Miss Civil War smarty-pants?" she teases me.

"The firehouse," I tell her. Robert E. Lee captured Brown and his men in the fire station, where they holed up after the townspeople discovered them stealing guns in the middle of the night.

As we follow the signs to the firehouse I look at the map again and see how this town is tucked into the edges of three states on the border of the North and South. Part of the reason Brown picked Harpers Ferry to stage his uprising was so he could easily escape by river or railroad to a free state. Aunt Laura told me a lot of New England abolitionists praised John Brown, even though they were nonviolent themselves. The writers Ralph Waldo Emerson and Henry David Thoreau said he'd done a good thing. Aunt Laura told me she isn't so sure. "You can be right as rain, but if you don't work with the other side you can't get anywhere. That's what King knew how to do," she told me. "He knew how to work with the other side. Of course," she said, "that was after he made us all stop to listen." I want to be that kind of person, able to get people to listen to me because I understand them.

We park and go through the firehouse. There is a small display of photographs from the same period as Brown's attempted uprising, but otherwise it's a small, almost empty building that smells damp and a little moldy.

We cross the street to the Harpers Ferry museum and go through the exhibits together. I expect Mother to lecture me about John Brown trying to end slavery, but she is quiet until the end and then she says, "Too bad someone with some sense didn't have the same idea and succeed."

"Aunt Laura says that nonviolence is the best way to change things."

"Well now," Mother considers, "she has a point there. But sometimes you have to fight."

We read about the armory, filled with the guns that John Brown tried to steal to use in his uprising. The exhibit says the town changed hands eight times during the war mostly because of the armory and its location on the border of North and South. The Union used it as a supply base whenever they had control of it. The battles here were down by the rivers and in the streets of the town as well as on the outskirts. Most of the residents had to move away during the war.

In the museum gift shop we find a portrait postcard of John Brown with his piercing eyes. Outside we sit at a picnic table and sketch. Mother's idea for mountains in the mist doesn't work well and she abandons it. Her rendition of the brick firehouse with its arched windows looks good, but she's afraid that no one will recognize it, so she adds a small portrait of John Brown in the upper corner. I draw the museum building and some of the people that come in and out until Mother agrees to take a closer look at the trestle bridge. The walkway that arcs over the river is built parallel to the bridge, and from the middle I wave to Mother, who has found a bench below. Cottony white clouds float in the sky between the green mountains on each side of the river. According to the map I got at the museum, these are part of the Blue Ridge Mountains. Up here the air is cooler. Below me the Shenandoah flows into the Potomac. The surface of the water is glassy, its powerful current barely visible, and I have a hard time believing that it can flood the whole town. Farther downstream, the water flows around shoals of white rocks and at several points it looks like I could almost walk across on them. It is so peaceful here, nothing like that violent night of Brown's raid—nothing like last night.

Harpers Ferry is an odd, contradictory place. John Brown was so wrong in what he did, but he was right in being against slavery. Later, during the war, the place was full of spies and troops, but no townspeople, and was both Northern and Southern, depending on who had won the latest battle. I'm beginning to think of myself as being both Northern and Southern, something I had not considered before. It's an unsettling idea.

Chapter Sixteen

We travel on a two-lane road to go from Harpers Ferry to Sharpsburg, Maryland, where the battle of Antietam took place. The map shows that we are closely paralleling the Potomac River, but we never see it. Our drive takes us through a valley of gently rolling hills and pastureland with fences here and there, past a few head of cattle or horses. In the bright afternoon light, the grass and trees are still the fresh yellow-green color that I think of as spring. I see fields of young corn, the plants knee-high with delicately flopping leaves. We didn't pass any promising-looking antique shops on the way to Harpers Ferry this morning and there are none on this road. But it's okay because we don't have that much room left in the trailer and we're likely to pass plenty of stores on the rest of the long drive to Maine.

As I stare out the car window, I imagine Jackson's troops hurriedly marching on this same route after they captured Harpers Ferry and Lee sent word that they should head north to Sharpsburg to reinforce the rest of the Army of Northern Virginia. I want to absorb everything as we drive by so I will remember how it looks. When Jackson passed through here in mid-September, the corn would have been much higher, as tall as a man. But for once, his men wouldn't have needed to gather the ears during their afternoon and evening march; they would have been loaded down with food taken from the Union storehouses at Harpers Ferry.

We get to the visitor center right before the filmstrip begins and Mother reluctantly agrees to stay for it. With Mother fidgeting next to me, I try to soak up all the details about Antietam. Lee had wanted to invade Pennsylvania and worked out an intricate way to divide his army in order to do so, but when Union soldiers found his battle orders, everything changed. He positioned his army on the ridge of Sharpsburg, a town east of the Potomac with the swift waters of Antietam creek running alongside it. Lee's first invasion of the North turned out to be the bloodiest single day of the war. More than 23,000 men were killed or wounded in the one-day battle.

On the screen is a photo of a tiny white building—Dunker Church. In the foreground are a dead horse, a broken two-wheeled artillery caisson, and many dead soldiers lying in a row. The next photograph shows the Sunken Road, a broad dirt path that lies some two feet lower than the fields on either side. After a three-and-a-half-hour fight there, the narration tells us, the soldiers renamed the road Bloody Lane. I grip the arm of my seat when the next picture comes on the screen. I've seen it before at Aunt Laura's. Two men in hats, slightly out of focus, look down from above the Sunken Road into the mass of tangled torsos, legs, arms, and upturned faces of soldiers who died there. The photo makes me queasy; the bodies are so much bigger projected on the screen. The narrator tells us that at the end of the battle Lee had to leave all the Confederate dead and many of his wounded when he retreated across the Potomac. Many of the dead in the pictures must be Confederates—the last to be buried.

I'm glad when we leave the dark auditorium to go outside into the sunlight, away from the gloom of those photos. Mother grabs a map of the battlefield and we drive along the car tour, not stopping until we come to the Sunken Road.

We get out, and Mother points to a statue in the distance of a soldier holding a flag that drapes limply over his shoulder. "Let's head to that monument." We walk along the Sunken Road. It's covered in grass now, but it's still lower than the field that borders it on one side and the park road that is on the other side. Walking on it, I understand how the Confederate soldiers thought it could provide them some protection from Union fire. A small boy in front of us clambers up the side to the low ridge. He makes a pistol with his finger and thumb. "*Pow, pow,*" he says, aiming down at those of us walking by.

"Get over here," his mother says sternly. The boy quickly runs down the short embankment. She holds one of his hands as he twists along, continuing to shoot his imaginary enemies.

I wish I'd eaten more of my breakfast when we stopped earlier at the drugstore counter in Harpers Ferry. This is what the Confederates felt, I realize, as I trudge down the road. They often felt hungry and thirsty. They were short on rations again by the time they got to Maryland. If they passed a farm, they tried to buy food with their Confederate money or trade for what they needed. Lee had hoped many Southern sympathizers in Maryland would give them food, but most of the residents refused to help. The filmstrip had said the Confederates ate a lot of green corn. Many of the soldiers must have stolen food. I would have. If that little boy shooting people with his finger had an apple in his pocket, I would grab his wrist hard and make him give it to me. Of course, I'd wait until we were out of sight of everyone. I decide not to say anything about being hungry. I imagine the dead Confederates, so thick on the road that the Yankees said they could walk down the whole length of it without stepping on anything but dead Rebels.

In the dark of night, the Confederate general looks back over her shoulder as the last of her men ford the Potomac River into the safety of Virginia. She has left thousands of her dead and wounded in Sharpsburg. To save the rest of her army, she has to leave them; but knowing this doesn't stop the aching in her heart. She is saddened by their fate, far from their families and comrades. She wonders if any battle is worth this many dead.

• • •

By the time we get to the monument, the sun is scorching hot. Mother begins to sketch and a kid walking up to read the inscription on the statue leans over to see what she is doing.

"How long is it going to take you?" I ask, flopping down in the grass, the rough blades sticking into my bare legs and arms. I fiddle with the metal snap on the pocket of my shorts.

"I swear, Katherine, you're all interested in the battlefields one minute and then the next minute you act like you are itching to leave. You got us going on this project and you'll finish, whether you're interested or not."

Arguing with her is useless, whether or not the sketches are my project. We'll leave when she is good and ready and we'll get something to eat and drink when she is good and ready. Soldiers had to endure the same thing; I can too, though I wish I had a canteen. After the battle was over, some of the soldiers left alive would have grabbed their canteens to cool their parched throats. The fight ended at one p.m. on a mid-September day. Not as hot as it is this afternoon in mid-June, but still plenty hot.

Lee didn't win at Sharpsburg, which the Yankees called Antietam, but he didn't lose either. The bloodiest day of the Civil War was a draw. McClellan stopped Lee's invasion, but he didn't defeat Lee once and for all because he was too cautious. Mother misunderstood me; I'm not bored here. So much happened at this site, probably not far from where I sit. Lincoln visited McClellan after the battle to congratulate him. In the visitor center, they sell a postcard of Lincoln sitting with McClellan in a white tent, a flag draped over a table where Lincoln's top hat rests. Lincoln counted the battle as a win and used the victory as an opportunity to sign the Emancipation Proclamation, cementing the fact that the war was about abolishing slavery. It was the one good result of the battle and one of the things that made Lincoln a great president.

I move my arms and legs into different positions and imagine I am a soldier dying on the Sunken Road, seeing my friends dead and crumpled all around me, rifles lying scattered among us.

"Katherine, Katherine, open your eyes," Mother calls. "And straighten out your legs. You look like you're crippled the way you're lying there."

I open my eyes and find a group of tourists walking around me. I sit up so quickly it makes me dizzy. When the sensation passes, I stand and walk over to look at Mother's sketches. She isn't sketching the statue. Instead, she is drawing soldiers in the Sunken Road. One who looks dead is leaning against the road bank and another is drinking from his canteen. The way Mother has done the shadows it looks as if it is evening, not midday.

In her sketch, the man leaning against the bank somehow resembles Eli, the handyman who used to work for my grandparents. Maybe it's the way his body is half-upright, with the shoulders slumped forward, the way Eli leaned against the shed when he died. Eli's face was ashen, drained of its normal soft brown color. His hat was on the ground beside him, just where Mother has put the soldier's hat in her sketch.

Eli, Daddy, and Poppa were building a pen for one of Poppa's bird dogs, Suzie. It was the beginning of the summer, but already it was heavy hot. I had just finished second grade with Mrs. Preston and that morning Mother had signed me up to go to Cherokee Day Camp with Milly. I sat on the dark green metal glider under the trees in my grandparents' backyard, watching Daddy and Eli use the posthole diggers to make holes for the new fence. Each raised their digger high in the air with the two wooden handles pushed together and slammed it hard into the soil. With a jerk they pulled the handles apart and raised up reddish dirt clamped in between the two blades. A mound of dirt grew beside the hole in which they would pour a little concrete and sink a post.

Sweat dripped off Daddy's chin and onto each clump of dirt that he pinched out of the ground. Eli took his hat off and wiped his face and head with a red bandanna. Eli Moore lived with his wife, Miss Phyllis, down the road in a small white house with a screened porch across the front. They still got their water from a well in their yard.

Whenever I went to their house, I drank from the aluminum dipper that hung from a nail on the side of the well. That water's cold metallic taste was better than any tap water.

Miss Phyllis had a tailor shop on the square. I liked to go there with Mother. While Miss Phyllis pinned the hem of Mother's dress or chalked a mark on her waistband to take it in, I looked at all the clothes on her metal rack with the bills safety-pinned to them, waiting to be picked up. Miss Phyllis's skin was blue-black—much darker than Eli's. During the week she wore a turban around her head that matched her clothes, but on Sundays she put on huge hats, bright yellow or red or brilliant blue—I had seen a few at her shop when she was making them. "Those are my Sunday go-to-meeting hats," she had told me. Eli worked as a handyman for a lot of people. He cut grass, planted trees, built things, patched roofs, cleaned out chimneys. "Nothing's made that Eli can't fix," he'd say. He fixed my bike when the chain broke, and he got under Poppa's blue truck and repaired it whenever it acted up. Eli had the idea to build the dog pen onto the shed so they only had to put up three sides of fencing.

Gramma came out with lemonade for everyone. Poppa and Daddy stood and drank theirs and Eli sat down against the wall of the shed. I couldn't hear what they were saying, but I saw Poppa gesturing and Daddy and Eli nodding their heads. I opened the book I'd brought out in the yard with me, one of my favorites—*The True Book of Dinosaurs*—and as I read the first page, I heard the clump and squeak of the posthole diggers start up again. When I had gotten to the chapter on *Brontosaurus*, I heard Daddy yell loud, "Mama, mama, come quick." I jumped up and ran to the chain-link fence at the back of the yard and saw Eli sitting against the shed with Poppa unbuttoning his shirt, raising a glass of lemonade to Eli's lips. The screen door slammed and Gramma hurried through the gate. When she got to Eli she motioned for the men to help her lay him flat on the ground, then she hit her fist against his chest, the blow so strong his body bounced a little and I was frightened that she had hurt him. She opened his mouth, pinched his nose, and put her mouth over his. I saw his chest rise when she blew air into him and fall when she turned her head to the side. In between breaths, she said firmly, "Bill, call the ambulance." Poppa undid Eli's belt and the button at the top of his pants. Eli was ash colored, gray. Gramma had on a maroon dress with paisley designs and as she knelt, the fabric of her dress trailed in the orange-red dirt. I couldn't move. Everything slowed down around me. I thought any minute Eli would get up, wipe his brow, put on his hat. I started wishing hard for him to get up.

Later, I watched the ambulance men pull a white sheet over Eli's head and pop the stretcher wheels up. One of them said to Gramma, "A big heart attack hits you, you're a goner. Doesn't hardly matter how fast we get here." Gramma turned away and motioned for me to come into the house with her. We sat together on the sofa and she put her arms around me. "It's a hard thing, someone dying," she said.

At first Mother said I shouldn't go to Eli's funeral, that I was too young, but Daddy insisted it would be better for me since I had been there when it happened. I wanted to go. Gramma always said a person could never have too many people at their funeral. We drove past Eli and Phyllis's church, Mount Gilead AME, all the time, going to the new post office. From the back of the packed church, light streaming in the tall stained glass windows, I watched during the whole service as Miss Phyllis sobbed, her fantastic lilac-trimmed black hat bobbing up and down with each shudder of her shoulders. Watching her made me sadder. Eli's silver casket was up by the altar and I could see only his profile from where we were sitting. A few white people werc there—the druggist, Sam Miller; Dr. Leslie; and Martha, the woman who ran the bakery next to Miss Phyllis's shop—but everyone else was Black and I didn't know them. All through the service I looked around to try to see someone else I recognized. Although we often drove by Mount Gilead AME and the Black section of town, we never stopped. In a world where I recognized at least half of the people on the street when we went downtown, the whole church was full of strangers to me.

Mother sighs and stands up from where she has been sitting. I look at her carefully. She has on a lot of makeup, but the dark circles underneath her eyes still show. Her turquoise sleeveless shirt is wrinkled and her blue jeans have a grass stain on the right knee.

"This place is dismal. I don't like these monuments at all—no grace in them. Come on. We'll go back to that little white church and I'll throw together a quick sketch of it." I am already up, but she waves impatiently. "Come on, come on. We haven't got all day. We still need to find a motel." I want to ask her questions about Eli and Miss Phyllis, but she's in too much of a hurry. I wish I could talk to Miss Phyllis in person. I've never thought about Eli and Miss Phyllis as having anything to do with the Civil War, but now I want to know what Miss Phyllis thinks about Lincoln and whether the Emancipation Proclamation freed any of her relatives.

I struggle to keep up with Mother as she hikes back down the Sunken Road. The heat doesn't seem to faze her, but sweat drips down the sides of my face. When we get to the parking lot, two kids in the backseat of the car next to us are drinking Sprites and I watch them tilt their bottles back and swallow. A red metal Coca-Cola cooler sits between them. I want to get in their car; I want to take the battlefield tour they have chosen. The father is reading out loud from a brochure folded out over his steering wheel and the mother is tying a scarf over her hair, though there isn't much of a breeze. They are following the order of the brochure, no detours, no surprises.

The Confederate general hates retreating. If her battle orders had not been carelessly wrapped around cigars and dropped, her troops would be marching victorious into Washington, D.C., right now. Instead of deciding the terms of the Union army's surrender, she is planning their nighttime escape back over the Potomac. She is a seasoned veteran, but she has begun thinking about home more often these days, particularly when the fighting doesn't go well. She can picture her porch, the rocking chairs, and her family coming out of the house to be with her in the cool of a summer evening.

Chapter Seventeen

We drive to the Dunker Church part of the battlefield, where the small, square white church sits on a rise looking out across gently rolling mown fields. Behind the church and off to the right a bit are the West Woods, where Jackson's troops hid behind rocks and ridges to surprise the unsuspecting Yankees. Mother sits in the car, leaning her pad on the steering wheel, and sketches the church. Another car pulls up behind ours and a family gets out—twin boys that look my age, a mother with a big straw hat, a father with a camera hanging around his neck, carrying a tripod, and a teenage girl walking behind the rest. The father groups them loosely in front of the church and then sets up his tripod. He changes its position several times while the mother pleads with the girl not to go back to the car.

"I can't stand the way he does this," I can hear the girl saying.

"Just a minute. I'm almost set, sweetheart," the father calls out.

Mother stops sketching and I glance over at her pad. She is finished with the little church, but she has begun adding cannons that aren't there. Without the cannons it certainly doesn't look like much.

"He's so embarrassing, Mother. Why can't he just use the Kodak?" I look back out at the family.

"There we go," says the father, glancing up from his camera. "I'm using my wide-angle lens. Say cheese!"

The mother turns her head to say something to her daughter right as the camera clicks.

"Let's get a few more," the father says as one twin pushes the other so hard that he falls down.

Mother puts down her notebook and cranks the Impala. "Ready to roll?"

Until now I hadn't thought about how strange it is that we have not been taking pictures of our trip. On all of our other trips, we have taken lots of pictures. When we get home we put them in scrapbooks.

"Why aren't we taking pictures to show Daddy and everyone when we get home?"

"We don't need any photographs," Mother says without looking over at me. "We've got our sketches." She is flying down the two-lane road toward the town center of Sharpsburg.

"But *we* aren't in the sketches." Mother ignores me.

The Confederate general spends a great deal of time on the battle reports that she sends to Richmond for President Davis to read. She knows the value of recording her actions and decisions, and she is upset that the photographer who was following her army to document the battles disappeared just before their current campaign. She has come to know that her notes and quick sketches are not enough record of something so important as this Northern campaign.

"Look at the map. Are we going the right way?"

I turn to the page marked with my folded notebook paper. We're on Highway 34, which is correct.

"We'll probably never find a motel. This town is tiny." Mother sighs and begins to drum the steering wheel with the heel of her right hand. The cornfields speed by and I see the beginnings of the town.

I hear a loud pop and the car swerves to the right. Mother slams on the brakes and we both fly forward. I feel the weight of the trailer pushing us from behind and close my eyes tight, waiting for the crash.

"What is it?" Mother screeches. "What's happening? The car won't steer. The trailer's fishtailing."

I hear a *flump, flump, flump* sound and open my eyes.

"Damn flat tire," she cries, looking around wildly. "We need a gas station, now." Mother drives in the far right part of our lane, but she has not pulled off onto the shoulder.

"See what signs you can read, Kat." The eye doctor says I am extremely farsighted. Mother and Daddy both test me all the time to see how far I can read signs. I strain to see if I can see the word *Shell* or *American* or *Gulf*.

"Yes," I sing out. "American Oil."

Mother speeds up a little and the tire flumps more. When we pull into the gas station, the attendant sitting outside on a chair next to the door shakes his head, takes his cap off, and rubs his hand over the top of his head. "Pull 'er over to the service bay." He points. Mother drives by the gas pumps, turning the car to face the open space that has a lift resting on the greasy concrete.

"Pull it on in," the short, wiry man says impatiently. He directs Mother silently with his hands.

"I got a flat tire on the way into town," Mother says as we get out of the car. "Could you . . ."

"Well I see, don't I?" the man exclaims. "Shouldn't run on a flat; you can ruin the rim. Where's your spare?"

"We don't have one."

"All that trailer space and no spare. Well, I'll be a monkey's uncle. You may have ruined that rim. Might have to get you a new one. Don't know how I'd get one. Have to see. Can't put a new tire on a bad rim. That much I can tell you. Simply won't do." All this time the man is bending, looking at the flat tire, running his grimy hands over the rim. "Don't know that I have this size tire in stock either. Might need to go across town to Shortie's and see what he has. Where are you two heading?"

I can tell Mother is mad. "Where we are going is no concern of yours. How much will a new tire cost?"

"Like I said, lady, don't really know what's the trouble yet. Need to figure out about this rim. Need to see how much Shortie wants for this size tire. Figure a retread will do for you unless you tell me different. Shortie's got all manner of retreads, any size, any type. You got whitewalls on now. You need a whitewall? It's a little more."

"Whatever's the least expensive. But is a retread safe?"

"Got to get this trailer unhitched. Hey, Ezra, give me a hand with this."

"Okay, Sam." A tall lanky man with a dark beard gets up from a chair behind the cash register and joins the attendant, and Mother and I sit on two metal lawn chairs on a grassy spot off to the side to wait. A black-and-white pointer ambles over, sniffs us a little, and flops down at our feet. I pet his head.

"Get your hands off that filthy dog, Kat." Mother looks disgusted, but the dog seems ordinary to me. "Go wash your hands." The bathrooms are on our end of the station. Inside, it is cleaner than I expected. I wash my hands and face. Then I cup my hands under the faucet and gulp mouthful after mouthful of cool water.

When I come out of the bathroom Sam is talking to Mother, telling her that the rim is fine and that he can get a tire, but we'll have to wait a little while. Mother is impatient and angry, but he tells us that we can use his phone to call a motel.

"We'll call in a few minutes," Mother says and doesn't get up from her lawn chair.

"Suit yourself," says Sam, grinning down at her.

"So here's the plan," Mother says as Sam walks away. "We'll go to Gettysburg next. Then the Cape. We'll try to find the old summerhouse and buy more antiques. I can make sketches of the marshes and the beach. But then, straight to Maine. We've got to rent a place for our shop and start selling things before the summer tourist season ends. Outside of Bar Harbor would be perfect. Rich people vacation there."

My muscles tense and I hold very still. What is she talking about? My heart is beating fast, but I try to stay calm. "We're going to live in Maine?" My voice is too quiet and I can't look her in the eye.

"Yes, I told you, we need a fresh start. A place we can be ourselves. Other people have been holding us down too long. I belong in New

England; that's where my family is from. I never wanted to be in the South, it wasn't my choice. The judge said I had to go live with my aunt Susan. I wanted to stay in Boston. I've never had any choices." Her jaw muscles flex and her neck is flushed red.

"You never said we were going to live in Maine," I whisper. Tears begin to well up in my eyes. I brush them away quickly with the back of my hand.

"Well, we are. We're moving to Maine. That's what I've decided." Mother's face is defiant; her lips are pursed and I look her in the eyes now. I wonder when she decided—has she known the whole time and not told me? She stares back at me without blinking.

"But we didn't say good-bye to Gramma and Poppa and Aunt Laura," I blurt. I start to add Daddy, but remember the notes Mother and I left on the kitchen counter.

A beat-up black truck with tires in the back pulls into the station. "Don't you understand," Mother says fiercely. "If we had said good-bye they would have kept us from going."

The Confederate general is troubled by the thought that President Davis isn't giving her complete information about his military strategy. She's desperate to know everything and it hurts her that he may not trust her enough to share what he's planning. Because of her sacrifices, he owes it to her to keep her informed. She is his top general! She stands up abruptly, her sword banging against her chair. "You will give me all the information you have from now on." Davis blinks and nods yes.

A man with a huge belly that peeks out from under the bottom of his tight T-shirt opens the tailgate of the pickup and bounces out one of the tires.

"Shortie!" Sam calls out.

"Gotcher tire here."

"When will we see everyone again?" I ask Mother. There is a little shake in my voice.

"Oh, for heaven's sake, Katherine. We've been gone less than a week. We'll see them sometime. I can't worry about things like that now." She turns away.

We sit in silence while Sam rolls the tire over to our car, now lifted on the shiny metal pole that rises out of the garage floor.

"That tire's like new, lady," Sam says to Mother. "All together, it's ten fifty."

Mother opens her purse and hands him the bills. "I never called up a motel," she says quietly.

"There's a Grover Inn right off the square that's pretty reasonable, with a restaurant so you can get dinner." He grins at us both and runs his fingers across the bill of his cap.

The Confederate general thinks about the family she's left behind. It may be six months before she sees them again. She's glad that they don't have to see the ravages of war. Still, deep in the night, she longs for them so much that she could come close to quitting the whole enterprise just to see them for one day from dawn until midnight.

At the motel, as Mother changes her clothes for dinner and puts on her makeup, I look at the letters I've been writing in my notebook to Aunt Laura, Gramma and Poppa, and Daddy. In the one to Daddy, I tell him about wanting to go to the drugstore again with him on Saturdays like we used to. I started writing to Aunt Laura about the VMI museum and I've finished a second short letter to Gramma and Poppa telling them about all the antiques Mother has bought. I shut my notebook. Letters won't ever be enough. I can't possibly tell them in writing everything I want them to know. I need to see them, talk to them.

"Why do we have to live in Maine?" I ask Mother. "Why can't we start an antique store back in Georgia?"

Mother turns around from the mirror in a fury. "Haven't you heard anything I've said?" She has her mascara brush in her hand and jabs it in the air at me as she talks. "I want to get away from the South, I don't want your father's family controlling everything in our lives, I want to be my own person now."

I see how angry she is, but I can't help replying. "I don't want to move away from everyone. I don't want to run away."

She drops the mascara brush on the carpet as she strides over to me. Her eyes are hard and darker than ever. She pulls back her hand and I shut my eyes and wait, but nothing happens.

Mother sits next to me on the bed. "Oh, my baby," she says, and her tone is softer now. "I know this seems sudden to you, but it's been coming for a long time. Your father and I simply can't live together any longer." I think she means a divorce; but divorce is bad, something that trashy people do. And why do we have to move so far away from everyone?

"What about Gramma and Poppa and Aunt Laura?" I'm taking a big risk by continuing.

"Listen to me," Mother says and puts her hand under my chin to make me look at her. "Do you want to live with your father?"

I don't say anything. I don't know how to answer.

"Well. Answer me. Do you want to live with your father?"

"I don't know." She lets my chin go. I drop my eyes to my hands resting in my lap. I like the way my blue veins fork at the knuckle of my ring finger. I don't want to live alone with my father because he's never at home, but I don't want to live away from him either, and I do want to live near Gramma and Poppa and Aunt Laura.

"You want to work at the antique shop, don't you?"

"Yes." I like the idea of the stone building Mother has in mind for the shop. I imagine the big black cash register and the cat in the window. But it is supposed to be in Marietta, not Maine.

"Good. Then you're my partner. You'll help me with the shop and I'll sell my sketches to the National Park system and start my painting again. Things are going to be good for once." Mother stands up and looks for the mascara wand.

I think about it hard before I ask my next question. "After we start the antique shop, can we visit everybody?"

Mother shoves the wand back into its container and throws it toward her train case; with a *thunk* it hits the counter and then rolls a little. She faces me again with the mirror behind her, and in the mirror I look into my own eyes and then turn back to hers. She stares me down and her shoulders are trembling a little. She turns and grabs her hairbrush like she's getting ready to hit me, and without thinking I am up and backing toward the door. I watch her warily. But suddenly she smiles. Her anger is gone as quickly as it came and she begins brushing her hair.

"I know it's hard, Kat, because you're still a child." She is looking at me in the mirror. "But you're grown-up enough to try to understand. We're going to have to be gone long enough to get started with our new life before we get back in touch with them. Your father and grandparents want to stop me from doing what's good for me. They don't want me to sketch or paint or move up north, they want me to be quiet and still. They don't appreciate people with drive and energy."

I think about this for a minute. Daddy and Gramma both were enthusiastic about Mother's art show in Atlanta, and Gramma always asks Mother how her painting is going. She's wrong about them. "Does Aunt Laura want to stop you?"

Mother puts the brush away and applies her lipstick. "No, I don't think Laura wants to stop me from doing what I need to do. She's always liked my paintings. She'd be a pretty good egg if she wasn't so hung up on all that genealogy stuff."

"She's a historian," I say.

"That's right. That's her excuse." Mother blots her lips gently on a Kleenex. "Now, start getting yourself ready for dinner."

First I put my notebook at the bottom of my book bag. I don't want Mother to read it.

"You don't need to change," Mother says loudly. "I'm starving. We need to get a move on."

I rummage in my suitcase and find my comb.

While I comb my hair, Mother looks at me as if she's sizing me up. "Do you want to try a little lipstick tonight? Just a pale, pale pink color?"

"No thanks," I tell her and put my comb back in my suitcase. I don't like the taste of lipstick and I like the color of my lips as they are.

"Listen," she says in a soft voice. "Sit down."

I do what she says and she stands over me. "I can't do this without you. You have to be on my side and help me. I'll need your help in the business and everything else. You're smart and you might even start making your own art that we could sell. But we have to keep where we are a secret until we can get established. And then, I promise"—she crosses her chest—"you can visit everyone for a good long while. You can even fly on an airplane so you'll get there really fast. Now, I have to have your word." She takes my hands in hers and looks at me intently. "Do you swear you won't tell any of them where we are? That you won't tell anyone else what we're really doing?"

Her hands are warm. Her eyes are pooling up with tears. "This means everything to me, Kat, you being on my side," she says.

Maybe she's mad at Daddy and everyone else right now, but after a while she's bound to come around. It seems impossible that we would really move away. Right now she needs me and I want her to have her trip to New England that Daddy always said was too expensive. "I swear."

"I'm so happy," she says, smiling. She lets go of my hands and dances around the room, swirling and dipping from one side and then the other like she's pretending to be an airplane. "My baby loves me!"

Loyalty is one of the most important qualities in an officer. The Confederate general turns this over in her mind as her heart races and her stomach clenches. Her commander is making plans that she believes will have devastating consequences, and yet, after voicing her contrary opinion, she now has to go along with it. In fact, she is now bound to support the plan in all the ways that she can. Obedience and loyalty are equal to bravery. She hopes everything goes the best it can and that at the eleventh hour, her commander will change his mind.

• • •

After her windmill dance, Mother picks up her purse. "We'll go get a nice dinner at the Chuck Wagon restaurant."

I go to the bathroom before we leave. While I sit on the toilet I examine the tiles, alternating yellow and white. In the corners, a tile might be half-size or quarter-size to make the row fit. I look for a mistake in the order but there isn't one.

"Come on," Mother calls out. "What are you doing in there?"

"In a minute." The gleaming bathtub faucet has a slow drip, staining the tub beneath with rust. I am hungry but I don't want to go to the restaurant yet. My head has started hurting, and by being very still it seems to throb less. Poppa and Gramma's bathroom has tiny black and white tiles. Sometimes when I take a bath there I count the tiles, putting soapsuds markers at different places along the wall so I won't lose my place. I like putting my toes up on the tiles, making them fit one per square. I don't know when I'll be able to spend the night with Gramma and Poppa again, rock on the side porch with them until it gets dark and then take my bath while they set up the coffee for the next morning and shut up the house for the night. I close my eyes and think about Maine in the summer. We'll eat lobster every day and walk on beaches covered in polished pebbles. Mother and I will sell antiques and art in Bar Harbor, get rich like Miss Jameson, and then Mother will want to move back to Georgia. Maine won't last. I'll convince her we have to go home and then I'll be with everyone I love.

"Kat," Mother calls sweetly from the other side of the bathroom door. "Tomorrow we're going to Gettysburg. You'll see the whole place. I'll buy you souvenirs in the gift shop. Be a good girl now and come on out."

Finally I flush and leave the bathroom. Mother stands by the door, ready to go.

On the long march the general considers the change of plans. Her cavalry has brought her news of enemy forces where she least expected them.

Even though her men are tired and many are barefoot, they must keep marching. They will camp next to the river and hope for good weather and decent foraging. She doesn't like the position that the Yankees have put her in—it seems to her they are dictating the terms, and she needs to figure out how to turn things around. She needs to find high ground from which to launch an offensive.

Chapter Eighteen

The next day the drive to Gettysburg takes us twice as long as it should. From the map, I estimated less than an hour, but Mother keeps stopping. First we leave the highway and drive into a small town to find a restaurant so she can get coffee. We sit in the booth for a long time while Mother sips.

"Don't you feel it?" she asks me, leaning forward as if we're sharing a secret. "Don't you feel different now that we're really in the North?"

I haven't noticed anything different except that it's hot and humid again since we left the mountains.

"But wait until we get to New England." She nods. "That's when I'll really start feeling at home. You're not going to forget what you promised me last night, are you?" She raises her eyebrows.

"No, ma'am." I shake my head. I've decided that by the end of the summer Mother will change her mind about staying in Maine and we'll head home in time to register me for school. I've seen her do it enough times before.

After only a short time back on the road, she decides we need to find a grocery store to buy ice for the cooler. At the third place we stop, a shack with vegetables, potato chips, candy bars, and a pot of coffee in the back corner, Mother buys a pack of cigarettes. I've never seen her smoke.

"Great way to stay awake," she says when we walk back out into the bright sunlight. She hands me her cup of coffee and opens the cellophane on the pack. She fumbles with the matches, finally striking one.

"Perfect," she says as she lifts her chin and blows smoke out of her mouth in a thin steady stream. "I'd forgotten how good these taste." She holds the cigarette in her left hand and flicks it with her thumb. The cigarette makes her look like a movie star in one of the old movies we watch. I wonder what else I don't know about her.

"Quit staring and get in the car," she says. I walk carefully with her coffee, wondering what her smoking means about her mood.

The general considers her good fortune in coming upon a perfect strategic spot to form her battalions. But for some reason her chief aide is behaving erratically. She wonders whether she can trust him to execute her battle plans properly. A nagging feeling in her gut tells her she needs to replace him, but she knows there is no one else with his experience. And as always, she is deeply loyal to those who have been in battle with her before.

"Hand me that," she says after I open my door, reaching across the seat to take the coffee from me. She blows on it, puts her cigarette in the ashtray, and opens her door to pour a little of the coffee out onto the ground. We sit in the hot car while she sips coffee and smokes her cigarette, staring ahead of her at nothing.

"Next time I'll ask for a cup of ice and have iced coffee. Go check the trailer, Kat." I do as she asks, but all I know to do is check that the chain and the hitch are still attached. Through the rear window I watch Mother smoking. Her cigarette appears and then disappears, appears, disappears. I walk around to the back of the trailer to make sure the door is latched and locked. I lift the padlock and drop it so that it clanks against the metal of the trailer door.

I'm glad Mother wants to go to Gettysburg, but I don't know why she's acting strange, like she's concentrating hard, but not on what we are doing. Usually she sees every detail around her; sometimes it even seems she knows what I am thinking. But right now she is irritable and far away. When she is painting in the basement she can get like this; that's why she forgets to pick me up from school. It's unnerving to have her here but not really with me.

Mother leans out of the car window. "Come on, already." As I get in the front seat, she flicks the stub of her cigarette away.

"Everything okay?" she asks.

"Looks fine." But what if it isn't fine? What if in a couple of miles the whole thing breaks loose and strews furniture and dishes all over the road? I position myself so I can see the trailer in my side mirror.

As we enter Pennsylvania, Mother lights another cigarette with the glowing coil of the car's lighter. Aunt Laura often tells me that I worry too much. "You need to leave the worrying to the grownups," she says. "Sometimes, the things that trouble you most aren't such big problems after all. And other times, the things that at first are bad turn out to be blessings in disguise." I try to follow her way of thinking. If something happens to the trailer, it might be for the best. We might lose all the antiques, but then Mother could change her mind about Maine. Of course, it could also make her turn around and go back home before we get to Gettysburg, which would be too bad. And if Mother loses the antiques, she won't have a chance to be happy. The blessings-in-disguise tactic isn't helping me; there are too many possibilities. I try telling myself that my worries are small ones, that I'm making a mountain out of a molehill, and that everything will be fine.

We're still driving through farmland and now in addition to cornfields, we pass apple orchards with low, sprawling trees in rows that roll away from us over the hills. Poppa has a few apple trees in his side yard and in the fall we make pies and applesauce. Rebel can have one or two apples at a time if they're good and ripe. In the side mirror, the trailer is doing fine, following right along behind us. The fields and orchards yield to tall groves of oak trees and other hardwoods. I see a sign for camping and the entrance to a state park. As we get closer to Gettysburg, there are more houses and roadside stores. I can wait and see what happens after we get to Maine. If Mother doesn't change her mind, I'll figure out how to convince her to go home. "When you're worried," Aunt Laura tells me, "try to think of pleasant things, things you enjoy." I look out the window and think of being in Aunt Laura's living room, standing at her shelves, picking out a book to read. In my mind, I pull out one on the battle of Gettysburg. I love its foldout map and the photographs of the battlefield from a few years after the war. I trace the red and blue lines and arrows depicting the movement of troops. Here A. P. Hill, there Hood, across the page Ewell, a tiny square each for Lee's and Meade's headquarters. A star for where Reynolds was killed—slash marks for Seminary Ridge and Cemetery Ridge. Visualizing the images from the glossy pages settles me down. Everything written and drawn there has already happened; its order will never change and I don't have to guess at how things will turn out.

When we enter Gettysburg, we drive past shops, restaurants, and old brick buildings, and at one point, we go all the way around Lincoln Square. Mother looks tired even though it is only two o'clock in the afternoon. We take a fork in the road and I see the Gettysburg National Museum. The sign for the National Cemetery is on the other side of the road.

"Can we stay near here?" I ask. Mother drives a little way and finds a picnic area to use as a turnaround, and when we pass the intersection again, she turns down the other fork. I yell out, "How about that Howard Johnson's?" I don't want to be far from the museum.

"Okay, okay," she says wearily and pulls the car and trailer into the motel parking lot.

Mother stands at the sink and splashes her face over and over with cold water. "I have forty layers of road grime on me." I bring in our suitcases and the cooler. "Come here, Kat, wash your face and hands." Mother plucks a second white washcloth from the stack next to the sink. After she wets it and rubs the soap on it, she begins scrubbing my face.

"That's too hard," I protest, pulling away. "Let me do it."

I can see the two of us reflected in the mirror. The damp bangs of my hair are pushed back from my forehead and my cheeks are red. Mother's peach-colored shirt front is wet and darker than her sleeves. The washcloth is streaked with dirt.

"Look at how filthy we both are." She wrinkles her nose. "Road grime."

I wring out the washcloth and with it my worries about Mother's mood. Aunt Laura and I have talked a lot about Gettysburg, and now I am here. She said that whether or not Lee won at Gettysburg, it wouldn't have changed the outcome of the war. Vicksburg was more important strategically. But Gettysburg was more dramatic for the history books with Pickett's Charge—one mad assault to save the Southern cause—and Lincoln's Gettysburg Address. More than anything I want to go to the visitor center and museum, get a map of the battlefield, and start exploring. I want to see Little Round Top, Devil's Den, and Seminary Ridge.

Mother looks at me in the mirror. "Pull your shirt back and scrub your neck too."

While I scrub, Mother takes everything out of her suitcase and mine, and begins putting our clothes in the drawers of the dresser. She works quickly but carefully. I wonder why she's changed the rule about keeping things in our suitcases.

"Finished," I say.

"I've got a little more organizing to do." She takes everything out of her train case and arranges the makeup bottles, shampoo, fingernail polish, cold cream, lipsticks, and sewing kit in rows on the counter next to the sink. Then she wipes the sink dry with a hand towel.

"When can we go to the battlefield?" I ask as she refolds the damp towel.

"Soon, soon," she says as she pulls all of her sketchbooks and art supplies out of her satchel and stacks them on a little table by the window.

"How does that look?" she asks. "Great," I say. When everything is arranged just so, she'll want to go to the battlefield. This is Yankee land. The most famous battlefield in America. I want to see where Pickett's Charge stepped off. She turns to face me. "You're enjoying this trip, aren't you?" she asks, her brows knitted together.

"Yes, ma'am."

"Well," she says, putting her hand on my shoulder, serious. "We'll have lots of trips. A lot of times like this. I'll grow old and you'll grow up and we'll still take trips together."

Though it's hard to imagine Mother being old like Gramma or Miss Jameson, I can see her always traveling—speeding through the landscape in a fast car. When I'm grown it will be different to take a trip with her. She'll have to treat me like an adult, talk over plans with me.

She changes her shirt, gets her purse and the motel key, jingles her car keys. "Let's go."

"We can walk," I say. "It's right across the street."

"So it is." She places the car keys on the dresser, lined up next to her hairbrush and perfume bottle.

One of the first displays in the museum has pictures, souvenir pins, and decorative ribbons from the reunions of Gettysburg veterans. I lean over the glass top of the case, staring at a sepia photograph of white-haired, bearded men in hats sitting at a long plank table with plates heaped with food. Each has a tin cup and fork and knife that look heavy, substantial. The ones closest to the camera gaze up, some with their forks in their hands. They are wearing their medals on their suit coats. The caption for the photograph says, "Union and Confederate Veterans Feasting Together at the 50th Anniversary of the Battle of Gettysburg." Another picture shows a group of maybe ten or fifteen old men, waving their hats and running through a field. Confederate survivors re-creating Pickett's Charge. They are grinning as they run through waist-high hay.

I know from Aunt Laura that my great-great-grandfather Gresham wasn't in Pickett's Charge. He fought under General Wofford in the

Wheatfield below Little Round Top on the second day of Gettysburg. They pushed back the Yankees and took the Peach Orchard, but they didn't get Little Round Top. On the third day fresh troops were used for Pickett's Charge. Aunt Laura hadn't mentioned whether he ever went back to Gettysburg for a reunion.

Mother walks up beside me. "They have an awful lot of stuff in this museum; some of it looks like they brought it in wheelbarrows and dumped it in the cases." She points to the upright case behind us. It is brimming with spent minié balls, pieces of trees with minié balls and scraps of shells embedded in them, and broken rifles. The identification card says, "Debris collected on the battlefield by J. Rosensteel." The case next to it has several hardtack biscuits with men's names written on them, a revolver marked "Found fully loaded on the field of battle," and a section of a bedpost with a bullet in it, marked "From Spangler Farm."

Someone blows into the microphone of the PA system. "In ten minutes, a guided tour of the National Cemetery will begin. Meet the registered Gettysburg guide at the front entrance of the museum. I repeat, in ten minutes . . ." I begin to walk toward the entrance and Mother follows close behind me.

A large group gathers and I struggle to stay in front, right next to the guide in his olive green pants and shirt.

"Will we see where Lincoln gave the speech?" a man asks as he pushes in front of me.

"Yes." The guide smiles. "We'll start in five minutes."

The man looks at his watch. "How long will it last?"

"Usually thirty minutes and then I answer questions." He smiles again. "We'll begin by crossing the street," he booms so the whole group will hear.

Across the street, we enter the cemetery grounds and walk beneath huge trees that cast pools of shade. The grass is lush under our feet. Mother lights a cigarette as the guide stops our group to begin talking about how difficult it was for the town of Gettysburg to cope with all the wounded and dead after the battle was over.

"It was hot, much hotter than it is today, and all the bodies of men and horses were decomposing rapidly, creating not only a horrible stench but a health hazard for the residents."

Mother puffs rapidly on her cigarette. I have seen pictures of the dead soldiers on the battlefield at Gettysburg in Aunt Laura's books.

The guide describes how the townspeople buried the soldiers in shallow pits or where they fell on the battlefield, but during a big rain shortly after the battle, the dirt washed away to reveal the bodies. Some farmers uncovered bodies as they plowed later in the summer. The guide walks our group to the edge of the carefully laid out semicircular cemetery with arcs of short white marble markers that unfurl in perfect waves for what could be a mile. The beauty of the white against the green and the sheer number of graves shock me. Mother drops her cigarette to the grass and grinds it out with the sole of her sandal. When she pulls her foot away I can see that she has dug a small hole in the grass. I wish she hadn't done that here, and I step away from her, embarrassed.

"A local Gettysburg attorney, David Wills, acquired this land to be used as a soldiers' cemetery. All this, of course, was while the war was still going on. The concern was to bury the Union soldiers. They had little or no interest in the Confederate dead." I suppose this was fair since they were still fighting, but it seems a shame.

The cemetery is beautiful, orderly, tranquil. I think the guide is looking at Mother disapprovingly as she lights up another cigarette, but then I notice that a man in the group is smoking too.

"In most cases, the names, when they were known, were penciled on wooden markers placed wherever in the field they were buried. Some of these became unreadable by the time the bodies were moved, so many of the men in these graves you see here are unknown soldiers."

Mother wanders away from the group, toward a cannon. "The central monument, called Soldiers' Monument or the Spirit of Liberty, marks the spot where Lincoln gave his speech. It wasn't finished until 1869." Mother leans up against the cannon. "The four statues at the bottom corners of the monument represent War, History, Peace, and Plenty." She gets out her lipstick and carefully puts it on. Mother may be bored; she probably thinks the tour is too slow.

"Who knows when Lincoln gave his speech here at Gettysburg?"

The guide is looking at a couple of kids to his right and they shrug their shoulders. A short woman behind me, holding the hand of her toddler, hollers out, "November nineteenth, 1863."

We follow the guide over to a short, squat monument with a bust of Lincoln and the text of the Gettysburg Address.

"Imagine," the guide says, "only a two-minute speech compared to the famous orator Everett, who spoke for two hours. As the story goes, Lincoln wrote it on an envelope during the train ride here, but that's not true. He spent a good deal of time on it."

Mother shadows us, staying at the edge of the group. I wonder if she wants to leave. I try to catch her eye so if she wants to she can motion to me, but she's looking off into the distance.

"Where's the cyclorama?" one of the boys in the front asks. The guide points back toward the museum.

"Where did they bury all the dead horses?" the boy next to him asks, and they giggle.

"An important question," the guide says. "Wherever they could dig a hole deep enough."

The group begins to disperse and Mother walks toward me. "This place gives me the creeps," she says and flicks her cigarette. "We're going back to the motel." As we walk across the street, down behind the museum to Howard Johnson's, she is silent. I am suddenly afraid we will leave Gettysburg before I get to see anything else.

The Confederate general continues to worry though she knows how useless worry is. Her chief aide still isn't himself—he sits on his cot smoking one cigar after another, staring off into space. And now as her army digs into the ridge, it seems the enemy may be pulling up stakes to slip away in the night. This latest intelligence could be faulty; her spy wasn't able to gather enough information to be certain. But what if it's true? Her mind spins. She doesn't want to be tricked into giving up such a good position, but there's no use in fortifying this high ground if there's no enemy to fight. Usually she has immediate and accurate instincts about these matters, but her instincts are being clouded by misgivings. She agonizes over their recent defeats and her growing sense that, in the end, her army will not prevail.

Chapter Nineteen

When we get back to the room, Mother turns on the television and sits on her bed. A soap opera blares, showing two women sitting at a kitchen table drinking coffee. One of the women is crying. "I hated to tell you this, Lorraine," the other one says.

"Oh, look at her, she loved every minute of telling her about her no-good husband," Mother says. "Bring me a Kleenex." I pull a couple from the dispenser at the edge of the counter by the sink. "I'm coming down with a cold." She blows her nose. "A summer cold."

All I can think about is whether or not she'll decide we have to leave. I can't bear not getting to visit the battlefield. Gettysburg is important—the High Tide of the Confederacy, where Lee failed and had to turn back. Where the Union generals finally came together and outsmarted the Rebs. Where Lincoln gave the Gettysburg Address to dedicate the cemetery before the war was even over.

"You know what would hit the spot?" Mother turns to me. "A Coke with lots of ice." She kicks her shoes off, swings her legs under the covers, and pulls the comforter up to her chin. "Go get me one and fill up the ice bucket, sweetie." She waves toward the dresser. "Get a dollar out of my train case, in the lining pocket."

I open her case and slip my hand in the silky lining pocket to get the money. I find a bank envelope with four crisp twenties, a few tens, and some dollar bills. I take a dollar and put the envelope back.

Mother has lit another cigarette. The smoke rises in front of her face as she watches the soap opera. "Hurry back," she says without looking at me.

Outside, the heat glazes the surface of the parking lot asphalt. A bell jangles as I enter the motel office and the man that registered us stands up from behind the counter.

"Looks like you need to know where the ice machine is. Out to your left, around by the swimming pool. Hot day, yes it is, hot day." He straightens the register book on his counter. Mother signed as Mrs. Dunfey.

"I want to get a Coke too," I say as I put the dollar bill on the counter. "Can I have change?"

"Why sure, little lady. Tootsweet. Say, have you been to the battlefield yet?"

"Well . . ." I put the change in my pocket. "We went to the cemetery on a guided tour but I haven't done anything else."

The man darts from behind his counter over to a display rack full of brochures that I hadn't noticed. "My name's Harvey," he says. "Like the six-foot rabbit that hung out with Jimmy Stewart. Only, I'm not invisible." He laughs. He does look a little like a rabbit with his big white front teeth.

"So many things you should see. Best way to do it is take the bus tour. My cousin is a guide for Gettysburg Original Tours. Here's their brochure. See, you'll look for the gray buses with the red stripe around their middle."

I open up the brochure to see glossy pictures of the monuments and battlefield areas the bus would drive you to see: the statue of General Lee, the looming boulders of Devil's Den, the Confederate cannons on Seminary Ridge, the huge domed monument for Pennsylvania. Underneath a picture of the National Cemetery the caption reads, "A shrine at which every American should stand at least once."

Harvey hands me another brochure. "You'll want to see the cyclorama. The building is new, built just for the Centennial, and now the painting will be preserved. Really impressive, that cyclorama. I bet you've never seen a painting like that before."

On the front of the brochure is a section of the cyclorama with a wagon exploding in flames and a cloud of smoke and clumps of men fighting in hand-to-hand combat.

"I've been to the cyclorama in Atlanta," I say.

"Oh, are you from Atlanta?" Harvey picks up another two or three brochures from the wooden display rack. I remember my vow not to tell anyone who we are or what we're doing.

"No, we went there on vacation."

"Sounds like you go on Civil War vacations."

"Mm-hmm."

"The Electric Map at the museum is a great way to learn about the battle. Of course, you kids love the wax museum. There are candlelight ghost tours, tours of the Jennie Wade House—she's the only civilian killed in the battle—died making biscuits, did you know that? And the Hall of Presidents. That'll set you up for sure. How long will you be here?"

"I don't know."

Mother will wonder where I am; Harvey has been talking for a long time. I wish I didn't have to worry about giving him too much information about us; I'd come back to ask him questions. I want to see every place he's mentioned. I've got to get Mother excited too, and make sure her cold doesn't get in our way.

"I have to go, my mother's waiting."

"Oh sure, sure. Show her these." He flaps the brochures and I take them. "Good way to plan what you want to do."

"Thank you."

When I get back to the room, Mother is asleep with the television still blaring. I turn the volume down and Mother opens her eyes. "Oh, baby," she says. "You brought my Coke."

I take the paper top off the glass by the bathroom sink and fill it with ice and Coke. Mother takes a few sips and then puts it on the nightstand. "Let's let it get good and cold. Bring me some aspirin from my case. I've got the worst headache."

After she takes her aspirin, I turn the television off and eat one of the peanut butter crackers I got from the snack machine.

"No, turn the television back on. It's keeping me company. What's that stack you've got?"

"The desk clerk gave them to me." I bring the brochures over to her. "All the things you can see at Gettysburg. A bus tour of the whole battlefield with a guide who tells you the history and explains all the monuments."

Mother opens up one of the brochures. "Here's the cemetery where all those poor boys are buried."

"I'd like to go on the bus tour," I say in my most polite voice. "Could we please stay tomorrow and go? I don't want to leave without seeing the battlefield. It's such an important one—more than any of the others. Please, let us."

Mother stares at me. "No one said we were leaving tomorrow. Can't you see that I'm sick?"

"Yes, ma'am," I say, holding very still. We're not leaving, hallelujah, but if she's sick we might be stuck in the room.

"Look. Tomorrow you go on the bus tour and scout it all out for me." She opens the brochure. "There must be hundreds of monuments. A lifetime of sketching. I'll stay here so I can get to feeling better and you'll make notes about which ones we should go back to sketch."

I smile at her, relief rushing through me. We're staying and she'll let me go off on my own. Perfect.

"A family place like this, you'll be okay alone on a guided bus tour." She takes another sip of her Coke. "I've got one horrible cold coming on."

I start making plans in my head. I know right where to get the bus tour—just down the street from our motel. The brochure has a map on the back. Maybe I'll have Harvey's cousin as a guide. And Mother is letting me go alone. I won't talk to her about it tonight, but I'll ask her tomorrow morning if I can also go to the cyclorama and the Electric Map. Both are practically across the street from our motel. There's a good chance she'll say yes. I am going to have a whole day at Gettysburg, a chance to see it all.

"Baby, what time is it?"

"Almost three o'clock." I eat another peanut butter cracker. On the television a man and a woman embrace briefly, but the woman pushes the man away as she begins to cry.

"Didn't it upset you when the guide talked about the dead soldiers?"

I swallow my cracker. "Not really." I had thought of the photographs I'd seen of dead soldiers at Gettysburg, but the cemetery seemed such a quiet, peaceful place.

"I can't help thinking about all those dead boys in shallow graves that got uncovered in the rain."

I drink half my Coke and try not to burp. I wanted to think of them as honored dead in a shady place with orderly white marble grave markers.

Mother lights a cigarette. "That's all I could think about—the rain pouring down, all the dirt washing away to reveal those dead faces."

I gulp more Coke. Mother has that overdramatic tone in her voice. I hope she's not getting ready to cry.

Mother looks past me, over the top of my head, then she focuses on my eyes and smiles. "Why do I say the things I say sometimes? Whaddya say we see if *To Tell the Truth* is on?" I nod and smile back. Sometimes after school Mother and I watch that show. We like to think up questions that will expose the fakes; questions too hard to answer unless the person is the real thing. I click the dial until I see Peggy Cass, Kitty Carlisle, and Orson Bean lined up on the screen.

"There now," Mother says. "We won't think bad thoughts. We'll watch the show and then maybe go for an early dinner." She settles onto her pillows and pats the bed beside her. I sit next to her in the cool air as she slowly closes her eyes, and I whisper questions to myself that I would ask the three men to figure out which one is a trick rider for the movies. "What's John Wayne's real first name?" Marion. "What do you do right before you tighten the cinch on your saddle?" Pop the horse's stomach so he'll let out any air he's holding. "Who invented the American Western saddle?" Mexican cowboys. No one asks my questions and sure enough they don't pick the right guy.

At 5:30 when the news comes on, I decide to wake Mother. I call softly first. She hates to be awakened abruptly. Nothing. I gently push her arm. "Mother, Mom. Get up. It's time to go to dinner."

She opens her eyes. "Just taking a catnap," she says in a gravelly voice.

"It's five thirty. Do you want to go and get dinner at the restaurant here?" Gramma loves to eat at Howard Johnson's and on Sundays after church we often go to the one on Highway 41.

Mother takes a sip of her watery Coke and lights a cigarette. "Well, now. That would be a good idea. But I don't really want to sit in a restaurant."

We never really had lunch, just peanut butter crackers, and I'm hungry but I keep quiet. Mother rests her cigarette in the ashtray and sits up a little straighter in the bed. Her face is puffy. If I rush her she might decide not to go at all.

"How 'bout you get our food and bring it back to the room. That would be fun, wouldn't it? You can order a clam dinner if you want."

I go to her train case to get out some money. "What do you want?"

"Oh, you pick out something. I don't feel that hungry right now."

I know without looking at the menu what I will get her. A steak cooked medium rare—even if she isn't that hungry she can eat it later as a snack. She loves cold steak.

At the restaurant I pass the soda fountain and the sign for twenty-eight flavors of ice cream and walk up to the podium where the hostess stands. "When your Mom and Dad get here, I'll get you a table," she says. Her name tag reads BETTY.

"It's just me," I tell her.

"Well." She takes a menu from her podium. "Where's everyone else?"

"My mother's in the room. I'm going to order something to take back with me."

"That's fine. Take a look at the menu." She hands it to me.

"Oh, I know what I want. Fried clams for me and a steak for my mother, medium rare."

"A kid who knows what she wants. I like that. You got enough money for all that?"

I take out the twenty.

"Yep. Okay, what do you want with the dinners? Baked potatoes? Salad?"

"Baked potatoes. And Cokes too."

"You got it. Wait right here." She points to a row of chairs across from her podium.

She puts in the order and comes back over to me. "So, what's your name? Where you from?"

"Katherine," I say. "I'm from . . ." I hesitate. I shouldn't say Marietta, Georgia, but I can't think of anything. My face is getting hot. "Virginia," I finally say. "We're from Virginia and we're on vacation."

"As long as it took you to figure out where you're from, you'd think you were making it up." She raises her eyebrows. My whole body tenses; she knows I'm a liar. Betty goes on, "I used to have trouble saying where I was from 'cause I'm an army brat. We lived in Germany and then on every coast this country has—California, Texas, Florida. Oh, got to go seat those folks." I smile at her. Everything's fine.

While she's gone I look at the bags of multicolored taffy on top of the ice cream counter. Mother likes taffy a lot. It might make her perk up and not get grumpy, which she always does when she is sick. I pick out a bag and take it back to my seat with me.

"I don't know about that taffy," Betty says when she comes back. "People buy it to take as a souvenir but it doesn't make sense. Gettysburg isn't a place famous for candy or taffy or whatever. I mean, if you come to Gettysburg, you ought to take home a souvenir of something military, right? A bullet or minié ball or whatever they call those things. A little cannon. Am I right?"

I nod. I'll get souvenirs of Gettysburg to put on my bookcase, and plenty of postcards of the battle and the generals to send to Aunt Laura. Betty sits down in the chair next to me and I'm pleased she wants to talk to me more. "Now, you see we're not busy right now. We won't be really busy until seven or seven thirty. That's when people get done taking their tours and what not. They come in here tired and sunburned and dragging kids that missed their naps. We have a heck of a time, excuse my French, if you know what I mean. And you should see this place during the anniversary of the battle. Lord, busloads of people coming in wanting clams and wanting them fast. They don't tip well either. I don't know why I stay here."

I'm at ease with Betty sitting next to me. She makes me comfortable being by myself in the restaurant and I like her slightly raspy voice.

I wonder how much the taffy is and how much I should give as a tip. Mother leaves money on the table after we've eaten at a restaurant, but I've never paid attention to how much.

"You said your mother's back at the room?" Betty asks.

"She doesn't feel well." Mother tells me it is nicer to say that you're not feeling well instead of saying that you're sick. And you aren't supposed to go into any details about what is wrong with you.

"Did you two go all over the battlefield today?" Betty rotates one foot very carefully. "Ankles are always killing me."

"We went to the National Cemetery. I'm going on the bus tour tomorrow."

"Yeah, that's a good thing. Lot better than driving yourself. They got good guides that can answer all your questions, and in between stops they have a nice recorded history made by real actors, you know."

Another waitress comes over with a huge brown paper bag. "I've got everything wrapped up good and went ahead and put it on real plates and gave you real silverware, so you be sure you bring it back. Okay?"

"Yes, ma'am," I say.

"Get that, Betty. A kid with manners."

"She's a Southerner, from Virginia. Right, Kathy?"

"Katherine," I say instinctively. Mother has always told me not to let people call me Kathy.

"Sure, sure. Katherine." The waitress winks and hands me a ticket and I give her the twenty. "And the taffy," I say.

When she gives me my change, there are only two dimes in coins, the rest in bills. I'm not sure what to do so I give her two dollar bills back. She smiles. "Thank you, Katherine. Have a good stay."

"See ya," Betty adds and goes back to her podium.

When I get back to the room, Mother is sleeping while the evening news drones on. I lift the foil from each plate and put them on the round table next to the window.

"Mother, dinner's here. I got you a steak."

She lifts herself up on one elbow. "That smells good. But really, I'm feeling worse. You go ahead. "

I slather my clams with tartar sauce and fix both baked potatoes with butter and sour cream. I eat quickly, first the crunchy clams and then a forkful of smooth creamy potato.

"Does the sour cream have chives in it?" Mother asks.

"Yes, want me to bring you some?"

"Maybe I'll eat a little."

By the time I finish, Mother has eaten a few bites of her steak and half her potato. "I hate to waste this," she says.

"We can keep it in the cooler."

"That's my smart girl."

In the time it takes me to wrap her steak in the leftover aluminum foil and store it in the cooler, Mother has gone back to sleep. I turn the volume down but leave the television on. I like the sound of the actors talking softly in the room. It is still early, only seven o'clock, and I'm not tired yet. I spread out all the colorful brochures on the bed, thinking about where I can go in the morning and everything I will see.

I'll walk where Great-Great-Grandfather Gresham fought in the bloody Wheatfield and Confederate sharpshooters hid behind boulders in the Devil's Den to pick off Union officers. I'll see Little Round Top, Spangler's Spring, the stone wall at the center of the Union line, and Jennie Wade's house.

Maybe Mother will feel better in the morning and want to go with me. But if she doesn't go, I'll be able to do exactly what I want. It will be like the days I spend alone in the summer playing in the woods and pasture around our house, when I lean up against a tree reading a book or uncover beetles from the moist leaves on the ground. If it's hot, I go to the creek to wade and catch crayfish and salamanders that scuttle out from under the rocks, kicking up small trails of mud that cloud the water. When I enter the woods, the buzz of the hot pasture gradually yields to soft chirps and the occasional thump of a branch falling to the loamy ground. In the woods, where it is darker and cooler, I can imagine myself far away from my parents and their house. There, I can't see them and they can't see me.

The Confederate general orders her staff to return to camp so she can have some time by herself. Their short reconnaissance mission has been fruitful, but tensions are running high because the army's next move is critical to the campaign. After the last of her staff trots down the hill along a narrow trail through the green canopy of trees, she turns to look out over a valley of orchards, a wheat field, and green pastures dotted with cows. Except for an energetic woodpecker it is quiet. Alone, not having to attend to the moods of her staff, she is serene. The war that has been wearing on her more and more seems far away. Right now in this restful place she doesn't have to make any decisions and she doesn't have to consider what's best for anyone but her.

I carefully fold up the brochures: The first thing tomorrow will be the bus tour. On television, the Jackie Gleason show is coming on, but I want to read the book I bought at Harpers Ferry, *Combat.* The cover shows a swirling Confederate flag in the right corner and a cannon pointing toward a group of Union soldiers, bayonets fixed, fighting hand to hand with the Confederates. The Stars and Stripes is small and the whole scene is engulfed in white smoke. The artilleryman next to the cannon is wielding his rammer like a club. I flip through the book to look at all the illustrations. Most are engravings from *Harper's* or maps with thick arrows showing Union and Confederate positions.

I turn to an account of Manassas written by a Rebel soldier. Outside our room cars are driving by. On the television, Jackie Gleason holds his drink high and flourishes a cigarette. "How sweet it is!" he exclaims.

McHenry Howard describes riding a train and then marching five miles to the battle. The train stops frequently on the way and the men get off to eat blackberries. They hear cannon fire when the train comes into Manassas Station, and as they march double-time toward the battle, dust from the road rises around them and makes it impossible to see very far in front of them. Because they are so thirsty, they drink water like dogs from the mud holes in the road when the column halts. As they march they pass the wounded and dead from the earlier part of the battle. Soon shells are exploding around them and bullets are whizzing and men to McHenry's left and right fall with terrible wounds. The Confederates are winning, though, and the Yankees retreat. McHenry feels as if he is in a dream. His unit reorganizes, raises rifles, and fires. During the long charge forward some men stop to eat blackberries because they are so thirsty and hungry, but the officers swear and threaten to get them to go on. At the outer edge of a pinewood, the columns stop to fire, but no one fires back at them. When the cannons are finished shelling, the Confederates march all the way through the woods, passing a good number of dead Yankees, and then halt at a stream to fill their canteens. McHenry goes back for a Yankee gun he wants. As he reenters the woods, he notices how quiet it is, how the woods shut out the sound of the battle going on near them.

I close the book with my finger marking the place. It's getting dark outside and the headlights of cars flicker on the walls. Mother sleeps. That soldiers would stop to eat blackberries in the middle of a charge is hard for me to imagine. I always thought soldiers ran during charges. Most of what McHenry talks about is marching, waiting, and hunger. He writes almost as if he isn't involved in the fighting at all. I expected his account of the battle to be about giving the Rebel yell and charging the Union soldiers and being brave but instead it's almost tedious, and the action seems to happen by accident. This isn't how I imagined it.

On the television *My Three Sons* starts. If Mother were awake she would change the channel. Ridiculous show, she always says. I open *Combat* again to continue reading.

Deeper into the woods, McHenry becomes afraid of running into enemy stragglers. But he keeps going, wanting to get the rifle. Suddenly a deep groan startles him and he jerks around, raising his rifle—he sees a Yankee leaning up against a tree, his middle torn away by a shell. "Kill me with your bayonet," the Yankee gasps. "Run it through my heart." McHenry knows the man is dying a horrible death but he can't bring himself to kill him.

I close the book. I don't understand McHenry. Why wouldn't he kill the Yankee to put him out of his misery? Daddy had a hunting dog, Charlie, that was his favorite, but when a car hit him and his whole hind end was paralyzed, Daddy told the vet to put him down. "Dog can get around on three legs," Daddy said. "But not on two." And when one of the cows got a mysterious illness that made her swing her head up against the side of the barn until she bled, I watched the vet give her two big shots that made her slump down on her front knees and finally keel over heavily on the stall floor. Putting her to sleep, the vet called it. That's the humane thing to do. When they're going to die anyway, help them not suffer. McHenry should have bayoneted the Yankee, but I suppose he couldn't because he was looking right at him. It would be one thing to fire into the woods, but something else entirely to see a man's face, talk to him, and then drive a bayonet into his heart. My stomach lurches thinking about what the man's guts looked like, bloody and spilling out of his torn blue Union jacket.

While I watch television, I sharpen all my drawing pencils over the trash can. I like the way the shavings of wood and different colored leads spiral out of my sharpener. When all the points are razor sharp, I begin to copy the cover of my *Combat* paperback. I sketch the scene lightly with a black lead pencil; then I color in the red and blue of the Confederate flag flying in the right-hand corner. I use sky blue over an undercoat of shaded pencil to create a sort of gray for the Confederate uniforms and combine yellow and brown for a glint of gold to top the Stars and Stripes in the background.

As I touch up one of the Union soldier's guns, I think about the woods McHenry had been in. They were probably like the woods behind our house, with lots of pine trees, but thicker, and an undergrowth of bushes and vines. Dense enough to cut the noise of a battle, but not enough to protect the Yankees from minié balls and shells.

Suddenly I feel so bad for the Yankee soldier, slowly dying at the base of a pine tree, that I ache. McHenry was wrong. He was a coward not to kill the man and put him out of his misery. The scene fills my head and on a new piece of paper I begin sketching the woods that McHenry describes. The woods I know. The tall pine trees reach up to the sky, and in between, maples and poplars and oaks spread their limbs. The ground is covered in layers of leaves and pine needles. At one end of my paper I shade a small stream. This is where the soldiers can lie down on their stomachs and drink from the running water. I draw faint diagonal lines across the open spaces on my page; the woods are dark and it's hard to see. Deep in the background of the sketch I draw a small figure seated against a tree. If you didn't know to look, you might mistake him for part of the tree trunk. I give the figure a tiny raised arm. If someone else comes, he wants them to know he's there and needs help.

Chapter Twenty

In the morning, sun pours into the room and I carefully put my sketch of the soldier in the woods into my notebook and tuck my drawing pencils into my book bag.

Mother opens her eyes when I come back to the room with cereal from the restaurant. "Close those curtains, baby, will you? I'm going to sleep a little longer." She looks pale and the circles under her eyes are darker.

I put her breakfast on the bedside table.

"You go ahead on your bus tour. I may go to some antique stores when I get up, if I feel better. You come back here and we'll eat lunch together, somewhere fun—we'll find a ladies' tearoom." She closes her eyes and rolls over. I doubt she'll get up before I come back.

"Better hurry," the woman in the kiosk says. "Tour's getting ready to leave." It didn't take me long to walk the three blocks from our motel, but I haven't finished reading the wooden board that explains how long we'll be gone. "When will we be back?" I hand the woman a ten.

"Says right there, two hours long, so if the bus leaves on time you'll be back at noon." She hands me my change. "Hey, wait a minute. You by yourself?" The woman leans forward to see over her wooden counter a little better.

I didn't expect this question and start to explain. "No, my mother's—"

The woman cuts me off. "Well, hurry up. She'll be worried sick if the bus leaves without you."

I hustle onto the bus and find an empty seat. The minute I sit down the driver closes the door, the guide stands up, and the microphone crackles.

"Welcome to Gettysburg Original Tours. We have a great program for you today; a journey back in time when our forefathers in blue and gray clashed in the bloodiest battle ever fought on this continent. The Union army under General Meade prevailed after three long days, July first through third, 1863, and General Lee's grand Army of Northern Virginia was defeated. But this place is more than the location of a battle. It represents the high-water mark of the Confederacy, the point at which the Rebels were repelled and the Union was saved. Lincoln bore witness to the significance of this place when he dedicated the National Cemetery with his brilliant Gettysburg Address—only two hundred and seventy-two words, but a monumental statement of why the war was fought, 'that this nation, under God, shall have a new birth of freedom—and that government of the people, by the people, for the people, should not perish from the earth.' "

The guide takes off his cap. "When we reach a stop on our tour you may get off the bus to look around, but when I wave my hat that means it's time to get back on the bus." A drumroll comes over the loudspeaker and then fife music. "Gettysburg," a deep voice from the loudspeaker intones, "is the shrine of all nationalities who cherish a living faith in democratic principles and ideals."

The man in the seat in front of me suddenly turns around.

"I don't know about you, but I didn't come here to get clobbered with Mr. Lincoln first crack out of the bag." He pulls at his beard, shifting in his seat so he is sitting sideways. "You a Yankee or a Rebel?"

"Rebel," I answer quietly. The tape is describing McPherson's Ridge and the beginnings of the battle of Gettysburg, and I don't want to miss it.

"Robert E. Lee never planned to fight in Gettysburg. The two armies ran into each other by mistake. Henry Heth had taken his Confederate troops into the town to forage for shoes."

The bearded man drums his fingers on the back of his seat. He has thick silver rings on his right hand: a wolf head on his index finger, a band with what looks like crossing cannons engraved on it—maybe an artilleryman's symbol—and a pinkie ring with a bloodred ruby. He wears a silver bracelet too, braided strands made to look like rope. The bracelet reminds me of the jewelry that the men and women wear who come to dinner parties at the art dealer Louise's house. Hippies, Daddy says and rolls his eyes. With his long hair, beard, and jewelry, this man resembles Louise's friends, but he acts serious and agitated, not easy and friendly and teasing like the artists at Louise's.

"I'm a Rebel too. Born and bred. Gonna do a reenactment up here come July. That's why I'm here now. To get the lay of the land."

The guide stands up. "We're coming to our first stop. Day one, July first, McPherson's Ridge."

"I like this part," the bearded man says. "Rebels whipped ass on the first day."

He has a tattoo of a spiderweb on his biceps and he sees me staring. "It's all right," he says when I look away quickly. "I have it there so people will see it." He flexes and points at the spider in the middle of the expanded web. "See the spider jump?" He laughs, and we all get off the bus.

McPherson's Ridge is actually a farm next to a small woods. "To your left you'll see McPherson's stone barn, the original structure here during the battle. Beyond that, the woods where General John F. Reynolds was shot by a Confederate sharpshooter." The guide points with his outstretched arm.

"Good for him. It's great to pick off an officer." The bearded man walks along beside me as we follow the guide. "What's your name?" he asks. I don't answer. I don't like this man talking to me and I don't want him to know my name.

• • •

The general considers busting this officer down to a private. He simply does not have the necessary decorum.

"Cat got your tongue?" asks the man, smirking. The guide is talking about the Iron Brigade capturing the Confederate general Archer, the first taken prisoner since Lee had commanded the army.

"Alice," I tell him, and walk closer to the guide, whose name, Sean, is on a badge on his shirt pocket.

"Alice." The man sticks his hands in his blue jeans pocket. "Alice. That's a good name. Alice, you better be careful of rabbit holes." He laughs loudly. "My name's Carl."

The general takes note of the odious officer's name. He will wake up tomorrow stripped of his rank and horse, walking for the rest of the war.

Sean is waving his hat for us to return to the bus. I wish Carl would leave me alone. He doesn't seem to care much about the tour. "When I was in Vietnam," Carl says as we step up to the line getting onto the bus, "we had to watch out for rabbit holes. Gooks dug underground tunnels, hid in them, and booby-trapped them to blow up if we came after them. It was bad shit, rabbit holes." He shakes his head.

When I sit in an empty seat, Carl slides in beside me. Sean starts up the tour tape. "In 1938, at the seventy-fifth anniversary of Gettysburg, Roosevelt dedicated the Eternal Light Peace Memorial. That is our next stop."

"If I had my own car, I wouldn't have come on this fool bus tour. All I want to see is Devil's Den and Seminary Ridge." He opens up his brochure, pointing his finger. "I did enough humping in 'Nam. I ride now. But I got to put up with this Yankee guide." He lowers his voice. "Yankees are shit and don't you forget that, Alice." I'm not used to men cussing in front of me and his angry tone of voice scares me.

• • •

The general lifts her chin and stares coldly at the officer. The man will know from her look that she has already demoted him and that he isn't to come near her anymore.

I open my brochure and pretend to read. Even when Carl isn't talking he seems to make noise and I have a hard time paying attention to the tape or concentrating on the next site in the brochure. I can only think of falling into holes or of Vietcong soldiers jumping out to shoot me.

At the North Carolina and Virginia Memorial, I stand close to where Pickett's men started their charge and am amazed at how far they had to go over an open field. Under the pine trees next to the line of cannons, I can barely make out the copse of trees and bit of stone wall they sighted on. Pickett's Charge seems so hopeless, even if the artillery had shelled the Yankees for a while, even if General Stuart was supposed to sneak up behind them. I walk slowly all the way around the statue of Robert E. Lee on Traveller. Lee has his hat in his hand. A band of Virginia soldiers circle the bottom of the statue. I watch Carl walk up the steps to inspect the figures.

When we get back on the bus, I am ahead of Carl and ask a woman if I can sit with her, but she says her son is sitting with her and I have to slip into a seat by myself again. I look out the window at the woods where Longstreet's men had been. Monroe Gresham had been part of Longstreet's corps. The seat creaks next to me as Carl sits down but I stay focused on the scene outside.

"You know," Carl says, "if Lee had listened to Longstreet, we would have won Gettysburg and probably the war." The bus lurches forward. Devil's Den is the next stop. "If we had won the war, little Rebel"—Carl leans toward me, a sneer on his face—"the country would be a whole lot better off. For one thing, we wouldn't have the n— problem we have right now. All them rising up. Wouldn't be happening, 'cause the Yankees wouldn't have thought they could put their fat noses in our business, sending Freedom Riders, agitators, and the like down to stir up trouble. Yep, everything was fine with us and the coloreds until the Yankees decided to step in. And why did they think they had the right to interfere? 'Cause they whupped us in the war."

I hate what he is saying. I wish I'd told him I'm a Yankee—it's half-true after all. I've seen men like Carl on television, their faces distorted by anger, spitting and yelling at small Black children walking to their new school. Daddy told Aunt Laura that all they show on TV are the rabid, crackpot segregationists and that people up North must think we're all KKKers down here. "It encourages those Freedom Riders to come down here and raise cain, which hasn't helped matters."

"Now, Bill," she pointed out. "Registering people to vote isn't exactly raising cain, and if all the good Southern white folks had done the right thing years ago, none of this would be happening."

"Well, I suppose good is coming out of it, but I still wish it didn't come across like the only hateful white people are in the South."

The bus stops and Sean announces Little Round Top. "Here's the site where Colonel Joshua Chamberlain led the Twentieth Maine, out of ammunition and holding up the entire left flank of the Union army, in an attack on the Confederates with only their bayonets. They surprised and repulsed Oates's Alabama rebels, which saved Little Round Top and may have saved the whole battle of Gettysburg. Chamberlain was awarded the Medal of Honor for his actions. We'll have a little extra time at this stop so you can walk to Devil's Den to see where the Confederate sharpshooters operated for the entire three days of the battle."

I remember the name Chamberlain from the guide at Appomattox. Chamberlain had ordered his Union troops to salute the Confederates as they surrendered their flags and weapons. He was a Yankee, but he was brave and fair.

It's our turn to get up and file off the bus. "I want to know about that bastard Chamberlain," Carl grumbles. A woman in the aisle hears him and gives him a glare. "Kiss my Rebel ass," Carl says to her. The woman sets her jaw. When we get out of the bus I see her talking to Sean. I hope she's complaining about Carl; maybe he'll get kicked off the bus. Carl sees her too, and he begins striding down the side road that leads to Devil's Den. I want to find someone else to walk with even if I don't talk to them and they don't talk to me. I wait for the guide. Sean begins walking toward me and the woman is with him.

"That's the little girl who's with him," the woman says.

Sean smiles at me. "Hello," he says. "My name's Sean McCoy."

"Hi," I say. The three of us begin walking toward Devil's Den.

"Is the man with the beard your father?" he asks.

"No. His name is Carl."

"See, I told you," the woman says to Sean. "Something's not right." I'm glad this woman has gotten Carl in trouble. Now maybe I won't have to listen to him anymore.

"If you don't mind," Sean tells her and turns back to me.

"I thought I remembered you coming on the bus by yourself. Did you know Carl before you got on the bus?" Sean asks me.

"No."

"Okay, that clears things up a little." Even though she's younger, the woman reminds me a little of Aunt Laura, maybe because she has short hair and a pocketbook that looks more like a library book bag.

"I'll speak to him, ma'am."

"Well." She seems as if she wants him to do more.

"The best thing would be to let the girl sit with you or one of your friends for the rest of the tour." Sean looks down at me. "How about that? Would you sit with Miss Pensky when we get back on the bus?"

"Sure," I say, relieved.

"What's your name?" Miss Pensky asks me.

"Katherine," I tell her. "But I told Carl my name was Alice." I want her to know that I can do things to take care of myself.

"That was smart, Katherine. My name is Elena. I'm here at Gettysburg with a few of my friends."

We've reached Devil's Den and a group of women wave at Miss Pensky. I don't see Carl, but I suppose he might be behind the boulders.

Miss Pensky's friends, Pat, Edna, and Barbara, are sharing a large guidebook to Gettysburg. No, they tell me, they aren't schoolteachers.

They're all lawyers who went to school together and now go on a trip once a year as a reunion. Edna shows me the picture in the guidebook of Devil's Den with the dead Confederate sharpshooter. I ask them a lot of questions because I've never met a woman lawyer before. I like the way they talk, fast but distinctly. They are impressive, especially as a group walking among the boulders, and I let them encircle me, pointing out sights and shielding me from Carl. Being around them is relaxing the way being around Aunt Laura is. I can ask as many questions as I want and not worry about how I say things like I need to do with Mother. When we get back on the bus, I sit with Elena, and Pat is right behind us. Elena asks me where Mother is.

"When I left she was at the Howard Johnson's, but she might be out buying antiques by now. She hasn't been feeling well since we got here yesterday."

"What's wrong with her?" Pat asks.

"She has a summer cold."

The women smell like shampoo, not stale and smoky like Carl. I catch a glimpse of him as he walks up to the bus. He sits in the front seat behind the driver. When Sean finishes his announcements, he sits down next to Carl.

The women don't talk during the tape, and I'm glad because I want to hear everything about the Wheatfield, where my great-great-grandfather was wounded in the leg. The tape doesn't mention General Wofford but I know that his brigade of Georgia soldiers pushed back the Federal line on the second day. It does mention the Union general Sickles getting shot in his right leg and, because he wanted to make sure his troops knew he wasn't dead, smoking a cigar as his men carried him on a litter to the rear.

I look out over the expanse of the Wheatfield bordered by woods. How could they have fought in this open field where there is no place to seek cover? In the middle of the field is a wooden sign, WHEATFIELD. Off in the distance, Sean tells us, is the Rose Farm. I imagine Monroe Gresham out in the middle of that field, struggling to get back to safety with his leg bleeding and the pain of the metal in his flesh burning like a torch. He wraps his shirt around it to help stop the bleeding. It is a good sign, he knows, that he can bear some weight on his leg. Maybe it won't have to be amputated. In the story that Aunt Laura heard from Great-Grandmother McConnell, Monroe refused to let the surgeons look at his leg. In the retreat from Gettysburg, his buddies helped him walk and he concocted a poultice for the wound. Long after the war, he told the doctors operating on him, "If they didn't cut off this leg at Gettysburg, I sure as hell better wake up with it still on me here in Atlanta!"

"Isn't it odd how beautiful all these places are," Elena remarks when we get off the bus again.

"My great-great-grandfather was wounded in battle here," I tell her. We both stand and look out over the field. Elena's right. During the battle with all the smoke, blood, and bodies, it would have been a horrible scene, but now it feels so tranquil, as if nothing bad could have happened here.

"Well, that certainly puts a different light on it. None of my relatives were even in the United States during the Civil War."

"Really?"

"My grandmother and grandfather came to America from Poland in 1910." Elena is the first person I've met whose grandparents weren't from America. It must be strange to live in one country and have many of your family's stories take place far away in another.

I consider this as we start walking back to the bus. Carl is standing by the door talking to Sean. He waves his hands around and his silver rings glint.

We walk past Carl to get on the bus and he looks Elena right in the eye, grins, and flicks his tongue in and out like a snake. Then he gives her a quick salute, a nasty look on his face.

"Don't let him worry you, Katherine," Elena says dismissively when we sit down. I have the sense that more than Mother or even Aunt Laura, Elena could stand up to anyone. It could be because she's a lawyer and has to be tough with witnesses in the courtroom, but I think it runs deeper than that. She's willing to make people mad for what she thinks is right. Maybe having family stories from two different countries, having a double history, gives her extra strength.

The next-to-the-last stop on the tour is the High Water Mark. The Copse of Trees that the Confederates sighted on as they charged the center of the Union line has now grown tall. Far across the field I see where I stood at the Confederate cannon line. Now I stand on the edge of the pavement, the top of my head baking in the sun, reading the inscription on the open bronze book that commemorates Pickett's Charge. Elena, Pat, Edna, and Barbara stand behind me reading.

"It seems a shame that the war couldn't have ended right here." Elena shakes her head. "So much suffering for two more years, when the outcome was clear." This is what Aunt Laura said, that the war should have ended in 1863 when Vicksburg fell and Lee was defeated at Gettysburg.

"All I can say is it's a good thing it finally ended the way it did," Barbara adds.

"Of course, we've got another kind of civil war today, what with King and Bobby Kennedy being assassinated. And now that George Wallace is strutting around upholding segregation." Edna stands with her hands on her hips. "Even here at Gettysburg, the Confederates seem to be glorified as if they were fighting for some wonderful cause."

"Well, this is it, as far as the Confederates got, and that's that." Elena peers down at her guidebook. "The next stop is the National Cemetery." She nods at Edna. "And Lincoln certainly didn't glorify the Rebels."

"Good point." Edna smiles.

These women remind me of Aunt Laura and her friends, including me in their discussions, asking me what I think. And the women talk about politics the way Mother and Aunt Laura do. They talk fast and switch subjects quickly but I listen carefully and I'm proud of the way I show them I can keep up. They're civil rights lawyers, they tell me, working to make sure school systems are integrated, all people can vote, buy a house where they want to, and not be discriminated against. They worry about what will happen to the civil rights movement now that Martin Luther King, Jr., is dead. I ask them if they will still be able to be civil rights lawyers or if they will lose their jobs.

"Oh, no." Pat chuckles. "It's not like that. We work in courtrooms trying cases for individual clients. We are making sure the laws that ensure civil rights for everyone are upheld."

Edna says King had started speaking out against the Vietnam War and we desperately need another leader who can think broadly like that. "Lyndon Johnson has been such a terrible president," she adds.

"But what about the Civil Rights and Voting Rights Acts?" I ask. They all look at me intently.

"True, very true," Barbara replies after a few seconds. "He did a great job pushing through civil rights legislation, but he's escalated a war that's morally wrong and has killed thousands in the process."

I want to defend Johnson because they are being too hard on him, but I can't think of anything to say other than repeating what he's done for civil rights. Aunt Laura says he is a good man, even though he's wrong about the war.

"No wars are good," Elena offers. "Even the Civil War should have been fought in the court system, not on the battlefield."

"Well," Edna says. "I do hope we're not really in for another civil war. I'm telling you, this violence could get out of hand quickly with no one at the helm." The others nod.

This is the first mention I've heard of some kind of second civil war, but then I think of Carl and George Wallace and all the other furious white people I've seen on TV. I don't know how this new civil war would be fought, but I know my family won't side against Black people. Of course, it's only Mother or Aunt Laura I can imagine arm-in-arm with Black people in protest marches like the ones I've seen. I think about myself at such a march, holding up a sign or one end of a banner. The white people yelling at us from the side of the road would scare me, but I wouldn't show it. I would look straight ahead as we all walked forward.

We get back to the National Cemetery around noon. The women and I stand in front of the memorial to the Gettysburg Address and read it all the way through.

"He must have been a heck of a lawyer," Pat says.

"I would have hated to go up against him," Edna replies.

We stand silent for a minute.

"Would you like to go to lunch with us?" Elena asks.

"Thank you. But I'm going to a ladies' tearoom with my mother." I look at my watch.

"My goodness." Edna giggles.

"I have to go," I tell them. "I'm already late." I would like to stay with these women longer. I want to ask them to explain the details of their court cases and what law school is like, but I can't disappoint Mother.

"Well, 'bye, Katherine." Elena smiles. "You take care of yourself."

I get back to our room a half hour late but Mother doesn't realize because she is still asleep. Her cereal box and milk sit unopened on the dresser. I wash my hands and face, even scrub my neck, then fold the hand towel.

"Turn that light off," Mother mumbles. I go over to her bed.

"Did you go antiquing?"

"No, baby. I can't go anywhere. I'm much too sick. Along with my cold, I've had a migraine all morning." She is sitting up a little in the bed. She speaks very slowly, as if she is still half asleep.

"Are you hungry?"

"No." She lights a cigarette. She wasn't waiting for me to go to lunch after all. I watch her smoke. She exhales hard, so that the stream of smoke shoots out of her mouth in a burst.

"I went on the bus tour. We got to see Little Round Top and Devil's Den." If we're not going to lunch, I at least want to tell her all about the tour and the women lawyers, but she interrupts.

"That's nice. Turn on the television for me and turn the volume way down." On the screen a golf course appears. I change the channel. "Put it back," Mother says. "Golf is perfect. Hit a little white ball all over God's creation and then try to tap it into a tiny hole. Do it over and over again until the day is done. Over and over. *Plunk*, down the hole. *Plunk*." She laughs.

Sometimes Daddy watches golf if nothing else is on. He has golf clubs that his cousin gave him. Once he took me to a driving range where we each had a bucket of golf balls that we placed one by one on a green rubber mat and tried to hit toward signs that had numbers on them—100, 150, 200, and 250. The man next to Daddy kept hitting his balls all the way past the 250 sign. Daddy tried to match his neighbor, but the harder he swung, the more his balls went crooked. He told me to hurry up and hit my bucket. Then he started hitting my balls too. When we left, the other man was still there, methodically hitting his drives well past 250.

"I'm going to go to the motel restaurant for lunch," I say. I have almost fifteen dollars of Mother's money left in my pocket, plus all eighteen of my own dollars in my book bag.

"Sure," Mother says, not really paying attention. "Have fun. Have a big time. We're on vacation." She doesn't look at me. She keeps staring at the television.

I tell Mother that after lunch I'll go to the cyclorama and the Electric Map show, reminding her they are close by. I have enough money and she doesn't seem to care if I'm gone the rest of the afternoon. At home when she has a migraine she stays inside all day with the lights off and the curtains drawn and she doesn't want anyone to bother her. The best thing I can do is leave her alone. I'd rather go without her anyway.

I wish Aunt Laura was here at the cyclorama with me. The building is brand new, all concrete, white, and clean. It doesn't smell musty like the Atlanta Cyclorama. I stand in line with a crowd of other people and while I wait I look in the glass window of the gift shop. The miniature cannons lined up on a shelf are flanked by figures of Union and Confederate soldiers in various fighting positions. One is crouching on his knee shouldering a rifle, another is astride a horse with saber drawn, and another is standing up shooting a revolver. All have hats, all have colorful uniforms. No ripped and torn jackets, no bare feet.

I hear the click of doors opening and people exit, streaming down the spiral ramp. My line moves forward and I run my fingers along the curved wall, touching each smooth glazed tile and the roughness of the grout. At the top of the ramp, I emerge in the middle of Pickett's Charge. In every direction, the battle races around the walls. The guide has a deep voice. "Look at the chaos at this point when the Confederates have breached the Angle." Because of people's heads, I have a hard time seeing a few of the scenes that the guide points to with his flashlight.

"The French painter Philippoteaux painted this cyclorama twenty years after the war," the guide explains. "They built a tower on the battlefield to make sketches and photographs. Many veterans, of course, were still alive and assisted the painter."

I like the purplish color of the mountain range on the horizon of the painting.

"Philippoteaux put himself in the painting as a Union soldier leaning against this tree." The guide flicks his light arrow onto the tiny figure.

Just as I catch a glimpse of the figure, a man in front of me puts his small son on his shoulders, blocking my view, so I nudge my way forward a little in the group. The guide goes on with his talk. "Here, a Federal hospital is set up behind the artillery of the Rhode Island First, which is north of the Angle, the focal point of Pickett's Charge." To the right of a road lined with broken cannons and white clouds of smoke billowing above it, men in bandages rest against an odd-looking haystack.

The scenes in the painting don't look like the battlefield I've just seen on the bus tour. The Copse of Trees stands at a distance from the Confederates surging over the wall at the Angle—it seems too far away.

The crowd claps and we're herded down the ramp. The next group, pressed against the tile wall, makes its way past us. With several other people I peel off into the gift shop. After I select a guidebook and two booklets of postcards, I roll a toy cannon back and forth on the shelf, considering it. I have a set of painted metal soldiers at home, but no cannon. I walk around the small store. Brass swords etched with the word *Gettysburg* stand in a container next to the cash register.

"Be careful," the saleslady says as I take one out. "They're letter openers—real sharp."

I hold the sword in my hand. It's heavy. I like the color of the brass and I like that it is sharp. I can open letters with it and keep it on my desk in my pencil holder, made from an orange juice can with fabric glued around. Two dollars. I put it on the counter, then go back for the cannon. First I take one cannon, and then on impulse, I get a second. Each side needs one, don't they? Behind me in line, a teenager is talking to his little brother about the Electric Map show.

"Wasn't it the best? Good thing we went there first. That way we know all about the battle lines."

Chapter Twenty-one

I go outside with my bag and over twelve dollars of my own left in my pocket. The Electric Map exhibit is in the next building over, the National Museum where Mother and I met the guide for the cemetery yesterday. The trees shading the path are huge; they must have been here during the battle. As I walk I imagine Rebel soldiers crouching at their bases, their rifles at the ready. It would have been the first time they were invading truly Northern territory—not a border state—and they would have been both excited and frightened. We'll take Gettysburg, they were probably thinking, then we'll storm Washington. Nothing turned out the way they thought it would. Circumstances can change fast when an army is on the move and even experienced soldiers can't always know what will happen.

I'm early, and while I wait I wander around the exhibits. The bloodstained table where Stonewall Jackson's arm was amputated. The cape John Wilkes Booth wore when he shot Lincoln. Lincoln's saddle from his ride to the cemetery when he gave the Gettysburg Address. Pictures of the last Union and Confederate veterans—the Yankee died in 1956 and the Rebel in 1959, two years after I was born.

I make sure I am near the front of the line forming for the show. By the time the attendant opens the double doors to the Electric Map, there are a lot of people in line behind me, but as I rush in I realize that I will have a good view no matter where I sit. The auditorium is a miniature stadium, with seats rising up all around the huge topographical map resting on the floor in the middle. The map is a mosaic of green and gold denoting the terrain, with clusters of small lightbulbs scattered across the undulating terrain. I choose to sit up high—the aerial view.

Just before the lights in the auditorium begin to dim, I catch sight of a familiar figure: Carl, in a front-row seat across the room from me. I duck my head; I don't want him to see me. The lights dim and a recorded narration begins. I can see Carl in the glow of the first yellow and blue lights of the Electric Map. He's much lower and would have to tilt his head up to see me. I watch him writing in a small notebook. For each of the three days of the battle, rows of lights illuminate the positions of the troops. Yellow for Confederates, blue for the Union, and green for landmarks. I watch as the lights blink on Chambersburg Pike, Cemetery Hill, Seminary Ridge, Devil's Den, Little Round Top, the Peach Orchard, and the Wheatfield. In between the days of the battle, small red lights represent the soldiers' campfires. When the narration turns to Pickett's Charge, I realize the show must be almost over. I am afraid of running into Carl as we leave the auditorium. I don't want to see his sneering grin, or hear what ugly thing he has to say about Northerners or Black people. I gather my bag from the gift shop and look behind me for an exit door. If I go out now, I'll miss the best part, and Carl might look up and see me when I open the door and let in light from the lobby. He could follow me back to the motel to get even with me. When we were on the bus tour he said he didn't get mad, he got even. In Vietnam he probably killed people. Lots of people. I decide to wait until the second the show is over and the lights come back on. If I hurry I can be out of the building before Carl gets out of his seat. But how will I know if he has seen me and is following? I wish my lawyer friends were here and I could walk out with them surrounding me.

Nothing can frighten the Confederate general anymore. She thinks about all that she has been through. Heavy shelling for days, hand-to-hand combat, a minié ball piercing her hat, and a bullet in her side. Any fear she has passes as soon as she begins to make plans and take action.

The music on the sound track swells. I shift from seat to seat until I'm at the aisle. As the lights come up, I have my hands on the handle of the heavy exit door, and I slip out. Once outside, I take off toward the trees and grassy lawn that lead to the street our motel is on. As I run through the parking lot, I catch sight of a few people coming out through a back door of the museum. What if Carl came out the back door? I stop running and stand near a group of kids who are piling off a church bus. I'm breathing hard. I can't see him.

I leave the group from the church bus and walk fast across the lawn, the back of my neck prickling. When I get to the main street, I know I need a strategy. Carl would be able to track someone without being seen. If I turn left and walk directly to our motel he will know where I'm staying. I won't be safe. But if I turn right, go in and out of shops, zigzag on side streets back to the motel, I could lose him.

The Confederate general is an expert tracker, which came in handy during the Indian wars. Now she can use the same skills in reverse to avoid being tracked. She knows how to move great numbers of troops with stealth. She makes them wrap their bayonets so the sun doesn't reflect on them. They move low and behind cover, and most of all they do not move in a predictable path. It is unnerving to proceed under these conditions; any minute they might be discovered.

I turn right and walk down to an intersection before I allow myself to look back. Lots of people, but no Carl with his beard and pony-tail. I cross the big avenue, heading for a row of stores, and spot the huge bay window of a bookstore that will give a clear view of the street. Once inside, I stand behind a tall wooden bookcase to watch the people who walk by. My hands are shaking and I make fists to stop it. If Carl is following me, I'll know it now. At least thirty people walk by, but no Carl.

• • •

The general is pleased with her quick success in shaking the pursuing army. Now they need to lie low for a while and make sure that their movements won't be detected. She chuckles to herself at her luck in coming across such an oasis tucked away in the middle of the forest where she and her men can wait.

I relax a little and begin to look at the books on either side of me. Some are old, like the books Mother and I have seen in antique shops. I am in the biography section and there are books on the lives of Lee, Grant, Davis, Lincoln, Meade, and Jackson. I refold the top of the paper bag with my purchases from the gift shop as I emerge from the row of bookshelves to the center of the shop. A white-haired woman with big red plastic glasses swivels in her chair to greet me.

"Hello. I thought I heard someone come in a few minutes ago, but when no one appeared I decided it must have been one of our ghosts." She laughs. "We have two ghosts of wounded soldiers who were brought to this building after the battle and then died. They're peaceful, though. And very helpful. If I've lost something, they'll find it straight away and deposit it back on my desk. Tell me," she says, peering over the top of her red glasses, "what do you want to find today?"

"Nothing . . . uh . . . I mean, thank you, I'm not looking for anything in particular." I've heard Mother say that to store clerks before.

"Well, we have a young readers' section in the far corner over there."

I watch her sort envelopes into cubbies in the desk. Are the ghosts something she's made up for tourists or does she really believe in them? I'm curious.

"What do the ghosts find?"

She looks up from her sorting. "Lots of things. My glasses, for one. And once they retrieved my sterling silver fountain pen. But the most important thing they found was my diamond ring. It had come off when I washed my hands in the bathroom. Five minutes before the plumber arrived, the ring appeared on my desk taped down to the blotter. The plumber swore that the pipe under the sink had recently been taken apart and put back together again.

"All I have to do is tell them out loud what I'm missing and ask them to hunt for it. I call them Elijah and Ezekiel; I've decided they're both Union soldiers. They're very polite. Never any moaning or clanking of chains, that sort of thing." She laughs. The woman's story is far-fetched but I'm not sure there aren't ghosts and I'd like to believe that if there are, some of them would help us.

"Too bad I haven't lost anything today. I could try to give you a demonstration. You seem skeptical." She gets up from her desk. "Never mind, most people are. That's fine with me. I prefer to have Elijah and Ezekiel to myself anyway. Let me show you the Landmark series books. I bet there's something there you haven't read yet." I follow her to the corner with the kids' books. She has a whole shelf full of Landmark Books, more than our Marietta library. "I shelve them in number order of the series. That is, I try to keep them in order—they get messed up."

"Thank you," I say. These Landmark Books have dust jackets, unlike the ones I check out at the library. I pull out a few I've already read to look at the covers. The biography of Robert E. Lee shows him with white hair and beard in his Confederate dress uniform, troops marching behind him. On Clara Barton's biography, a white flag with a red cross is front and center and Clara stands next to it in long skirts. All around her are individual scenes: a man dying, a man riding a horse, a flood and a house washing away. The compositions and colors appeal to me—maybe I could be a book cover artist! I can't wait to tell Mother. All day long I could read books, sketch, and paint. I bet I could even meet the authors.

I pick up one that I haven't read, the biography of Abe Lincoln: *Log Cabin to White House*, Landmark Books #61. On the front of the book is a profile of a young Lincoln in a buckskin-fringed jacket, his black hair blowing in the wind and his right hand holding a double-bladed ax. The first chapter starts with a quote from Lincoln, "The story of my early life can all be condensed into a single sentence and that sentence you will find in Gray's Elegy—'the short and simple annals of the poor.'" I'm not sure what "annals" are but it must have something to do with troubles. I hold on to the book while I look at others. I've never read a biography of someone on the Union side before, but now I want to. Lincoln's face appears everywhere at Gettysburg. He helped save our country and freed the slaves, the exhibits say. I know from school that he split rails for fences when he was young, educated himself by reading borrowed books, was a lawyer, and that he was assassinated by John Wilkes Booth right after Lee surrendered. When I was with Elena and the other lawyers from the bus tour, I told them I didn't know anything about the Gettysburg Address. They clucked at me and asked if I had been taught to hate Lincoln, and when I said no, we hate Sherman, they laughed. They told me I should learn more about Lincoln, that he was a brilliant politician and writer. They also told me that, like the Kennedys and Martin Luther King, Jr., Lincoln had been assassinated in his prime, before he had a chance to fulfill his greatest legacy. Rebuilding the country and the South after the war would have gone so much better under Lincoln; the South probably wouldn't have had Jim Crow at all. I want to learn more about Lincoln than I've been taught in school. I want to understand all the things Elena and the other lawyers know.

I hear a typewriter and turn around. The bookstore lady pecks the keys with two fingers. *Ding*, she makes the machine begin a new line. She is rolling index cards into the typewriter. I bring the Lincoln biography over and she pulls a card out of the book.

"This one's a dollar ninety-five," she says and sticks the card in one of the slots in her desk.

She wraps my book up in brown paper like a package to be mailed. "There you go. Enjoy. I like to see a young person buying books for herself. Build a library, pass it on to your children. That sort of thing." I want a library like Aunt Laura's—built-in bookshelves along one whole wall.

A door behind the desk opens, revealing a man in a dark beard holding a small stack of books. I jump, thinking of Carl.

"Easy now." She laughs. "I bet you thought my Woody was a ghost."

Woody puts the books on the table next to the desk. "Has Momma been telling her ghost stories again?" He winks at me.

Before I leave the store I check the bay window one more time. It's safe to go back to the motel.

Mother is asleep when I get back. I'm surprised; she must still feel sick. "Hey," I say and sit on the end of her bed. The air in the room is cool, even a little moist, and it smells of cigarette smoke. "Don't you want to wake up? I'm back."

"Uh-huh," she groans as she rolls over.

"I went to the cyclorama."

Mother still has her eyes closed.

"Then I went to the Electric Map show. It's in the same building where we were yesterday." I consider telling her about Carl and that I thought he might be following me, but that seems like a bad idea.

I bounce on the bed a little even though I know I shouldn't if she's still got one of her headaches. I'm tired of her being asleep. "Wake up. I went to a bookstore too, and I've decided I'm going to be a book cover artist," I say.

"What?" Mother asks thickly.

"Get up. Time to get up." I turn the lamp on over her bed.

"No."

"Time to go to dinner." I pull the bedspread and blanket off her the way she does to me sometimes when I don't want to get up.

"Leave me alone," she mumbles. Her eyes open into slits. "You leave me alone," she says louder. She turns the lamp off.

I move over to my bed.

"But it's dinnertime."

"Don't care. I'm sick."

"What should I do?" I hear the whine in my voice.

"I don't care."

"You don't want any food?"

"Just hush, Katherine!" She rolls to the far side of her bed.

I want to do something to make Mother feel better, but I don't know what's wrong with her. She never wants to eat when she has a migraine, but they usually last only a day. Maybe this one is worse than the others. She says she has a bad cold, but it's not like any cold she's had before—she always eats when she has a cold. Starve a fever, feed a cold, she tells me.

A weight lies on the Confederate general's shoulders, the hope of Virginia and the rest of the South, and if she doesn't figure out how to turn this failing campaign around, she will let everyone down. Early on she won battles, but now the landscape is more complicated, the Union generals more competent. The Union army has her outnumbered, sometimes two to one, and her men lack shoes, food, and even enough guns and ammunition. But no matter what the odds, her job is to read the lay of the land, second-guess her opposing general, and guide her army to victory. Whatever happens, she must figure out what's working and do it more, and uncover what's wrong and fix it.

Maybe what's wrong with Mother now is like what happened two Christmases ago. I overheard the doctor telling Daddy then that it was exhaustion. Nervous exhaustion. She took pills for a while to keep her calm, but later she flushed them all down the toilet because she said they made her feel like she was underwater.

On Christmas Eve that winter, Mother locked herself in her bedroom. It was afternoon and I had walked home through the pasture from visiting Gramma and Poppa's. When I came in, I heard Daddy pounding on their bedroom door, yelling, "Let me in. You're not going to do this to me." He stopped pounding when I came into the hall.

"Go to the den, Katherine," he said. "Your mother's pitching a fit."

Even in the den with the television turned up loud, I heard him pleading with her. "Please. You have to come out. It's Christmas. We have to do Santa Claus and everything." I didn't know what their fight was about, but it wasn't a good sign that it was happening on Christmas Eve.

That night, with Mother still in the bedroom, Daddy and I ate peanut-butter-and-jelly sandwiches in the den. Mother's projects were all over the dining room table. She'd been needlepointing pillows for everyone in the family. She had created elaborate designs, all on tiny-weave canvases that almost required a magnifying glass to see where to put the needle. None of them were finished. After I ate my sandwich and Daddy went into the hall to call Aunt Laura, I went back to the dining room. On the ironing board was one very small canvas of an artist's palette dabbed with splotches of color; behind it emerged a bundle of brushes, tubes of paint, pencils, and calligraphy pens. It was freshly blocked and waiting for its backing. The colors were amazingly vibrant—cobalt blue, magenta, fuchsia, chartreuse, lemon, ebony, turquoise, and teal. In tiny white stitches in the bottom right corner, Mother had put "From MCMc to KCMc." It was my Christmas present. I took the canvas over to the Christmas tree next to the brick fireplace, plugged in the lights, and sat cross-legged next to the tree with the picture in my lap. I had asked for art supplies for Christmas, which I knew Mother had bought because I had spied the bag in her closet one afternoon. But she had wanted to create something lasting.

Ever since Thanksgiving she had been working until the wee hours of the morning on the gifts. She hadn't cooked, or cleaned, or even picked me up from school regularly. The bags under her eyes were deep and dark. Almost every night she and Daddy had a fight. "Damn it, Margaret," he said. "Just buy some presents at the store and quit making such a production out of Christmas."

"Your father doesn't like beautiful things as much as we do, Katherine," she said to me later.

I didn't think it had anything to do with beautiful things. I was tired of the fights and having to heat up cream of mushroom soup for Daddy because Mother was too busy with her projects. Daddy switched from beer to bourbon and that made their fights worse. At first when she began staying up late, watching old movies and doing her needlepoint, it had been fun. She let me stay up too, and make popcorn at midnight. But as Christmas got closer, Mother didn't act like we were even around anymore. I started walking through the pasture to visit Gramma every afternoon after school. She fed me tuna fish sandwiches and helped me with my homework, and she never asked me about Mother.

After Aunt Laura arrived to take care of us, Daddy settled on the couch with a glass of bourbon and Coke, watching Christmas specials. Aunt Laura got in my bed and I rolled out my sleeping bag on the floor. We closed the door to muffle the buzzing of the television in the den, and she read out loud from my favorite book, *Linnets and Valerians*, about orphan children living with their uncle. I fell asleep while she was reading, and the next morning we both got up early, as the sun was rising. She made me hot chocolate and toast with grape jelly cut in strips, and let me eat in the living room while I pulled down my stocking. I expected Mother to fill the stocking with art supplies and a Christmas toy. The year before, my stocking had held a new set of watercolors and a Santa that rode a windup trike with a tall flag on the back. This year it held an orange, some nuts, and one of Aunt Laura's presents to me, a tiny stuffed bear. Mother hadn't come out of her room to do my stocking. I was angry with her; it wouldn't have been that hard. Daddy didn't get up until eleven thirty, when Aunt Laura pulled all his covers off, and although Mother hadn't appeared, neither Daddy nor Aunt Laura went to knock on her door. After Daddy took a shower, we went to my grandparents' for Christmas lunch just like always, but without Mother. No one asked about her. It felt as though there was a big secret that no one would tell, but we all knew. During dessert my stomach started hurting and I couldn't eat my pecan pie. Everything about Christmas was being ruined and it was Mother's fault. That evening Aunt Laura sat in the hall and talked with Mother through the closed bedroom door for almost an hour. I couldn't hear what Mother said, but Aunt Laura kept mentioning me. Mother still wouldn't come out.

Aunt Laura told me that Mother was sick. That she had something wrong with her like the flu or the measles. It wasn't a matter of her not trying to get better, she said. Mother needed a doctor and medicine. As soon as Dr. Haskins saw her and gave her some pills, she would be fine. I shouldn't worry, Aunt Laura said, but I still couldn't understand why no one had talked at Christmas lunch about Mother being sick. I waited to see what Mother would be like when she came out of her room and saw the doctor.

She emerged late Christmas night. I had already gone to bed, but she and Aunt Laura woke me up to give me the bag of art supplies. Mother had stuck a red bow on the bag. Her eyes were bloodshot. As they sat on the edge of my bed, Mother began to cry. Aunt Laura patted her back and said, "There, there." I felt bad that I had been so mad. Mother hadn't meant to ruin anything.

The pills did help, though Mother said she felt washed out and stupid. Aunt Laura came over twice a week to cook dinner and Daddy quit drinking bourbon and only had one beer at dinner. When Mother told me she was afraid of her paintings, but that I shouldn't tell Aunt Laura, I helped her wrap them all in brown paper and stack them in a corner of the basement. She packed away her easel and paints too. "Sketching is okay," she told me. "But when I'm painting I think about all the things I want to forget." I had no idea what she was talking about, but I did know some of her paintings looked scary to me. Maybe she had been thinking about frightening things when she was painting.

Every week, Aunt Laura picked me up at school on Friday to take me to her apartment for the weekend, and sometimes I even stayed through part of the week. I loved being there even if we didn't do anything special. While she graded history tests or homework at her kitchen table, she let me play her hi-fi in the living room. I liked her opera records, especially Caruso's arias. My favorite was from his role in *Pagliacci*, and sometimes I played it over and over before I listened to the rest. The music was so tender, the clear high notes haunting.

Aunt Laura said she knew it was hard on me that Mother wasn't feeling a hundred percent yet, but that she would be well soon. Everything was so easy at Aunt Laura's. We had a routine—definite times for meals, walks in the morning, reading in the evening, trips to the library or the history center on Saturday afternoons. But gradually Mother got her energy back, and I spent less and less time at Aunt Laura's.

I decide that Mother needs rest. The trip and all the driving and staying up late sketching has exhausted her. I won't try to wake her or make her eat. She needs to be left alone. She'll be better before long.

The Confederate general often feels very alone; after all, everything is up to her. Even if she gets advice from her staff, the decisions are hers. She can't reveal her uncertainties to anyone. Her men and her staff need to be confident in her, confident in her abilities; it wouldn't be good for them to know about the times that she is unsure and confused. To know that she questions her own resolve.

"I'm going to get some dinner and bring it back," I say softly.

"Okay." Mother's voice sounds distant, muffled by the pillow that she has put over her head.

Chapter Twenty-two

The sky has grown cloudy and the wind blows my hair across my face as I walk back from the restaurant. When I open the door with my key, Mother is sitting up in bed, smoking a cigarette, and crying so hard her chest is heaving up and down.

I run to her. "What happened?"

"What am I going to do?" she whispers. Her tears have wet the front of her yellow pajama top. She has a bit of ash near one of her top buttons. "I feel so bad."

"It's okay. You'll be okay in a couple of days. I'll take care of you."

"Oh, Kat," she says. She crushes her cigarette in the ashtray and slumps down in the bed. She stops making so much noise, but she is still crying. She puts the pillow over her head.

"Maybe I should call a doctor and get you some medicine."

"No, no. Don't call any doctor; this isn't something for a doctor. You hear me? Come over here. I can't see you."

I go to the other side of the bed where I can just see her eyes underneath the pillow. "No doctor. You understand me?" She looks at me hard. "Just you and me." Her nose is running and she wipes it with her sheet.

"Yes, ma'am."

I sit at the table and pick at my hamburger while I try to figure out what's happening to Mother. The medicine she took when she was sick at Christmas sapped all of her energy. That's why she doesn't want me to call a doctor now. I'm not sure what I should do. I swore to her that I wouldn't tell Daddy or anyone where we are. I can't call anyone. I will look after her and she will get better. A distant thunderstorm rumbles toward us and a soft but steady rain starts. I open the curtain to watch. Small canals of rainwater start to flow next to the sidewalk. The flashes of lightning glow in the distance. The thunder between the flashes might be drumrolls or artillery fire. But in real battles the noise would be much louder. I read it could be unbearable—it could make you go deaf in a second.

The Confederate general knows when to wait and watch, and when to take immediate action. This is a wait-and-watch time. There won't be any harm in a short delay right now. She needs more idea of what is going on outside their valley of operation. She will wait until she receives word back from the officers she sent out on reconnaissance.

The raindrops are fatter, and it's coming down hard. After one huge flash of lightning, I count—one thousand, two thousand—then I hear the faraway boom. Two miles away. Mother says never to sit in front of windows in a thunderstorm or take a bath or wash dishes.

The storm moves in right on top of us and I shift my chair back from the window. A big jagged bolt of lightning cuts down to connect the sky to the ground. One thousand—*boom*. Mother turns over. The sky lights up with a mesh of light. One—*boom, boom, boom*. Mother hates thunderstorms. She is always afraid they will develop into tornados. During a lot of storms, I sit with Mother and a transistor radio in the northeast corner of our basement. A huge spidery trail of lightning shoots down into the field across the street from our motel. Instantaneously the thunder splits the quiet of our room.

Mother moans. "Is it a tornado?"

"A thunderstorm," I answer. I stand in front of the window even though it scares me, and watch the sheets of rain crashing down.

"I was having a nightmare," Mother says. "I was walking down a narrow, dark corridor. It snaked around, like it was a fun house or maze. Every so often I touched my palm to the wall to try to find a door or a window—any kind of way out." She sits up. "Close the curtains. Maybe we should go into the bathroom to be safe." But she doesn't get out of the bed and I don't close the curtains.

Mother's eyes are big. Her hair is tangled and oily. I listen carefully to her dream. She is talking softly and sometimes the thunder drowns out her words. "I felt in my pocket for my gun, but it was gone. I tried to retrace my steps to find where I'd dropped it, but all of a sudden there were forks in the corridor behind me that hadn't been there before. A window appeared with light streaming through it.

"Kat, it was the strangest thing. I opened the window, pushed the screen out, and started to climb through it. Then the window started to dissolve, melt just like ice cream. I lunged through it into a bright white room. Spotlight bright. All over the walls were knives attached by brackets. I tried to get a knife. They wouldn't budge. While I was pulling at one of the knives, the bright room turned into a boat."

Mother gets out of the bed suddenly. She yanks the dresser drawers open one by one, looks through the contents, then slams each shut. The way Mother is acting and this dream she's telling me about make me uneasy.

"So I was in a boat, waves washing over the side. I could taste salt water in my mouth. The waves started washing bottles of pills into the boat. I tried to grab them. If I did manage to get my hand around a bottle it turned into a flopping fish with sharp fins. My hands bled from trying to hold on to the fish."

She turns on the lamp between our beds and I can see that she's trembling. "It felt so real, Kat. I really thought I could see my hands bleeding." She examines her palms under the light. "See"—she holds her hands out for me to look—"there's nothing wrong with my hands." She climbs back into her bed.

"At the end of the dream, I was alone in a room. No door, no windows. In the middle of the room was a chandelier with a coiled rope and a chair underneath it. I picked up the rope and found that it was glued together. It couldn't be uncoiled. I wanted it uncoiled so badly."

She pauses. The thunder rolls. The lamp flickers. "I wanted to use that rope so badly."

Mother is staring blankly in front of her, her lips pressed tightly together. Her dream is awful and the way she describes it seems so real. She checked her hands for blood like maybe she thinks it *is* real. A chill makes my shoulders jerk.

The Confederate general tightens her reins. She listens. In an instant, she slips from her horse's back and flattens herself on the ground. A second later she hears a mighty crack and a limb on the tree next to her drops with a thud. Her horse shies; she has the reins in her hand and he drags her a short distance but she keeps him from running off until she can get to her feet. She pulls the rifle from her saddlebag, then positions herself and her steed behind a large boulder. She waits until she sees the glint of steel in a tree across the way; she aims and fires. The glint disappears. No more Yankee sharpshooter. The instant before she dropped from her horse's back, she felt fear. And then the fear was over. It was as if the fear simply worked as a warning to help her take the right action.

When I was little I had the same nightmare over and over again. I dreamed that the Frankenstein monster came through my bedroom window, picked me up out of my bed, and threw me down a well. When I would wake up crying, Mother comforted me. "I shouldn't have let you watch the movie. It's just a scene from the movie. It's not something that could ever happen. Nightmares aren't things that can really happen."

I look at Mother sitting straight up in the bed staring at the blank television screen.

"Kat," she says finally.

"Yes, ma'am."

"You need to watch me. I'm not feeling well. I need to sleep, but I don't think I can go to sleep unless you say you'll watch me."

"I'll watch you, Mother."

"Good." She lies down and pulls her covers up. "Don't let anything happen to me."

She reaches up to the lamp.

"Mother?"

"Yes, baby."

"Nightmares aren't anything that can really happen. That's what you told me."

With a click she turns the lamp off. I can still see the outline of her face because of the glow of streetlights outside our room.

"Just watch me," she says. "Forget about other things I've told you."

I sit at the table by the window and watch the lightning recede into the distance. I watch the bolts become thinner and more fragile until they are barely more than tiny scribbles on the dark sky. Mother thinks something bad might happen to her, that's why she wants me to stay awake. But nothing bad can happen to her here in the motel room. She's disturbed by her nightmare and the thunderstorm and her mind is playing tricks on her. My stomach hurts like the time I ate two banana splits. Maybe there is something I don't know about that could happen to her. I've sensed sometimes that Mother doesn't tell me things I should know, things that could keep us both safe. There were times two Christmases ago when I wished I could stay forever with Aunt Laura, but I felt guilty for thinking that way. I look at the luminous dots on my watch face—10:30. I am so tired, but I don't dare go to sleep. I open my new Lincoln book and tilt the shade on the floor lamp before I turn it on. Mother doesn't stir. I begin reading about Abraham Lincoln being born to Nancy Hanks Lincoln in a log cabin. The first drawing in the book shows Lincoln's cousin Dennis in a fringed jacket and coonskin cap holding the infant Abe. As I do with all the books I read, after I read to the first drawing or picture, I pause to turn through all the pages to see the rest of the illustrations. One of them is of young Abe kneeling beside his mother's gravestone. The entire picture is framed by branches of an oak tree and leaves that have fallen to the ground. It is a small drawing centered in the middle of the white page. The artist should have made it larger to fill up the space more. The book says Lincoln's mother's grave site was peaceful. "The leaves of autumn and the snow of winter drifted down almost without a whisper. It was a place where Abe could go when he felt sorrowful and alone."

A car horn wakes me up. I glance at Mother. She's still asleep. I was sleeping with my head down on the table, next to my Lincoln book. The sun is coming up and a mist is hovering over the parking lot, making things look pink. It's a little after six thirty and outside our room everything is quiet. The last time I checked my watch it was two a.m. My stomach still doesn't feel good; I wish I had a glass of milk to make it settle down. Before Mother wakes up, I need to think of a plan that will make her forget her nightmare and get her out of our room and into the world.

The Confederate general thinks about all the things that can be done to help a soldier get over the trauma of a battle or to prevent him from being too anxious about an upcoming fight. Occupy the soldier with tasks: close-order drills, digging trenches, cleaning weapons, currying the horses. Having the chaplain conduct services. And then some soldiers make their own diversions—playing cards or gambling.

When I couldn't stop thinking about my Frankenstein nightmare and fall back asleep, Mother would read to me from one of the Thornton Burgess books that were hers as a little girl. A happy story replaces the disturbing one in your mind, Mother explained to me. Everyone needs a healthy dose of distraction from the negatives in life, she said.

Mother needs a major distraction now. Getting to Cape Cod—the place she's wanted to go back to for so long—will help her snap out of this. I dig the atlas out of my book bag and begin writing down on notebook paper a route from Gettysburg to Cape Cod. Flipping to Massachusetts, I pass the Maine map. I don't want to mention Maine, and I definitely don't want to move there. Maybe Mother can be just as happy starting a shop in Marietta, or even near her artist friends in Atlanta. I stare at the notebook paper filled with place names and highway numbers. Looking forward to the Cape will get Mother moving, I'm sure of it. She'll feel better when we're on the road with the windows rolled down. Who knows what could happen after that? Maybe I'll map the shortest route home from the Cape while I'm at it.

Reminiscing about the Cape has always made her happy. She has told me endless stories about summers at her family's house there. Her father would pack their station wagon with suitcases, her mother's easel and painting box, a deflated yellow raft, and a cardboard box full of clean linens, and they would drive the hour and a half from Boston. They would stay at least a month, sometimes more, while her father commuted on weekends from his bank job. She told me how her golden cocker spaniel, Ralph, ran in the surf, his ears flopping in the spray. "I used to have hundreds of sketches of him," she told me. "Ralph running in the surf, scratching out crabs from the sand, lying on the beach towel with his fur all wet and ruffled. I don't have any idea where they went. I lost track of a lot of things when I moved to my aunt's." She hated moving to Georgia to live with her aunt Susan, uncle Roger, and their only child, Reginald, who was one year older than Mother. It wasn't just that her mother had died suddenly, she told me. It was that Susan, Roger, and Reginald Spaulding were mean people. She couldn't wait to get out of their house. She met Daddy the first Thanksgiving she was in Georgia; he was older and had dropped out of Georgia Tech to work construction.

Every year for as long as I can remember, she has talked about driving north to the Cape, but until now we've never gone. She hasn't been there since her mother died.

Chapter Twenty-three

Six months after the awful Christmas, Daddy decided we had enough money to go to the beach for a week—not Cape Cod, but Jekyll Island off the coast of Georgia. Still, Mother was ecstatic. Daddy drove the Impala. He had bought it a couple of months earlier, used, from Bob and Joe's car lot. He washed and waxed it every other Saturday—I helped him buff out the wax with a chamois cloth. While he drove, he sang to the radio—rock and country songs. "Down every road there's always one more city . . . ," he wailed along with Merle Haggard. Mother and I covered our ears, but his voice wasn't bad. In the rearview mirror, I saw him smiling at Mother and she smiled back.

Once we got to Jekyll, Daddy found a used bookstore and loaded up on novels while Mother and I stayed down at the ocean all day with Scout and our pink-striped umbrella. Daddy came down in the mornings and we took pictures of Scout chasing the waves and us posing under the umbrella. Toward lunchtime, Daddy retreated to alternate between the pool and the motel room. He wasn't big on the ocean. "Too sandy, too salty. Give me a pool deck any day." Sitting in a lounge chair reading a paperback made him happy; he didn't want to tour around looking at sights either, he said.

But Mother and I did, so we rode our bikes to see all the abandoned mansions. Riding across the scrub grass with patches of sand that were once lawns, we tried to find windows we could peer into.

"I don't know why they don't fix these up and charge admission," Mother said.

At a white frame mansion Mother called, "Come look, but be careful where you step." I picked my way across the porch to peer through the dirty windowpanes and saw humps of furniture pushed to the middle of the room and covered in sheets. Old drapes that looked to be made of velvet drooped heavily at the edge of the windows. Across the huge room was a beautifully carved wood mantelpiece.

"Like scary movies," I said. In a spooky voice I added, "It's dark and raining; their car breaks down and they go to the mansion on the hill and it so happens the big front door is open . . ."

"*Creeeeeeeeeeek.*" Mother joined in. "They go in and pull off all the sheets from the furniture and dust flies everywhere." She made her voice sound ominous. "And they definitely disturb the ghosts." She raised her arms and flapped them and laughed a witch's laugh. "A-ha-ha-ha."

We rode our bikes to the chapel that had Tiffany windows and was open to the public. "See, these people really understood the importance of art," Mother said. We sat on the wooden pews in the cool interior. "They knew you had to nourish your spirit with beauty—even if you were on vacation." We sat in the chapel for a long time, long enough for me to be worried that she was getting into one of her moods. But after I read through practically half the hymnal, she got up cheerfully and took my hand. "Let's go find your father and get some shrimp for dinner."

I watched them as they cooked together in the tiny kitchenette of our motel suite. Daddy danced a little, announcing into a potato, "Welcome to the luxury suite, ladies; step right up to the five-star restaurant. On tonight's menu—famous shrimp à la McConnell with roasted ears of succulent corn and the scrumptious Carter hush puppies." He lunged at Scout to make her bark, then sang, "Hush puppy, hush puppy." I laughed and stood on the foldout couch where I slept. "Madam," Daddy said, "what is your opinion of your accommodations?"

"A million stars," I shouted.

Mother laughed and put the potatoes, wrapped in aluminum foil, into the miniature oven. "Let's sit on the porch until it's time to boil the shrimp. Here's the sunset." Mother grabbed a sketchpad and drew outlines of the beach while Daddy and I watched the waves roll in.

After dinner Mother went back out on the porch and sketched in the moonlight. She must have had twenty sketches torn out of her pad and lying on the floor when Daddy went out there. I heard them talking quietly. I went to sleep and woke up when Mother bumped against my folded-out bed. "Sorry, sweetie," she whispered. My watch said it was four a.m.

The next morning, though, she was cooking breakfast when I woke up. She wanted to ride bikes all around the island, she said, first on the beach, and then we would carry them over the rocks and finish up our ride by the mansions. She wanted to go swimming in the freshwater pool next to the old Jekyll Island Hotel. Daddy went down to the motel pool with Scout.

We rode and rode down the beach on the hard edge where the tide came in, and my legs were sprayed with a thousand tiny dots of sand and salt water. As I pedaled, the surf drowned out the *click, click, click* sound that my loose chain made.

We passed sunbathers coming down from their weather-beaten cottages toting aluminum lounge chairs and towels. A shirtless runner jogged by in red gym shorts with white piping, his hairless chest glistening with sweat. He smiled and waved. After a while I stopped looking around me and focused on pedaling in a rhythm. I looked at the sand in front of my handlebars and occasionally lifted my head enough to find Mother up ahead. Soon she had gotten out of shouting range and I was falling farther and farther behind. I was hot and tired and my legs ached.

With the glare of the sun it looked like Mother was flying above the sand on her bicycle. Any minute she had to stop, I thought. Please stop, please stop, I chanted under my breath. Waves curled white and then thundered to the shore. I started picking landmarks ahead.

When she reaches that house with the flag, she'll stop. When she gets to that weird rock, she'll stop. When she gets to that set of wooden stairs, she'll stop. I stood up and pedaled hard to try to catch her, but I lost my breath and had to slow down, even slower than before. So slow my front tire wobbled. Mother was only a dot of red shirt when I realized she must have stopped because her figure finally started getting bigger. "Hey, slowpoke," she said when I made it to her.

I got off my bike. "Can we rest?"

"Sure," she said. "We have a little farther to go and then we'll cut across and go to the pool." I flopped down on the sand. I was thirsty and felt sunburned and didn't know why we couldn't have gone on a simple, easy bike ride. Mother walked up and down. After a few minutes, she hopped on her bike. "Come on," she said. "Up to those rocks"—she pointed—"and we can ride to the drugstore for something to drink, then off to the pool."

At the drugstore, I sucked down two cherry Cokes and Mother bought some zinc oxide to put on my nose. The air-conditioning felt good. In one aisle I found souvenirs of the island, including a book with old photographs of the mansions, their rich owners playing croquet on the lawns. I read in the book that the millionaires got scared and left during World War II because they thought German submarines might torpedo them. "But why didn't they come back?" I asked Mother.

"That's rich people for you," she said. "They've got so much they can throw away a house and build another one somewhere else."

The photographs were brown and faded like the mansions looked now. But the people in the pictures looked happy in their pale linens and straw hats and white shoes. They were relaxed and having a good time. They were not afraid yet. I wanted to buy the book but I didn't have enough money.

Mother hurried me. I asked her if we could get the book and she said maybe when we were up here in the car. "You can't carry it back on your bike because you don't have a basket."

The Jekyll Island Hotel and the pool weren't far from the drugstore. Mother marched through the gate, stripped out of her shorts and shirt, revealing her blue tank suit, and dived right into the deep end. "Whoo, it's cold!" she said after she came shooting up out of the clear water. I walked into the shallow end and dipped my foot in. The water felt like it had ice cubes in it. "It's fed by an underground spring," Mother said. "That's why it's so cold. And it doesn't have any chlorine, so we won't ruin our eyes."

I inched down the steps, splashing water on my arms and face to get adjusted, but finally gave up and did a quick dolphin dive. When I came up I felt immediately revived. Mother began swimming laps and I floated on my back letting the water wash away my sweat and soreness.

After a little while, I got out and lay down on the warm concrete. Mother was in her rhythm, doing the crawl back and forth the length of the pool. I watched her and saw how little she splashed; her kicks just made whirlpools. She was always trying to teach me how to use the water the way she did instead of fighting against it. I was ready to go back to the motel, but I knew how much Mother hated to cut her laps short when we went to the YWCA. I closed my eyes. As the sun dried my hair and bathing suit, I went to sleep. When Mother woke me, I was dreaming that I was floating on a red raft in the ocean, shooting flares into the sky to try to attract the attention of a small plane flying by.

"Hungry?" Mother asked.

"Starving." I hurried to put my clothes on over my bathing suit. Mother had already dressed and I could see where her wet bathing suit was soaking through.

"If we ride down the main road, we'll pass that little stand that has ice cream and hot dogs."

By the time we got back to the motel, Daddy was taking a nap and we needed to figure out what we were going to eat for dinner. He woke up while Mother was in the shower and wandered out into the living room–kitchenette part of our motel room. I was watching television on the floor right up close to the screen so I wouldn't have to turn the volume up very high. An old movie was on—I recognized Jimmy Stewart—and I was trying to figure out what was happening.

"Well, Kat," he said cheerfully, "where did y'all go?" I told him and he whistled. "You must be tired."

"And hungry too." Jimmy Stewart was talking to himself and the other people were looking at him funny.

"I was thinking we might try that seafood restaurant we saw on the way in. When I went to get a paper, while you two scalawags were gone, the guy at the grocery said it was a real good place. We can get some deviled crab. I don't think you've ever had that—it's good stuff." He patted me on the back.

We didn't go out to restaurants much because Daddy said we had to save our money so he could start his own construction business; this was a real treat.

Daddy sat on the couch and watched the movie with me, and Mother came out of the shower and went into the bedroom. "Hey, Margaret," he called out, "let's go out to eat. I got a line on a place that has great crab." She didn't respond. Daddy leaned forward on the couch. "We want your mother to relax a little; she's starting to get all wound up like she does," he whispered to me. "You know what I mean, don't you, Kat? A nice quiet dinner. Everyone agreeable. She stayed up way too late last night."

"Okay," I whispered back. I thought she was fine now. She was never agitated after she swam. On the bike ride home she and I had ridden abreast, talking about how we could restore the mansions, fill them with period antiques, and make money charging people to tour through them.

When Mother came out of the bedroom she was dressed in white pants, sandals, and a black sleeveless shirt. Her hair was up and I could smell White Shoulders, the perfume that Daddy got her every year for her birthday.

The restaurant was as good as Daddy had promised, and I had deviled crabs in their own little aluminum-foil crab shells. We took Scout, but left her in the car with all the windows down a quarter of the way.

Halfway through the meal, Mother took her hush puppies out to feed Scout. Daddy smiled at me, his eyes shining. "Great vacation, huh, Kat?" I nodded, my mouth full of baked potato. He was right.

The next afternoon Mother and I came back from reading on the beach to join Daddy at the pool. Earlier we had walked up and down the shore, collecting a whole pail of shells, and Mother had taught me how to make a sand castle by first building the shape of the castle, then dribbling handfuls of watery sand all over it. The more I dribbled, the more the castle turned into an otherworldly sort of structure that seemed made of clouds or popcorn or melted dollops of chocolate. When we got to the pool, we saw Daddy walking Scout in the grassy strip across from the motel.

"Let's do some cannonballs," Daddy said, and he climbed up the diving-board ladder. He made a huge splash, and Mother laughed and shook her head. I followed and she laughed even more. She watched as we tried to bounce high off the board to get a big splash, but when another family came to the pool, we had to stop. A few more families and a group of teenagers came down. All the lounge chairs were filled. Daddy walked Scout around again, and then went back up to the room to get his book. He was gone a long time. Mother was quiet, and I thought she was watching all the people, but I couldn't tell for certain because she had on her dark glasses.

Not many people were swimming. One of the teenagers tried to do a swan dive and he landed with a loud splat on the surface of the clear water. When he climbed out of the pool, his stomach was bright red.

Daddy came back down from the room with his book and a big tumbler full of Coke. He hadn't had anything but beer that I knew of since he gave up liquor after Christmas, but as he walked by me I smelled the strong sweet smell of bourbon, the liquor he usually drank only after he and Mother had their worst arguments. He grinned at Mother. She frowned, then stood up. "Come on, Kat, let's work on your strokes. Do your racing dive and then go into the American crawl."

Mother hissed at Daddy as she walked by his lounge chair. "Watch yourself, Mister."

"We're all having fun, Margaret," I heard him say. "Don't ruin it."

I hurried to the end of the pool and waited for the pink-float woman to drift out of my way while Mother took up a position on the side of the pool with her arms crossed. I did my racing dive, coming up in a crawl stroke. Mother watched for two laps, pacing up and down. I could see her when I turned my head to breathe. I watched the black line undulate below me. "You're not lifting your elbow first. Elbow out of the water first!" she yelled at the end of my second lap. She stood on the pool deck, beautifully golden with pink toenails, demonstrating while I hung on the side and nodded my head. As I watched her in the glare of bright sunlight, I knew exactly what she wanted me to do to improve. I saw her fingers held tight together, slicing into the imaginary water in front of her, and her elbow lifting in the air ahead of her forearm. With a little squiggly motion, she represented the push of each palm against the water. After she thought I had gotten the idea, she added rhythmic breathing. Her chin tucked and then she rolled her head to the side, exaggerating a huge suck of air. Then she stood there, pointing sternly to the other end of the pool. "Go on, swim," she said.

I plunged back into the water and started my lap to the other end. I tried to kick four times to each arm stroke like Mother had said, but I could never get in that many. This time I didn't try to look at her when I took a breath on my right side—seeing her walking and windmilling her arms, obviously talking to me, was a distraction. She had lettered in swimming in high school and could do the butterfly.

"No one can do the butterfly worth a damn," she often told me. "It's the hardest stroke. And I was the best on my team." Sometimes she still tried to get me to do it even though she said it was hopeless, that I had inherited my father's awkwardness.

She stopped me after another lap. "I want you to get out," she said sharply, "and watch me. I want you to start trying to glide through the water and not fight it so much."

I got out and stood dripping as she did a perfect racing dive that took her halfway down the pool. Two more surging crawl strokes brought her to the shallow end. She turned and swam back to the deep end. People around the pool were watching; she was going fast and making no noise. She did a flip turn at the deep end. "Wow," said a little kid. Daddy looked up from his book and smiled.

Mother got out and told me to get my towel. "We can grill steaks," Daddy said. "There's a grill on the other side of the motel. I can go to the store now and get the charcoal and the meat." Mother stared at him without saying anything.

"Well, if you don't want to have a nice dinner, that's fine with me." He shrugged, then went back to reading his novel. Mother strode back over to the pool, dived in, and swam five perfect butterfly laps. Now everyone watched. "What's that?" one guy asked his wife. I wrapped my towel tighter and watched too. With each lap, she got faster and faster. She was flying through the water like a skinny dolphin. As she turned it always looked like she'd break her legs, but then all of a sudden she was headed back the way she came, lunging in huge powerful strokes, like she was capturing and subduing the water.

I sat on the lounge chair next to Daddy. I could hear his ice cubes clinking in his glass. "Your Momma is showing off, isn't she?" he said. I didn't answer him. I knew Mother was mad. I watched how long she surged underwater after her flip turn. A human torpedo.

Mother got out of the pool fast with a swift push of her shoulders that lifted her body expertly up out of the water and deposited her seated on the side of the pool. She called to me. "Get in again, Katherine."

I shed my towel and padded over to the deep end. "I'm tired," I told her.

"That's okay; you can swim when you're tired."

I dived in and began my crawl. I knew she was watching me carefully. I swam five lengths of the pool before she stopped me and told me to get out. My eyes were burning and my muscles felt tight.

She had put on her terry cloth swimming jacket. "How many times have I told you to reach? Do you want to swim well? Come here."

I went over to her. Mother took a rubber band off her wrist and gathered my hair into a short ponytail. "Can't you remember what I tell you?" She was talking too loud and I glanced at Daddy. He was staring at us.

"Yes," I said. "I was working on my kicking and trying to glide through the water." I wanted to keep Mother from getting angrier, but I didn't know the right thing to say.

"You have to want it, Kat. It's a mental thing. Not everybody has the mental thing." Her voice was growing even louder. "You can have the best body in the world, the best instincts in the world, but if you don't have the mental thing you'll never get there. You hear me, Kat?" She was almost shouting. "You'll never get there!" Daddy came over to us and put his hand on Mother's shoulder.

"Don't touch me," she said sharply.

"Now, Margaret."

"Don't 'Margaret' me." She started walking away and waved her arms at everybody watching her. "What are you looking at?" She slammed the chain-link gate. "I'm leaving. You two do what you want."

Daddy moved as quickly as he could. In the process, he tripped over his lounge chair. "Get Scout and go to the room." He tossed me the motel key and jogged after Mother, trying to catch up as she headed to the parking lot. I felt sorry for Daddy; he often missed the signs that Mother was getting ready to explode. I wondered if she had the car keys in her terry cloth jacket pocket. The jacket was bright aqua—she had made it, and one for me too. If she had the car keys, there was no telling when we'd get dinner. Sometimes when she went off in the car she was gone for five or six hours.

Daddy and I waited for her in the room. He drank coffee and we watched *High Noon* on television. "She's too sensitive," he said. "Every little thing throws her for a loop. You understand, Kat? A man has one drink and it sends her to the moon." I was glad that Daddy didn't pour another drink. We didn't need Mother any madder. The movie was almost over when Mother returned, and I was so tired I could hardly keep my eyes open. She had bought steaks and frozen french fries and she cooked them in two frying pans on the stove in the kitchenette. Daddy told her he was sorry that he had upset her, and Mother shook her head and held up her hand. "Let's not talk about it, Bill. Let's just eat."

Before we left Jekyll Island we stopped at the drugstore. Mother asked if I wanted the book on the history of the island as a souvenir of our trip. I stood in the drugstore aisle, chilly from the air-conditioning, and carefully leafed through the book. The pictures all looked eerie to me now. Their sepia tones seemed dull, lifeless, as if no one was having a good time. Maybe the people had never been happy; maybe their mansions had never been well cared for. Maybe they never came back to the island after the war because it had been a horrible place for them all along. I told Mother I didn't want the book. Daddy bought an *Esquire* magazine and peanut butter crackers. Mother stood next to me. "Are you sure you don't want it?" She added, "I'm paying."

"No, thank you." I shook my head.

Mother looked perturbed and quickly picked out a T-shirt for me that said *Jekyll Island* with bicycles riding diagonally across the front of it. "You need a little souvenir," she said, handing me the bag.

Chapter Twenty-four

After we got back from Jekyll, Daddy told Mr. Price that he was quitting to start his own business. He built Mother a cabinet for her paints and supplies, and they got along better for a little while. She set up her easel again in the basement and began creating large, wild splatter paintings. Every afternoon she and I swam laps at the YWCA. The monotony of swimming laps got on my nerves but I didn't complain because Mother enjoyed it so much. Occasionally she forgot about lunch until I reminded her, but every night without fail she cooked dinner, sometimes from elaborate recipes she cut out of magazines.

The morning outside the Howard Johnson is unfolding. More cars begin driving by. A truck rumbles into the parking lot next to the restaurant. It will be good to leave this brown-and-orange room and get to the coast where we can hear the ocean.

I mull over the atlas, tracing with my finger the big green Interstate 81 to Scranton, then the connecting highway to 6, which will take us to Danbury, Connecticut, and Interstate 84. On the way, we will drive past West Point and across the Hudson River. But we don't want to stop anywhere. We want to go as fast as we can to Cape

Cod. On Interstate 84 we can go to Hartford, but then we'll pick up 6 again, the smaller red highway, to drive to Providence. We'll have to drive through the city even though Mother hates to do that. Highway 6 leads all the way to the tip of the Cape. On the map it looks like an elf's slipper. I love the names of the towns. Buzzards Bay, Sagamore, Sandwich, Yarmouth, Orleans, Wellfleet, Truro, Provincetown. I whisper the names softly. Mother will be happy again when I show her the route. I figure it's about 450 miles. If we take two days it won't be that hard on her, I think—four or five hours a day driving at most.

At 7:30, I nudge Mother's arm that lies outside the covers.

"Mother, wake up."

She opens her eyes. "Is it morning?"

"Yes," I tell her, being careful to speak softly. I wait to see if she will keep her eyes open. She does. I pause a little longer and she yawns.

"Listen, I've looked at the map and figured out that we're only ten hours from Cape Cod. Let's leave this morning!" If I'm enthusiastic, maybe she will be too.

"Slow down, Squirt." She frowns a little, but she sits up in the bed and straightens her bedspread. This is a good sign. Already my plan is working.

"Well now." Mother clears her throat. "Tell me more."

I bring the atlas over to her bed, opened to the page with Massachusetts, and she pulls me next to her. "You're my baby."

"Look, here's Cape Cod," I point out. "You can drive five hours today and again tomorrow and then we'll be there. I have all the highways figured out." I'm excited. I realize that I want to get to Cape Cod too. This is not only Mother's trip, it's mine. Mother nods and looks at the map, moving her finger along the coast. I can tell she is perking up. Cape Cod is a good distraction.

"Well," she says. "I still feel sick."

"Don't say no, Mother. It's time to leave here and buy more antiques." I make my voice strong, convincing. I need to keep encouraging her. Daddy says Mother's biggest problem is that she never finishes anything. That she is always biting off more than she can chew and choking on it. Just once, for Christ's sake, he says, I wish you'd decide to do something easy and do it without a whole lot of drama. It's easy to drive to the Cape. I will help her and then Mother will have accomplished something she has been wanting to do for a long time.

"You know," Mother sighs. "If I eat something, get cleaned up, and take it real easy today, maybe walk outside and sit in the sun, I could start driving us to the Cape tomorrow."

"Yippee." I jump up and down.

"Now I need you to go get us some breakfast, because I'm not presentable yet. Okay?"

"Yeah," I yell.

"Sshh." Mother holds her index finger to her mouth. "Not so loud, sweetie. Get the money out of my train case. How about scrambled eggs?"

When I get to the restaurant, a large family has walked up to the hostess's podium. Betty sees me and smiles.

"Say, kid, wait a minute; I'll be right back." She takes off with menus and the family of six trailing behind her. Two of the kids are identical twins. It would be nice to be a twin. To have someone else around who is just like you, who knows you better than anyone else. Someone you can tell secrets to.

I smell bacon and it is making me hungry. I'll get eggs, bacon, and maybe even pancakes. Since Mother hasn't eaten much for two days, she'll be hungry too.

Betty comes back to her hostess station. "Okay, kiddo. What'll it be, here or takeout?"

"Takeout, please. And Mother's feeling better."

"Well, that's good. So how come she's not coming over here to eat?" Betty rummages in her pocket that has a fake white handkerchief sticking up out of it. "Thought I had a little packet of aspirin, but I guess I used them yesterday. This place gives me a major headache."

"She says she's not presentable."

"Lord, honey, I understand that. After you've been sick, you're weak as a kitten and look like heck. What'll you have this morning, then?" I tell her. Before she takes the ticket to the kitchen, she pulls a coloring book and a pack of crayons from underneath her podium. "Here you go. Something to do while you're waiting. Sit over at the ice cream counter." She turns quickly on her white rubber-soled shoes, making a slight squeak.

I like sitting on the orange vinyl stools. It reminds me of Dunkin' Donuts, except here I'm the only one at the counter. I am too old for coloring books, but I pick a page to color and overlay soft shadings of blue and red crayon to make a purple ice cream cone. In the margin, I draw the Howard Johnson logo—a silhouette of a baker, a boy, and his dog.

Betty comes over with two plates covered with aluminum foil. "Hey, that's great. If I'd known you were a real artist, I wouldn't have given you that coloring book."

"It's okay," I say, putting the crayons back in the box. "I like to color," I add, fibbing a little.

Back at our room, Mother is out of bed, dressed, and folding clothes at the dresser, putting them into her suitcase.

"Hey there, kiddo. That breakfast smells good. Put it on the table and we'll eat it right up."

Mother has cleared off the round table—my books and papers are neatly stacked on the end of the long dresser. She has put all my pencils away in their case and even leaned my book bag up against the dresser. As I uncover the plates, Mother keeps talking.

"Yes sir, I need a day to finish recuperating and then we're off to Cape Cod. I'll be able to show you all the places my mother took me. One huge nostalgia trip. And history. You love history, Kat. This will be the history trip of all history trips, only it will be your family history. Your legacy. All that we have to look back on and to look forward to. Your grandmother Katherine in all her splendor and your mother, Margaret, and what they both mean to you."

She sits at the table and uncovers her eggs and bacon. "Pancakes too. What an amazing child you are. I was thinking while you were gone that I wanted pancakes and see, you got them for me. I've always told you you were psychic, haven't I? That we have a bond between us?" She smiles, but the way mother talks scares me a little. Not just that it is too fast and she is too cheerful, but that she's mentioned me being psychic. Sometimes right before she is mean to me she tells me I am psychic and that we have a bond. Then she will yell at me for disappointing her, for not living up to my talents and abilities. I've learned to be wary when she says these things, so I wait. She puts salt and pepper on her eggs. "Go on, Katherine, eat your breakfast before it gets cold." Her voice is a little softer now, her eyes kindly; she isn't changing into her mean self. She's fine. She has gotten up and gotten dressed. We are going to Cape Cod. I take a bite of eggs; they're cold.

"Yum, aren't these eggs good." Mother swallows some. With her fork, she pushes the rest around her plate. Mother usually complains about cold eggs. You have to eat them hot or not at all, she says.

Across from me at the table, Mother opens a packet of butter and spreads it onto her pancakes. Outside our room the parking lot is noisier—car doors slamming and people cranking their engines. "While you were getting our breakfast, I went through your stack of brochures. It looks like there are lots of things for you to do today that are close by."

"Don't you want to go with me?"

"I need to get my strength back. I'll stay here and organize our things. Let's look together and see where you want to go." She moves to my bed, where she has spread out the brochures I got in the motel lobby.

I pick up the Jennie Wade House brochure and one for the Hall of Presidents. "I haven't done these yet."

Mother opens up the map of the town of Gettysburg with all the tourist spots marked on it. "Let's see where everything is." There is a list of restaurants, all within walking distance; we can go to one for dinner tonight. She points out a spot marked in red. "Here's the Jennie Wade House. It's not far. Then you could go to the Hall of Presidents, right up the street."

"I'd like to go to the cyclorama again. It wasn't very expensive." I think of the circular ramp and the dark platform, the painting lit by individual spotlights and red-arrow light pointers. The painting is so big it's impossible to take in on one visit.

"Don't worry about money, Kat. We're on vacation. If you want to go again, go."

I have only ten dollars of my own left, plus less than ten dollars of Mother's money. There are a few twenties left in her train case, but the money hidden in the trunk of the car is gone and I'm concerned that we might not have enough for the motel bill and the rest of the trip. But she is in such a good mood, I don't want to ruin it by talking about money. Even little things can make Mother fly off the handle, and money is never a little thing. I will keep my mouth shut. When we choose a restaurant tonight, I'll make sure it's inexpensive.

"Why don't you take your sketchbook, Katherine? If you want, in between places, you could take some time and draw. You'll be right by the cemetery again; there's that wonderful statue on the spot where Lincoln gave the Gettysburg Address." Mother takes a small tote bag out of her suitcase. "Here, use this to carry your pad and pencils. If you buy some souvenirs, you can carry them in here too." She also hands me a twenty-dollar bill from her pocketbook. She has money I didn't know about, and I'm relieved. "Buy a book or anything you see that you want. I want you to be happy on your last day here."

Mother sits down on her bed and puts her feet up. "You know, sugar," Mother says, "there aren't many times when you get older that you'll be as happy as you are when you're eleven."

• • •

The general senses other people's moods with painful accuracy. She knows when any of her officers has had a disturbing letter from home or a fight with another member of the staff. It's a curse in some ways, she feels, to always pick up on strong emotions in others. She can't determine exactly what the trouble is—only that it's there. So she spends a lot of time trying to figure out how to keep everyone's mood steady. As a good general, she keeps her own moods hidden as much as she can.

Chapter Twenty-five

The guide in a long skirt, apron, and a blouse with ruffled sleeves unlocks the door to the Jennie Wade House with a key on a leather lanyard. The group and I follow her into the tiny kitchen, where Jennie had been making bread for Union soldiers when she was shot.

"Jennie Wade was the only citizen casualty of the battle of Gettysburg," the guide begins. "If you look behind you, you'll see the bullet holes in the thick wooden door we just came through, and again in this door, which is open just as it was when Jennie was killed." She points to an interior door. "Jennie was kneading bread dough in this wooden bowl when a Confederate bullet passed through both doors and struck her in the back, killing her instantly."

The interior door has a framed notice above the bullet hole. "Any single woman who puts her ring finger through the hole will be married within the year, so the legend goes." The hole has been worn into a large pendant shape. One of the women in our group puts her finger through the hole and laughs. "You have to marry me now," she says to the young man next to her. He strokes his chin hairs with the thumb and forefinger of his right hand as if he is thinking very hard, and she hits him on his upper arm. "Ow," he says and grins. "We're going to be married next week," the young woman says to the group.

The guide picks back up with her spiel. Jennie's sister had been in the next room in bed with her day-old infant when Jennie was shot. That was why the family hadn't evacuated with everyone else on the first day of the battle. Then Union soldiers had holed up in their house and Confederate sharpshooters peppered them with fire. As we walk upstairs I guess that the Union soldiers were lying on their bellies on the second floor with the tips of their rifles stuck out the windows.

The guide leads us to the other side of the house through a hole in the wall upstairs that was created by an exploding shell. She continues telling us the story. The owners of the house, who shared it with Jennie and her family, had left when the battle started. After Jennie was killed, the Union soldiers brought her mother and sister and baby through the hole and down to the cellar beneath the house. Jennie's mother made them go back to get Jennie's body. Then, after everyone was settled in the cellar, the soldiers asked the mother to go back to the kitchen and finish making the bread. She did, producing fifteen loaves. The guide shows us the entrance to the cellar and tells us we can tour it on our own.

Our group walks down the brick steps into the cellar, where several figures are set up to represent a Union soldier, the mother, daughter, baby, and dead Jennie. The cellar smells like mold and the figures are awful-looking, just store mannequins. The dirty face of Mother Wade looks exactly like a man's. And the baby in the daughter's arms is a dime-store baby doll. The cellar is a dark and freakish place, more like something in a haunted house. I don't like it. I walk up the steps into the light of day. The Yankees got Jennie killed. The Confederate sharpshooters didn't know there were any women and children in the house. And then the Yankees made the mother finish making the bread. That was wrong. I can't believe that they would ask her to risk her life after her daughter had been killed. I'm surprised the mother didn't refuse. Maybe she did and they ordered her back into the kitchen.

I walk around to the door where we entered. To kill Jennie, the bullet went through two thick wooden doors. When I walk around on the battlefields there are no bullet holes, so I haven't thought much about what it is like when a bullet hits something. But here I can imagine the sound of the bullets slamming through the thick wood of the door or shattering half-inch holes in the red brick, sending shards in every direction.

Thinking about Jennie being in the cellar for two days before they could bury her makes me mad. Her family had to be cooped up with her dead body, every minute thinking about how senseless it was that she died making bread for soldiers who had plenty of rations. The Yankees should have left as soon as they realized civilians were in the house. They knew they would be drawing fire. If they had to stay, they should have helped the family to safety in the cellar first.

I like being out in the warm sun again. The cellar was too cool, too damp. The Hall of Presidents will be a better place. It'll be all about brave men—not like the cowardly Union soldiers getting Jennie killed and endangering her family. Aunt Laura helped me memorize the presidents for extra credit in school. She had me write their names on construction paper that she bought at the drugstore, and under each name I wrote the president's number and a few facts. From George Washington, number one, to Lyndon Baines Johnson, number thirty-six.

Aunt Laura was mad that Johnson wasn't running for reelection. "He's letting us all down," she said. Aunt Laura reads everything in the newspaper about politics. "I'd never vote for a Republican; they're always just for the rich, no matter what they say," she tells me. Daddy said he'd go with Humphrey if that's who the Democrats nominated, but he needled Aunt Laura occasionally by saying that now he owned a business he might change his mind at the last minute and vote for a Republican, maybe Nixon if he was the one nominated. "Don't you dare," she warned. When we watched Bobby Kennedy's funeral, Aunt Laura said it was a sad day for the country. "I'm afraid," she said. "There have been so many assassinations—I'm afraid of who might be next." She and Mother had talked about how the loss of Bobby Kennedy would change the country for the worse for years to come.

"The Great Society" is what she told me to write under Johnson's name. "Don't forget it. That's what he did that Jack Kennedy started but never could have finished by himself. Whatever people say about Johnson, he helped poor people and Black people and he's a Southerner." When I did the presidents project with Aunt Laura I found out that a lot of Southerners had been president. Washington, Jefferson, Madison, Monroe, Jackson, Harrison, Tyler, Polk, Taylor, two Johnsons, and even Lincoln, if you count that he was born in Kentucky.

At the Hall of Presidents I open the door to a rush of cool air-conditioning. "Welcome!" the woman behind the counter says. Inside the first room of presidents, I press the red button on the display and sit on the metal bleachers across from a row of six presidents standing on a small stage. I didn't think about Carl while I was at the Jennie Wade house, but now I consider whether he might show up here. A big group is ahead of me in the next room, but I am alone for the time being. I tell myself that Carl would think this place was for kids. A spotlight illuminates Washington and he begins talking about himself: "I wanted to make sure the presidency never resembled the monarchy. I lived in Virginia."

The presidents are wax, not mannequins like in the Jennie Wade cellar. All their faces resemble pictures I have seen of the presidents, but the hands sticking out from under their cuffs are peculiar—some too big for the bodies, some too small—and Herbert Hoover's fingernails seem to be painted with pink polish. I notice that some of the figures' feet aren't in proportion either. The very tall Jefferson has tiny shoes; the very short James Madison's feet are clownlike. But I like the voices—they are deep and soothing. Even though the lips of the figures aren't moving, I feel as though they are talking to me. When each president finishes giving details about his life, he introduces the next.

Lincoln, the sixteenth president, has his own room, where he is seated at a table in front of a window that looks out on the unfinished Capitol building. His right hand rests on an open book and his left hand holds papers. Behind Lincoln's voice, the "Battle Hymn of the Republic" is playing. His face appears youthful, not at all like the pictures of him taken even as early as his second year in office, with dark circles under his eyes and deep wrinkles on his forehead.

The Confederate general has to admit it—she admires President Lincoln. In her mind, he is a far better leader than Jefferson Davis, who is sick all the time. Lincoln has guts and, so she hears, a sense of humor. Deep in her heart she knows that they will lose the war and she hopes beyond hope that Lincoln is president when they have to surrender. Lincoln alone is capable of putting the nation back together.

When I come out of the Hall of Presidents, I hear banjo music. I follow the sound several doors down the street and find an antique and Civil War relic shop. Through the plate-glass window I see a man behind a high counter, playing a fast and furious bluegrass tune with lots of picking, the kind my father and Poppa like. The counter in front of him is a glass case in which books lie flat on the shelves with typed information on index cards beside each of them. I enter and peer into the tall cabinet nearest me. Behind the glass hang Union and Confederate cavalry coats—both double-breasted, full of brass buttons. They are labeled with the owner's name, where he fought, and what he did after the war. Also in the case are belt buckles, ambrotypes in velvet and brass frames, a sword, and on a lower shelf, unexploded shells, a rusted canteen, and a leather haversack. Next to it is a cabinet with rows and rows of rifles. I'm surrounded by Civil War relics. Looking at the prices, I wonder how much Miss Jameson's things must be worth. The man stops playing.

"The souvenir shop's down the street on the right," he says in a clipped though not unfriendly voice.

"Oh, I want to look at the antiques," I tell him. I draw closer to the glass display case in front of him to read the labels for the books: "Personal Diary (1861–1863) of Private A. E. Bledsoe, CSA. Killed in action at Gettysburg ($800)." "Muster Rolls of the 45th Maine

($200)." "Bible carried in action at Shiloh by Colonel Charles Brady, USA ($250)."

Before I know it he has come around the case with a huge ring of keys. "Take a look, young lady." He places Bledsoe's diary on the counter. It is small, no bigger than Mother's checkbook, and covered in cracked black leather. He gently turns a few pages for me. The writing, in both faded ink and pencil, is cramped. I imagine Bledsoe sitting on a wooden box writing in the dim campfire light, this small diary resting on his thigh. He's getting down all the details he can remember even though he's desperately tired.

"This guy's a good writer—he says early in his diary that he wanted to be a journalist. Hoped he would be able to sell a newspaper article about Gettysburg when it was all over. That's practically the last thing he wrote before he died." The man rubs the whiskers on his chin. His thumb has a long pointed nail on it for banjo picking.

"Such a shame, dying before he even had a chance to get his article published. I don't get many diaries, and those I do get are usually dull as dishwater. You know: 'It rained today, we marched twenty miles, I think we're in Maryland or Pennsylvania,' or 'I've got the dysentery.' This guy's different." I remember being surprised by all the waiting and marching, and waiting more, that McHenry Howard's account described in my *Combat* book. But then he went into the woods and found the dying Yankee. I hate that image, but it is also true that I wish I could read Bledsoe's diary from cover to cover and know the horrors that he saw too.

I had set my sketchbook on the counter while I looked at the diary, and the man flips through it. "Hey," he says. "These are good." He starts turning the pages more slowly. "I've got something that you'll want to see. Hold on a sec." He locks the diary back in the case and walks to the rear of the store.

While he is gone, I wander up and down looking in the wall cabinets. The store is like a museum. I think about Jennie Wade dying in the middle of rolling out bread dough. She left nothing behind to tell us who she was or what she looked forward to.

Halfway down the left wall of the shop, a folded quilt hangs over a rod inside a cabinet. The quilt itself is beautiful, with tiny postage-stamp-size pieces of fabric in every pattern and color combination imaginable. One section, though, is discolored by a faded rust stain. Even before I read the card, I know it is blood. The quilt was used by Major John Cobb's slave, Rory, who accompanied him in battle, to wrap his body and bring him home to Virginia, the card says. I have a hard time imagining the slave having to follow his master in battle and then not running away when he is killed. Instead he acts as a brother would. I think the slave was definitely more honorable than his master.

When the man returns he puts a big black scrapbook on the counter and carefully turns the pages. A colored-pencil drawing of a battle or an encampment or a fort overlooking a harbor is pasted on each page. Whoever drew them had a perfect sense of composition and perspective, but couldn't draw the human form well. It doesn't matter, though. Some pictures burst with action, heat, smoke, and horror. Some convey the languidness of soldiers relaxing in their winter camps. The artist captured the smallest details—keys hanging from a quartermaster's belt, a colonel smoking a short stub of a cigar. Though Mother's sketches are beautifully done, the drawings in front of me have a personality that fairly leaps off the page.

"This guy Reardon was a Union private—made all these sketches throughout the war," the man tells me. "When he got wounded toward the end, he was sent to a hospital in Washington, D.C. That's where he pasted the sketches in this scrapbook. He knew he was dying and he wanted his nephew to get his artwork. He wrote out a will. You see how the glue ruined some parts of the sketches?" The owner turns through every page. Each sketch is done with colored pencil and some are embellished with watercolor. I can't imagine how Reardon managed to keep up with his art supplies and paper during battles or on the march.

"I'm hoping some historical society will want to buy this. I'm talking to one right now," the man says.

"Where did you get it?" I ask.

"Some old lady's attic, in a trunk of Civil War letters she sold me." He laughs. "Of course, I thought I was going to sell it right away, but it's been six months now. Hard for a historical society to scare up fifteen hundred dollars. I may have to give up and sell it to a private owner. Seems a shame, though. I'm afraid it'll get cut up and sold as individual sketches, but it's the scrapbook as a whole that tells his story." I can tell that the shop owner loves the stories behind all his objects. That's the part I like best too. He would rather everything be in a museum so that the stories can be spread around to anyone who wants to hear them.

Reardon and Bledsoe both died too young—before they each had a chance to become a famous artist or writer—just like my Grandmother Katherine. That's what Mother always says—that she was cut down in her prime, right as she was beginning to show paintings in New York galleries. "Such a shame," Mother says. "All that talent."

"How long have you been drawing?" the shop owner asks. He carefully puts the scrapbook in its box and looks at my drawings again.

"I guess since kindergarten."

"Well, I mean, when did you start lessons?"

I took tennis and swimming lessons at the YWCA, but I didn't know you could take drawing lessons. "I haven't," I tell him. "Mother shows me things. She's an artist."

"You're a natural, then. Inherited talent. Wonderful thing being a natural."

A man in a black suit hurries in the shop door. "Darrell, Darrell. I need to talk with you immediately."

I move back from the counter to let the round-faced man in the old-fashioned black suit and bowler hat step up. He looks a little like a preacher in a cowboy movie.

"Excuse me, young lady," he says and bows slowly at the waist. "A thousand pardons for my rough and overly excited entry . . ."

"Leonard," Darrell sighs.

"Despite your doubt, I have been successful in my entreaties to

Mister Calhoun concerning young Lieutenant Bayard Wilkeson's pocketknife he used to complete the amputation of his right leg after it had been partially cut off by an exploding shell. I can also buy the sash that poor Wilkeson used as a tourniquet. Unbelievably brave lad, don't you think, young lady?"

My face freezes. I can't nod or say anything. How can anyone cut their own leg off, especially with just a pocketknife?

"You're making the kid turn green, Leonard."

"Oh, my apologies, young lady. I should have thought to be more delicate. War can be a terribly gruesome topic. A thousand pardons, please."

I manage to nod and smile a bit to show that I'm not really upset.

"Leonard. Remember what I said about provenance. Calhoun doesn't have any paperwork or other real proof of the knife's ownership, does he?"

Leonard slowly shakes his head no.

Darrell picks up his banjo, strumming a few long, lonesome chords. "The truth is that Calhoun has a Civil War–era pocketknife that his granddaddy picked up off the battlefield. It's no more Wilkeson's than the one I have in my own pocket."

"Did he die?" I blurt out.

Darrell picks a few high, fast notes and stops. "Yes," he says quietly. "He died. His father was at Meade's headquarters—he was a newspaperman covering the war—and he went to get Bayard's body. I'm sure the real knife is still in the Wilkeson family."

"Well." Leonard stuffs his hands into his pockets. "I should get to work on sorting that new bunch of regiment buttons." Leonard bows to me. "I take my leave, young lady. My best to you in your future endeavors. May you prosper."

After Leonard shuts the rear door behind him, Darrell lets loose with some measures of the "Orange Blossom Special," then he puts the banjo down again.

"Leonard's a little tetched. Most of the time he acts like he's living in 1863. But he's really good at running the metal detector."

I glance at my watch and find that it's much later than I thought. The cyclorama might not have another showing after four thirty. I should leave soon if I'm going to make a sketch for Mother and be back at the motel in time to get ready for dinner.

"Hey, I bet you'd like a minié ball as a souvenir. Let me get you one—on the house—Leonard finds them by the hundreds." Darrell opens a drawer under the counter where he laid his banjo. On top of my sketchbook, he plunks down two minié balls, one smashed flat and the other intact.

"Thank you very much." I examine the gray pieces of lead before I put them in my pocket. Now I have a genuine piece of the Civil War to take home from Gettysburg.

"Enjoyed looking at your sketches," he says. "Keep it up."

I walk out of the relic shop toward the gate to the Gettysburg cemetery. I liked the way Darrell talked to me and showed me things, not because I could buy them but because he felt I would appreciate them. It was the way Miss Jameson acted toward me, as though we shared something significant—a love of stories about our families and the Civil War.

An unexpected image of Lieutenant Wilkeson fills my head. Blood covers his hand that holds the pocketknife; it pulses thick and dark red until he pulls the sash tight and twists it with a stick. I stop on the sidewalk, blinking. I've reached the clanking flagpole in front of the Hall of Presidents. I feel ill. My mind shifts abruptly to the floor of Jennie Wade's small kitchen. She lies facedown, blood pooling beside her body, the dough abandoned in the big wooden bowl on the table where a minute before she had been standing. An old couple wearing matching red vests with patches all over them comes out of the Hall of Presidents. Trying to erase the images of blood, I stare at them as they walk to their truck with a travel trailer hitched to the back of it. They are as old as my grandparents. I remember the quilt with the faint rust stain. The rust stain isn't as scary as the other blood I've been thinking about. I take a breath.

• • •

The Confederate general sits with the soldier who wails about his fallen buddy. Other generals wouldn't do this, but she too, has fallen apart amid the carnage of a battlefield. In her first battle her friend died in her arms of a terrible neck wound. Blood soaked her uniform. She didn't rejoin her unit until nightfall and she thought she would be broken forever. She had not been prepared for the fact that war and battles were personal, not just troop formations, maneuvers, maps, and cannon positions. Even now, though she has secreted the blood away into a small corner of her mind, the Confederate general lives with the sorrow of all the dead that the battlefields have stolen.

Chapter Twenty-six

Somehow the war is more real in Gettysburg than it was at the other battlefields. All around me here are stories of people who were killed. Even the museum has large portraits of common soldiers, labeled with their names and what befell them in the battle. It's as if this place is asking me to think of the separate faces of the men who charged up Little Round Top, fought in the Peach Orchard, or defended the Angle. Before we got here I rarely thought about the soldiers in the ranks as individuals; they came together as armies, as battle lines, marks on a map. As I walk the arc of the grave markers in the cemetery, a wave of sadness comes over me for each of these dead men. This must be what Mother felt the first day we were here. She knew right away that this place, with its battlefield, graves, and bullet holes, is full of sorrow. I believe now that Gettysburg itself is making Mother sick. A place can have a powerful effect, especially on someone as sensitive as Mother. And we've brought with us to Gettysburg pieces of all the battlefields we've already been to. All the war, for us at least, is piled up here. That's why I want to get her to Cape Cod, a place that can cure her sadness. I need to go there too, to rest on the sand with the sounds of the ocean lulling me to sleep.

After a big battle, the general makes sure that her men have a proper rest—extra rations, passes to a nearby city or town, or some form of recreation or entertainment. They love to bathe and swim, swinging from a rope they've rigged up on a tree and landing in the river with a huge splash. They always look so happy out of their uniforms, clean for a change, baring white chests and brown arms, frolicking without a care.

I walk more quickly, pausing only for a minute in front of the huge Soldiers' Monument that Mother said would be good to sketch. It marks where Lincoln stood to give the Gettysburg Address. I can see it will take a long time to draw all four statues on the base, not to mention the figure of Liberty at the top. Longer than I now want to be around all these graves. Mother won't care if I don't do the sketch. I hurry through the rest of the cemetery, past huge trees and the smaller monument to Lincoln that has the text of the Gettysburg Address on it.

As I cross the road at the National Museum, I veer left toward the cyclorama. It's quarter to five, so I'm too late to see it again, but I can go to the viewing area at the back of the building and look across the battlefield. I don't need to be back at the motel until five thirty or so to get ready for dinner.

The viewing area is built like a concrete fort with walls all the way around as high as an adult's waist. Plaques are mounted at the corners and in the middle of the wall to identify everything in view. From where I stand, to the far left is the house that Meade used for his headquarters, at least until the Confederate artillery began shelling it. Ahead is the Pennsylvania Monument and, a ways behind it, Little Round Top. Slightly to the right is the Copse of Trees, which marks the apex of the Confederate charge, and then to the right of that, the statue of Meade on his horse, Old Baldy. I see the field where the men from Pickett's Charge marched and then ran toward the trees.

A smiling red-haired woman waves at me. She wears a funny outfit—bright pink Bermuda shorts, a pink-flowered shirt, and red tennis shoes. Around her neck, along with her camera strap, she has a scarf with a design of the American flag. I hesitate. We are the only ones at the overlook.

"Ah, ah," the pink-and-red lady says and hurries toward me. She pulls the camera strap over her head and holds her large box camera toward me. "I wish that you could take my picture. It is easy." She has a thick foreign accent. I have never seen a camera like hers. Its shape is rectangular and the woman shows me how to look down into the camera to see the image reflected through the lens.

"It's good, no?" she says as she stands next to the wall of the overlook. I center her image in her unusual camera. She waves enthusiastically as I push the button.

She has me take pictures of her and of the landscape to either side of her. "So to get all the view," she instructs. "I will tape them together," she says, "and have a panorama." She holds her hands far apart to show how long the picture will be.

"You are the best," she says halfway through the pictures. "What is your name? I am Anna Maria." I shift the camera to get Little Round Top above her right shoulder, and tell her.

"Katherine is a good name. I would have named a daughter Katherine, but I have all sons." She laughs. "They are all grown now."

I take the last picture—the green of the field where Pickett and Lee's army made their last ditch charge. In the viewfinder it could be any field. Nothing to distinguish it.

"Now I have a picture for my walls like the one inside the building—right? Panorama!" She slaps me on the back. I wish I had pictures of the places where Mother and I have been. I would like to look back at them and remember. Already our short trip contains too much for me to recall. If I had pictures, I could make better drawings of what I've seen. I could paint a landscape of this battlefield as it looks now, wiped clean of death and dying. "I am with a tour from Germany. We visit American sites. Mostly war things. I am not so interested in war, but my sons will enjoy the pictures. I wish to talk with more Americans, but I have to escape the tour to do it.

Otherwise all I do is talk German to Germans. Silly. We go sit. Tell me about America." Anna Maria smiles and points to a bench at the back of the overlook. I think about the time, but decide it won't hurt to talk with her for a few minutes. I like her accent, and that she hasn't stopped smiling.

"Where are you from?" I tell her the truth instead of making something up, because she won't be in the country long enough to tell anyone where we are. "A Rebel." She whistles. "This is good. What do you think about Gettysburg?" I don't know what to say. Since meeting the women lawyers, I have begun to think of Gettysburg as being as much about Lincoln as about the Confederate High Water Mark. I've also thought about King and Bobby Kennedy being assassinated, as Lincoln was, before they had a chance to finish their life's work. And about the lawyers' comment that our country might now be in a new kind of civil war. A week ago, before the trip, I would have told her a story about the insurmountable odds of Pickett's Charge, and how the Confederates made a valiant but failed effort, earning the admiration of even their foes. But now everything is jumbled in my head—assassinations, Lincoln, slavery, and the Rebel army shoeless, hungry, but brave and fighting for the wrong reasons. I shrug my shoulders.

"Ah," she says. "It is a bad question. I ask another. The Rebels lost at Gettysburg and then lost the war. Do people in the South still get a lot upset by this?"

I nod, yes.

"Uh-huh." She nods back. "This I figure."

We sit in silence for a few seconds. I want to tell her something I think about Gettysburg. "Gettysburg is a sad place," I say. "Full of the dead from both sides, but the North saved the country here."

"Ah, well. So you think differently than others in the South." Anna Maria stands up. "Why are you alone here?" she asks.

"I'm not alone," I say quickly. "My mother's back at the motel."

"I ask because children usually go places only with their parents when they are your age. But I am older and think differently than a lot of parents now."

A large group spills out onto the overlook. Several greet Anna Maria. She takes my hand. "Katherine," she says to me. "I go with you back to your mother so you will not be alone. Which way?"

I don't want her to go with me. Mother might find out that I gave Anna Maria my real name. I point to the driveway that leads from the cyclorama out to one of the main roads through town and practically to the lobby of the motel. "I'm okay. We're at the Howard Johnson's. Just at the end of that driveway. Mother let me come over here because it's so close." I look at my watch. "She expects me back in fifteen minutes. We're going to the Farnsworth House for dinner." I remember seeing that name in a brochure.

Anna Maria looks over the wall at the drive. "Ah," she says. The members of her tour fan out along the other side of the overlook. She gazes intently at the driveway. You can see a tip of the orange roof through the trees.

"See, there's the roof of the motel."

"Ah-hah," she says. She looks at me intently and cups her hand under my chin. "You will be careful, yes?"

"Yes," I say. I'm not sure why she seems worried about me.

"Okay then. But I think she must make you too separate—no, I don't mean separate—I mean alone. One need not be so alone, especially so young. It's not fun, being alone." Anna Maria's not entirely right. At home, being alone *is* fun, and when I tire of being by myself I can run up the pasture to Gramma and Poppa's. I'll be fine for now, with Mother ready to go to Cape Cod, but if we really end up living in Maine I'm sure I would be too alone. I push the thought away. It won't happen; Mother's going to change her mind.

"Listen," Anna Maria says. "The Farnsworth, we eat there last night, have food like in the Civil War—something called game pie, peanut soup—don't eat it. Ugh." She wrinkles up her nose. "Get a steak."

"I better go now," I tell her.

"Bye-bye, American Katherine." She waves to me as I go down the ramp. "Wait," she calls. I turn around. "I have a picture of you, quick." I stand still while she focuses and snaps. Now one picture exists of me on this trip, even if I won't ever see it. Halfway out the drive, I turn around and she is still watching me from the overlook. We wave at each other.

Looking up at Anna Maria, I think of Robert E. Lee at his headquarters near McPherson's Ridge, watching and waiting for the outcome of Pickett's charge. Winning the battle of Gettysburg was a long shot. He must have known he would never get that far north again—he would have had a good idea that Gettysburg was a last chance to gain the advantage for the Confederacy and maybe get Britain to back them. The charge was a desperate plan—it could work only if every piece fell into place. Longstreet was against it. He wanted to slip around Meade's rear flank and make Meade attack them. Instead, Lee sent fifteen thousand men in a charge across one mile of open field. His artillery on Seminary Ridge couldn't support them—not from a mile away. Men died by the thousands, five hundred killed by enemy shells in Pickett's division before they even stepped off for the charge. In the end, the failure of the charge was right. The North needed to push back Lee's invasion, otherwise the union might not have been saved. I know all this now, but I can't help wishing the Confederates could have had their victory against such odds, even if it meant they had to lose eventually elsewhere. Mother had known—Gettysburg is sad. I walk toward the motel, its orange roof glinting between the tree branches.

The Confederate general faces the photographer as she holds the reins of her horse. Her army has begun its retreat. While the photographer sets up his tripod and gear, she ponders her conflicting thoughts about this battlefield, this place. She has lost the fight here, but she doesn't know what to make of it yet. There is a deep unease coiled in her chest about what will come next and whether they are meant to fail. She looks hard into the camera lens as if she might find a clue there that will help her.

When I go into our motel room, I don't see Mother, and the bathroom door is shut. She must be taking a bath, getting ready to go out to dinner. I'm looking forward to it—I don't want takeout food again—I want to go somewhere nice with Mother, maybe a fancy restaurant like the one where we met Miss Jameson, our plates and silverware resting on a tablecloth, our glasses full of ice water, and big menus in leather folders opened up in front of us. I want to spend time with her when both of us can be happy. "Mother," I call at the shut door, "I'm back." I hear her turn on the water full blast. "Okay," she calls back. I can barely hear her over the water. "I'll be out in a little bit."

Soaking, adding more hot water as her bath cools, she likes to stay in the tub forever. I settle on my bed with my new guidebook about Gettysburg and begin to read a familiar story. General Jeb Stuart, the book says, was Robert E. Lee's eyes and ears, his most trusted cavalry officer, and Stuart had been absent at Gettysburg when Lee needed him most. I study the map of Stuart's ride around Hooker's army. If Lee had known more about the position of the Army of the Potomac, he might never have fought at Gettysburg. The book says Lee would have battled the Yankees at a location better suited to his style of fighting. Stuart let him down and had nothing to show for his week-long ride except the mules and wagons he captured. When Stuart arrived a week late, Lee said, "They are an impediment to me now." I shut my eyes, leaning back against the soft pillows. I see Stuart galloping, waving his hat with a huge plume on it.

When I wake up, it seems I've been asleep ten or fifteen minutes, but my watch says it's quarter to seven. An hour has passed since I got back to the room. I knock on the bathroom door.

"Mother?"

I hear her crying.

"Mother, are you all right?" She doesn't answer. I am afraid she'll be mad at me, but I turn the knob to open the door. She is sitting naked in the empty bathtub with her left elbow resting on the soap dish. Parallel lines of blood snake down the inside of her forearm.

"You're bleeding." With the words, my throat closes with fear. She stares at me like she wants me to go away, but I can't move. I stay in the doorway. Somehow Mother has gotten hurt in the bathroom. I saw Daddy cut himself once trying to get a window open that was painted shut. He pushed and pushed on the sash and when the window finally let go, his hand slipped and slammed against the glass, breaking it. He held his hand up and wrapped his white handkerchief around it. "Damn, that hurts." I watched the blood flow down through the hairs on his arm. "It's nothing to worry about, Kat. Probably not even bad enough for stitches. But I better clean it up a little." I went with him into the kitchen, where he washed it under the faucet in the sink and spread antiseptic cream on it. I asked him if he had to get a shot for it. "No, baby," he told me. "I had a tetanus shot last year when I cut my leg on the job, remember? Those shots last seven years."

"What happened?" I ask her. I am stuck in the doorway. I want to move toward her, but I can't make myself.

"Katherine," she says. "It's not bleeding much now." Her face is pale, though, as if all her blood has drained away.

While I was sleeping and even before that, maybe, Mother has been bleeding in the bathroom. How did she cut her arm? I need to move to the tub to help her. Even if she doesn't act like she wants me to help, I have to. I take a breath and walk to the side of the bathtub. Her skin is so white; all her freckles look washed out. There's a bloody cut across her wrist. I pull a clean hand towel from the rack over the toilet. Kneeling beside the tub, I can see that the blood on her arm is mostly dried. She holds out her wrist to me and I wrap the towel tightly around it; she holds it on with her right hand. Only then do I see that in the soap dish lies a bloody razor blade. Pink blood streaks down the shiny white porcelain of the tub below the soap dish. A swirl of pink stains the area around the drain.

The bathroom is hot and humid; it's hard to breathe. My head feels wobbly on my neck and I grip the side of the bathtub, staring at the soap dish. It seems to be moving, like when my father held my hands, spinning me around and around in a circle in the front yard so that my feet left the ground. When he stopped and we both collapsed on the ground laughing, the world kept whirling.

I look at Mother, her face swimming in front of me. She doesn't seem to want to move, but I need to get her away from that razor. I need to get us both out of the bathroom so the spinning will stop. My mouth is dry.

The Confederate general reaches inside herself to remain calm. She ignores how her body is feeling. A general must push through unpleasant sensations and not succumb to them. People depend on her.

"Maybe you should get out of the tub."

Her face looks blank like she has no idea what I mean.

"Do you want to get out of the tub?"

She doesn't answer me right away and then she says yes a little too loud. "*Yes*, I want to get out of the bathtub."

Mother is tall and I have always thought of her as strong, but in the tub she looks like a child, small and weak. She acts as though she doesn't know what to do and this frightens me even more.

"Come on," I say and put my hand on her back to gently guide her up. She uses her right arm to help herself stand and the white towel falls off her wound. When she steps out of the tub, I get another folded hand towel to put around her wrist. I wrap her in a big towel too—as she has taught me; one end tucked under to make it stay put.

"Let's go get on the bed," I say as I lead her out of the bathroom. I think of Lieutenant Wilkeson's razor-sharp pocketknife and all the blood soaked into his tourniquet when he cut his own leg off. Mother has cut herself with the razor, but I don't understand how or why.

She keeps her arm elevated as I pile pillows behind her. She presses her right palm against the towel on her wrist. "If I keep pressure on it, it won't start bleeding again."

"Mother, you need to go to the hospital. You need to get stitches." I really don't know whether she needs stitches or not, but I want to take her to a doctor. I want to get us out of this room, find out why this is happening.

"No. No hospital."

I sit on the end of her bed. Her wet hair is making large dark spots on the pillows. How much blood has she lost already? People can bleed to death. That is probably why Lieutenant Wilkeson died. No blood is showing through the towel now, though, and the blood around her cut had been mostly dry when she was in the bathtub.

The general knows that wounds can be deceptive and that a wound on one soldier will kill, but a similar wound on another will merely lay him up for a few days. She has seen a man hurt so badly she knew he would never live through the wagon ride to the rear of the line, and then two weeks later, there he was standing up on crutches smoking next to the hospital tent. But another boy who was barely nicked had keeled over dead after he undid his uniform coat to find his wound. As if the sight of his own blood had stopped his heart.

"Katherine, listen to me. I have to tell you something." Suddenly Mother's eyes are focused, intent.

"But you're cut. We need to do something." I want to convince her to go to the hospital. I'm sure something serious is wrong with her, something I can't help or fix. "It might get infected if you don't put some ointment on it. At least let me go to the drugstore. I can get bandages too."

"No." She hasn't raised her voice, but the *no* is sharp, harsh. I know better than to ask again to leave.

"Listen to me. This is so important that everything else can wait. I have waited so long as it is. Almost too long. I should have told you the truth from the beginning. I should have talked and talked and talked. But I didn't. I kept quiet. Ssssh." Mother holds her finger up to her lips. "That's how I have been practically my whole life. Ssssh." She shakes her index finger. "Never, never did I say what I should have. I tiptoed around, quiet. Don't say anything that might upset things. Well, that's the wrong way to be, Katherine. You understand? That's the wrong way." Her eyes, red and watery, search my face.

I nod. I will agree with whatever she says right now, no matter how confusing. I want to make sure she doesn't get angry with me, that she stays calm.

Sometimes the general concurs with whatever is said to her to keep the peace, to maintain calm. Situations that involve terrible consequences may require a delicate, quiet touch. Sheathe the saber, holster the gun, speak softly.

"I'm cold," she says.

I get the spread from my bed and put it over her. She pulls it up to her chin with her good right arm. The towel dangles open a little from her left wrist. The cut is only bleeding a little—one small trickle has inched down her arm. She sees me looking and pulls the towel tighter.

"I have to talk to you now. It's a second chance I've got and I want to make the most of it." She shivers a little.

"After you left this morning, I started thinking the bad thoughts that I think a lot. I felt that if Mother couldn't beat the thoughts back, then how in the world could I do it? My mother was so strong. I wish you could have known her, you are so much like her." She is quiet for a long time, staring into my eyes.

"I went to the bathroom, prepared everything. Got in the bathtub, ran the water."

I know now that she cut herself with the razor to let all her blood flow out into the bathtub and then down the drain. She wanted to die. But it wasn't quite like the soldier in the woods at Manassas who was dying of a physical wound and wanted someone to bayonet him to put him out of his misery. Her *mind* made her feel so bad that she wanted to die. Aunt Laura says Mother is the most artistic person she knows and that artists are aware of things in the world that other people don't even notice. "It's hard on her," Aunt Laura said, "seeing things we don't see."

"But I couldn't do it," Mother says. "It was you. I thought about you and I couldn't do it. I wanted to so bad. I guess I still do. But I thought about you coming back to the room, finding me in the bathtub, and I couldn't finish it. I knew I couldn't leave you with that—it's what I was left with, and I know how bad it is." I don't understand what Mother was left with. "I try to think about something else, think about something pleasant, fun, cheerful. But I can't think of anything. I'm deep, deep underwater—water that's pressing me deeper. And then, when I'm so deep I can't come up, I think of Mother." She pauses, silent.

I know what it is like to be underwater and I'm struggling to understand what Mother means. I can swim the entire length of the pool underwater without taking a breath, but I've never felt I was so far underwater that I couldn't rise to the surface.

"I kept thinking of my mother's face. I can never erase her face. You left and I started to think about Mother. Everything's worse when I'm alone. I'm afraid, and when I'm afraid like that, Mother's face sticks in my head and won't go away. Nothing I can do will make it go away." Her voice is almost a whisper.

Mother trembles, her arms have goose bumps, but the air in the room feels hot to me. Because of the silence, I can tell that the air conditioner isn't running. When it's on, the rumble of its motor fills the room.

"I heard that a razor in a hot bath is easy," she says. "But it wasn't. I kept thinking about you." She stares at me.

Like a bayonet, I think. A razor-sharp bayonet.

"Listen, Katherine, I have to tell you what really happened."

Her voice is shaky. She is about to tell me what made her so sick she couldn't get out of bed. She didn't have a cold or a migraine, but she was sick just the same, with a sickness that made her deeply sad. That made it hard for her to be in the world. Like Aunt Laura had tried to explain to me before.

Chapter Twenty-seven

Mother begins in a quaky voice. "The house was dark when I came home after school. I opened the front gate, went through the garden, as I always did. The flowers were just beginning to come up. It always felt like a surprise in the spring when their leaves began inching out of the ground. I was late because I'd been sitting on the wall outside our school with Albert from the tenth grade. He was hinting at asking me to the school dance."

I already know the story she is telling me. And I hate it. She is coming to the part when my grandmother Katherine has a stroke. I want to get Mother's wrist bandaged properly. It worries me that it is getting dark; Mother is worse at night. I fidget with the bedspread, bunching it up into a lump and then smoothing it out.

"When I shut that huge front door behind me, I realized there were no lights on. I called to Mother. Nothing. No sound. I turned on the lights in the front hall. Then the parlor, then the living room. I went to the kitchen. Maybe she had gone out, maybe she was upstairs in her bedroom. I took the steps two at the time. I wanted to tell her about Albert, the dance. That he was going to ask me. I kept calling her. I went into her bedroom. Her easel was set up with the partially finished canvas of me at the beach, at Cape Cod. But no Mother."

Tears roll down Mother's cheeks, but her voice is stronger. This part of the story I don't recognize; before, it always ended in the parlor.

• • •

The Confederate general puts down her field glasses. Something bothers her about what she sees up ahead. The cannon positions of the enemy don't make sense. She fears a trap and scribbles out a hasty order for all battalions to halt. She'll send her best scout out for more reconnaissance.

"I looked in every room of the house and decided that she had walked to the store to get something for dinner. I waited in my bedroom, doing my homework. It was six thirty and beginning to get dark when I decided something must be wrong. Even if she had stopped to visit her best friend down the street, she wouldn't stay past when we usually started cooking dinner. I went downstairs to the kitchen to look up Anne's number in Mother's address book." Mother wipes her face. "I got the address book from the end of the kitchen counter. That's when I noticed the basement door was halfway open. We stored things down there."

I'm not fidgeting anymore. I pay attention. The way Mother is telling this frightens me.

Keep collected and calm, the Confederate general thinks. No matter how badly the fight is going. The men mustn't see their general rattled. Morale makes more difference in the outcome of a battle than you can imagine.

"I called down the steps. No reply, but the light was on. I walked down and saw the neatly stacked cardboard boxes, and the shelf with tools that no one used. Everything in its place. Things my father didn't take with him when he moved out. Then I got to the bottom step."

I know about her father dying of a heart attack two years after he divorced her mother and remarried. She hated visiting him when his new wife was around. And she hated him for telling her once that he was much happier with his new wife.

Mother looks at me closely. "When I stepped off the bottom step I had the strongest urge to look behind me. So I did. And I saw her.

A kitchen chair was under her, kicked over. Her face was swollen. She had tied the rope to a beam. I stood there for a long time. Then I walked over to her and touched the hem of her dress. She had on her nicest dress. The pink one with tiny white polka dots that you could barely see."

Once, in the middle of the carnage, the general had wanted to stop everything. To give out the order that everyone should lay down his arms. At that moment, she felt that if she gave such an order the war would end and all the men would live. It was a strong feeling, so strong that she got out her pen and pad and actually started to write. But she didn't go through with it. In the end she knew her order wouldn't bring the end of the war. The end had to come after all the battles were fought.

"Stop," I whisper. I don't want to hear any more of the story. I don't care how important it is for me to know.

She stops telling the story and takes my hand. "Don't think I'm a bad mother," she says. "I had to tell you. I couldn't let you find me. I've barely been able to live with it all these years. I couldn't let that happen to you. You're my baby. Come here." She opens her arms. "Sit next to me. I'll hold you." I move stiffly to her. She puts her right arm around my waist and then holds her left wrist again. I feel locked into her body. My arms are pinned to my sides. She begins rocking from side to side.

The general knows that to be successful in battle you have to act as if you aren't afraid, even though you are, desperately afraid. In battle you have to react quickly—fire, charge, and fire again without hesitating. You can't let fear in because that will slow you down. When a comrade falls, you fill in the ranks. This is being brave, keeping the fear at bay.

"Everything's all right now, baby," she says.

It isn't all right. The story about my grandmother is so terrible, and today it could have been Mother too. I'm not sure what is going to happen next or what I am supposed to do. I close my eyes and wish away this day and the whole trip. I don't want to think about my grandmother's basement.

I don't think I can help Mother anymore. I don't think I'm strong enough. I may fail her like Jeb Stuart failed Lee at Gettysburg. I know the story of Stuart's ride around Gettysburg by heart.

The Confederate general's horse picks up his front hooves, one and then the other, in small stutter steps. She reins him around in a tight circle, puts on her plumed hat, and faces her staff. "While we march toward Ewell's division, we'll wreak havoc on the Yankees where we can." She leads the cavalry off at a trot. Here is an opportunity, she thinks, to show Lee that her recent defeat at Brandy Station was a fluke, that the Southern cavalry can beat Northern cavalry any ol' time they want.

Mother holds me tighter, but it's no comfort. She keeps rocking me and I get a faint whiff of her lemony perfume and of cigarette smoke in her hair. She is humming. I am held tight in her arms, but I feel far away. I have heard of people killing themselves before. There was the story about Shelley Gaston's great-aunt lying down on the railroad tracks north of town because she wanted to die. The train ran right over her, brakes screeching, whistle screaming. Gramma had said Mrs. Gaston was going through the change and it made her crazy. "Doesn't make everybody that way," she had said. "But some women suffer more than their due. And her husband was no treat to live with."

The Confederate general's cavalry finds Hooker's long stretch of Federal troops. She puts her binoculars away in her saddlebag and orders her six cannons to fire on the troops even though she knows it will only be a minor irritation to them.

Lee wants her to find General Ewell and give his troops protection. But Hooker and his Union troops are blocking her way. "By God, if there were fewer of them we'd give them more than distant cannon lobs. We'll have to go out of our way to get around them," she tells her aide.

She clicks to her horse and gently taps his sides with her spurs. There's still plenty of time to rest and graze tonight, she thinks, and find Ewell tomorrow.

Mother begins to sing very, very softly: "Hush, little baby, don't say a word, Momma's gonna buy you a mockingbird . . . if that mockingbird don't sing, Momma's gonna buy you a diamond ring . . . and if that diamond ring turns brass, Momma's gonna buy you . . ." She sings so slowly it seems as if she is pulling every word out of the air one by one. She has sung this song to me over and over again since I was a little girl. Her warm tears drip onto my shoulder. Mother likes the mockingbird song with all its verses and she used to make up new verses to make me laugh. She often sang it to me when I couldn't get to sleep or after she and Daddy had a fight.

She doesn't like the look of this ford, but they have to cross the Potomac soon, and the Federal infantry is posted upstream at the easier fords. She is already late. The water here is deep, but her men can carry the ammunition boxes over their heads to keep them dry. In the wee hours of the morning they finish crossing, everyone sopping wet. The cannons had been underwater coming across.

I feel Mother's breath against my back. She keeps singing slowly and softly, "And if that looking glass gets broke, Momma's gonna buy you a billy goat . . ." I try to think of a plan. Generals planned campaigns with other generals. At Gettysburg, Lee didn't have Stonewall Jackson to plan with anymore. I have lost my right arm, he said. Of everyone, he trusted Stonewall the most. But even without Stonewall, Lee had Longstreet and others, and he asked for their advice. In the end, of course, Lee took full responsibility. When you were the head of an army and were honorable, that was what you did.

Her cavalry comes upon Federal supply wagons pulled by fat mules. It's easy to overtake them as they try to escape toward Washington. They're loaded to the gills with bacon, sugar, hardtack, whiskey, and oats. It's the oats she wants most, for their hungry horses. But she is also thinking of Lee, who said gather supplies as you can. She takes their weapons away and paroles the Union soldiers. It will be slow enough to move with the captured wagon train; she doesn't need prisoners too. She is beginning to worry she will never find Ewell. Where is he?

Mother lowers her arm; she is still singing. I look carefully to see if her wrist is bleeding through the towel. It isn't. "And if that billy goat don't pull, Momma's gonna buy you a cart and bull . . ."

All of a sudden, while she is searching for Ewell, trying to link back up with his troops, whose flank she is supposed to be guarding, a Federal cavalry charges them. She is forced to make her horse jump a wide gully to avoid being captured. Now she has to make another costly detour to avoid having to stand and fight. Days have gone by and she still has no idea where Ewell is.

The towel around Mother's left wrist comes unwrapped again and I stare at the wound. The skin around it is stark white and puckered. "Momma's gonna buy you a dog named Rover . . . and if that dog named Rover don't bark . . ." I'm horrified by the image of Grandmother Katherine that Mother has described. Her face would have looked like the bloated men left dead on the battlefield. If I am just like her, maybe I will die that way too. I try to wipe the image out of my head.

Her horses and men are beyond exhaustion. They have finished their fifth night march in just over a week and still haven't reached Gettysburg. She has to rest them at dawn. That afternoon she rides ahead to Lee's headquarters at Gettysburg. It is the afternoon of the second day of the battle. "Where have you been?" General Lee says to her. The look is enough. She has failed in her mission. Lee doesn't need the mules or wagons of supplies. He had needed information on Union troop positions.

He had needed her cavalry for the first days of this battle that is now raging at Gettysburg. She would rather fail any other person in the world. Lee is like a father to her.

Mother starts on the last verse. "Momma's gonna buy you a pony and cart, and if that pony and cart fall down, you'll still be the sweetest little baby in town." She kisses me on the top of my head. "See," she says, "as long as we're together, everything will be fine."

I don't believe her. Things aren't fine and aren't going to be fine. Mother needs someone besides me to help her. She keeps rocking, she is rocking herself mostly. Mother's breathing is slowing down; she might be falling asleep. I will have to do something, but she won't let me leave the room. She thinks everything is over, that the danger has passed. When I close my eyes and don't make myself think of something else, I think of my grandmother Katherine, whom I have never met. I think of her polka-dotted dress; her dead face like those in Mathew Brady's photographs. Mother has always told me how much I look like my grandmother. I am named for her; Mother tells me I am just like her.

I wait and think. If you try to kill yourself, you're crazy. Crazy people get taken to the asylum at Milledgeville and that's where they have to live. It's like a jail; they're locked in because they're not safe. That's what Gramma said. It's for their own good; they have to be taken care of. I don't want Mother to have to go to Milledgeville. I wait and think some more. If I call a doctor here in Gettysburg, he'll have Mother taken away to an asylum. I will never see her again. I would have to break my oath to Mother to call home. I'm not sure I can do that. There must be some other way to get help.

Mother lies back on the bed and I sit beside her. Until she falls asleep and I come up with a plan, I practice my multiplication tables in my head; I try to remember stop-by-stop the route I'd taken on the bus tour of the Gettysburg battlefield; I list all the Civil War generals' names I can remember, matching each Confederate with someone from the Union. Lee-Grant, Jackson-Sherman, Hood-McClellan,

Longstreet-Meade, Pickett-Burnside, Stuart-Custer, Johnston-Hooker, Early-Chamberlain, Hill-Hancock. I name every battle I can remember—Southern and Northern names. Finally, I slip off the bed.

Mother stirs. "Where are you going?"

"I'm going to read my book. You go back to sleep." I sit at the round table reading my Lincoln book. After each half a page, I look over at Mother. I have to be patient. I read on.

The Confederate general is known as the most patient general in the army. It's important to take action, but it's not good to take action without thinking through what the consequences will be. She needs to think things all the way through to anticipate all the different ways the battle can proceed. When she is doing serious planning, she considers her mind to be an orderly vessel. A place where ideas step forward in clear, recognizable patterns.

Aunt Laura told me once when she picked me up from school after Mother had forgotten me again that we had to be patient with Mother, that Mother couldn't cope with the world as well as other people, that it took her twice as much energy to get through a day as anyone else. She said that Mother had had more sadness in her life than anyone should have. "Try not to be angry with her," Aunt Laura said as she drove me home.

Chapter Twenty-eight

Mother is sleeping. I make sure that I have money and the room key in my pocket. I crack the curtain; it's twilight. I tiptoe into the bathroom and fold the bloody razor blade into a washcloth. Then I go through Mother's train case to find the rest of them. I put them all in my pocket and stand staring at Mother. She doesn't wake up. I watch her chest move up and down. She is sleeping; she is fine right now. I slowly, slowly turn the knob until it makes a soft click. I slip outside the room still holding on to the doorknob, then gently shut the door. I see through the opening in the curtain that Mother hasn't moved.

I have no idea where I'm going or what I will do. The air is heavy, humid. I need to be away from Mother so that I can think clearly. Near her, all I hear in my head is her voice. All I feel is her despair. I need to be by myself. She's safe for right now.

I walk toward downtown Gettysburg, first passing the kiosk where I bought the bus-tour ticket, then the Farnsworth House Inn, which has bullet holes in its walls from the battle. People are coming out of restaurants, strolling in the coming dusk. No one pays attention to me. I sit down on a bench, but it's no place to concentrate—I need trees, ground, the smells of soft rotting wood, pine needles, and grass. Some place like the woods at home. I think about Seminary Ridge—the canopy of tall trees lining the road, cannons positioned along the way, their bronze muzzles pointing toward the stone wall a mile away across the field. In my mind I map the landmarks, turns, and street names from my bus tour. We drove north on Baltimore Street, where I am now, and then we turned left at the courthouse. I'll recognize the intersection when I get there. From the courthouse we drove a long way—maybe ten blocks—before we turned left onto Confederate Avenue, and that's Seminary Ridge. I head out.

On the march is the best way to be, the Confederate general thinks. To be headed somewhere is soothing, even if you're not sure what will happen when you get there. Sitting and waiting is almost never the way to obtain the advantage in a battle. You have more to risk when you move forward, especially if you don't know the possible future scenarios, but there are times when it is absolutely necessary.

Soon after I make my first left turn, there are hardly any other people on the street. The rest of the way is along a two-lane highway. There's no sidewalk, just scrubby grass with trash that people have thrown out of their cars. I go slow, careful where I step. Cars drive by and I move farther away from the shoulder of the road and begin to walk faster. I don't want anyone stopping to ask me what I'm doing. By the time I reach Confederate Avenue, I'm sweaty and thirsty. This is exactly what the soldiers felt like. Their feet were sore and heavy; their throats were parched, raspy hollows.

At the first cannon I stop. I am here. I touch the cool bronze. I imagine myself as a soldier.

We have left our large packs behind the lines. On me I have my rifle, a cartridge belt, an ambrotype of my family, a pocket watch, and my lucky leather journal and a pencil. The journal has a split in its cover and a few of the pages are ruined, but it stopped a piece of shrapnel at Sharpsburg. I keep it in my breast pocket without fail now, in every battle. Only a few more of its pages are blank, just enough to write about Gettysburg. Sitting down with a pipe after a battle and recording everything I can remember gives me such peace of mind. There's always so much to put down—even the color of the light on the leaves, little things like that. And there are the images I describe to try to purge them from my mind—the bodies, dull in their dirty butternut or navy blue, dark stains seeping along the threads of the cloth, around the buttons, pooling at the stitching.

I look across the mile-wide field of Pickett's Charge. I can hardly see the Copse of Trees, and a hundred years ago they would have been much, much smaller. Mother made me swear I wouldn't let anyone know where we are and I don't want to be disloyal. Helping her is up to me, but all I want to do is run away. I stare into the distance until I seem to see the air itself. My grandmother's polka-dot dress floats in front of my eyes, rippling like a flag.

The generals ride by, waving their arms, their hats. Ready, men, they say. Steady, men. We soldiers are steadier than the generals are. We know what we're up against. We've done this before.

Our cannons begin their booming. We stand shoulder to shoulder in the heat, shifting from one foot to the other, itching to have the damn thing start, whatever the outcome. When the charge begins and you quick-step off, the release of adrenaline jolts your senses, sending all your worries packing. For a few moments you are free and powerful, heart pumping hard, marching and then running with your mouth wide open screaming bloody murder. It's a false freedom, stripped away as the roar of the battle deafens you to your own voice, acrid smoke fills your lungs, and your eyes are assaulted by the agony and blood all around you.

I step off with my regiment toward the trees. I am a foot soldier. The generals are elsewhere; we will cross to that stone wall, fighting our way over into the swarm of Yankees.

The grass is high where I march, up above my knees in some places. It's prickly on my bare legs and quickly soaks the bottom hem of my shorts. I pick up the pace. My grandmother's dress flutters in the breeze. I can make it to the stone wall and then over the wall. I'm sure of it.

• • •

In the darkening sky, I see the smoke and fire from exploding canisters. On either side of me soldiers fall, bleeding. They know that I can't stop for them—that all of us still standing must press on to our objective. The noise rises to an unbearable volume. I start running. Getting there is the only thing that matters, getting away from the dying soldiers around me. Escaping the cannonballs and canisters spewing shrapnel and shot everywhere. I'll be one who reaches the stone wall. We'll break the Union line in two this time; we'll show ol' Lee what we're made of—iron and steel. Sweat rolls down my forehead, stinging my eyes. I brush it away. I'm closer to the copse now—close enough to see the Yankee rifles waiting for me, waiting until they can see the whites of my eyes. I see their dark blue kepis above the wall. I keep running, but now I'm yelling again at the top of my lungs, a Rebel yell. The yell that puts the fear of God in the enemy. Here's the wall—no minié balls have found me. I climb over, pushing the Yankees down in front of me. They fall like dominos—all the way down the wall. Our flag bearer crosses over. We've taken the wall.

I am panting, sucking in the heavy evening air. I rub the middle of my chest where my heart feels like it will burst from my ribs. I fall to my knees. None of it can be changed. Brave Confederates fought and died for the wrong cause. Honorable soldiers killed one another by the hundreds of thousands. A war that should have ended at Gettysburg dragged on for two more years. It can't be changed that my grandmother took her own life. Can't be changed that my mother tried to do the same. I sit on the ground next to the Copse of Trees and hug my knees.

As the sky turns ink blue, I watch the lightning bugs rise from the grass. One appears, blinking its slow signal, then more join it, some sailing high above me. They float inside the trees like someone threw glitter into the branches.

This place is so big it seems to be swallowing me up. I turn away from the trees, toward the wide expanse of field. Overhead, wisps of clouds are blowing away, the stars are coming out. First star I see tonight, I wish I may, I wish I might, have the wish I wish tonight. Across the field, the few remaining Confederates regrouped after the charge. They tried to gather strength in case Lee wanted them to charge again. But they didn't charge again; they retreated. Some of them must have wanted to go home so badly, even if they did love General Lee and wanted to do their best by him.

I see the North Star, the Big Dipper, and the Little Dipper. That's all I know by name, but some of the other clusters are familiar. I strain to make sense of the patterns, trying to pretend they are connect-the-dots pictures from which I can create an outline that will form an archer or a bull or a bear, but I don't know which stars are belts, which are horns or claws. Aunt Laura probably knows—I'll ask her when I get home. If I do get home.

The soldiers must have looked up at the stars at night after a battle. Did they talk about the constellations, teaching one another all they knew, so that by the end of the war the whole company could name everything in the sky? Did the night sky and the familiar stars bring them any comfort?

I lie down beside the stone wall and gaze upward. Right here the Confederacy was stopped. The lost cause that needed to be lost. No one knows I'm here. I could stay out all night, sleep under the trees like the defeated Confederates.

I am honorable and brave, and I am in retreat; the battle is over. It is time to gather the wounded and get them to safety. I get up slowly. The lightning bugs flicker around me. I begin walking toward the motel on the park road, a shorter way than I came, then trotting, putting more distance between me and the stone wall, the Copse of Trees, and the battlefield. All the truth needs to be told now. I am running. I'm tired, but I push myself to keep going. I picture the lobby—the front desk, the brochure rack, and next to it, a telephone booth. Just past the cyclorama building, I run across the parking lot to the street. Only a short distance now between me and the motel.

No one is at the desk when I open the big glass doors underneath the orange arched roof. I step into the phone booth, close the folding door behind me. It's hot and I'm breathing hard, not just from running, but because of the dark feeling coursing through my whole body. I need to do this. Now. In my head, I recite Aunt Laura's phone number. I take down the black receiver, dial zero, and wait for the operator.

"I'd like to make a collect call to Miss Laura McConnell in Marietta, Georgia. I'm in Gettysburg, Pennsylvania. My name is Katherine McConnell." I hold my breath until I hear Aunt Laura's voice.

Author Notes

This is a work of fiction; though I used names of real places, discussed historical figures, and recounted historic events, I did so in the service of a fictional narrative. When necessary for the story, I altered facts. For instance, while most of the references to the Civil War and battlefield parks are accurate, I also create fictitious diaries and records, imagine events and tours, invent museum exhibits, and pass along apocryphal tales. In addition, all of the history is filtered through the sensibility of an eleven-year-old. Among the nonhistorical characters, no reference to any real person is intended or should be assumed; and though the characters travel on real roads and highways for the most part, the journey of the novel is a product of my imagination and was never taken.

Multiple sources informed me as I wrote the book: visits to Civil War battlefields, historic sites, and museums; late 1960s publications from selected Civil War sites; the Atlanta History Center's permanent Civil War exhibit, "Turning Point"; a Civil War seminar taught at the Atlanta History Center in 2000; *The Civil War,* the documentary film by Ken Burns; and children's books about the Civil War from the late 1950s through the late 1960s, particularly biographies in Random House's Landmark Books series and *The Golden Book of the Civil War,* adapted by Charles Flato from the *American Heritage Picture History of the Civil War*. AAA kindly sent a photocopy of a 1968 road map that helped me plan the journey described in the novel. National Park Service staff generously provided crucial information.

Other books I consulted included: Roy Blount, Jr.'s *Robert E. Lee*; Don Congdon's anthology, *Combat: The Civil War*; Shelby Foote's *The Civil War: A Narrative*; Alexander Gardner's *Photographic Sketch Book of the Civil War*; William E. Gienapp's *Abraham Lincoln and Civil War America*; Robert Knox Sneden's *Eye of the Storm: A Civil War Odyssey*; James M. McPherson's *Hallowed Ground: A Walk at Gettysburg* and *Antietam: The Battle That Changed the Course of the War*; Fletcher Pratt's anthology, *Civil War in Pictures*; the Time-Life American Civil War series, including volumes on individual battles, *Tenting Tonight: The Soldier's Life*, and *Spies, Scouts and Raiders: Irregular Operations*; and Sam R. Watkins's "*Co. Aytch.*"

Contemporary guidebooks and handbooks from various battlefields and historic sites were indispensable. In particular, I benefited from the following titles in the National Park Civil War series: *The Campaign to Appomattox* by Noah Andre Trudeau, *The Battle of Chancellorsville* by Gary W. Gallagher, *The Civil War's Common Soldier* by James I. Robertson, Jr., *Life in Civil War America* by Catherine Clinton, *The Battle of Gettysburg* by Harry W. Pfanz, *The First Battle of Manassas* by William C. Davis, and *The Second Battle of Manassas* by A. Wilson Greene. Another series published by the National Park Service was also very useful, in particular, *John Brown's Raid* by William C. Everhart and Arthur L. Sullivan, and *Antietam* and *Gettysburg* by Frederick Tilberg. Other publications that proved helpful were *Hands Across the Wall: The 50th and 75th Reunions of the Gettysburg Battle* by Stan Cohen, *Gettysburg: The Story Behind the Scenery* by William C. Davis, and *From the Riot & Tumult: Harpers Ferry National Historical Park* by James V. Murfin.

Acknowledgments

Many people and institutions sustained me as I worked on this novel, and I am grateful to all of them. The Georgia Council for the Arts, the City of Atlanta's Bureau of Cultural Affairs, and the Money for Women/Barbara Deming Memorial Fund provided financial support at critical junctures. The literary journals *The Crescent Review* and *Kalliope* published "The Confederate General" and "Lamb of God," which developed into portions of the book. The Corporation of Yaddo, the Hambidge Center, and the Virginia Center for the Creative Arts awarded me residency fellowships that supplied solitude in which to write, and the engaging company of other artists. The Decatur Library of the DeKalb County public library system granted me the use of their Author Room for a summer. Independent bookstores were havens for me—especially Charis Books and More, where I first read my work in public. Over the years, colleagues and students at Emory University, Denison University, and the Georgia Institute of Technology generously offered support and good wishes. I appreciate my new academic home as a student in the creative writing graduate program at Georgia State University.

Good friends followed the progress of this book, and I thank them for their interest and care for me. They kept me on track and continued to believe in my efforts even when I was flagging. Artist and friend, Anita Edwards drew the frontispiece map. The Martin family listened to my dreams and cheered me on.

The members of my writing groups over the years have given me good advice and companionship—thank you Websters, Emory ILAers, AOL, and Zona Rosa. I have also been graced by a number of teachers who have made all the difference in my fiction writing. In particular, I am indebted to Clark Blaise and Bharati Mukherjee, in whose workshop I wrote the short story that developed into this novel, and to Rosemary Daniell, who has shared so much of what she knows and has been a champion of my work.

I am incredibly fortunate that Jacques de Spoelberch is my agent. His enthusiasm for my writing and the lessons he has taught me by his example have been invaluable. I knew that Samantha Martin at Scribner had my novel in her head and heart from the first time I talked with her. She is an exceptionally gifted editor and my book is much the better for her work on it. Many other people at Scribner also made it possible for my novel to be published and introduced to readers; I thank them very much for their efforts and expertise.

Esta Seaton, an exacting reader of my work, provided years of absorbing talk about books and writing. My parents, who love books as much as I do, always encouraged my writing and never wavered in their belief in my abilities. Finally, I am grateful to Julie Martin, who lived with this book from the beginning and immeasurably enriched it and all things in my life.

About the Author

Amanda C. Gable's short stories have appeared in *The North American Review, The Crescent Review, North Dakota Quarterly, Kalliope, Sinister Wisdom, Other Voices*, and other publications. She has been awarded residency fellowships by Yaddo, the Hambidge Center, and the Virginia Center for the Creative Arts. A native of Marietta, she currently lives in Decatur, Georgia.